BURDEN

TONY WALTERS

 BURDEN

St. Martin's Press ❦ New York

www.stmartins.com

Designed by Lorelle Graffeo

Library of Congress Cataloging-in-Publication Data

Walters, Tony.
    Burden / Tony Walters.
      p. cm.
    ISBN 0-312-28705-4
    1. Young men—Fiction. 2. Married women—Fiction. 3. Suicidal behavior—Fiction. 4. South Carolina—Fiction. I. Title.

PS3623.A45 B87   2002
813'.6—dc21

                                            2001048647

First Edition: March 2002

10 9 8 7 6 5 4 3 2 1

To Mary, my bright and shining path
And to my family, who had the first faith

ACKNOWLEDGMENTS

No book springs straight from an author's mind to a publisher's press. In between, there are numerous people helping to shape the words and to make publication possible. Among those who were especially helpful in the former, I'd like to thank my good friends Caroline, who had the first look, and Steve, who offered wise advice on the finished product. I would also like to thank my fellow members of the Titusville Writers' Roundtable: Ruth, Leslie, Irene, Kim, and Mr. Richardson. A special thanks to Valta, simply because she didn't want her name mentioned.

I also want to thank the people who shepherded *Burden* toward publication. These people are, in order of appearance: Leonora Hart, Lauri Jon Caravella, Andrea Greenbaum, my agent, John Talbot (thanks for your faith in me, part one), my editor at St. Martin's Press, Elizabeth Beier (thanks for your faith in me, part two), and assistant editor Michael Connor. I'd also like to acknowledge the proper alignment of the planets, the Illuminati (thanks for keeping things running on schedule, guys), Lady Luck (I'll always remember our night in Milwaukee), and of course, the little green fellow on Antares, through whom all things are negotiable.

Last, I'd like to thank my wife, Mary, who has remained a guiding voice throughout.

BURDEN

"**Get your pants on,** Burden," Eugene Boaz's wife protested. She wanted to sound stern, to sound in command. But her voice faltered and the urgency drained, making her words seem silly. *Get your pants on.* . . . As she spoke, she struggled against Burden's reluctance to pull on his jeans and her own desire to reclaim her mount a final time before sending him into the night—this *after* the headlights of her husband's truck had swept across the front yard.

Only by good fortune had she caught those beams, betrayed by twin reflections drawing illumined fingers across the sheers of the second-story bedroom window. At that moment she had been straddling Burden. She had been straddling him for several long minutes before that also, her fingernails in furious motion as they teased across his chest and belly, her body bending backward in a sweaty, athletic arch. The ceiling's troweled texture ("They look like clouds, don't you think so, Burden?" she had remarked the first time they'd made love in this bed) had been a mere distraction to her eyes, the ceiling fan's spinning blades no more than a lost detail as her loins slurped the glans pleasure swelling inside her. She had been absolutely pulsing—*pulsing*—swelling wetly, enveloping Burden in a way she hadn't Eugene in years, her mind intoxicated by the humid bouquet of sexual perfume scenting the air.

But then the telltale halogen reflections had swept across the sheers and she had sprung forward so quickly she had nearly struck foreheads with Burden.

"Jesus, Pru, that felt good," Burden said. "Do it again." His words were slurred, his mind steeped in that same sexual perfume. A lazy, crooked smile adorned his face and his eyes were closed, his senses abandoned, lost somewhere beyond the bedroom's pink walls. Instead of doing it again, Pruella had leapt off her moistened toy and scrambled for a T-shirt and floral pedal pushers.

"Eugene just pulled up. *Lord*, he's home early! Get your clothes on, Burden, get them on *now* before he comes in and shoots us both." Knowing that Eugene moved like a sloth kept Pru from becoming hysterical; still, it wouldn't do for Burden to be so, so *goddamn* deliberate.

But Burden's consciousness was a sail unfestooned from a mast; he was floating just above a tropical sea, his canvas edges skimming the waves, buoyed by the barest breeze. An indolent sun burnished a blue sky, lulling his sail-self nearly to sleep. He felt prepared for Eugene. He felt anesthetized for the task at hand. *Burden?*

Burden! Pruella pinched his cheeks, pulling his mouth into a narrow slit. She pressed her face to his, their noses touched. When she spoke he could smell her words, warm and wet and foul with sex. "Eugene's gotten home!"

Yes, Eugene, Burden thought. He appreciated the precarious turn the evening had taken, delighted in that turn. *So this is it. At last*, he thought. Eugene, 230 pounds of stimulus-response. Eugene, with muscles at the ready for the slightest provocation to demonstrate their power, simmering underneath curls of coarse black hair. The coital opiate spiking Burden's blood dulled his sense of self-preservation, making him, for the moment, carefree. With deliberate ease, he slipped on a rumpled shirt then bent ass up over the edge of Pru's bed and felt for his jeans, determined to take his time.

Pruella slapped his ass (she had done so many times this evening) to get his attention. Burden turned to her, wagging his ass like a censer, his impish smile telling her he liked the sting her delicate hand left on his buttocks.

It was then that she said, "Get your pants on, Burden," as she handed him his jeans. "And get off the bed. *Lord!*" She pulled the bed sheets and cover to the headboard, creasing them under the pillows and folding them on top. She smoothed the cover as well as she could, then leaned over to a mirror and worried her fingers through sex-tousled hair. Henna strands caught fire in fragments of errant light, and she couldn't help but smile noticing how vibrant she looked after a good fuck.

Burden pulled Pru from the mirror and ran a hand under her T-shirt, groping a breast and buying time. "Just once more," he insisted. He thought of Eugene—surely he was in the house by now.

"Burden, *no*." But she hadn't the conviction of her refusal and her lips were soon to his, their tongues darting past parted teeth. Only the sound of the garage door jangling closed separated the two. "*Lord*, what am I doing? Get your pants on and get them on *now*." Pruella pushed Burden away and hurried to the window. Why hadn't she kept it open? *Jesus, the room reeks of sex!*

"*Pru?*" Eugene's voice bellowed from the kitchen. "*Pruella?*" Her name sounded as though it had been blown out a busted exhaust pipe.

Pru slid the window open. Moist air crawled over the sill and she could see rain puddles in the sidewalk and street reflecting lamplight and lighted windows from across the way. She turned back to Burden and cursed. His jeans were only to his knees and he gave no indication they'd be fully on and zipped up before her husband lumbered into the room. The sound of muffled footsteps carried from below, telling her that he was nearing the stairs. Pru took Burden's arm and ushered him to the open window.

"Hold on, Pru, give me a chance—"

"*Shush!* He'll hear," Pru whispered tightly. She tilted Burden's head and guided it under the window sash.

Burden stretched out a hand and clasped the window's frame to buy a few moments more; surely even Eugene was only so slow. Yet even now the opiate of Pru's sex was dissipating in his blood, returning him to his better senses and to doubt. He glanced at the bedroom door and then back at Pru. "Give me a kiss," he pleaded. *Yes, a kiss would help*, Burden thought. "You can't send me out without a last kiss." His head gamboled and his lower lip jutted out in a wonderfully effective pout as he silently counted the risers Eugene's feet were fouling, carrying him nearer.

"*Burden*," Pru pleaded, but she kissed him just the same. "Now get, you," she said, pushing him through the window. As he slid down across the porch roof the friction of its shingles worked Burden's jeans over his ass. He splashed down in the wet grass unscathed, then turned to face Pru as he pulled his zipper closed. "Pru," he called to her.

"*What?*"

"My shoes, I need my shoes." With a silent actor's dramatic flair he pointed to his wet, white socks, the only clothing he'd retained during their lovemaking.

"Oh, *shit!*" Pru scanned the bedroom for Burden's sneakers, saw them discarded beside the bed table. She scooped them up and tossed them down to Burden. After he pulled on his shoes Burden lifted his face to Pruella, his eyes betraying a certain disappointment, almost dissatisfaction with how the evening was ending. At length he offered her a final kiss, placing it wetly on his palm and tossing it up to her. Pru caught the kiss. When Burden turned away, she wiped it on her pants.

"*Pru?*" the exhaust pipe bellowed.

Pruella thought to close the window but preferred that it appear she'd been standing by the open window for many minutes, caught in idle fascination by the quiet, dampened Walterboro streets resting sleepily below her. Composing herself, she relaxed against the wooden frame and closed her eyes, relieved.

When Eugene opened the door, he did so the way a husband does who perpetually suspects he will one day open it to find his wife in bed with another man, which is to say with a mixture of apprehension, belligerence, and relief.

"Pru," he continued more softly, "why didn't you answer me?"

"What? Oh, hello, dear." She held a hand out for her husband. "I must have been lost in my thoughts." She drew a long breath as she took his hand in hers. The storm had exhausted its fury somewhere in hidden eastern vistas, leaving the late evening air cooler as the sky darkened from peach to plum; tea olives opened their many mouths, exhaling honeyed breaths; a dog bayed, and a conversation from next door—only one end of which could Pru discern—carried up through the open window. "I do love the smell of the air after a thunderstorm, it somehow makes all the fragrances more . . . *alive*. Don't you think so?"

Eugene harumphed gruffly but all the same drew in a deep breath and imagined that under the smell of freshly scrubbed air and the delicate fragrance of tea olives he detected the odor of detergent. This was what he thought cum smelled like.

Burden broke through the doors of Buck's and entered a darkness different from that of the night. Three patrons, clumped like trash at the bar's far end, tended to their drinks under a television bolted high on the wall. Only one of the patrons paid more than passing attention to the screen, and its volume was lost below Merle Haggard's plaintive voice as he sang out from a small jukebox. The television threw its pale light across the room, dressing its walls and furnishings in a flickering palette of faded, mutable colors. Frankie stood behind the bar, conducting the drunken crescendo his three performers were slouching toward. Bobby Cort held First Chair, and it was his face that the television held most vividly alight, which was a shame. Cat Burrows, at fifty-five, ten years older than Bobby, thought he belonged in the First Chair. Blind Willie sat in a rounded, unkempt but not undignified heap, oblivious to his poor position or the televised chiaroscuro playing across his flannel shirt.

"What'll you have, Burden?" Frankie asked.

Burden sat softly on the fourth bar stool. The seat of his jeans was still damp from his fall from Pruella's bedroom window. "Corona."

Frankie grinned, for Burden always ordered an import after having sex. Domestics meant he'd done without. Frankie pulled a Corona from the cooler, popped its top, and wedged a lime quarter in the bottle's mouth. "How was it, good?" he asked as he set the bottle in front of Burden.

Burden shook his head in a manner indicating he could not say. "I'll let you know once I'm done."

"Interrupted? What happened, the old man come home?"

Burden cast his gaze mirthfully down toward the counter like a shy young boy.

"What quarter? Third? Fourth?"

"Overtime."

Frankie grinned again. "Sudden death."

"Not sudden enough for me," Burden muttered quietly.

Frankie started to ask Burden to repeat himself when Cat called out from his seat. "Hiya, Burd." He raised a sweating can of red and white in greeting, giving Burden an informed smile when he saw the Corona that Burden volleyed with a cheerful grin of his own.

Burden looked up at the television. Cheerleaders frolicked the way very responsible, very directed people frolic, forcing geometric shapes from apparently chaotic movements. "Who's ahead?"

"*Fucking Cocks.*" That was Bobby, spitting his words out on a spray of chilled bourbon. Of the five present, only he perceived Merle's deeper meaning.

"Go Cocks," Blind Willie said without inflection.

"Fuck your Cocks," Bobby said. He loved the Game Cocks, but superstition demanded he bad-mouth them at every opportunity, lest Fate learn of his love for them and crush them to dust.

"After your wife finishes with me. Go Cocks," Blind Willie repeated with unforced equanimity.

Bobby Cort shook off the mental image of *anyone* having sex with his wife, then said, "Well, it isn't going to last, so don't get your hopes up." And it wouldn't. No Game Cock lead—in itself a rare phenomenon—was so great that it could not be overcome by well-coached incompetence.

"See you in November."

"Think so?"

Blind Willie sucked down more of his Bud. He never ordered imported.

"You interested in laying money on that?"

Willie turned and regarded Bobby Cort with impassive eyes. "Ten dollars."

Cat hooked his toes under the bar rail and leaned backward on his stool till he had cleared Blind Willie. "Hey, Burd, you want to head out to Monck's Corner in the morning? Cousin of mine up there—you remember Clyde—got himself a new motor. Wants to try it out on the lake."

"What kind'd he get?"

"Johnson. Got one hundred and twenty-five horses just chomping to lead us to some fat-assed bass."

"Good motor." Burden upended his bottle to his lips. He brought the beer into his mouth in measured amounts, watching the tiny bubbles as they floated heavenward through the bottle.

"What do you say, Burd? You in?"

Burden brought the bottle down to the counter. "I don't know. I got to make some deliveries tomorrow. Promised my dad I'd get them done before one o'clock," he lied. "But you can sure bring me back some bass if you like."

"I didn't lay ten-dollar piddly ass amounts when I was in fourth grade, betting whether Skunk Johnson had the balls to look up the teacher's dress," Bobby said to Blind Willie.

"Okay, make it fifteen," Blind Willie returned calmly.

"I wouldn't screw my own wife for fifteen dollars."

"He's telling it straight," Frankie said from behind the bar. "Offer twenty."

"Can't you deliver whatever you've got to deliver in the afternoon? We could get back by one o'clock. I'd help you. We could get it finished up in no time."

Burden considered Cat's proposition and was about to respond when the door opened. He turned and watched Eugene Boaz force his mass through the door's slender frame, feeling as though he were witnessing a type of sexual violation. He also grew a degree cooler. He leaned into Blind Willie's ear and said, "I been with you fellows last couple of hours. Hear?"

Blind Willie looked at the beer in Burden's hand. "Drinking imported. Suddenly afraid when Eugene walks into the place." He spoke his conclusion into his beer can, then said to Bobby, "Twenty's as high as I go."

"It's a bet. Did you hear him, Frankie? You heard him, right? Twenty dollars. Clemson is going to whoop the ever-living shit out of your Cocks."

"Your wife couldn't do it, what makes you think Clemson can?"

"Would you lay off my goddamn wife?"

Eugene carried his mass to the bar and heaved it on the stool next to Burden. He smelled vaguely foul, as though he had collected the vagrant odors of the cities he'd made runs through in his rig.

"What're you drinking tonight, Eugene?"

"Whiskey. Straight. And a beer." Eugene surveyed the group. "Christ, *women*," he confided as Frankie set a mug of beer and a shot glass on the counter before him.

Burden edged closer to Blind Willie.

"Know what you mean," Frankie agreed, filling the shot glass with whiskey.

Eugene made a show of sniffing the air then hesitated, casting a suspicious glance toward Burden. He sniffed again.

Burden turned to him. "Cock or Tiger?" he asked as a distraction. "What?"

"Cock or Tiger? Blind Willie put twenty on the Cocks."

"Shit, tiger'll whip a fucking rooster any day."

"Amen, brother. Goddamn got that right." Bobby raised his glass to Eugene. His beloved Game Cocks would lose, but not on his account.

Eugene leaned into Burden and sniffed again.

"Look, do I smell like shit or something? Did I maybe step in dog crap and don't know about it?" Burden demanded, countering Eugene's sniffs of suspicion the way a baboon might turn to challenge an attacking cheetah.

"Where you been earlier, boy?"

"Why I got to tell you where I been?"

" 'Cause I asked." Eugene brushed a hair-coarsened forearm against Burden's naked hand.

"Been making deliveries all day." Burden's pinky finger twitched spasmodically, tapping the Corona lightly.

"*After* that."

Frankie refilled Eugene's shot glass. "Burd's been with us past couple of hours, Eugene, watching the game."

Burden took a sip of Corona, its flavor leeching under Eugene's shadow. *Goddamn, Eugene*, he thought. Away from Pru, away from the moment, Burden didn't have the courage to provoke him.

Eugene downed the shot and took a quarter of the beer into his rough-rimmed maw. He held his eye to Burden. His father had raised him to trust a bartender's word, but he also believed he detected the faint odor of detergent. After a few moments' hesitation he settled back on his bar stool.

Cat leaned forward and said to Eugene, "You want to go up to Monck's Corner tomorrow morning, get some fishing in?"

"Can't. I'm making a run at four to Ashville, be gone most of the day."

"You leaving four in the afternoon?" Burden asked.

"Christ no, boy. I'm leaving four o'clock in the morning. You had a real job, you might know what a real man's working hours were."

Burden let the insult slide off his ego and sipped his beer. Its taste was returning. "What time'll you be back?"

"Now what the hell business is that of yours?"

Burden didn't press the point.

"Of course," Eugene offered confidentially to Frankie, "I *am* planning on getting home by one tomorrow if I can; thought I'd surprise Pru and take her out for lunch some place nice."

"Got something special going on?" Frankie asked.

Eugene glanced at Burden then drank the last of the whiskey. "Just keeping her on her toes. It won't do to let a woman get too comfortable."

Frankie tried to pour a third shot into Eugene's glass but Eugene raised a blocking hand, finished what remained of his chaser, brought the mug down sharply on the bar counter, and stood. "Got to get home. Won't be much sleeping done tonight." He slapped Burden soundly on his shoulder. "Enjoy the rest of your game." Burden offered him a smile of angelic benignity. Eugene threw a five-dollar bill on the bar counter and walked to the door. When he reached the door he turned and said, "I ever catch the prick fucking my wife, he's going to wish he'd been born a nigra."

"Why so, Eugene?" Frankie asked.

" 'Cause a lynching ain't nothing as much as what I'm going to do to that goddamn cocksucker when I catch him." Eugene dipped his head in parting. "Ya'll have a good night."

Blind Willie turned to Burden and said, "You best stick with domestics, son."

"Why's that?" Burden asked. Having come so close tonight with Eugene, he was determined to have another go tomorrow.

"Because that imported shit's going to get you killed."

"What, Eugene? I'm not afraid of Eugene."

"Well, you should be. I don't know what this game is you're playing, son, but one of these days you're going to take it too far."

Burden waved away Willie's words.

"No, you listen to me: Pru's using you for the thrill of it. Let Eugene catch you and her in bed; you think for a second she wouldn't beg Eugene to beat God's holy living shit out of you for what *you've* been making her do? That woman is poison."

"Pru's not so bad."

Now it was Willie's turn to dismiss Burden's words. "And another thing, rile a man like that Eugene and he'd just as soon kill you as look at you."

"Yeah, well, if that's so, what's he waiting for?"

"You know what I'm talking about, son. I've done delivered too many friends to their everlasting peace. I don't care to do the same for someone as young as you."

Burden stood and patted Blind Willie on the back. "Thank's for watching out for me, old man, but I know what I'm doing. Oh," he said, bending close to Willie's ear and speaking softly, "I never play games."

Burden drove through the dampened streets. Above the quiet noise of the road passing under his wheels he could hear also the sound of Eugene's footsteps as he trudged up the stairs and his voice, so full of menace and doubt, calling out to Pru and to whomever might be with her. *Poor Eugene*, he thought, *if you weren't such a sloth this would have all been over with long ago. But maybe tomorrow you'll do better.*

When he reached the cemetery Burden turned into the entrance and pulled to a stop. For several minutes he sat there, studying the dark beyond the fence work. He could have just as easily started the van again and left, but he'd not been by to visit for what, a month, more? This sense of neglect provoked him at last and he stepped from the van, and looking both ways for approaching cars, he mounted the iron and stone fencing and touched down inside the grounds.

The early evening rain had gathered up the humid air and removed its heaviness, leaving the night cool and easy to stroll through. Cicadas sang unseen and bullfrogs grumbled from their freshly wetted lairs so they would not be forgotten below the bright full moon. Cooler breezes, discarded remnants of the earlier rain, occasionally hurried over the grounds and lifted into the trees, finding their voices in the limbs. Burden dug his hands deeper into his pockets when these breezes came up beside him to take him by his arms with their cold embrace.

Burden followed the clay road to the heart of the grounds. Massive oak trees, their backs broken and bent with age, towered above the graves. Most of the oaks were older than the least well-remembered soul interred below Burden's feet, and had themselves taken on the afterlife's tallow glow, their craggy faces bearing the impassive expressions of so many death masks. They wore these stolid expressions for good reason, for it had been their task to usher generations of souls into that undiscovered country. Rising on all sides, they protected Burden from the moonlight—protected him also from those mislaid souls who prowled these hallowed grounds. Frivolous-spirited azaleas pawed at the oaks, whispering rumors and telling tales out of turn, hoping to bedevil the separate lines of slumber and death and secret a departed soul through the gates, if only for an evening's sojourn through the town square. Be *reasonable*, they entreated the oaks. Burden took no note of these quarrelsome voices rising all around. Instead, he pressed forward. When he reached the third crossroad he hesitated, kicked at the damp clay below his heels, and turned down the narrower lane.

Fifteen yards down the lane Burden turned again, walking a final twenty feet over the grass, passing many older headstones that rose high into the air, declaring the dearer value of their residents. He stopped at a simple granite marker whose verdant brass shone dully in the oak-filtered moonlight. The name it bore in raised letters was illegible through the night's ebony veil, so Burden spoke the name for any who might not know who was hiding under this particular rectangle of sod. "Evening, Peedie."

A gust of wind curled through the oak limbs, then died.

"Haven't been by for a while . . . thought I'd stop to see how you were getting on."

The fragrance of newly mown grass and the crisp odor of juniper strode upon a gentle breeze winding through the headstones. Burden ran his palms over his arms to warm them. He leaned back on a tall stone, felt a cold circle spread on his back where he pressed against its granite face. For several minutes he remained silent, absently listening to the breeze's vacant voice.

"We came pretty close tonight," Burden said. "Thought you'd want to know." There was no answering breeze to his remark, so he closed his eyes against the fragile moonlight and remained silent also. There had been evenings, as a teenager, when he had passed hours alone under these same limbs, counting the souls in their coruscant larks, holding his cheek to the leaf-littered sod, listening with youth's melancholy ear to the murmuring voices interred below. But those evenings were hours and a lifetime ago. Each passing year found him in these grounds with increasing infrequency, till at last he could fairly say he neglected Peedie. Well, it was no wonder Peedie had grown taciturn; Burden figured he would too if he felt he'd been abandoned.

"Blind Willie thinks we're playing a game, you and I." Again there was no breeze, only the mournful light and the feel of cold against his skin. *A game, is that what Willie thinks I'm up to?* Burden laughed sourly at the thought. "If this is a game I wish it was a game I'd lose pretty soon." But saying this to Peedie, Burden heard the doubt, subtle but present, in his tone. It was this doubt, a presence he felt with increasing insistence each day, that kept him from coming to the cemetery as often as he used to. It was this same doubt that stole the peace he used to feel here in Peedie's presence and made him fidget his feet through the grass and trace a fingertip's greasy trail over the lichen-tinged headstone he rested against; it was this same doubt that made him cast anxious glances about in the darkness, a darkness in which he'd once felt comfortable. Finally, in a single motion he stood and twitched his shoulders, unwilling to linger even a moment more. "Look, Peedie," he said at length, "I should be getting home. I'll come 'round to see you sometime soon, in a couple of days, maybe. Sure I will. We can talk then if you want." He turned his back to the grave and started to leave, then, twisting his body without shifting his feet, he regarded the plot a last time. In the darkness and from a distance he looked like a miniature oak curling toward the sky. " 'Night, cousin."

TWO

Burden grabbed the yellow grocery slips that had been called in for delivery and read through them. As he scanned the items, he thought of his near encounter with Eugene the previous night, of how it had come so close to happening with him. Had Pru not hurried him out the window . . . But he could do nothing about that now, so Burden concentrated on what had to be done this afternoon. There was still an opportunity with Eugene, still a chance that Eugene would do the job Burden needed doing. All that was necessary was for him to get to Pru's before Eugene. Having no idea her husband was to be so soon home, she would gladly take Burden to bed to resume last night's love play. Burden had only to imbibe the anesthesia of her sex and bide his time, waiting for Eugene and the lethal wrath the scene would bring down on his head. Once Eugene did Burden's dirty work for him, he and Peedie would be square.

Who do we have today? he thought, scanning the names on the lists. There were a great number of requests today, and if he made deliveries to all those who had called in groceries, he couldn't get to Pru's in time. He would have to lose one or two lists. Very quickly he selected two customers—Ada Baggett and Stuart Smalls—who lived at opposite ends of Walterboro. Misplacing their lists would buy him the time he needed. Neither was indigent, Burden reasoned, nor otherwise in need of his services, so not getting their groceries would pose only a temporary inconvenience.

Burden took a shopping cart and made his way quickly along the aisles, retrieving various items with machinelike grace. Errantly he thought of Eugene and was seized by a burst of energy, which he dissipated by hopping onto the back rail of the cart and pushing off. Momentum carried him three quarters down the aisle, and he was about to push off a second time when his father rounded the corner. Jumping from the rail he blindly grabbed a can from the nearest shelf.

"Those today's lists?" his father asked.

Burden held up a clenched hand sprouting yellow slips of paper.

His father nodded approval. "Need you to hold off on those. Birch called in sick, so I'm going to need your help trimming and packaging the meat this morning."

Burden's cheerful expression fluttered and he had to catch up its slackening lines. "But—"

His father cut Burden off, communicating with subtle flexes of mouth and brow muscles that he would tolerate no argument. "I shouldn't need you much more than an hour. That still leaves you plenty of time to make your deliveries."

"Yes, sir." The late start gave Burden all the more reason to discard Baggett and Small's grocery lists. He decided to lose another name just to play it safe. When his father left he scanned the lists a second time. After much consideration, he pulled Maude Whitman's list from the others. Maude was the wife of Dr. Whitman, who, at the age of sixty-one, was twenty-five years her senior. How it was that she had not killed the doctor Burden did not know, for she was a woman of tremendous sexual appetite, eager to explore her imagination, no matter how demented or frivolous. It must be, as she had explained to Burden, that they no longer had sex. Yet this abstinence was more a function of priority than physical consideration, for, although Burden was supremely bored with her, Maude was a woman of considerable beauty. Her breasts were modest and pliant, her eyes bewitching, sparkling with a green splendor. And her legs. . . . Legs, Lord yes, legs. Her legs were very fine and because Burden had lost his virginity to those legs, he could not shake a lingering loyalty to her that made him hesitate a moment before secreting her list in his pocket. It was unfair for Burden to feel bored with Maude, for it had been she who had devised the solution of how he should effect his final exit. His continued liaisons with her over the last six years had been an oath of loyalty, a show of gratitude for her unwitting brilliance.

The slip balanced in his palm a moment longer, suspended on the scales of indecision as he considered her legs, then he closed his eyes and balled the slip up tightly. A twinge of guilt pricked him as he shoved her list in his back pocket with the other two. Sex with Maude, he reasoned to assuage a gaining guilt, had never held any purpose. With Pru it was different: Sex with Pru was a means to an end . . . *his* end.

The hour had wonderfully transformed the day's outlook; a higher wind had peeled the skin of gray clouds, revealing the blue pulp of afternoon. Every yard held azaleas in bloom, and their pink and white faces dressed the avenues nicely as Burden made his deliveries. Not that he noticed the blue afternoon or azaleas themselves, they merely provided a pleasant backdrop, encouraging his light, slightly frantic mood. His mind was occupied by vital thoughts of Pru and of his forfeited encounter with Eugene last night. These thoughts emboldened him to take chances with traffic lights and stop signs, all to speed his rendezvous with the Boazes. He accepted tips graciously but quickly, the smile on his lips less from gratitude than for his anticipated tryst with Pruella Boaz and of the return of her husband.

It was 12:10 when he made his final delivery, giving him fifty minutes to set his trap.

———

Burden turned the van's engine off several houses shy of the Boaz residence, coasting to a quiet stop in front of Pru's house. Because there was no sign that Eugene was home yet, his steps danced lightly across the flagstone walkway, at the end of which he rapped his knuckles with a reckless confidence against the front door. As he waited, his foot tapped out the rhythm to a song he was surprised he remembered and which he recalled he didn't like. Feeling sufficient time had passed without a response, Burden rapped against the door a second time. When he rang the doorbell his foot had lost its rhythm.

"Pru?" he called, walking to the living room windows. Winter-colored sheers obscured the room's careful arrangement of furniture, but clearly there was no sign of life, no telltale shadow sliding across panelled walls. Perhaps Eugene had come home earlier than anticipated and already spirited Pru away. It was likelier she was out on her own somewhere, thwarting not only Burden's plan but Eugene's, as well. Because he had not called to warn her of his coming, he could not reasonably feel disappointment; Pru's not being at home was the price he must pay for not wanting to give her the chance to decline his inopportune visit. Yet even though Burden could not reasonably feel disappointment, he felt it nonetheless, and returning to his van he was carried by steps which did not dance but which barely lifted from the flagstones' rippled surfaces.

He clambered heavily into the driver's seat. The high emotional state he had enjoyed as he contemplated arranging his own death was now offset by an equally persuasive despair. Whereas this morning his life had contracted into a single bright afternoon, now his days stretched once again before him in an unending reproof.

Burden was painting milky swaths of water and bleach across the packing room's concrete floor when his father entered. Weariness from the day's long hours had overtaken the older man, slackening muscles used for presenting pleasant faces to customers. Half-light falling from beyond the door only exaggerated the crags delineating his face.

"Sue tells me she took calls from Mrs. Baggett, Stuart Smalls, and Maude Whitman wanting to know why their groceries weren't delivered this afternoon."

Burden eased his back toward his father before lying. "I delivered to all the homes Sue made lists for this morning." He set the mop in its bucket and pulled out the sheaf of yellow paper from his pocket. "Here, these were the ones on the counter this morning, these are the deliveries I made; all of them I made, and before one."

Burden's father took the lists and absently leafed through them, then refolded the pages and held them in his palm. "Look, Burden, it's important that our customers stay *happy* customers, especially someone like Dr. Whitman, who carries weight in the community. You have to constantly cultivate customer loyalty, son, or one morning you wake up to find your customers have all gone over to the Pig or Winn Dixie."

"I made the deliveries. If some of the pages got lost, then I'm sorry, but I can't help that."

"Of course. But don't forget what I said about loyalty. Whether we forgot to make a delivery or we didn't isn't what matters. What matters is that Ada, Stuart, and Mrs. Whitman *think* we forgot them. Tomorrow I want you make their deliveries first thing—oh, except for Mrs. Whitman. She asked if you wouldn't mind making her your last delivery, says she'll be out most of the early part of the day. I'm going to give Ada and Stu a couple of cartons of strawberries for their inconvenience. I'm giving Mrs. Whitman a shank of ham. Point this out, only don't be obvious about it, understand, son?"

Burden nodded.

"Oh," his father began, then paused. He creased the folded edges of the lists and tossed them into the trash can. "Sue told me something else that I thought you should know."

His father's hesitant tone made Burden look from the milky water drying at his feet.

"Jo's coming home for the summer."

Burden painted another swath on the floor, pretending disinterest.

"Sue says she's taking up her old job at the Sonic, probably getting some cash together for books and other expenses for next year."

Was there nothing his little sister didn't know? Burden wondered.

"I thought you should know, just in case—"

"Thank you," Burden responded shortly.

"She'll be in town this weekend. Don't know when. Sue'd know better. You might ask her."

Burden nodded and pressed forward with his mop.

"Well, when you're finished here you can go. Just see that you get in early tomorrow. Hear? I don't want those people waiting long for their groceries."

When he was once more alone, Burden stuffed the mop in the bucket and churned the water and bleach mixture into a frothy lather, then slapped the mop hard against the floor. His sour mood made swift work of his task, not minding the filthy crescents of floor that remained untouched.

Tossing his apron on the cutting table, Burden hurried outside and jumped into the truck. His heart felt as though it had swollen within its prison. *Christ*, he thought as the engine turned over. *Jo.*

Burden drove as far as Johnnie White's roadside stand. Overturned shipping crates formed ad hoc tables upon which Johnnie displayed warm, wet bags of boiled peanuts. Two five-gallon pots, fired by gas-fed flames, cooked the peanuts into soft, salty bullets. Johnnie had turned the crates right side up and was packing the bags in their bellies when Burden pulled in. Seeing his friend, he pulled a bag from among its brethren and tossed it to Burden.

Burden dug a hand in his pocket, fishing for two quarters.

"No worries."

"Thanks."

Johnnie's night-colored skin glistened wetly in the failing evening light as he packed the bags. He had rolled his shirt's sleeves above his elbows; the shirt's front was open, revealing a thin tank top made semi-transparent by sweat.

Burden rested on a full crate. "What you doing tonight, Johnnie? Want to go get a drink?"

"Can't. Got to head over to Garnett tonight. Promised my uncle I'd help him work on his truck. Told him I'd stop over this evening so we could get on it first light tomorrow."

"Okay. One drink, then. I'll buy."

Johnnie piggybacked two crates in his arms. "Here, help me put these away and maybe I can see my way to one drink."

Johnnie popped the tab on his third Coors and walked back to Burden's delivery van and rested against its hood. They had stopped by the package store for a six-pack of Coors and then parked on the dirt road hemming a small rise overlooking the drive-in. Through the fuzzy limbs of pine trees two women as tall as a two-story building frolicked; they were topless and wore only champagne-colored panties and in their romp their breasts danced with much animation. A man sat to one side, content for the moment to watch.

"Lord have mercy," Johnnie said, holding his beer before him, saluting the topless, frolicking women. "How come the women 'round here don't act that way?"

"They do, Johnnie, they do—somewhere out there." Burden used his beer can as a compass to roughly indicate the direction where topless, frolicking women could be found in Walterboro.

"Yeah, well, this boy ain't found none."

Burden stood and walked to the line of trees. The man was standing now, kissing the redhead. The second woman, a blonde, walked up behind him, wrapped her arms around him, and began unbuttoning his shirt, her pelvis swiveling lustily against his buttocks. "Damn, that's sweet," Burden whispered in reverence.

Johnnie leaned against an opposing tree trunk, sipped his beer, and said nothing.

"Jo's coming home," Burden said, implying by his tone that he hadn't stopped talking about the risqué scene playing before them.

The man on the screen began suckling the redhead's nipple and Johnnie blew out a breath and said, "She quitting school?"

"Not sure. I think she's just coming back for a semester. Sue said she's low on cash, wants to work for a while. Probably get her old job back at the Sonic for a few months and then head back."

"Well, I know one boy ain't going to the Sonic for a while—*goddamn.*" The actors were in bed now, apparently nude but with a rumpled sheet discreetly covering their bodies below their hips. The redhead had her hands hooked under the headboard as the man worked her. The blonde was kissing the nape of the man's neck, her breasts flattened against his shoulder blades. Suddenly a far door burst open and a man, a furious, hulking, crimson-faced colossus, filled the door jamb. The three frolicsome lovers spun around and the women screamed tin box screams of horror through the hundred small speakers below, and Johnnie and Burden both started in surprise, as well.

The furious, hulking, jamb-filling colossus lunged into the room and uprooted a floor lamp. The women drew the sheet to their necks, either as an alibi against their nudity or an attempt to escape an X rating. The man leapt from the bed; he had on boxer shorts after all, and black socks and no hard-on, and made comic attempts to evade the lamp-wielding behemoth.

"Nah, I figure I ought to see her. I don't have anything to run from. Anyway, we're bound to bump into each other sooner or later so it might as well not be by accident."

"When she coming in?"

"Saturday evening. I'll probably call on her then, get it over with."

Burden turned back to the screen but the women and the hulking figure were gone; past the pine limbs he could see the lover's legs jutting beyond the foot of the bed. The man lay there immobile, but he couldn't tell if the attack had been fatal or the man had merely been beaten unconscious.

Johnnie drank the last of his beer, then crushed the can. "Better be on my way." Taking careful aim, he tossed the can through the van's open window. "You going?"

"Not yet. Think I'll stick around, see if those women don't come back." Burden winked at Johnnie. "You take care."

"You, too. Hear?"

Burden kept his eyes to the screen but he wasn't waiting for the women to reappear; his mind had transported him to recent years and another life that had been consumed in lust and trouble. Images rolled along, blurred through the cataract of time, but intermittently there appeared in his mind's eye perfectly focused simulacra of past events that made him wince with pain in the dark.

THREE

Maude Whitman was a woman whose fortune masked Irony's continually laughing gaze. Blessed with an indomitable spirit, she was nevertheless encumbered at birth by a name—Maude Clements— unpleasant to every ear, and which spoke perfectly of her appearance, which was throughout puberty unexceptional. Her striking beauty was a surprise to all when it blossomed late, not the least to the high school boys she'd thrown herself upon as a teenager, only to be rebuffed at that most tender age, a prisoner to plain features and an oblique figure.

Throughout those desolate, affectionless years when her lovelier self hibernated beneath a homely husk, her mind nurtured enmities against her peers, imagining that a great many thousand illicit delights were escaping her simply because she was plain. These thoughts preyed on her adolescent mind, sickening her, knowing her body—a sensual wire sheathed below an ugly casing—was being neglected by the likes of Beau Gisson and Pretty Pete Peterson and Champ Wilson. Those boys had preferred the whores on the cheerleading squad, who stood close to the boys during P.E., pressing their breasts against the boys' arms, smiling *prettily* at them. Maude could not smile prettily.

But then, following the thaw of a particularly harsh winter, in the bitter depths of which she had emersed herself in the false warmth of impossible dreams, a miracle seized Maude. Now twenty-one years of age, it was for her the first spring of undeniable womanhood. When judged by the span of a lifetime, it seemed that overnight the cocoon of homeliness within which she had been imprisoned broke open to reveal a shapely, lovely butterfly. Only a master sculptor could have perceived the goddess waiting to be carved from the common marble as full, curving calves and delicate ankles were cut from thick, clubbish legs. Hips emerged where before there had existed only parallel lines spanning an unremarkable distance; perfect breasts surfaced as though driven from the depths by rapidly approaching landfall. And her face, unchanged in any detail, became a thing of absolute beauty. The components had been there all along; anyone who cared to look carefully could have seen them, each particular requiring only to be moved the slightest degree to the left or right, or lifted, or brought forward until each was in its preordained quadrant of space.

However, as with every other moment in her life, Irony had delivered this miracle of fleshly metamorphosis on its own demonic timetable, for by the time her late debut had been announced, the pillage of her psyche was complete. Countless hours spent gazing into mirrors revelling in her no longer latent beauty could not displace the recollection of how plain she'd been as a child and adolescent. Her memory mocked her newfound beauty, superimposing over it the image of her former homeliness. These mnemonic quirks caused her to become self-protectively arrogant, vain, and insecure, none of which she'd been prior to her awakening.

Suddenly, the uninterested and scornful boys of her youth became aroused young men, appealing to Maude with tardy courtships. To her credit, Maude Clements would have nothing to do with these latter-day converts. Instead, she collected her savings, bought a one-way bus ticket for Charleston, and encamped near the medical school, determined not to quit her habitation until she came away with a fine gentleman doctor freshly graduated.

Yet even with her beauty, her early social deprivation made her poor bait to attract a decent fellow. For two semesters she tossed about from post-grad to post-grad, becoming by turns a pretty ornament, a pal, a sexual aid, but never a friend. She was far too abrasive and insecure for friendship. Whenever potential suitors felt the nascent stirring of true affection for Maude Clements, she would turn suddenly mean toward them, rebuffing them as callously and with as little effort as the high school boys had rebuffed her years earlier. She was, unconsciously, sliding the marks one by one back to her side, betting that when she had evened the score there would be a last, fine specimen awaiting her.

Hubert Whitman was not the fine specimen Maude had envisioned. Hubert was a dull fellow who, at the age of forty-eight, entered college to pursue his life-long dream of becoming a physician. A Charleston native, he'd made a small fortune selling German-made bathroom faucets to wealthy homeowners. Eight years and a dissipated fortune later he graduated a respectable distance from the bottom of his class, and when dressed in a white starched shirt, blue tie, and physician's white lab coat, looked very much the doctor.

Hubert discovered Maude his last day on campus. He had been loading his suitcases into the back of his automobile when he chanced to look up to see Maude drudging along the sidewalk with suitcases of her own. "She looked for all the world as though she'd only just surrendered, that she was dragging behind her her dearest belongings as she slouched toward exile," Hubert often said when recounting his first impression of his wife and how he had "rescued" her from her surrender. Her forlorn expression, so uninhibitedly and honestly displayed, spoke of limitless bewilderment as she stopped at the corner and set her cases at her heels, her fortune—both real and metaphorical—gone. How had she managed to *fail*? fail *now*? now that she had become so *beautiful*? A homely line of displaced persons bracketed her, each waiting for the Greyhound bus to take them someplace other than where they were, someplace where skies were bluer and hours easier.

Perhaps it was that graceless line of displaced persons standing beside Maude, making her appear unimaginably lovely in the golden June light, that seized Hubert—*Dr.* Hubert—Whitman's heart, or perhaps it was that in that moment he realized he'd lived more than half his life without having yet enjoyed a woman's tender touch that roused his mind to sudden panic; whatever his motive, at first sight of her, Hubert strode to her with all the confidence a medical degree confers upon a man's ego, tipped his hat and stated: "You will marry me."

But Irony had one last laugh at Maude's expense, for while she had found her doctor and lived a life of ease, it was Irony's final touch that her doctor had heard The Calling, taking the Hippocratic oath to heart to the point of neglecting his beautiful wife. In the years since their marriage began she had become a lovely work of art shut away, as far as Hubert's affections or libido were concerned, in a dark empty room. And really, thirteen years after that fateful June afternoon, how much sexual satisfaction could she find in the arms of a sixty-one-year-old man?

The afternoon heat and the day's work had painted a patch of sweat on Burden's back and chest. His thighs and crotch were damp and occasional musty gusts billowed up from the neck of his shirt as he lifted bags from the van. Rounding the corner to Dr. Whitman's house, he saw a Cadillac parked in the driveway. That meant the doctor's sister was with Maude. Burden was glad to see the car. He didn't feel sexy in his sweat-dampened shirt, and he didn't feel like pretending to feel sexy, which was what Maude Whitman always demanded of him.

Burden eased the van to a stop, got out, and grabbed the remaining three bags of groceries from the back.

Maude waited at the open doorway letting onto the mud room. Confederate jasmine carpeted an arched trellis framing the brick stoop, and she stood below the arch looking, in her ivory, knee-length dress and matching pumps that were never scuffed, like a bride anticipating her groom. This is just what she imagined herself to be. She fantasized that as Burden mounted the steps to the mud room he would throw down his bags and embrace her, that he would find her neck with lips moist from a day's hard toil. He would hold her tightly against his body—that glorious instar still exhibiting the taut angles of youth—so that her breasts compressed almost painfully against his chest. Holding her, his hands would seek out the flesh of her buttocks underneath her dress (his fingers would soil her bride's dress!) and lock onto them as he lofted her upward against his body; his grasp separating their pale hemispheres ever so slightly, and in the act she would experience the erotic tug in her anal muscles as they stretched. Through the fabric of her dress she'd feel the outline of his ripening penis, warm and bloated, stiffened by his desire for her. Her mouth watered.

"Afternoon, Mrs. Whitman."

"Good afternoon, Burden. It's a warm day, isn't it?" Maude's eyes glided over Burden's matted shirt as a thin smile ruined the poise of her lips.

"Yes, ma'am, it is." Burden looked beyond Maude to the shadow slipping across the mud room's rear wall. He dipped his head and said, "Afternoon to you, too, Miss Whitman," without seeing the doctor's sister.

Maude straightened at her sister-in-law's approach. Her mouth watered a little less as she eased from the doorway to admit Burden. As he passed, she breathed in his musk scent and dabbed a finger to her exposed collarbone and then to her lips, wetting her finger. "Can I get you something cool to drink, Burden?" Maude asked, looking askance at Marlene, silently damning her for her unexpected visit. "I made sweet tea fresh this morning. A cool glass would do you good."

"That sure sounds fine, Mrs. Whitman, but I need to get back to the store." But Burden wasn't sure he wouldn't like some iced tea. The day was hot, after all, and he'd made his final delivery. And Maude was looking fine in her ivory dress, its material gathered tightly at her waist, as though its fabric wrapped itself around her body and said to him,

"See, Burden, see what a fine hourglass has been blown into this dress? Its curves were specially made for grasping in your hands." *And my God, those legs.*

Burden coughed to drown out the voice in his head.

"There," Maude Whitman said, seizing on Burden's cough, "tell me you couldn't do with some of my sweet tea."

Burden had begun making deliveries for his father when he was fifteen. From the start, the Whitmans were one of the grocer's best accounts, and Burden's father had instructed him to be especially polite and helpful when delivering to their house. Mrs. Whitman, likewise, had been unfailingly friendly and kind to him, growing increasingly generous with her tips. On an afternoon that was blue and warm and bright like today, he'd come to deliver the Whitmans' weekly request. Upon arriving, he had found the mud room's door ajar. When he knocked, Maude, her voice captive to a room deep within the house, called for him to enter. "Just put the bags on the counter," Maude had instructed, still unseen. Burden had put the bags on the counter and then he heard her say, "Burden . . . Burden, dear, can you come here? I need your help. I'm upstairs . . . in the bedroom."

Suspecting nothing, he had crossed through the foyer, mounted the staircase, and strolled down a hallway that was lined—at that time— with tintypes of the doctor's ancestors. A rectangle of afternoon sunlight rested hard against the wall opposite the master bedroom and within the rectangle Burden saw the foreshortened shadow of a figure standing improbably tall. He hesitated and scratched his head at the odd image.

"Burden?" Mrs. Whitman called, her voice sounding for the first time a mixture of fear and shame.

"Coming," Burden called back to her. When he reached the door and looked in he hesitated at a second odd image: Maude stood on the bed, the expression on her face a perfect realization of her voice. She wore a sheer white blouse illuminated like a makeshift aura by the light slanting through the window behind her (the blouse was pulled open at the neck, revealing a triangular swale, delicate and opalescent, while

the cuffs were tightly clasped about her wrists); a pearl necklace, matching pearl earrings; a wedding band whose three-carat pear-shaped dia-
mond sparkled with a pirate's avarice in the strong afternoon light; pale
ivory panties that peeped shyly from below her blouse—and nothing
more. On the floor next to the bed, crumpled in a heap, lay a pair of
forty-dollar jeans that were such a deep, deep blue that Burden thought
they must never have been worn yet.

"Thank *God* you've come, Burden. I've been like this for an hour,
an *hour*."

"Are you okay, Mrs. Whitman, ma'am?" In his shyness, Burden was
unable to look her in the eye, so as he spoke his gaze drifted balloon-
like around the room until, by the force of an unanticipated windshear,
it plummeted, becoming fixated on Maude's legs, pale, perfectly formed
in their silhouette, with full calves crowned by shadowy dimples pressed
into tensed knees.

"This is so embarrassing, Burden, really. You see, I was getting
dressed to go out and as I was about to put on my pants I heard the
squeak of a rat—a *rat*—come from them. I swear to God in heaven that
I saw two beady yellow eyes staring back at me from inside a leg, its
filthy rat snout twitching at me in my own home—*my own home.* Can
you imagine that, Burden, a rat in *this* house?"

Burden considered the tasteful assortment of dustless family heir-
looms and Ethan Allen furniture and the moteless shafts of light slanting
into the room. "No, ma'am, Mrs. Whitman." He stared again at her
kneecaps, oblique crowns fashioned from the most delicate, palest porcelain. *How cool they would feel against my cheek,* he thought and then
blinked the thought away.

"Oh, but I do hate rats, Burden, I simply can't abide them. I must
have a rat phobia because as soon as I saw that beast I tossed my jeans
to the floor and leapt up on this bed"—she pointed at the bed and
Burden followed her finger to her feet, which were partially hidden in
the thick comforter—"which is where you've found me, God bless you.
And I've been here an hour and now I have to *pee*. God in heaven, my

poor bladder is about to burst—*burst*—Burden." Maude twined her legs at the knees, touching them for the barest moment. Her expression begged sympathy.

"Why don't you?"

"Because, Burden, dear, the filthy beast is still in there," she said, pointing an accusatory finger at her crumpled jeans. "Do be a dear and check them for me."

Burden shrugged his shoulders. He liked rats. Without fear, he knelt before the virgin blue cloth heaped on the floor; Maude held her hands to her mouth and said, "Careful." Burden looked up to reassure her he would indeed be careful and in so doing spied her panties below the cleaved hem of her blouse; he saw her mound of pubic hair pushing against the pale ivory fabric of her panties, like straw pushing at a scarecrow's junk clothing; he saw the irregular forms of hair running in thick thatches and could distinguish individual strands rising in curled loops over those thatches; he could see the narrow fleshy cleft cut between twin hillocks just below the thatch of hair; he could see the milky rise of her belly above her silk panties' elastic waistband and the sudden plunge of thigh below. After so intimate an examination it was impossible for him to look her in her eyes, and so his gaze fell once more to her knees. They were eye level now, two feet away, no farther. A hothouse garden of fragrances swept over him, a piquant mixture of loam and orchid, intoxicating his mind and making him want to kiss her knees' perfect-shaped pale mounds, to suckle their shadowed dimples, and to wrap his fingers around their nether sides where he could feel the warm creases pinch his fingertips as she bent her legs.

"Can you see the furry devil-beast?"

Yes, yes I can.

"Not yet." Burden curled the ends of the pants legs closed and held them in one hand, grasping the waist in his other. He rolled the legs toward the middle, his ear intent for high-pitched protests and his eyes alert for the rat's round body trying to effect its escape. When the pants were rolled up, Burden looked at her knees and said with a dry mouth, "There's no rat in your pants, Mrs. Whitman."

"Perhaps he's run under the bed. Oh, but I do *so* have to pee. Would you please—no, no, never mind."

"What?"

"I shouldn't ask you, really. But. . . . Well, if it's no trouble, before you check under the bed, would you be a dear and carry me to the bathroom? *God,* I sound like such a coward. But what am I going to do? I just have to pee and the thought of that furry, evil beast running loose under my bed petrifies me."

"I can do that, I can carry you, Mrs. Whitman."

"You *are* a dear," Maude purred, holding her arms out for Burden.

Rising, Burden was aware his dick had betrayed his thoughts, stiffening slightly in contemplation of Mrs. Whitman's knees. Deftly, he rose and swept her into his arms before she could notice. She squealed and kicked her feet in fear of the rat she imagined lurking unseen below her. She was heavier than he'd imagined but was handled easily, and she felt wonderfully soft in his arms. With speed and care, he delivered her to the bathroom. His exertion had dissipated his nascent erection and so he stood confidently, facing her at the door to prove he had entertained not a single impure thought about her and that he certainly had not thought he might kiss her perfect knees.

Maude held Burden's gaze for several moments, a hint of invitation lingering in her green eyes. "Well," she said at last, "I really must pee. You check under the bed for that ratty beast, won't you?"

She closed the door and Burden listened to the toilet lid as it clipped the porcelain tank and then he heard the fabric of her panties slide down her thighs. He knelt and lifted the bed skirt and swept his hand in a broad arc across the carpeting. There was no rat. He heard the toilet flush but could not remember hearing Maude pee.

"Well?" Maude asked, opening the door enough to peer with a single eye into the room.

"No rat. It must have run off. Probably down in the basement, or," he added, seeing she was not reassured by that prospect, "halfway across the neighborhood by now, if you ask me."

"You think so? You *really* think so?"

"Yes, ma'am. I do."

Maude opened the door and entered the bedroom. "You're a brave young boy, Burden. But then, after what you've been through this last year, I suppose a rat is nothing for you."

Burden looked down at the carpeting where Maude stood. A delicate finger of pain stroked his heart but as he gazed at her toes with their red-painted nails easing into the plush carpeting, the finger withdrew. He looked at her knees again. *Jesus, just one lick. That would be enough.*

Maude walked past Burden and the breeze carried after her was scented with orchids. She bent at the waist and picked up her jeans, pressing the folds from them. "Well, I should finish dressing."

Burden remained motionless.

"If you wouldn't mind closing the door on your way out," Maude said softly.

"Oh, oh yes," he said, starting from his thoughts. "Yes, ma'am. Of course." Burden hurried for the door.

"No, wait," Maude called after him, setting her jeans on the bed. She walked to her dressing table, retrieved her purse, and withdrew a ten-dollar bill. "A little extra this time for your trouble." She held the bill toward him, intending he should cross the room to her.

Which he did.

When Burden took the bill, Maude clasped his hand in hers, trapping him in the plush prison of her palms. "Thank you," she said, holding his gaze. "I simply don't know what I would have done had you not come when you did." She placed a hand around his neck and leaned toward him and kissed him softly on his cheek; her nose brushed near his ear and a quick hot breath warmed his lobe.

Burden took the bill from her hand and wondered at the blaze of warmth heating the right side of his face and the smell of orchids in his nose. "It wasn't anything, Mrs. Whitman," he managed as he turned to leave.

When he was at the bedroom door, Mrs. Whitman said, "I'll see you next week?"

"Yes, ma'am."

In the open air and sunlit warmth, Burden had looked back at the house. It somehow was now more than a house, but he couldn't comprehend just what it had become or that, as he studied its elegant paneled door and true French windows and expensive Georgia brick skin, it was not the house he saw but the promise of the woman who lived inside. At length, he got in the delivery van; a deep breath brought the faint odor of detergent into his nostrils. He glanced down at his crotch; a pea-sized circle of pre-cum glistened darkly atop his jeans. He took his sweat towel and wiped at the stain. As he wiped he regarded the house a final time, blissfully unaware that the following week he would kiss her knees. Well, that was where he would start.

"A glass of tea would be nice," Burden now said at last. It was safe, Marlene was with them and not even Maude was brazen enough to pounce atop him with her husband's sister present.

"I believe I'll have some also, if it wouldn't be any trouble," Marlene said.

Maude turned to her sister-in-law and regarded her with stern affection. "But of course, love, it would be no trouble at all."

"Sulah, these here're my cousins, Peedie and Burden. They're from Walterboro."

Sulah looked askance at the two fourteen-year-olds and turned away.

Peedie leaned into Burden. "Nice tits," he whispered and both boys laughed. Burden nodded; few girls he had met had larger breasts than this Sulah Russell who was, in every way, the polar opposite of Jo, his wonderful new discovery. He and Jo were to see each other again tomorrow evening and when they were together he would take silent stock of Jo's many hundred superior qualities.

"Are they comin' or *what*?" Sulah asked Whalie. Her voice was grating.

"Hold on, Sulah, they'll be here soon enough."

Sulah was a Cottageville girl, eighteen years old and twelve pounds overweight, most of which was accounted for by her bosom. She wore a tube top and tight blue jeans; her jeans were dark blue save where the stress of pressing flesh and the erosion of passing palms had faded them. Under Whalie's porch light their copper rivets shone brightly. Her tube top was a poor covering for her chest and her cleavage jutted darkly upward like a burned Charleston palm. The top's cherry-colored material was puckery and soft looking. Peedie bent toward Burden and whispered, "Dare you to grab her tits."

"*Shush,*" Burden shot back, worried Sulah would hear. But Sulah was in her own world, impatiently waiting for Ricky and her boyfriend, Sutton. Ricky had the car, Sutton had the beer.

Whalie had picked Sulah up at Sutton's request and brought her to his house. Ricky and Sutton had spent the last two days in Garnett hunting and had intended to pass a third there. But a heavy rain, at first a manageable drizzle that became a persistent downpour, forced their early return. Filled with ill humor that he needed to blow off, Sutton had called Whalie to say they would be late but that he'd have a case of Coors in a cooler, and could Whalie please have Sulah waiting for him at their house?

A yard's worth of raking and cutting and the promise of ten dollars each had brought Peedie and Burden from Walterboro to their cousin's house in Beaufort. Whalie was about to take them home, some thirty miles away, when Sutton had called, agitated and in no mood to wait. "Shit, take 'em along," had been Sutton's response. He had met Peedie once and hadn't hated him. He hadn't met Burden. For his part, Burden was reluctant to stay over, and only when Whalie promised to take him and Peedie home first thing in the morning could he find pleasure in the approaching joyride.

"When'd he say he'd get in?" Sulah asked again. Her voice pilled Whalie's eardrums like a metal file drawn over their membranes. Little wonder, he thought, that her voice was so grating, blown through so misshapen a mouth. Her lips were pale pink like her skin, and too fleshy, with black freckles dancing so close to their edges that they made her lips appear to be skirted by a bruise. When she became pissed and started fuming, the freckles would jump between nose and chin; if she carried on long enough, a sheen of sweat would squeeze from her pores and moisten their black eyes till they were weeping tears of rage. Whalie could not imagine how distasteful it would be to kiss those lips or to thrust his tongue in her mouth's black hole; bad enough he had to hear what spewed from that hole.

"Soon, Sulah, soon," Whalie said, turning to Peedie and rolling his eyes. "How 'bout running in and gettin' me another beer?" he said to his cousin.

"Should I get one for me, too?" Peedie asked with a pleading smile.

Whalie was about to say "no" when Sulah huffed and looked derisively at Peedie for his impertinent suggestion. "Sure, go 'head." He looked at Sulah, who turned away, her chin rising on a wave of disapproval. "Just see you go slow with it."

"What about me?" Burden asked.

"Share with Peedie," Whalie said and Peedie shot Burden a dark glance.

The two cousins raced inside and Sulah looked at Whalie. "Real smart, Whalie, giving a couple of fourteen-year-olds beer."

"Aw, what're you talkin' about? Shit, I started drinkin' when I was eleven."

Sulah opened her misshapen mouth in retort but closed it without speaking. Headlights swept the front yard and behind him Whalie heard the sound of gravel being crushed under tires. He turned as Ricky's '78 Monte Carlo pulled into the driveway.

"*Finally,*" Sulah huffed, and Whalie was thinking the same thing.

Peedie and Burden burst from the house in a storm of noise and motion. They hadn't heard the car pull up, and as they rushed down the front steps they struggled for the beer they were to share.

Sulah shook her head, wounding Whalie with a cutting glance, then turned to the car.

When the boys saw the Monte Carlo they stopped struggling. Burden let go of the beer and walked slowly to the car, admiring its fine lines. The car was a lime green wonder shining in the evening like a counterfeit saint. Its skin of rain only heightened this illusion.

"We going riding now?" Burden asked. Between the beer and the car it was now not so important he get home that moment. Peedie upended the beer into his mouth and Burden forced the can back down as he spoke.

"Sure we are," Whalie said, and Sulah puffed out another breath of disapproval.

Sulah approached the passenger door as Sutton, a broad-shouldered giant, stepped out. He stretched the restlessness from his muscles and wrapped his arms around Sulah. The sweat from an open Corona bottle in his hand darkened a crescent of the tube top's material. Sulah looked up at him and stretched on tippy-toe as they locked in a breath-stealing kiss. Whalie said to Peedie, "Give me that beer," so he could drink it down and chase the imagined taste of her tongue from his mouth.

"We ready to roll?" Sutton bellowed when he'd finished with Sulah.

"Sutton, these here—well, you remember Peedie—this here's my other cousin, Burden."

Sutton nodded politely to Peedie and Burden. "I see you boys drink. Good." He turned and flipped the passenger seat forward. Forcing his giant's frame into the backseat, he retrieved two Coors. "Here go, boys. This'll start you two off better than that shit. Later on we'll get into the really good stuff." He held up the half-consumed bottle of Corona and gave it a shake.

Whalie glanced at Sulah to catch her reaction. She only smiled.

"I gotta take a piss and then I say *let's hit the goddamn road*," Sutton bellowed, bounding into the house.

Burden looked at the Coors, then his gaze passed between Peedie and Whalie. Whalie nodded, and Burden pulled the tab and knocked back a large gulp.

"Slow down, Burden, ain't no rush. Plenty more where those come from."

Peedie took Burden aside while they waited for Sutton. The beer made him smile, and when he spoke he lost none of that smile. "Dare you to grab her tits."

"*Shush.*"

"Coward."

"You're the one so damn interested in them, you grab 'em."

"I dared you first. Look at them. They ain't tits, they're more than that. They're boulders big enough to break a man's back. . . . Dare you to grab 'em."

Burden considered Sulah as she leaned against the Monte Carlo. She was not at all to his liking, still, set against the car's green body the cherry red of her tube top looked like a baboon's ass jutting high in the air, provoking attention. Her breasts were not attractive, yet they were in their own way tantalizing. As the dare wormed into his young mind, the prospect of grabbing her tits became less an outrageous thought and more a matter of fate. "When?"

"As we're driving. It's simple: Just reach over the top and take a tit in each hand and give them a good squeeze and let go. Shit, do it fast enough and likely she won't take any notice."

Burden gave his cousin an incredulous look.

"Still . . ." Peedie persisted, "just grab 'em for one second. I swear if you don't, as you're lying in bed tonight you'll be cursing yourself for why you didn't."

The confluence of Peedie's words and the few sips of beer in his empty stomach and Sulah's baboon-assed tube top lulled Burden into a space of quietude. He visualized himself in the backseat. He visualized Sulah's tangled coil of hair lifting from the front seat like burned sprigs of curled rye grass. He visualized the serpentlike attack his hands would make as they struck her tits, his fingers sinking into their flesh as the tongues of his palms gagged at the oversized prey they'd seized. Then he visualized his unmolested retreat into the shadows of the backseat.

The screen door sprang open and clattered against the porch framing. "You girls ready?" Sutton barked. *"Let's go! Let's go! Let's go! Let's go!"* With each repetition he slapped his giant's hands together and they made miniature thunder claps in the cups of his palms.

The thunder claps wrested Burden from his reverie. He turned to Peedie and said: "Okay."

In his dream, Burden was running blindly through the rows of a long-dead cornfield. Stalks snapped to either side as the sun, bloated and obscene looking, listed on the horizon. "Boy!" a raging voice cried after him, its fury articulated by a personage so ancient that it seemed to be the voice of death itself pursuing him unseen beyond the desiccated rows. His lungs burned hotly within his chest, starved for air and polluted with the dust of decay. "Boy, don't run from me," the voice cried, drawing nearer. Burden dug deeper to find a final ounce of energy, but an errant step sent him tumbling to the ground. Sprawled between the furrows, his body assumed the heaviness of lead, and he was helpless to lift himself up to take flight. A slender figure parted the corn stalks just beyond Burden and he wanted to close his eyes for fear of who he might see. But it was only his cousin, Peedie. In the haze of twilight his cousin looked fair and unblemished, and regarded Burden where he lay on the ground, a half smile parting his lips and his eyes soft and open. He offered a hand to Burden. "Come with me."

"I can't," Burden answered pitifully. "I can't move."

Peedie's expression darkened with his cousin's words and he turned away from him. "He's over here!" he called out.

Burden snapped his head around to see behind him. From the wake of felled stalks a withered man approached, a shotgun cradled in his arms. Burden looked back at Peedie. "Why are you doing this to me?"

"Boy," the old man said, "I've been looking for you." As he spoke the man raised his shotgun level with Burden's face. He cocked the hammer back. "What are you doing in my field?"

Burden struggled awake as the sound of gunfire died in a fading echo. Sweat matted his T-shirt and stung his eyes. He searched around the room, and when he was satisfied that he had risen from his dream alone, Burden threw back the covers and walked to the window. Unhooking the latch, he raised the window's sash and fell to the floor and breathed in deeply the muggy night air, his arms crossed on the sill and his cheek pressed against the screen. "Jesus," he whispered after he'd caught his breath.

The night was still, with bushes and yard ornaments forming a frozen processional, made ghosts for a short time by the moon's cold, haunting light. Burden wondered if Peedie saw this same pale light, wondered whether he felt its chill rays against his cheek. Or had he given up the use of his eyes in the endless midnight of his grave? Had his own cheek, cooled by an unceasing slumber, become numb to the moon's cold touch? And was that slumber wrecked by dreams of living just as Burden's were of death?

Burden squinted and studied the yard for movement. A figure stood just beyond the reaches of light, skulking in the boundary of shadow and blackness. "Is that you, cousin?" Burden asked quietly. "Jo's come back, cousin. Jo's come back for me so you better hurry."

He sighed and for a moment all the breath was out of his lungs and he felt light enough to be carried along by the strong moonlight pressing through his bedroom window. If he let go of the sill he would rise, a mote swimming in the eddies and currents of lunar light; an illuminated ghostly speck, haunting rather than being haunted.

"I asked: Is that you, Peedie?"

The figure danced in the shadows. From his window Burden could hear soft, erratic footfalls barely crushing freshly fallen leaves and browning blades of grass. Across the field, a hound howled at the solitary figure hiding in the dark. After a few moments the figure stopped dancing and cocked an ear toward the rough voice. Burden held his breath against the inevitable and then let it go when the visitor receded through the trees and darkness in search of the hound.

Burden watched as far as he could as the figure made its way to the baying animal, a mere shadow borne by the line of stronger shadows thrown by boundary trees against the fallow field. When he could no longer follow the figure, he eased around and rested against the wall, his head tilted back on the sill. He closed his eyes and followed the steps with his ears, listening as the hound's calls grew louder and more frantic till at last the night visitor had reached the hound and commanded it to be silent.

He told himself he wasn't afraid, not of Jo, not of Eugene . . . and certainly not of his cousin.

FOUR

Burden woke before first light Friday morning. Remaining in bed, he cast off the sheets and let the ceiling fan churn the room's humid air across his skin. In the dark he thought of his dream of last night and then of Jo. There had been, from the beginning, a unique bond between them, an intangible ease in each other's company. She'd been his saving grace following Peedie's death, lighting many dark moments, carrying him through his despair in the wake of the days that followed. With an uncanny selflessness she had known when to speak, when to listen, when merely to sit with him in silence as the moon keened above the pine and there was only the voice of quail and whippoorwills in the dark distance and the sensation of spirits moving about them.

Yet he understood when he'd determined the avenue of his demise that she could not continue being a part of his life. For her to remain so would create doubt in his mind, undermining the resolve he must maintain for the task at hand. And if she had indeed been his saving grace then he had understood hers was a grace he must reject. Even so, when she told him she would be attending nursing school in Charleston, he had experienced a fear for her absence greater than that for his own impending mortality, forcing him to confront the first consequence of his irrational desire.

Burden turned to his side and gazed out his window. A slender ribbon of color graced the horizon. How much better would it be that Jo had not returned; how much better that Eugene had finished things two nights ago and that he was nothing more now than a memory in so many people's hearts? Soon it *would* be finished, he felt. Soon Eugene *would* catch him in bed with Pruella and that would be the end. But Jo had returned and he would see her a last time. Perhaps he would meet with her as soon as she arrived in town. No, later. There was no need to rush. But soon. Soon.

He twisted again onto his back and closed his eyes to the morning sun.

Sue was sitting at the breakfast table, finishing the last of a bowl of oatmeal when Burden descended from his bedroom. Her eyes lit upon his sleepy figure and held him in her gaze an uncomfortably long time.

"What?"

"Nothing." Sue scraped her spoon across the bowl, conjuring up the remaining traces of oatmeal.

"You need a lift this morning?"

"That would be nice," she responded flatly.

"Just give me a few minutes to get ready."

"What'cha doin' tonight?" she asked casually, giving her brother another odd look. She ran a finger along the side of the bowl and then stuck her finger in her mouth and sucked it.

"Nothing special. Why?"

"No reason." She smiled and stood and took her bowl to the sink.

"What about you?"

"Oh, I don't know. Thought maybe I'd catch a movie with Carla. Buddy asked me out, but I don't think I want to go. Of course," she continued innocently, "I might head out to the Sonic, get a burger."

"Sounds great, knock yourself out."

Sue turned and leaned against the sink counter. Without inflection or stress she said: "Jo got in last night." She smiled.

Burden hesitated. "Thought she wasn't getting in till tomorrow," he said at length.

"Well, things change—you know how that is—and now she got in last night. I figure she's probably working at the Sonic this evening. You want to come along?"

Burden stood. "Can't tonight." He walked to the refrigerator and retrieved a carton of orange juice, poured a glass, and headed for the stairs. He would go out tonight. "Look, I'm going to take a shower. Give me fifteen minutes and I'll be good to go."

Sue smiled again as she felt the blade scrape the bone. "I'll be waiting."

"No, no, do it slower, like this," Burden said. "Like we did it before." He took the string from Jo's hands—could she feel the chill that had overtaken his skin in the afternoon's heat?—and tossed the catfish head back into the shallows. The bait landed near the blue claw, which seemed blind to the easy meal. "Now wait, just wait. You gotta give him time to smell it."

"*Smell* it, under *water*?"

"Oh, yeah. They can smell just like us. Well, not just like us, but they *can* smell . . . sort of."

After a few moments, the crab shrugged off its blindness, twitching a claw and shifting to face the bait. "See? He's getting it. He's getting the smell of it."

Jo used the crab's movement as an excuse to shift also, so that now her forearm touched Burden's. She felt the warmth of his skin and the slight cord of muscle flexing under that skin as his fingers manipulated the string. Her eyes followed the spidery movements of his fingers to his wrist as it pivoted in its joint; she continued along the length of forearm to where their arms touched near their elbows and the hairs on his arm stood on end. His skin was tawny colored, almost golden next to the blue paleness of her own flesh. She thought to withdraw her arm for all its paleness, but delighted too much in the pleasure of their touch to do so.

"Now, slowly start to pull it in. Here, take the string with me." Burden studied Jo from the corner of his eye, her own eyes the color of empty green bottles, floating atop pale skin and sunscreen. Black hair hung in wet strands from underneath the fisherman's cap he'd given her for the afternoon. Her hair, moistened by the bay's salt water, had darkened almost to jet and set off the lovely color of her flesh, which in its blue-tinted paleness, seemed a virginal terrain that the sun had not tarnished but had merely painted the impressions of pink petals on her high cheeks and the line of her nose. Burden pulled her cap down and smiled and then returned to the string and crab as though he'd never left it. "Slowly—"

"Ain't this a touching sight," Peedie remarked. Burden and Jo turned to look behind them. Peedie stood, a bucket and surf casting pole in his hands.

"Quiet, Peedie," Burden said.

"I'm not saying anything. Oh, look at what I caught: a couple brim and three whiting." Peedie tipped the bucket for Burden and Jo to see inside, pleased to show off his catch. He leaned over to look in Burden's bucket, saw the two blue claws. "Is that all you got, just two?" he asked, teasing.

Burden shrugged his shoulders, trying to twitch his cousin from his presence like a horse trying to rid itself of a nuisance fly. "Soon it'll be three if you'll quit bugging us."

Peedie stretched tanned shoulders and set his bucket in the shallow water. "I'm in no hurry to go anywhere," he said as he sat on the bucket's rim. "By the way," he added, holding a hand out for Jo, "I'm Peedie."

Jo took his hand. "Jo Simon."

"Oh, yeah, Peedie, this here is Jo—"

"*Simon,* we've already met," Peedie said easily.

"She's from Walterboro, too. Her family's spending the weekend with some friends who have a condo on the beach."

Peedie whistled. "A condo on Edisto?"

"They're retired," Jo explained. "Daddy used to work for the owner, Mr. Jeffries. Burden's been teaching me how to catch crabs."

Peedie laughed and felt snot warm his upper lip. He wiped himself clean with the back of his hand. "That so?" he remarked.

"She's a fast learner, too," Burden said. "She helped me catch the second one and she's going to get this one for sure." Burden tried hard to keep his voice level. If Peedie suspected how much it bothered Burden having him here he'd never leave.

"Make it quick if you can; Pa's going to want us to wash up so we can get some lunch."

"Tell him I'll be along in a bit."

"You come to Edisto often, Jo?"

"Me? No." She refused to look at her pale arms and paler legs.

"Didn't think so."

"Stop distracting Jo, would you, Peedie?"

"Sorry. Look, I'm going to put these fish in the ice chest. I'll see you back at the car when you finish. It was fine meeting you, Jo Simon."

"Would you shush, Peedie?" Burden asked. He wanted Peedie away from Jo. Peedie, who was older; Peedie, who was better looking; Peedie, who was taller; Peedie, who was smoother talking. *Just go away and let me enjoy the afternoon and the breeze and this pale young girl next to me. Go now. Go.*

"Well, don't be long. I'll tell Dad you got one on the line. He'll wait."

Burden didn't turn to acknowledge his cousin, only kept his eye on the line and the blue claw and, surreptitiously, diminutive thirteen-year-old Jo at his side. At length, he heard the splashing sounds of his cousin sloshing away from them and he breathed more easily, aware he'd been keeping his breathing in check while Peedie had stood with them. "You remember, slow. You don't want him to think he's in a race. He's just out for a leisurely stroll and by a stroke of good fortune has happened upon an easy meal." The string, held by Jo but really held by Burden, fell and rose in periods of tautness and laxness, its vibrations echoing Burden's own nervousness.

On any other occasion he'd have a dozen blue claws this late in the afternoon, but he figured Jo was a much better catch than any number of blue claws. He had been casting for the crabs in the estuary where the cooler water of the South Edisto River flowed into the warmer Atlantic. The temperature difference created thermoclines, liquid walls that attracted the crabs. His cast net was new, a gift from his parents for his fourteenth birthday, but he only used the net to catch the blue claws when he was impatient. Most times he would carry a coiled string with him and a bucket of catfish heads for bait. Coming across a blue claw, he'd thread the string through the eyes of the fish head and toss the bait near—but not too near—the crab. Then, with a patience verging on sun-induced stoicism, Burden would wait for the crab to scent the head, and once it had its claw on the head, Burden would slowly, slowly, slowly reel in the string. When the crab was within arm's length, Burden would take his scoop net and reach behind the blue claw and collect it. Victory. Catching blue claws this way, with the sun on his shoulders and the sea clothing him in its salty breath and the sounds of laughter and music and cresting waves in his ear, was a thing of sublime pleasure.

He'd been working on his second blue claw when a small voice called from behind him. "It looks like fun." The voice had startled him, for he had been enveloped in the silence of the hunt. When he turned he saw a pale waif of a girl staring at him from several paces along the shore. She squinted at him in the bright sunlight, her hand to her brow for shade, the skin of her nose crinkled. Her skin was delicate like Chinese rice paper, and varying hues of blue swam below its covering, and the sun feathered pearl-pink brush strokes on the tops of her shoulders and the crowns of her cheeks and her knees and the tips of her ears. He said nothing to her, merely held up the string. She hesitated and Burden said, "Want to give it a try?" In her presence, he felt transformed into a figure of extreme inadequacy. He sucked in his gut and straightened his back, which was until that moment relaxed into a homely French curve.

The girl stepped toward him—he noticed that she was slightly knock-kneed—and stood above him. She wore a plain and unflattering bathing suit. The nascent budding of breasts showed underneath the material, casting the barest shadow in the late morning sun. As she stood next to him, Burden could smell the coconut fragrance of her sunscreen and he was overtaken with the urge to eat her as if she were food, to lick her fingers one by one till he had stolen all the flavor from the bone and let the rice paper sweetness dissolve on his tongue. "What do I do?" she asked shyly.

"Kneel here, here beside me," Burden managed, patting the water, which was warm against his shins and ankles.

The girl knelt. A greasy white line of sunscreen ran around the flesh of her right nostril. Burden reached up and rubbed it into her skin. "Thanks," she said and Burden smiled at her in a silly fashion. He was operating on ignorance and instinct, and instinct told him not to think too hard, simply act and react. "Now what?"

"Would you like my cap?" The girl said nothing. Burden removed his cap and placed it on her head. "This'll help with the sun. Although it looks like harm enough's been done already. Well, this'll keep it from getting worse. My name's Burden."

"Jo Simon."

"Ever caught blue claws?"

Jo shook her head. "I don't come to the beach very often. I don't fish either." Burden observed the light sprinkling of pale brown freckles across the bridge of her nose and cheeks; pale on pale. A few oval splotches graced the crowns of her shoulders, antipodal stars dimming in a white heaven.

"What *do* you do?"

She thought silently for a moment. At length she shrugged her shoulders and replied: "I read."

"Read?"

The girl nodded shyly. "Poetry, mainly."

Burden nodded. How dull, he thought, and at the same time, how wonderful.

"Well, this morning"—he cast a quick glance to the high-mounted sun—"or what's left of the morning—you're going to have your first lesson on catching crabs."

Had he glimpsed Jo from across the crowded beach, had he been standing in the waves as she was passing just where the waves lapped the sand at low tide, Burden would have admired her but he would have remained silent. He could be swell pals with homely girls and the sisters of friends and cousins, but it was a much more frightening proposition to approach a girl so comely as this Jo, with her green eyes and pale, opalescent skin and perfect hands and delicate fingers.

How fortunate for him, then, that Jo had spied him and spoken to him first.

They returned their attention to the crab Burden had been trying to lure, and, with his guidance, she enticed the crab to its prison. The operation took fifteen minutes. When the crab drew near, Burden reached stealthily out with his scoop net and said to Jo, "Watch this," because he was feeling important next to her and he wanted to show off. With the net behind the crab, he splashed violently in front of the blue claw with his other hand and it skittered quickly backward to what it thought was safety. Burden laughed gleefully as he hoisted the net high in the air with its treasure of sweet meat. Jo clapped her hands and squealed in that half-frightened, half-delighted way that young girls so easily affect. He handed her the net and had her shake the crab into the bucket and then they spent the following hour searching for other blue claws.

But the search was mere pretense. Mainly they had splashed through the shallows and fluttered through the waves and kicked the sticky beach sand with their toes and laughed and giggled and screamed non-sense into the sun-drenched sky. Burden had known the girl instantly; the passing minutes confirmed his knowledge of her. He wondered if she felt the same as he did, but lacked the courage to ask, as though were he to inquire, the spell or lie or foolishness or whatever it was would vanish and he'd be left with a stranger he did not and could not ever know. Still, something inside told him that he loved her; he loved her instantly. And because he'd never been in love before, not truly in love, he did not know to be afraid.

Blue claws were forgotten all together until they happened on one by accident in a tidal pool. So cleansing had their afternoon folly been that he had to reteach her everything he had shown her earlier.

And then Peedie had intruded upon them and the magic had vanished and it was just the two of them among hundreds of other beachgoers and not the two of them and no one else.

"Was that your brother?" Jo inquired when Peedie was gone.

Burden snorted at the suggestion. "Gosh, no. Peedie's my cousin."

"He your age?"

"Yeah." A worried voice began whispering in Burden's mind. It told him the spirit of Peedie lingered between him and Jo, and that his own presence was waning. Between himself and Peedie, Peedie was the fairer of the two. Peedie stood an inch taller, with hair so light a brown that the summer sun each year burned it to a dusty blonde. His cousin was also broader and if he wasn't muscular, still his body possessed a lean, efficient quality that spoke well of his future. By comparison Burden's physique was soft and, he felt, unimpressive.

"I bet he can't catch crabs like you can," Jo said finally, and the nagging voice in Burden's mind quieted.

"Hell no, he can't."

Jo smiled at his curse and he laughed with relief.

Burden's eyes darted over the beach images. Brightly dressed, large-breasted beasts lumbered in the waves while on the shore other girls lay in long-held oil-slicked poses, their limbs seemingly seized by rigor mortis, while boys like himself prowled the shore, judging the various poses. Where the sand softened and sloped upward, a vendor was renting floats and umbrellas from a cabana. Everywhere music looped through the air as songs competed for space like kites tangling in the transparent blue above the beach. With his eyes still darting, he asked: "Would you like to have lunch with us?"

"Yes," Jo responded without hesitation. "Oh, but I'll have to ask my dad."

Burden nodded.

They were silent for a few moments. As they crouched in their silence, the crab tested the fish head with a tap of its claw. In another second the fish head was in its grasp. Burden did not feel the faint tug on the line at first, but when it finally registered he started and Jo started sympathetically and they stared at the strange sight of the crab and fish head before them. "Slowly," Burden said, guiding the string's movement within Jo's fingers. When the crab was near enough, Burden took the net as he had earlier and placed it behind the crab. Without making a show of it this time, he scooped the crab into the net's belly and lifted it high. "You're mine now, Mr. Crab."

"Ours," Jo corrected.

Burden turned. He gazed into her eyes without thinking to do so, falling into them because they had opened for him in a way a girl's eyes had never opened for him before. His breath became short but this did not worry him; he'd become wrapped within a warmth greater than the sun's.

"Shouldn't you put him in the bucket with the others?"

"What?—Yes. Yes, of course. Let me have him."

Jo brought the bucket around front, and Burden upended the net and shook the blue claw into the bucket. "These'll taste great boiled," he said.

They fell silent again. Burden wanted to fall forward, fall forward and taste the wonderful fresh flavor of her skin with its marinade of coconut sunscreen. He became aware suddenly how naked his desire was reflected in his eyes and he withdrew them into the shadows. He thought he might have blushed.

"I think we should find my dad and ask him about lunch."

"Yes."

The Monte Carlo sped along the rain-slick road so quickly that at times Burden could not discern the friction of rubber to pavement; at these moments he assumed either they had taken sudden, brief flight, or the tires had merely lost their traction and the car had begun to hydroplane and that at any moment a tree would catch them up in its deadly hands. The compartment smelled of beer and a miasma of smoke levitated around them, slowing speech and thought and action; only the car itself remained in real time.

Sutton reached back a giant's hand. "Give me another Corona," he demanded of no one, everyone. Burden bent awkwardly in the backseat, pinned between Peedie and Whalie. The beer cooler rested tightly between Peedie's feet. Burden thrust a hand into the ice, burrowing past the Coors, grasping for the Corona bottle's telltale form.

"Last one, I think—wait, there's another one." Burden withdrew the bottle and passed it forward. As he did so, several drops of ice-chilled water dove from the bottle onto Sulah's bare shoulder and hurried down her breast. She pulled her shoulder down in retreat from the sudden chill and spun around to face Burden. "Watch it, jerkoff!" she spat. "That's the third time you've done that and I'm getting goddamn sick and tired of it." As she spoke they passed an oncoming car and its headlights lit her sprig of hair in glorious incandescence, transforming the confused tangle into a pilose emanation. The details of her face became lost in silhouette, with only the black circles of her mouth and raccoon eyes discernable. Then the car passed, or they passed the car, and the red glare of taillights strobed across her face, bringing her angry eyes to brief, glistening life. Peedie pinched Burden's thigh.

"Damn, Sulah," Sutton said, laughing, "rip him a new one, why don't you?"

"I'm about to if the goddamn son of a bitch doesn't watch it—don't you smirk at me, you little shit. I'll climb back there and slap that smile off of your fucking face."

Burden wished she would turn away so he could laugh at her. "It was an accident, Sulah, I swear."

"Don't call me Sulah. Don't call me anything. Don't talk to me. I won't have no jerkoff shithead like you saying my name. *Got it?*"

Burden nodded.

Sulah held him with her angry gaze a few moments longer to make sure he "got it," then settled back in the front seat.

Peedie leaned close to Burden's ear and whispered, "Do it now. Grab her tits." Burden snorted laughter into his hand and his palm smelled of stagnant beer. In his mind he watched his hands curl over the front seat, felt their twin jaws clamp onto her tits, even anticipating the slight give and spring of the flesh as it struggled beneath its cloth covering.

They had spent the last two hours joy riding, with no destination in mind save to feel the road roll under their wheels as they drank beer and cussed loudly. Each time he finished a Corona, Sutton would hang out the window, resting his hip on the door, and toss the bottle at the next approaching speed limit sign. He never missed, and each time the glass shattered with a sharp sound that fell away quickly behind them. For an hour it had rained so hard Ricky couldn't see the road ahead, and Sutton was unable to launch his bottles. But Ricky didn't slow down, Sutton wouldn't let him, taunting him to go faster if he wasn't afraid. Then the rain slackened and finally ended. When they passed the Old Sheldon Church Sutton yelled for Ricky to stop.

"Back up," Sutton ordered.

"What do you want to do?"

"Just back up, goddamn it," Sutton barked back, not angrily, but petulant and drunk. "I want to go to church; I ain't been in a long while and I need to pray. What the fuck difference does it make?"

So Ricky backed up to the church and pulled off at the entrance. It was only raining from the trees now, and then only when the breeze shook the limbs. They got out and Sutton hurried to a tree and unzipped his pants to take a leak.

Whalie peered through the darkness at Sutton pressed against a tree. "What are you doing?" he asked, his voice sloppy from drinking.

"I'm making holy water. What the fuck does it look like I'm doing?" Sutton's laughter echoed coarsely through the headstones and ruins.

Ricky fumbled for a flashlight in the trunk, found it, and trained it on Sutton.

"Get that goddamn light off me."

"Ah, come on, baby, turn around," Sulah said. "Show everybody what it is you got in your hands."

Sutton refused, but Sulah continued goading him as Ricky gyrated the light like in a strip bar, and finally he turned around and wagged his dick—which was pale and large and semilimp—at everyone and then quickly pushed it back into his pants. "Ooo, baby," Sulah cried out. "You're making me hot."

Peedie took Burden's arm and led him toward the church. "I think I'm going to puke," he said under his breath.

"Dare you to grab it," Burden teased.

Peedie stopped Burden and spun him around. "That ain't funny, cousin. Don't even joke about a thing like that," he said, heading again toward the church.

Old Sheldon Church had been twice desecrated, once by the British, after which it had been rebuilt, then by the Federal Army, after which its burned-out hulk was left to stand as testament to the unbridled fury of war. A visitor could only guess what beauty it had once possessed. Now the ruins lifted high among the surrounding limbs, a ghost of brick and mortar. Windows had been punched out, leaving grand, hollowed-out arches. Pillars rose into the air but supported nothing, while all that remained of the altar was its stone pediment.

Peedie and Burden stepped through an archway and walked to the center aisle. On clear nights one could come here and peer up through the ruins and discover a ceiling of stars hung overhead. Tonight there were only clouds above them, but occasional breaks in the cloud cover threatened to spill the pale rays of pooled light.

There came the sound of the trunk opening and closing a second time, followed by a heated exchange between Ricky and Sutton.

"You going to do it?" Peedie asked Burden.

Burden kept his eye on the clouds, at their many semilucent patches. After a moment, he said, "I don't know."

"Do it."

Burden shrugged his shoulders. "I might," he said, turning to his cousin.

"You ain't afraid, are you?"

"No," Burden insisted.

"I mean," Peedie began, his voice placating, "I can understand being scared. Nothing wrong with that. Why, just last night . . ." he said then fell silent.

" 'Just last night' what?" Burden asked, prodding him to continue. The beam of the flashlight swept over the walls and Sutton called out for the boys.

"We're over here," Peedie answered.

" 'Just last night' what?" Burden repeated.

Peedie looked shyly at his shoes. "I shouldn't say anything about it," he began slowly.

"Come on, Peedie, tell me."

"Well . . ." For a moment Peedie seemed an embarrassed young boy, an innocent lad ashamed to reveal a secret sin. "Last night I met up with Pruella Lovejoy. You know her?"

Burden shook his head. He'd heard the name but couldn't place her.

"She's in high school. Nice looking. Got a crazy boyfriend, though."

"Peedie," Burden pressed, annoyed by his cousin's dissimulation.

"Like I said, I met up with her last night. . . . We ended up behind Parker's Hardware, a little bit back in the woods."

"Goddamn it, Peedie," Burden said, his voice strained, "just tell me what happened."

"Okay, cousin, okay, since you're in such a godawful hurry, I'll tell you the short of it. I gave her five dollars and she took her shirt and bra off and showed me her titties. Happy?"

Burden flew in into a rage. "Why wasn't I there? Why didn't you tell me this girl—"

"Pruella."

"—was going to do this? You should've come got me."

"Calm down. You were having dinner with your new girlfriend—"

"She's not my girlfriend."

"Whatever. Anyway, it wasn't like I knew she was going to do it beforehand, one thing led to another and it just sort of happened."

Burden turned and walked to a window arch and looked back at the others. Sutton had his hunting rifle out of its bag and was having a difficult time loading it in his drunken state. Whalie was lying on the hood of the car, his arms over his eyes. Ricky stood at Sutton's side, trying to help with the rifle. He didn't see Sulah. But these images didn't register with him, for all he could see in his mind was a faceless girl baring her tits. His anger increased, and he felt like a child who had been singled out for punishment rightly deserved to be shared by all.

"I got it, goddamn it," Sutton said in the distance, his voice a peculiar mixture of irritation and humor.

Peedie approached Burden and placed a hand on his shoulder. "Honest, I would have brought you with me if I'd known ahead of time. We always do things together, right? I go, you go. Only you weren't around."

Burden shrugged Peedie's hand from his shoulder. The initial flash of anger was gone, but in its wake he felt a dull regret pressing against his chest.

"Careful," Ricky said in the distance.

"That's the funny thing about a girl, how she always manages to screw things up."

"What does that mean?" Burden asked, still hot.

"If Pru hadn't shown me her tits you wouldn't be mad at me now. Then again, if you hadn't met Jo you would have been with me last night and you would have gotten a look at Pru's tits for yourself. But I suppose maybe she'll do the same for you someday and I'll be the last person you'll want around."

Burden shot Peedie a hard look. "Shut up about Jo. She isn't like that and you don't know what you're talking about."

"No need to get all hot about it, Burden, I'm just telling it like it is. Everything is square until a girl comes around and then there ain't nothing but trouble. Look at what Pru did between you and me just now."

Burden took several steps toward the wall, away from Peedie.

"Look, Burden, I'm sorry what I said about Jo. She's a good girl, sure she is. No hard feelings?"

Burden remained silent and Peedie walked to him and poked him in the shoulder as he gazed into the dark distance. Without warning the night exploded into brief, sharp light as a muzzle flashed in the near distance. Burden froze and felt the air in front of his face disturbed and then there was the sound of brick shattering to pieces behind them as a bullet bit into the wall.

"Jesus Christ!" Peedie yelled. He glared furiously at the point where the shot had come from, and instead of falling to the ground or ducking behind a wall, marched toward the gunman in a high rage.

Burden hung back in the church, half hiding behind the window arch. "What are you doing?" he called after his cousin. "Are you nuts? You'll get shot!"

Peedie ignored Burden's warning and continued toward Sutton. "You goddamn prick," he screamed. "You goddamn, fucking prick. What are you doing shooting at us?"

Sutton lowered the rifle, a grin on his face, as though what he had done had been only a harmless prank. "Have a little faith, kid, I wouldn't've shot you. I'm a better aim than that."

When Peedie reached the two older boys, Ricky looked down at the ground, his complexion pale and his expression sheepish.

"I don't care what you would or wouldn't do, asshole: You don't goddamn shoot at people."

Sutton lifted the rifle and pointed its barrel at Peedie's chest. "Oh, no?" he asked in a taunting tone.

Peedie swatted the rifle away. "And don't fucking point that at me, either."

Sutton laughed, shrugging off Peedie's anger. It was evident he was amused by Peedie's reaction, and had no wish to further provoke him. "Okay, kid," he said, pointing the muzzle to the ground. "No hard feelings?" Sutton held a hand out to Peedie. Peedie regarded the gesture with disdain and stalked back toward Burden, his heels dogged by Sutton's laughter.

"Can you believe that idiot," Peedie asked, still fuming.

"I can't believe you just walked up to him like that."

Peedie brushed off Burden's concern. "He's just lucky I didn't shove that rifle right up his goddamn ass."

Burden shook his head; he was smiling now but he tried to hide his amusement. He could not picture Peedie ever being able to do any such thing to so big a body.

"Hey, ladies," Sutton yelled. "Tour's over, time to leave."

"Prick," Peedie said quietly. "Look, Burden, I'll say it again: I'm sorry what I said about Jo. And I'm sorry I wasn't able to take you with me to Pru's. To tell you the truth, her tits aren't even that great. They're too small. They're not at all like Sulah's. Don't stay mad at me, not over a girl. Okay, cousin?"

Burden agreed quickly. The sound and feel of the gunshot was still too fresh for him to be angry with his cousin. Indeed, he was in a heightened emotional state and felt the very chill of the night as though it had slipped underneath his skin.

His emotions had not come down at all when he reached the car, having bottled up his fear and anger rather than venting them as Peedie had done. This emotional energy made his limbs shake and seemed to increase either the moonlight or the acuity of his vision, for now the grounds appeared to glow with a silvery luminance. Sulah approached the car, walking through this newfound ethereal light, and Burden had to rub his eyes at what he saw. Surely this was not the same Sulah he had spent the last two hours with. That Sulah had been homely, stirring not the slightest sexual desire. She was certainly as homely now as before the shooting, but now Burden felt the sharpest urge to touch her just as Peedie must have touched Pru. It would be recompense for that loss but more than that. He recalled Peedie's dare, which he'd dismissed out of hand and then slowly accepted, only to relinquish it once more. For Burden hadn't found the courage to grab her, and had devised many reasons why he should not, the most convincing of which was simply that he didn't find her appealing. Now, however, Peedie's dare, combined with the need to regain ground lost to his cousin, stirred within him like a command he could not refuse.

He stood next to Sulah for a moment, doing his best to exchange glances with her to see if this new feeling had possessed her as well. But she turned haughtily away.

Undeterred, Burden squeezed into the back, and when Sulah heaved her bosom into the front seat he watched her attentively. Her movements seemed graceful, artistic, the gulf between her and Jo not so great. He wanted to caress her. He understood now the evening would not be complete until he had.

FIVE

On the first-year anniversary of his cousin's death, Burden lay in bed unable to sleep. Seldom was the night when he did not experience some unwanted remembrance of their final evening together. If it was not a dream made sick with cruel violence, then it was a phantom sound just beyond his window or deep within the woods that recalled Peedie to mind. And there were his thoughts also, returning always to the final seconds of Peedie's life when, in a moment for which Burden could not account, Peedie was suddenly no more. These were the hallmarks of his guilt, the evidence of the death laid at his hands. That he held within him a secret from that fatal evening, a secret he could not speak to his parents or Jo or even to a stranger in passing, only increased the unceasing weight of responsibility he felt.

He quickly came to understand his guilt and to accept the obligation that guilt demanded. It would not be enough to confess his secret; that would do nothing to bring Peedie back. No, it was necessary to complete what had been begun that fateful evening.

We always do things together, right? I go, you go. How cruel Peedie's words were now. But if it was not possible to bring Peedie back, it was possible—and it was Burden's responsibility—to follow after him. Doing so would make him and Peedie square with each other; following after his cousin would absolve his guilt. And with the release of guilt there would be no more voices calling for him at night beyond his window or within his dreams.

At 12 A.M. Burden rose from his bed and padded quietly into the kitchen. There, with the greatest care, he searched through the utensils drawer for the paring knife. Finding it, he returned to his room, pulled on a light jacket, and placed the knife in his jacket pocket. For several moments he stood peering out his window. He searched the yard for signs of his cousin and believed he saw him as a fleeting shadow moving beyond the light of the street lamp. "Hold on, cousin, I'm coming," he whispered wearily as he lifted the window sash and removed its screen. On the ground, he opened the van door and put it in neutral and pushed it along the road. When he'd gained enough distance between himself and his parents' house he leapt in, started the engine, and followed the shadowy figure to the cemetery.

Burden parked at the front gate of the grounds. Making sure there was no one nearby, he stepped from the van and hurriedly scaled the tall fencing, landing in the grass and rolling onto his side. He rose, dusted the dead blades from his pants, then proceeded into the heart of the cemetery.

The night hanging over the graveyard had not brought silence but a cache of sounds undreamed of during daylight hours. Birdsong unfamiliar to those who sleep at night echoed among the many headstones, holding to the darkness like the moss holding to the limbs of trees. In this relative quiet a falling leaf striking the clay road made a sharp sound like that of a cautious footstep, and the flutter of a wing took on the curious sound of a lady's skirt being shaken. Then there were the murmuring voices hiding in the stronger voice of the breeze, so lazy and careless in the lost hours of night. So much time had Burden spent in the cemetery at this hour that these noises were as familiar to him as his mother's voice, and disturbed him not at all. He pressed forward, intent on his destination.

An overcast sky stole what light there was from a half-moon, and so he rushed along nearly blind, his memory carrying his steps over the cemetery's familiar terrain. Such familiarity was sufficient to give him considerable confidence as he moved through the darkness, yet was not absolute, and the careless way he strode made him hit the ground that much harder when a stray root reached out from the sod to trip him. For several seconds he lay there breathless and blind, the taste of grass on his lips and the grit of clay between his teeth. In no hurry to get up, he rolled onto his back, resting as he found his breath and letting the false light produced from landing hard fade from his eyes.

A form moved in the distance and rustled through the bushes. Burden turned toward the sound but saw nothing, not even the trailing movement of leaves. Standing, he dusted himself clean and continued toward Peedie's grave, moving this time with greater care.

When he reached Peedie he hesitated, unsure of every next moment, knowing that each action he took now led to an irreversible action he wasn't certain he could take. "Evening, cousin," he said softly, his voice as unsure as his resolve. He twisted his foot in the sod and pushed his hands deep in his pants pockets against the chill. He didn't want to sit; sitting was commitment.

Don't be afraid.

I'm not, cousin, but my eyes are open to what needs doing.

Don't be afraid. It'll be over in a flash.

But not like it was with you. I need to tell you something, Peedie. I need to tell you something about that evening before I do this—

Tell me after. Time's wasting.

But why does it have to be this way?

There was only silence. Burden hesitated a few moments longer then sat cross-legged on the grave. The grass was damp and cool and he could feel its dampness through his jeans. "All right, cousin," Burden said aloud. "All right, I'll tell you after. First things first." As Burden spoke he reached into his jacket pocket for the paring knife; it wasn't there. He fished through his other pocket and then, alarmed, stood and searched his pants pockets as well. "I . . . I've lost it, Peedie. The knife. I had it but . . ." He turned and peered into the dark, back along the path he'd taken. "I tripped . . . the knife must have fallen out of my pocket."

Excuses.

"No, it's the truth. I'll find it; just give me a minute."

Time's wasting.

Burden retraced his steps as best he could. When he reached the general area close to where he had fallen, he got down on his knees and began sweeping his hands across the ground. He continued this way for ten minutes, patiently feeling his way through the darkness, feeling also his resolve, which had faltered while at the graveside, redouble in the knife's absence. It occurred to him as he groped about that had he not dropped the knife he would be dead now and his troubles over, for in hindsight his resolve and courage had multiplied and he'd forgotten his momentary lapse of will that may have kept him from applying the fatal touch. But every minute without the knife in his possession emboldened him toward committing the act. That it was the act's very impossibility of taking place securing his determination did not enter his thinking. When at last he gave up ever finding the knife, his confidence was increased by its loss, certain now he had possessed the mettle all along to draw the blade across his wrist. But if he couldn't find the knife, well, what was he to do?

He stood and turned to walk back to Peedie's and kicked a small object at his feet. Even with the sparse light the knife's blade shone in sharp relief against the surrounding black. His heart sank at the sight of the glimmering blade, which pricked the vain puffery of his ego and made him feel the fool for his imagined bravery. *I know I have to go*, he said to himself, *but why this way?*

Time's wasting, cousin.

"All right, damn it," Burden said, squatting to retrieve the knife. Acting quickly was the key to doing the job and so this time, unlike at the grave, he brought the blade's edge to his wrist without hesitating. But he did not draw it, only held it there. "Help me, Peedie. I can't do it; I can't move my hand."

Against the broad backdrop of night an unwanted—or much

wanted?—light swept the grounds. Burden swiveled around and peered back at the gates; a police cruiser had pulled up behind his van. The policeman got out and swept his flashlight inside the van's rear compartment and then again through the passenger area. Burden remained on the ground, his breath stilled, the knife at the ready against his wrist. The policeman next passed his light over the ground, apparently tracking Burden's footprints as they led to the gates.

Burden tensed his hand around the handle of the paring knife, felt the blade scratch at his skin. "Just do it," he remonstrated himself, the words carried on the barest breath. But as he thought he just might pull the blade, the policeman panned his light across the cemetery grounds and called out "Who's there!" in a voice so commanding that instead of drawing the blade across his wrist, Burden flung it into the dark distance.

"I said who's there?"

Burden stood, his legs weak. "It's me, Burden, sir," he called out.

"Who?"

"Burden, the grocer's boy."

There was a long pause and Burden wondered if maybe the policeman hadn't heard him. He started to repeat himself when the policeman finally called out from the distance: "All right, grocer's boy, what're you doing here this time of night?"

But Burden was constrained from answering by the distance and how loudly he had to speak to be heard, for he feared Peedie's overhearing the truths and lies he would have to tell. Instead of answering he started toward the gates. He was in the beam of the policeman's flashlight now and the light he walked toward blinded him with its intensity. The patrolman didn't lower the beam from Burden's eyes until he was at the gates.

"Climb on over and let's talk," the policeman said.

Burden did as instructed and the policeman told him to sit on the stone pediment.

"Now, tell me again what you're doing in a graveyard at one in the morning."

Before answering Burden glanced over his shoulder, looking back to the drape of night and the young boy hidden there. "I came by for a visit," he said, turning back around. "That's all."

"Who're you visiting this hour?"

"My cousin," Burden offered honestly. He spoke quietly, and did not look up from the ground. "He died a year ago today. Thought I'd stop by."

Burden's words seemed to soften the officer's stance. He directed the beam to the van. "That yours?"

Burden nodded.

"Your parents know you're out this late?"

"No, sir."

The policeman flicked off his flashlight. "Look, I won't give you a hard time just this once, but I want you to go home now, come back in the morning when it's light out and the gates aren't locked. I'll follow you home to make sure you get there safe."

Burden stood.

"But if I catch you out here again I'm going to have to take you in and call your parents; I don't want to have to do that. Understand?"

Burden told the officer that he did and got into his van; the policeman got in his cruiser and together they drove along the deserted Walterboro streets. They had just passed through downtown when suddenly the cruiser's blue lights came on and for a moment Burden thought the policeman had changed his mind and was going to arrest him after all. But instead the officer did a U-turn and sped away in the opposite direction.

Burden pulled over at once, sick to his stomach with fear and exhaustion, stepped from his van and vomited. "Jesus, Peedie . . ." he said when the heaves had left him. He looked up. He had stopped in front of a bar; the words "Buck's Tavern" lit the night in green and red neon, the letters flickering every few seconds like a candle's flame in a passing breeze. The strains of a song passed through the closed door, its melody smoothed over by the door's filtering touch. Without thinking it wrong to do so, Burden went inside.

At first he thought the bar was empty, that the music and dim lighting had been left going by mistake, for there were no patrons sitting among the tables. But then as he looked about the room he saw three men sitting at the bar, clumped together at the far end, their bodies all curves dressed in plaid flannel. A fourth man stood behind the bar, his hands resting on the counter's edge. This fourth man was the first to notice Burden and then the others seemed to sense there was some strange object behind them, so they turned also.

"Can I help you?"

Burden hung by the door.

"What is that?" the man farthest from Burden asked.

"It's a boy," the middle man replied.

"I can see that," the first man replied testily. "What's a boy doing in here?"

"Maybe he heard you were finally buying a round."

"Can I help you?" the bartender asked again.

"Pour him a drink, Frankie," the first man said and laughed and then the other two men with him laughed.

"Come here, son," the third man, the one closest to Burden, said. He stretched his hand out to Burden and motioned him to come to him. Burden did so with slow steps. When he reached the man, the gentleman studied him closely with a keen eye. "Name's Willie. My friends call me Blind Willie. What's your name?"

"Burden."

"Well, it's nice to meet you, Burden." The man motioned to the bar stool next to his. "Have a seat."

Willie turned to Frankie. "How about a drink for our new friend. What'll you have, son?"

Burden looked at Blind Willie's glass. "What are you drinking?"

Willie didn't tell him, only laughed and said to Frankie to get Burden a Coke. "There, that's half of what I'm drinking, anyway. I'll buy you the other half when you're old enough."

Willie raised his tumbler to Burden. "To new blood. Drink up, son."

Burden downed his drink. It was good to get the taste of bile off his lips and tongue.

"Care for another?" Willie asked.

Frankie's hand hovered near Burden's empty glass, waiting for his answer.

Burden nodded.

" 'Burden,' " Willie said, "now that name sounds familiar, but I can't quite place it."

"I'm the grocer's boy. I may have delivered to your house," Burden replied. For all the newness of this strange environment, he felt welcome. Perhaps it was simply that he hadn't been chased out as he had been at the cemetery that gave him this impression. Still, whatever the reason, he did not feel unwanted and that meant a great deal at the moment. The bartender set a full glass of Coke on the counter and he took it and drank less hastily from it than before.

The man sitting next to Willie nudged him and whispered in his ear. As Willie listened his eyes darkened in understanding, but he soon rediscovered his more pleasant expression.

"Do you believe in ghosts, sir?" Burden asked, having finished his second glass.

Willie considered Burden's question, but also still thought about what his friend had told him. At length he pushed his tumbler toward Burden. "You care to try this?"

Burden regarded Willie with a questioning look. Frankie offered Willie a questioning look as well but Willie dismissed his concern.

"Try it, just a taste. Don't need a full glass right away, but it might make your Coke taste a bit better."

Burden took the tumbler in hand and brought it to his lips, then brought it instead to his nose and sniffed it.

"It works better if you drink it," Willie offered.

Little whiskey remained in the glass, and although he wanted to do as Willie instructed and drink only a bit, Burden found he'd consumed it all in one gulp. It burned going down and with the rawness of his throat it felt like threads of fire trailing down toward his belly.

"Feel better?"

"Yes."

"Now, Burden, I'd very much like to buy you another drink, but I suspect you ought to be getting home before someone notices you're gone. You all right to go home?"

"I was heading that way when I stopped here."

"You go home and get some rest. If you want, you come back some other night, maybe not so late; you'll find us here most times. I'll buy you a drink then. But for now you go home and get some rest."

In his exhaustion Burden found he was running on automatic, and the suggestions made by others, whether it was the policeman earlier or now this man at the bar, seemed more to him like commands that he sought and willingly followed. It would be good to be in bed and to be asleep. Whether restful sleep was possible he didn't know; he doubted it. When he was at the door he turned to look back at the men. Willie nodded to him and he understood it was best that he go now. But he also knew that he could come back sometime and that he would be welcome here. That felt good.

So exhausted was Burden when he returned home that he succumbed to sleep entirely and without reserve. If any visitor had come to him, either from beyond his window or within his dreams, he was blissfully unaware of them.

Still, although he felt somewhat rejuvenated when he awoke, there remained with him the night's melancholy. He felt the dull rebuke of failure, as well, as though his cousin's eyes were heavily on him. The day only compounded his dark mood, for the morning had been miserable when he started out on his deliveries, with gray clouds promising neither rain nor afternoon sun, merely hanging overhead in damnable irresoluteness. Cooler air intimated rain, but occasional breezes argued conversely that the morning gloom might soon blow away.

Certain only that the morning was uncomfortable to move through, Burden had loaded the day's orders in the delivery van and started on his rounds. By eleven o'clock the breeze had become cold gusts of wind that, far from blowing aside the gray gauze of clouds, ushered in billowing rain clouds, whose bellies cut black wakes through the darkening sky. By lunchtime their bellies had opened, drenching the town—and Burden especially—in a hard, cold rain.

Despite the poor turn the weather had taken, Burden pressed on through the rain as unthinkingly as though by instinct. It was two-thirty when he reached Maude's. He was thoroughly soaked, having neglected to take a raincoat. His T-shirt had become sheer, his faded jeans had darkened to navy and had begun to emit a thick, vaguely unpleasant odor, and his socks were cotton weights squishing in soaked tennis shoes. To keep the paper bags from becoming too wet (he'd lost only two since the rains began), he rushed quickly from van to stoop.

So also had he rushed to the stoop of Maude's mud room. With practiced dexterity, he stretched out a pinky and pressed the doorbell. After several seconds and no Maude he pressed the doorbell again, impatient in the cold and rain, which, though it had slackened, still gusted with a cutting chill that assaulted him beneath the stoop with open-handed slaps. When there was still no Maude, he kicked the mud room's door. Standing in the rain, Burden felt the uneasiness of one being secretly watched, sensing that from an upstairs window eyes narrowed with mirth as they peered through blinds. A finger of cold water leaped from his hair to the nape of his neck and he shook off the sudden tickle it provoked. Then, from the periphery of his vision he thought he'd caught the fluttering of drapery; he kicked the door again. "Miss Whitman, ma'am?" he called out, his voice drowned out by a thunder clap. "Miss Whitman, you home?"

Maude Whitman opened the door quickly, as though making amends for her tardiness. "Why, Burden, you're soaked, absolutely soaked, soaked to the *bone*." She stood back to appraise Burden's condition. A smile crested her lips and she reached a wet hand—trails of sudsy water slid past her wrist toward her elbow—to her chin. "*Mm-mm*. My, my—oh, but here I am keeping you in the rain. What*ever* am I thinking. Come in, dear."

"Thanks, ma'am."

Maude stood slightly aside as Burden entered the mud room.

"It's awful weather out today, and there you are in the midst of it, working away, no regard for your health. Here, put the bags on the washer and I'll put them away presently."

Burden set the three bags down and took a step back. He hesitated, waiting for a tip, which he knew was coming, but also waited, no, hoped for . . . what?

Maude took a towel and blotted her hands dry, then closely and without pretense examined Burden where he stood. After a few moments' silence she said, "I believe I can see straight through you."

"Ma'am?"

"Your shirt, it's so wet I can see the color of your skin and every other detail as well." The smile crested a second time.

Burden looked down in self-examination: through the shirt's fabric, dark brown nipples stood out against pale skin, and a small circle of white showed where his belly button tucked into his stomach. He pinched his shirt between his fingers and drew it from his body, obscuring the painting Maude was so obviously enjoying.

"Well, you're certainly in no condition to continue."

"Ma'am?"

"At least, not until I've taken care of you."

"Ma'am?"

"Your clothes. Here, take them off for me and I'll dry them."

"Oh, Miss Whitman, I don't know if I should do that."

"And why not?" Maude spoke to him now as a teacher might speak to her student, that is, with assumed authority, utterly bland, utterly persuasive. "You *have* met my husband, haven't you?" Burden nodded his head. "And you know that Dr."—Maude emphasized *doctor*— "Whitman is a man who approaches his calling with the utmost seriousness. Now, how do you suppose he'd react knowing that I, a doctor's wife, had allowed a young boy like you to go back out in this horrid weather . . . in absolutely *soaked* clothing . . . caring not at all that you might catch your death of cold? I'll tell you how he'd react: He'd have my hide." Maude stepped closer to Burden. "Indeed, he'd take me over his knee and have my hide. So, I don't intend to stand here and have you argue with me. Now, off with them." She placed one hand resolutely on her hip and the other palm up in anticipation of his impending nakedness. When she saw that he was still hesitant, she added, "We won't have to wash them. Only dry them."

Burden remained motionless. He very much wanted to stand naked before Mrs. Whitman, she was a fine-looking woman; indeed, he wanted for them both to be naked. But how strong the fear? In his statuary stillness, she could not know the ferocity of the fight waging in his mind, a battle between fear and desire. And by touching her he believed he might relieve some of the weariness from his mind.

At length, she changed her tactic. She lowered her hand and made a feint toward the kitchen door. "Tell you what, I'll just give your father a call—"

"No," Burden interjected quickly, "you don't have to do that."

"Very good, dear. Now, off with them."

Burden made a furtive tug at his shirt, looking toward Maude with questioning eyes; she returned his look with her own dispassionate gaze. When at last his shirt was off, he shivered visibly, not from the cold alone, but also from a thought that would not release him and which set his nerves to wagging maniacally; he saw himself kissing Maude, and more, touching her the way he'd seen the young man touching the girl in the field last year just before Peedie was killed.

Maude applied the towel she'd dried her hands with to Burden's shoulders, then pulled the towel over his head and giggled as she chased the rain from his hair. "You're as soaked as a homeless mutt," she said, withdrawing the towel.

Burden knelt to untie his shoes. As he undid his laces, his eyes became fixated on Maude's legs just as they had the previous week; full calves swept upward to dimpled knees that, in turn, joined with inscrutable thighs that seemed to Burden pillows of pale flesh. Those thighs disappeared under a short, billowy white skirt printed with delicate lavender flowers, twined to one another by verdant vines. Pigmentless peach fuzz dusted her thighs, their strands glinting softly under electric light. Burden worked slowly on his shoes, feigning a knot had tangled the wet laces. As he knelt before her, Maude lifted one leg slightly, drawing its knee closer to its companion. Her foot lifted from its shoe, revealing a pink, uncallused heel. She held her foot in this semiclothed state for several agonizing moments, then smoothly slipped it once more into its shoe. "I'll put on some fresh coffee to warm you up. You do drink coffee, don't you?" she asked. "Oh, but of course you do," she continued before he could respond that he did not much care for coffee. "You're a young man, now, you are."

The knots in Burden's laces evaporated when Maude left the room. He stood and pulled off his shoes and socks. He pulled off his jeans, which in their wetness clung tenaciously to his thighs, then, hesitating for a moment to make certain Maude was not returning to the mud room, removed his underwear. He quickly wrapped himself in the towel, which allowed only a small triangle of milky upper thigh flesh to show.

Footsteps.

Burden straightened.

"Here," Maude said, a man's bathrobe in her hands. She passed the robe to Burden. "I believe this will fit you better than that towel." Her eyes lingered over the triangle of flesh cut in the cloth.

Burden took the robe, thanked Maude. He slipped on the robe, tied it, then reached up and undid the towel, letting it fall to the floor.

Maude knelt to retrieve the towel, her face hovering inches before Burden's robe-clad cock. She looked up at him, and he could see the glorious blue of her irises through thick lashes that fluttered soundlessly over her eyes. "Might as well dry this along with your clothes," she said, standing. At fifteen, Burden was not exceptionally tall, but then neither was Maude. Her 5'6" frame brought her eyes just below Burden's own; standing so close to him, he could feel her silent breaths on his chin. Her lips parted just as from the kitchen the coffee pot percolated toward completeness. There was a quick show of tongue, a pink, glistening animal approaching the bars of its cage, peering out to see who was peering in. Then, connected to nothing else that had passed between them, she asked, "What do you know about plumbing?"

"Ma'am?" Burden replied. A nascent erection twitched between his legs; he hoped the robe's thick material hid its movement.

"Plumbing. Come, the coffee's ready."

Disoriented, Burden followed after Maude. His skin was flushed with heat and chilled and trembling by turns; a type of mental vertigo plagued his mind and he found that as he walked, trying also to tamp down his waxing erection, he lurched slightly to his left. Once he was in the kitchen, he took hold of the counter and steadied himself. Maude retrieved two cups and saucers from the cupboard. His eyes drank in as much of her as he dared while her back was turned to him. Hair that was not entirely blond fell in generous, moussed waves, just brushing the nape of her neck. The triangle of her back fascinated him tremendously, the assured way that her discretely broad shoulders dovetailed into her waist before exploding into round buttocks. And then, supple trailing vines, her legs rooting her marvelously to the ground. His groin burned and he felt the familiar involuntary twitch as his penis suffered toward life.

"Here you go."

Burden took the cup she offered him.

"I don't know how I could have been so careless, really," she said, looking toward the sink.

Burden followed her gaze. The sink was half filled with milky water. Suds, which had largely evaporated, clung to the basin's porcelain sides while archipelagos of food light enough to float hid just below them.

"I clogged the drain and was trying to clear it when my ring slipped off my finger." Maude spoke as though accusing the ring of treason.

"Your wedding ring?" Burden asked with alarm.

"Oh, no, dear child, worse: my husband's mother's family ring. It has three precious stones set in it, one for each of her children. She willed it to us, the love. Well, I shouldn't have worn it but I had no idea I was going to be up to my elbows in *filth*. It slipped off and I didn't notice until it had worked itself well down in the muck. Oh, it would just kill my husband if I lost that ring."

Burden sipped the coffee and burned his tongue. Without making a face, he asked, "Is it gone?"

"I don't know, Burden, dear. I hope not. I think maybe that it's in the trap. Oh, I do hate calling plumbers, they're such . . . *common* creatures. Aren't they?" Maude smiled, drawing Burden into her prejudice. It excited him. "Not that I know how to take the trap off."

Burden brought the cup to his lips and made as though he'd taken a sip, then lowered it and placed it on the counter. "I could take a look at it for you, if you'd like. Do you have a wrench?"

"What a saint you are. It does seem that every week I present you with some new emergency. I hope you don't believe me to be so helpless as I appear. Really, there are some things I'm *very* good at. It's just these . . . *manly* things that confound me. But you're certainly capable, aren't you?"

Burden shrugged.

"Now, a wrench. Yes, I believe Hubert keeps one in the garage. I believe I know where it is. I won't be a minute."

While Maude foraged in the garage, Burden paced the kitchen, patting down his increasingly indurate penis. He walked stiffly to the table, studied Maude's coffee cup with its half moon of currant-colored lipstick folded over its rim. Swayed by a whim, he took the cup and carefully matched his lips to the imprint left by Maude's. The remnant felt waxen on his lips and unpleasant, yet the faint floral fragrance it emitted under the earthier odor of coffee, combined with the fact that they were lately dabbed on her lips, made the experience strangely erotic. His penis jumped and he restrained it with the table's edge till it subsided.

"Here we go," Maude announced from the garage and Burden set the cup down and drew his hands across his lips, erasing the evidence of his crime. He rushed to the sink, opened the cabinet doors below it and stuck his head inside, pretending deep inspection of the plumbing.

"See anything?"

"Uh, no. Just looking." Burden slid onto his back, making sure the robe did not open inopportunely. *But what if it did?* his mind asked before schizophrenically banishing that thought.

Maude knelt and handed Burden the wrench. "Will this work?"

Burden craned his neck and looked at Maude as he took the wrench. Of her face, only her lips and chin dipped below the open cabinets, but her legs were in full view, her knees provoking him by their nearness. From his vantage point he could see along the pressed line of her thighs, a valley that disappeared in a wedge of shadow. "Yes, that should work, ma'am."

"Burden?"

"Yes?"

"I want you to do something for me. I want you not to call me *ma'am* anymore. It makes me feel, well, *old*. I don't want to feel old. From now on I want you to call me Maude."

"Oh, I don't know—" He wanted to say *ma'am* but stopped himself. "Miss Whitman."

"Well, I suppose 'Miss Whitman' is better than 'ma'am.' We'll just try that for a while and see if we can't get to Maude later. How's that?"

Burden screwed open the monkey wrench, test-fit it to the nut, then opened it more. "I could do that." He slipped the wrench around the nut and tightened its jaw. He tested the nut for give; he didn't want to bang the pipe unless it was necessary.

"Fine. How is it?"

"A little tight. Might be frozen. A little elbow grease should get it, though."

"No," Maude continued, her voice growing softer, more deliberate, "old is not good."

"I wouldn't call you old, Miss Whitman," Burden said with a grunt. "I don't know who would." The nut remained stubbornly unmoved. He worried that he might not be able to loosen it, and how would that make him look in her eyes?

"You wouldn't?"

"What? Oh, no, ma'am . . . uh . . ."

"You *are* a sweet one. You'll make some lucky girl a fine husband one day." Maude stood and walked to the table and retrieved her coffee. When she approached Burden, she placed one foot between his legs, lingered above him, then knelt. With deft movements which implied nothing more than casual contact, she swayed her shins against his knee-caps. Burden started at her touch, craned his neck to see what was going on. Her legs were no longer pressed tightly against each other; as she swayed, the wedge of shadow became a patch of sheer lace covering a black bulge. He looked away quickly when he felt his crotch grow uncomfortably warm.

The nut gave under suddenly increased pressure. "There," he announced, his voice quivering. He looked again toward her legs. Maude had placed a hand on her knee, which had bleached white from being bent. Fingers chased imaginary dirt from her skin then fretted over her skirt's hem. He could not see her face. She placed her coffee cup on the counter.

"Of course, growing old is inevitable," Maude said, her tone almost wistful. "And when people grow old there are certain things that become, well . . . *difficult* for them. The Sweet Bird of Youth, Burden, you don't understand its magic, its power, its fleeting nature, not until its song has died. Money can't buy it back, only forestall its eventual departure."

"Miss Whitman?" A dribble of brownish water dripped near Burden's ear and he retightened the nut.

Slender fingers took the robe's belt and tugged at it without loosening its knot. Her actions seemed as innocuous as if she were merely worrying over an already well-arranged doily. Burden felt his penis twitch from her fingers' proximity; only fear stayed it from standing tall in turgid glory. "Yes, dear boy, a woman's position becomes cold comfort for her when . . ." Maude released the robe's belt and stood. "You're such an able young man, that's what you are, really, a young man, not a boy anymore. Not anymore. I shouldn't think of you as a boy; still, you're pure, even with the tragic things you've seen. My, such things. I look in your eyes and something stirs inside me, Burden; I must confess that something stirs in my breast that makes me want to comfort you. Is that so wrong? Is it so wrong for me to want to hold you? To comfort you?"

There was silence between them for several moments. Burden lay motionless, voiceless under the sink, the trap half an inch from his face. He saw his reflection in its pitted chrome, his face distorted as in a funhouse mirror; he studied his eyes, searching for some quality in them, any quality resembling that about which she spoke.

"Come," Maude said at length. "Come."

"Ma'am?" Burden replied, forgetting himself.

"Come. Come here." She waved fingers beside her legs.

Oh, God, he thought. *Oh, God.* His body was a core of fire wrapped in a skin of ice.

"Please. . . ."

Grasping the pipe, Burden leveraged himself with slow movements from below the cabinet; his joints felt as though they were squeezing glowing coals in their sockets. He lay now between her legs, staring up at her as though she were the Jolly Green Giant and he an ear of corn or pea pod discarded in a furrow. *Yes, but this Giant sported a pussy!*

Maude gazed down at Burden, her hair falling veillike around her face. Shadows of rain striking the kitchen window coursed down her face and made it appear as though she were crying. In that moment she looked to Burden very sad indeed, very distant, and very old. "Do you want to touch me, Burden?" she asked quietly.

Burden did not respond.

"Don't be afraid. Not of a touch. Never of a touch. Now—do you want to touch me?"

Burden's body trembled. After several moments of constrained silence he nodded his head.

"Then touch me."

The first contact was a fleeting connecting of fingertip to shin. *God, how soft.* But the touch was instantly withdrawn. His tongue flicked across dry lips. He looked into her eyes; she encouraged him wordlessly. A second approach was attempted; fingers, not only their tips this time, pressed lightly against her calf. He drew his hand down to her ankle, experienced the infinite spokeshaven softness of her foot just above its arch. His hand rose, as though carried aloft on some upward sweeping current of warm air, and caressed her kneecap. She took his hand and pressed his palm against her flesh.

"How does that *feel*, Burden?"

"Not old," was all he could think to say.

Maude laughed gently. With care, she guided Burden's hand beyond her knee to her inner thigh. Burden took in a breath. His penis leapt below the cover of robe. With slow motions, Maude painted the flesh of her inner thigh with his fingers. "And this?"

"It's as warm and soft as an angel."

"You couldn't have imagined it'd be so warm, could you, dear boy? It's the warmth of comfort. I would comfort you with this warmth." With her foot, Maude pushed aside the portion of robe covering Burden's swollen penis. She brushed him gently with her ankle. "How does that feel? Does it feel nice, Burden?"

Burden nodded but said nothing, could say nothing.

Deftly, Maude brought his fingers over her panties, applying the barest pressure against her pubic hair. "See, there's no need to be shy." She released his hand. As if by magic, his hand remained against her crotch. Fingers spread out and stroked her through the material. She felt to him like an old, well-used down pillow. He would never tell her this.

In the distance, thunder rolled sullenly through the streets; Burden could feel its voice in his spine as it rolled over the house.

Maude stepped back. Fear seized Burden's heart. Had she changed her mind? Had she been merely teasing him? He'd heard about such women, women who would talk to a man with deliberate ease, coaxing him, leading him on only to cut him off as suddenly as a slamming door. But as Burden lay paralyzed by this thought, she held her hand out to him, relieving him of his fear.

"Come, dear," she said softly.

With a single motion, Burden rose to his knees and grasped Maude's legs, smothering them with dry kisses that quickly moistened.

"Yes, yes, my dear Burden, yes." Maude stroked his hair. "All this and more, so much more. But we should go upstairs. Come."

They had wrestled up the stairs to the bedroom and fallen into bed, limb grappling with limb, tangling in sheets that finally were stripped to the floor. Kisses became explorations and touches of the hand became passive acts of aggression. The storm still threatened from outside but they were creating a storm all their own, with thunderclaps of flesh sounding in their ears and sweat drenching the mattress that had become their field of play. After he came and it was over, Burden was surprised to find that it had taken only five minutes for his world to change. Yet the ecstacy captured in those few moments of ejaculation could not be denied, as though all cares had been for a time abolished, all sensation not bent to the will of pleasure banished from his flesh and mind. He lay on the bed, his mind quiet as in the aftermath of a tremendous whirlwind, elated that the sex had occurred but empty inside now that it was over. Shortly he had had to urinate and went into the bathroom. When he came back Maude straddled him a second time and purred into his ear, and he was delighted that his penis responded again so quickly to her coaxing fingers as they never would have to his. "Now that I've broken you in," she had said, "let's see what you can really do." The Sweet Bird of Youth swelled. They wrestled again, and he came again but only after a much longer period of time, and the elation he felt was not so strong as at first. And then they engaged in a final bout at the end of which he was defeated, having simultaneously lost the ability to ejaculate or even to sense Maude around him. His penis had become an insensate, blunt object and this suited Maude perfectly, for it allowed her time to reach her own climax, which, to Burden's mild discomfort, was a long time coming. Afterward, Maude rose and went to the bathroom and Burden heard it as she turned on a faucet. She remained in the bathroom for several minutes and when she returned he saw that Maude had a wet towel in her hands. Without warning, she draped the towel over Burden's penis, which, although fallen, still twitched with the spasmodic movements of a beheaded snake. The towel might just as well have been soaked in ice, for Burden did not care to move or protect himself, so steeped had his mind become in the anesthesia of intercourse. He felt detached, set aloft like a leaf in the arms of a breeze. Still, he was glad to find the towel was warm, pleasantly warm, soothing him, relaxing him further against the mattress. "We bury the dead," Maude had said as she dabbed it across his crotch. Then she took the towel back to the bathroom and draped it over the curtain rod and returned to lay next to him.

They rested there on the denuded bed, their heads on pillows propped near the footboard, their feet pressed against the headboard. Burden felt very lazy, very decadent as they lay listening to the rain, falling with a slackened exhaustion all its own, mirroring their own physical dissipation. What an odd thing, Burden thought, to lie so near a naked woman, to be able to turn his head and see the details of her body, its every rise and gentle sloping away; its permutations of color and texture, to breathe in the fleshy odors so dark, so satisfying. He glanced down the length of Maude's body; her breasts had relaxed toward her armpits as she rested supinely, her pubic hair was a dark cloud on her belly's pale horizon. Her legs swayed lazily, the left becoming entwined with Burden's right.

Burden was exhausted, his body drained of energy down to his toes. As he lay next to Maude, satisfied, his mind more composed, he thought of Jo. They had never been intimate with each other, only kissed, and that not well. He had once pressed a hand to her breast and felt such instant remorse for his action, even though she had been gentle in her rebuke, that he swore to her he'd never attempt such a coarse act again.

Now he felt he must. There was little time left, for although his attempts to kill himself last night had met with failure, still he had faith that soon the door would be opened to him, the way made known. He had to introduce Jo to this wonderful discovery of motion before that moment arrived. He wanted to be in her, for her to want him to be inside her, that they might taste each other fully as he and Maude had tasted each other this afternoon. Peedie's continual gaze, alternately teasing and scornful, beckoned Burden to join him. *But now there are things, Peedie, you know,* things *that have to be done before I can run with you again.*

What things? That's just selfish talk. Sunlight's wasting. When you coming, cousin?

Soon.

Soon? That's a scared person talking. You're not scared to join me, are you, cousin?

'Course not.

But he was. It was a certainty that he must join Peedie, the obligation, as was his fault, was clear. But how? There was too much pain in the passage, and the deliberateness made the journey impossible to begin. It had been easier with Peedie, the unexpected suddenness of the end had stolen the pain. It was the very deliberateness of his trying to take his own life that made the act impossible.

Peedie, why have I got to go like you?

'Cause we always did things fair that way. We were blood brothers, that's more than cousins, more than real brothers 'cause we made it that way when it wasn't before. And everything we did, we did together. So, when you coming home, cousin?

But now he did not want to be with Peedie, not till he'd shown Jo these new tricks he'd learned at Maude's hands. *Let me finish with Jo, Peedie, let me be with her and then I'll come home.*

You'll just chicken out like you did last night. When you coming home?

I can't say.

When?

Soon—

"What are you thinking?" Maude asked, her question displacing Peedie's voice from Burden's mind.

"Nothing," he replied quickly.

"You can tell me."

He didn't think he should.

Maude bent her legs at the knees and twisted onto her belly, a nipple tickling Burden with a feathery touch where it brushed his arm. Absently, she stroked soft-skinned fingers through his hair. When she spoke her tone was very open, lacking now any pretense or manipulation. "I still remember everything about my first time. He wasn't much of a lover. Probably didn't know what to do any better than I did. Still, I was afraid and excited all at once, like I was getting on a ride that would be terribly frightening and absolutely satisfying. Afterward, turns out it was neither." Maude kissed Burden's chest. "I hope it was more than that for you."

Burden stiffened: How could she tell this had been his first time?

"A twenty-one-year-old virgin—not a curse I'd wish on anybody." Maude pressed her ear against Burden's chest. "I can hear your heart; it's beating hard. It must have been much more than that for you," she teased, smiling. She kissed his chest again, drifted upward along the valley of his neck, across his collarbone, wetting his skin along her course with moistened tongue and lips. Then, drawing back and slitting her eyes, Maude studied the three elongated scars, like furious scratch marks, on Burden's shoulder. She hadn't noticed them in the heat of engagement. She brushed her fingertips across them in fascination. "Those are from the shooting, aren't they?"

Burden shifted uneasily and shielded the scars with his hand. He nodded.

"Such young eyes to have witnessed so horrid an event. It must have been awful for you being there and helpless to do anything. I can only imagine what it was like for you. Oh, but it only makes me love my Burden all the more."

Burden turned away, wanting desperately to close his eyes to Maude's voyeuristic gaze yet fearing that to do so under the influence of her words would bring to mind afresh the violence of that evening.

Maude leaned forward and kissed him gently on the lips. "I'm sorry. I shouldn't have said anything."

"That's all right, Miss Whitman."

"Burden?"

"Yes?"

"Burden, I believe it's safe to say we've moved beyond the 'Miss Whitman' stage of our relationship. I must insist you call me Maude. Let me hear you say my name. Say 'Maude, you're the best lover I've ever had.' Go on, say it."

"You're the only lover I've ever had."

"Then you won't be lying. Now, please, for your lover: Maude—"

"*Maude?*" Hubert's voice sounded from downstairs. Burden sat bolt upright in bed. Maude moved more slowly. With deliberate ease she stood and slipped her dress over her head. "Would you zip it up for me, please, Burden?"

"Shouldn't I hide?" Burden asked, his voice sharpened by panic's keen edge. Gone was the opiate that had so recently dulled his mind.

"Don't be silly. Here, zip me up and I'll go see what Hubert wants and then send him on his way."

Burden did as he was told, marvelling at Maude's composure, her evenness of manner, for he could not feel his fingers as they grasped the zipper's tongue. When she reached the door, she turned and said, "If it makes you feel any safer, hide in the shower, he won't look for you there."

When she was gone, Burden gathered Hubert's robe and put it on. He tiptoed to the door, careful not to make a sound as he listened to their conversation. Maude's voice rose with gay animation from downstairs. Hubert's remained calm throughout. With rough accuracy, Burden followed their movements as they strayed from kitchen to front parlor and then to kitchen again. There was the sound of the refrigerator opening as Maude offered to cook Hubert dinner. Hubert insisted he could not stay, had only stopped by to retrieve some papers he needed at the office.

"But I would have been happy to bring them to you," Maude said.

"Nonsense. No need to trouble you . . . especially with the weather as foul as it is. And anyway, I wasn't certain myself where they were."

When the papers were found, Maude and Hubert's cool parting tones drifted up to Burden. The front door opened and Burden eased against the bedroom door's frame, wanting to feel relief or something akin to it. But he did not hear the door close and this absent detail spurred his anxiety. Then the doctor spoke again and Burden felt the chill of being found out.

"Where's the delivery boy?" Hubert asked.

How quickly Burden's emotions had changed. Only minutes earlier he had been lost in the haze of consummation, his thoughts for a moment at rest, his body in repose. But Hubert's question, spoken without even the hint of accusation or suspicion, was an antidote to that peace, rending it utterly.

"Dear?" came Maude's reply and Burden felt not at all reassured of his safety despite her composure.

"His van's outside."

Burden tapped his finger against the door frame, counting the seconds passing in silence as Maude conceived her answer.

"Oh, yes. He was here earlier. After he dropped off our order his van wouldn't start. I offered him a ride but he called a friend who picked him up. Said he'd be back with tools to fix it if he could. I'd forgotten all about it. I hope he won't be much longer."

Burden could hear no response from Hubert save for a measured breath and then the door closed and Burden sat back on the bed, the strength having leeched from his muscles.

"That was a pleasant surprise," Maude remarked when she returned. She held Coronas in both hands. The bottles were sweaty with condensation. "Congratulations," she said and offered a bottle to Burden.

Burden took it, brought it to his lips.

"A toast to Burden's first beer—it is your first beer, isn't it?"

Burden hesitated, then shook his head.

"Well, then, your first Corona?"

Again Burden shook his head. "My second, actually," he said, offering her an apologetic look.

Maude's expression darkened for several moments. Then light returned, first to her eyes and then her lips. "But your first after having made love to a gorgeous, succulent, physically ravishing woman."

"Yes . . . *Maude*."

Maude beamed, more by his mentioning her Christian name than by his agreeing. "Well, then, to Burden's new life. May there be no regrets and no turning back."

Maude lightly touched her bottle to his. Burden regarded her deliberately, unable to get a secure hold on his feelings; beyond the exhaustion of his climaxes, he felt a nagging melancholy, a disturbing awareness of something having been lost in their exchange. At length, Burden beat down his uncertainty, tipped the bottle and took a drink. "It's good."

Maude stood and walked to the bathroom, lifted her skirt and sat on the toilet. A spray of water sounded sharply. "In Europe women use bidets," she said as she wadded toilet paper in her hand and reached forward between her legs to wipe herself.

Burden remained on the bed. He took another drink of beer, liking its taste better now. "What's a bidet?"

"A kind of reverse sink. It sprays water upward."

"Upward? So it's a fountain."

Maude laughed gently. "Lord, no. A woman uses it to clean herself after she pees."

"Oh," Burden said, still not understanding, not caring that he didn't understand what it was that Maude was saying.

"Society is so much more civilized in Europe than in America. For instance, take what just happened between you and me. In France it would be *celebrated*—two people finding such free, pure expression of their sexuality. Here? We'd be driven from town. Well, *I* would be driven from town. You'd fare better; half the town would see you as victim in need of comfort and the other half as hero, a golden boy touched by an older woman's transforming hand."

"Maude," he said at length. "Weren't you afraid?"

Maude sat next to Burden and placed her hand on his. "Whatever of, Burden?"

"Your husband. That he'd catch us. I've seen it in movies: The husband comes home and catches the wife and her fellow in bed and he gets a gun and kills them both."

Again Maude laughed. "That doesn't sound like my Hubert. Lord," she began, then fell into quiet reflection. "Maybe right after we were married, *maybe*. You see, Hubert is a husband more to his calling than he ever was to me. And at his age, perhaps that's for the best. A woman's position," she repeated from before but fell silent, leaving her thought unfinished. "At any rate, I wouldn't worry about Hubert coming after you with a gun." Saying this she placed a finger to Burden's temple as though it were the barrel of a pistol and pressed her lips against his ear. He could feel her words again, warm and moist and threatening as she spoke. "Of course, some *other* husband might not take kindly to your sleeping with his wife, so you best stick with your Maude," she said softly, pretending to pull the trigger of her pretend gun. "Or else someone *will* put a bullet in you, and that will be the end of Burden." There was the faint undertone of Peedie's tenor in her mellowing soprano.

Burden drank from the Corona and thought silently; a glimmer of radiant light bore through the dark chamber of his soul, for as fruitless as his suicide attempt had been he now saw what he naively believed the perfect manner for killing himself, which wasn't to kill himself at all but to goad someone else into doing the dirty work for him. Recalling the sense of remove he experienced at the point of orgasm and the lingering calm afterward as he lay next to Maude, he could conceive of no better end than to be killed under the anesthesia of sexual bliss. This passing was not too painful, perhaps not painful at all. This passing through the bliss of sex led to the greater bliss of release from his guilt. This passing was certain because it rested not in his hands but another's. He turned to Maude and smiled for her. At length he replied, "Yes."

SIX

"No," **Jo said, extracting** herself from Burden's arms. He had pinned her against the trunk of a beech tree whose branches spread upward in a broad parasol. They had been necking for several minutes, making a game of innocent kisses, Burden's hands flitting across Jo's body, landing here and there. They had played this game often in the past month, Burden with trembling eagerness, Jo with engaged resignation. She had accepted his awakened inquisitiveness about her body, flattered that he found it such a worthy object when she felt it held nothing exceptional. With deft ability, she deflected his more amorous explorations, choosing when to restrain mouth or hand.

Burden had tried hard to honor her boundaries, offering profuse apologies and retreating to seemlier ground whenever he trespassed too greatly. But with the passing weeks he'd grown more aggressive, his mind unable to comprehend the opiate effect his encounters with Maude had on his psyche, how the effect grafted onto a heightened desire for Jo. Now, when she took a hand that had sufficiently explored her breast, that hand did not quickly retreat, but instead lingered, giving ground only with the greatest protest. Lips ranged farther from her own, darting over rise of cheek and swale of collar, suckling the pulp of earlobes, scheming to engage the long march down the shallow valley of her chest.

Jo grasped Burden's head as he kissed her through her cotton blouse. She covered his ears with her palms, her fingers threading through his hair. His scalp sweated in the noonday heat, darkening and becoming matted where her fingers pressed. She struggled against her desire, against the reciprocal longings Burden's insistence stirred within her own breast. *This is wrong*, a voice spoke to her; how like the tenor of her mother's voice it sounded. *Shame, shame.* Yes, but it feels so . . . so . . .

"*No.*"

Burden was on his knees. He held Jo's hips in his hands as his mouth sought her breasts. The cotton grew damp with his kisses. Hoping her mind was racing with the same blind fury that impelled his own, he pulled out the sides of her shirt and slipped his fingers underneath its material. Her skin was warm; fingers twitched over flesh rising and falling with the syncopated breaths of one caught in free fall as thumbs traced courses over a supple belly seeded with peach fuzz. Burden brought his hands to Jo's breasts as his mouth descended to her navel. He took the clasp of her jeans in his teeth and unbuttoned it.

Forward! his mind commanded.

Jo's lips yielded a delicate moan of pleasure and its sound frightened her. The abandon in her moan recalled the stern voice within her mind. "No, Burden. That's far enough." But the words were difficult to get out. With a deliberate show she pushed him from her and tucked in her shirt. She tried to appear cross, but she was as frightened by her own desire as by Burden's advances.

"Christ, Jo," Burden said, his tone hiding none of his frustration.

"Don't you use those words with me," Jo said in a scolding voice.

Burden slid his thumbs through her belt loops and tugged at them, pulling her from the tree. With saintly innocence he rested the side of his face against her belly. "I didn't mean anything by it, Jo," he offered in a placating tone. "Believe me." He imparted a single kiss on one of her tiny pearlescent buttons. "It's just that . . . you make me feel so godawful *funny* when you're this near me. I wouldn't hurt you."

"I know you wouldn't."

"I'd just as soon die than hurt you, Jo." Burden slid his thumbs farther through the loops and his fingers wrapped around till he could feel her flesh underneath the material of her jeans. "Honest, Jo. Put a bullet in me and you'll be free."

"Hush with such talk." Jo was stroking his hair; she could not remember having begun doing so.

"It's just that, God, you're just like a gift, you know, a gift I can open fresh each day like it was for the first time." As he spoke, he felt his words coax the rigidity from Jo's muscles and he eased his face against this softer pillow.

"Burden. . . ."

Burden brought a finger to his lips, "Shhh," he said quietly.

"What are you listening to?"

"Your heart."

"You can hear my heart beating all the way down there in my stomach?" she teased.

"You've got a strong heart; it's beating thump-thump thump-thump thump-thump. Wait, it's saying something."

"Is it?" Jo realized what a fool thing Burden had said. Still, a hopelessly wistful, innocent part of her wanted to believe it was more than foolishness to be in this boy's arms and to listen to him talking sweetly to her under this tree and the bright afternoon. "What's it saying, then?"

Burden hesitated. "It's faint, wait, I've got it. It's saying: 'Burden, be a fool and kiss her again'."

"Is not," she said, giggling.

Burden buried his face in the material of her shirt and growled as he kissed her in the hollow of her belly button. "I could eat you up like pecan pie."

"So now I'm a pecan pie, am I? Before I was a present."

"You're a present of pecan pie and I'm going to eat you up." As he spoke, his hands wrapped around her hips and clasped her buttocks firmly.

Up to now she had been laughing, content to let Burden talk like the perfect fool she knew he was. But now his mouth was on her jeans' button again and a rage flashed in her eyes. "*No*," she said harshly, pushing him away from her. In the motion he lost his balance and stumbled backward, landing hard on his haunches.

He thought to curse as he had earlier but held his tongue. With an exaggerated display, he sighed and fell onto his back; leaves lifted and scattered to all sides, returning to their accustomed rest on the death of his sigh. How quickly he'd ruined the mood. It was Saturday, but instead of sleeping in, the two had made a date to rise early and to walk through the woods so that they might catch the first painted rays of morning color.

They had broken the woodline while the sky was still healing from its bruise of night; above them they heard a warbler's clear, ringing voice welcoming the morning. Soon the forest floor fell away in a steep swale and the ground became damp, giving like new carpeting under their steps. The air was cool and wet, and the woodland odors and sense of space filled Burden with an animating energy that made him want to shine. He took Jo's hand in his, entwined his fingers with hers and hurried her forward. He thought of the slender present in his pocket and when he might give it to her.

"Where are we going?" she had asked, slightly breathless by their quickened pace.

"Nowhere," had been his answer. And truly, he had no destination in mind, merely knew he had to—*had* to—run through the morning light. In his rush, he felt the many morning webs breaking across his face. He wiped these away and continued forward. Occasionally the flotsam of these webs became attached to Jo's face, as well, or her clothing and she would squeal, half in delight at her bravery, for she too continued forward. Twigs and small branches snapped at their arms and dampened leaves groused from their slumber but moved very little.

Overhead, the treetops were sparkling with new life. Above their highest limbs Burden could see the blueing sky, the sunstruck leaves shimmering against this pale background. He knew that the light would be fully upon them soon, that it would spill over the rim of treetops and flood the ground and baptize them in its brilliance.

They were rushing through the Negro cemetery when the first ray fell to the ground, striking a slanting, pink-granite headstone planted more than two generations before Burden and Jo had been born.

"I have to rest," Jo pleaded, and she tore her hand from Burden's. She dropped to her knees, laughing with barely the breath to carry the sound. As she lay on her back she felt the damp grass cool her heated skin. It was a wonderful sensation.

"Just a little farther," Burden insisted.

"No, rest first." Jo rested her head in the cups of her palms. She lay quietly for several moments, with only her breathing betraying her separateness from the others in this sleepy ground. After her breath returned more easily to her, she rose to her elbows and asked, "Where *are* we going?"

Burden insisted that he did not know. "But it's not far." He looked around, his glance skipping across the many plain grave markers. The most recent had been planted a generation ago, and although the cemetery now lay fallow and nature had reclaimed the ground, even so fresh carnations and daffodils dressed several graves. Burden wondered at the dedication their bearers felt. What animating instinct drew them this distance through these woods to place flowers on the graves of kin whose voices they'd never heard? Was it instinct or will that drove them to tend their memories so unfailingly? A sting of reproach pricked him and he started visibly. "Are you ready yet?" he said to obscure the pain. "Want me to carry you?"

"Would you?"

"Of course I would, to the end of the world." Burden stood and offered Jo his hand. "Only not today. Now get up."

They walked more slowly through the quickening morning. The occasional gust shook high in the trees, sending leaves fluttering from great heights, twirling on loops of breeze like miniature carousels descending to earth. Burden caught a leaf and held it to the morning light. Veining showed strongly through its body and he imagined blood pulsing through those veins, and then he thought of Maude and her sex and how each time it had swelled around him. So caught unaware by the suddenness of this erotic thought was Burden that he cast a quick glance toward Jo, worried she could sense it.

She regarded him naively.

"I don't know where we're going, but it's not far."

And it had not been far.

The ancient beech tree rose from the ground with assured intimidation. With its girth of nine feet and height stretching forty more, with its roots threatening to lift the ground itself, with its moss hanging gravely from its gnarled limbs, the beech tree looked like a hoary-headed ogre, transformed by a witch's spell into this unmoving figure. A gaping wound, starting near the ground and continuing in a rough oval rising to a height of five feet, marred the tree's western face. Far from weakening the tree's appearance, this shadowed wound only increased its sense of dark menace, as though the wound were a mouth threatening to consume the careless traveler.

But where would I be digested if you swallowed me? Burden thought as he touched a hand to the wound.

In the cold, cold ground, the tree responded, and Burden stepped back. *To dust I'd chew your bones.*

Burden grasped the lip of the wound. Peering upward he spied the stalactites of decay that had eaten into the tree's flesh. He breathed deeply of the wound's dank odor and found it oddly satisfying. "This is the place," he said finally and they had fallen together to the base of the tree, ready for their games. From a middle distance they had looked like only one more root cresting above the dampened ground.

Without drama, Burden pulled the present from his back pocket. It was a book of poetry Jo had found in a used bookstore in Charleston. The book had been printed in the early '20s and had grown worn, hiding within its pages the odors and stains of multiple generations. Yet its very age increased Jo's interest, as did the barely legible inscription written on the book's first page in flowing, careful script, and although the ink had faded and the page yellowed, the sentiment seemed more real for having endured so long. "Here," he said, holding the present out for her, almost sounding ashamed.

Jo's eyes widened upon seeing the gift. "What is it?" she asked, her voice bright.

"It's for you."

"I know that, silly." Jo snatched the gift and held it for a moment. "Open it."

"The paper is so beautiful, I almost hate to spoil it," she said as she turned the present over, studying its pattern from every angle. "Did you pick out the wrapping yourself?"

Burden blushed deeply. He wanted to take the present back and forget he'd ever brought it. He made a grab for the book. "Give it here, I'll open it."

But Jo pulled the gift back. She laughed and then slid her thumb under a seam. Folding the paper back, her laughter quieted and her face took on an almost somber expression.

Burden shifted uneasily.

"Oh, Burden, I love it," Jo said at length, flinging her arms around his neck and kissing him deeply. Then, sitting back, she removed the book from the wrapping to examine it more closely, skimming through its pages. "What's this?" she asked, finding a poem lightly underlined in pencil.

"It's nothing," Burden mumbled, making a second unsuccessful grab for the book. Why had he gone back to the bookstore to buy it for her? he wondered, embarrassed. And why the hell had he gone and underlined *that* poem? *Because*, a voice answered, *it's her.*

Jo straightened and began reading the poem aloud in a faintly dramatic voice. " 'She walks in beauty like the night—' Now who do you suppose he's talking about?" she asked as an aside.

Burden clutched the book and pulled it down but Jo retrieved it and stood. She continued, her eyes bright with mirth. "Where was I? Oh yes: 'Of cloudless climes and starry skies'—Are my skies really so starry?" Jo asked as she paced backward through the trees, Burden in half-hearted pursuit.

"Come on, Jo."

But Burden's protests only made her speak out more gaily. " 'And all that's best of dark and bright, Meet in her aspect and her eyes.' Why, Burden, I didn't realize you were such a wonderful writer. Ah, this part is very nice: 'Thus mellowed to that tender light, Which heaven to gaudy day denies.' " As she continued, her voice followed the melody of youthful female joy and it was evident the gift pleased her greatly.

Burden retreated to the beech tree and rested against it, resigned to having to endure her recitation. He didn't like her making such a show of the gift, and thought sourly that had he to do it over again he wouldn't have bought her the book. For apart from the pleasure it gave her he understood now how it bound them closer, making it more difficult for him to leave.

Perhaps not wanting to cause him too great a discomfort, Jo continued in a more subdued voice, till as she read the poem's concluding lines she'd grown quiet and deliberate. " 'The smiles that win, the tints that glow, But tell of days in goodness spent, A mind at peace with all below.' " Here she paused as she contemplated the final line. " 'A heart whose love is innocent.' " She closed the book and brought it to her breast, remaining silent for several moments; silent and still. When she approached Burden it was with steps treading lightly over the leaf-littered ground. "Am I that girl? Is that really how you see me?"

Burden turned his face to the limbs and sky above him, his face flush.

"It's okay," she whispered into his ear, kissing its lobe.

How was it possible that the cause of his greatest agony was also the source of his greatest joy? Jo touched a finger to his cheek and he took her hand. There was so much now he could not comprehend. Irreconcilable desires tore at him, demanding he experience her fully and yet demanding equally that he exile her from his life.

She's coming between us. I knew she would the day I met her at the beach. She's coming between us, cousin.

The voice had made him take hold of Jo and kiss her desperately, anything to drown out the words. And in kissing her he felt again the surge of desire for her flesh that Maude's touch had awakened, the need to be a part of her, to erase their boundaries of flesh and soul.

But how badly the morning had ended. Now they sat apart under the old beech tree as the afternoon brought bluer skies and straggling clouds. Burden lay on his back, his feet propped against the beech's trunk. He pitched tiny stones into the air, watching their ascent, anticipating their inevitable fall as they hung suspended, for a moment motionless. Jo was an unfocused form in his peripheral vision that he tried not to see; he was thinking of Maude and seeing her mature body in his mind. They had made love on three other occasions since that first rainy afternoon. Always there was an eagerness in Maude that she should lead Burden to some new sensual diversion. He could not appreciate the desperate quality of her embraces or the abrupt emptiness behind her raw kisses, which at times stole his breath and bruised his lips. It did not seem odd to him that a fifteen-year-old should make love to a thirty-six-year-old; certainly this was no more peculiar than his desire to find his death at the hands of a jealous husband, a desire whose potency increased daily.

But finding that husband was going to be a more difficult search than he had anticipated. He had assumed other wives would react to him as Maude had, that they would draw him into their bodies with angel's wings and dust him with their kisses. And then, in that moment of climax before the emptiness, the husband would burst in on them, gun in hand, and in a jealous fury kill Burden. It was a mocking thing to find the narcotic necessary to face his death only in Maude's arms. Still he held out faith the right husband would soon be found.

Just one bullet will do the trick, he thought.

Or you could just do the job yourself, cousin.

I've tried that; it's no use. I just can't do it on my own. Help me find the right woman and her husband'll do the job for me.

Then I'll help you.

"Burden?" Jo's hand rested tenderly upon his hip, but he found nothing erotic in her touch. "What are we going to do?"

Burden cast another stone into the air. It fell very near his right ear and he heard the flat thud of its impact on the sodden ground.

Jo crawled atop Burden's chest, weaving her fingers in his hair. "I love you so much," she began. "I do and I wish a kiss could take away all your sadness. But you want too much and I can't keep up with you anymore . . . I don't want to. I won't."

Burden remained silent. He felt the tiny heaves of breaths echoing against his ribs as Jo fought not to cry.

Jo had met Peedie only once that afternoon at the beach when Burden had taught her to catch blue claws. What she knew of him she'd learned from Burden, who relived their adventures through the tales' retelling. Only to Jo did Burden speak of his and Peedie's relationship, and these reminiscences were a cord binding him especially to her. He did not speak often of Peedie when the wound was new, and never of the sudden violence of their final evening together, as though those last moments did not exist for Burden. But in the weeks that followed, the scarring over of the hurt began and she observed that although time had not healed Burden's wound, it had begun callousing it over with distance, so that with each passing day he grew more numb to the hurt.

When the hurt had numbed sufficiently, Burden began to speak to Jo of his and Peedie's adventures, of their hours in the woods pressing new trails, or of hunting quail and climbing into deer stands and pretending to hunt deer, waiting patiently for a buck to appear, their prize the creature's nearness.

Recounting these stories and others, the evening often would sneak up on them and yet they would remain under its brilliant dome well into nightfall.

How distant those evenings were. How distant from being here now with Jo in the grass underneath the beech tree.

"Jo?"

Jo's hand flexed and grew relaxed against his chest.

"I don't ever want to hurt you. I don't like it when you're mad at me."

Jo clasped Burden more tightly.

"I can't tell you why I keep messing up. I'm thinking . . . I'm think-ing this . . . that maybe we shouldn't even kiss. That's how it always starts. And then I do something to make you mad at me and it ruins everything."

"That's a hurtful thing to say." Jo pressed her face into the crook of Burden's neck and shut her eyes tightly. "It's hurtful and mean. I don't want you to stop kissing me."

"No?"

"I like it when we kiss. I want you to kiss me. But I like it just as well sometimes when all you do is hold me the way you're holding me now."

They remained by the tree, lying silently under the day's slow prog-ress. Jo fell asleep at one point, and Burden concentrated on how her hands twitched as in a dream and he tried to imagine what that dream might be. The sun was warm on his face and the air felt clean in his chest, smelling of verdant life exhaling breaths into his lungs. Under this delusion of peace he drifted away from his cares for a short time. Then the beech tree loomed over him, staring hard at him beyond Jo's shoulder. *To dust I'd chew you, boy*, it whispered to him.

SEVEN

"I need a change," Jo said to Burden the evening she began working at the Sonic. She and Burden were sitting in his van finishing their meal. Their conversation up to that point had been sporadic and unfocused, the silences in between no longer marked by a contentedness at being together but rather by the self-conscious awareness that so much wasn't being spoken of. Burden's pursuit of his ambition had made him grow lazy both emotionally and physically. If he was not dead in fact, he at least *was* dying to all those around him, including Jo . . . especially Jo. Growing accustomed to his desire, he found it was not important what the day brought; if it didn't bring the right husband, what else could it give him beyond another day?

"I need a change."

The strong fluorescent lighting chased away the immediate surrounding dark, throwing harsh shadows all around like a failed sun. Everything touched by this failed sun looked sickly. It fell across Jo, as well, and as Burden looked at her she too appeared pale and not at all well.

"I need something more stable."

Burden was uncertain what Jo was referring to at first, but assumed she meant her job. She worked at a lady's boutique where her hours were sporadic and the pay was poor.

"Well?"

Burden stuck a fry in his mouth and regarded her with a deliberately uncomprehending expression.

"What do you think? Don't you want something better than what you have right now?"

"I like working for my dad. The work is easy."

Jo turned and gazed hard out the window through the light of false day. "Lindsey is applying for a scholarship to attend college in Columbia. Have you thought about what you're doing after school?"

"What do you mean 'after school'? I'm barely a junior, it's too early for me to start thinking about that stuff." Burden felt uncomfortable when Jo spoke of the future, for when she did so it brought into focus for him that he—they—had no future, at least no certain future. Such focus made his desire an ugly thing to him.

Jo faced Burden and regarded him with unyielding eyes. "Don't you want out of your father's store? Don't you want something better than this someday?"

"Well, someday I guess but—What's got you all riled up, Jo? Is it this Lindsey girl going off to college?"

"It doesn't have anything to do with her, Burden, it has to do with you; it has to do with you and me."

Now Burden offered Jo an honestly befuddled expression. Jo took his hands in hers and stared hard into his eyes with an earnestness that caused him to retreat in his own gaze. "Tell me what you're going to be doing ten years from now? Tell me just a little. Where will you be?"

"How can I know that?"

"Then tell me what you'll be doing five years from now?"

"Jo—"

"Or one year. Tell me what you're going to be doing tomorrow, Burden. Can you tell me that? Wait, I'll tell you: You'll be making deliveries for your dad. And that's what you'll be doing next year and the year after and ten years from now."

There won't be a ten years from now, Burden thought spitefully. *There won't be a next year, and if I have my way there won't be any days after tomorrow. So stop talking about my goddamn future.* He felt provoked and wanted to explain Jo's mistake to her as he would to a young child, but he was damned if he was going to tell her the first thing.

Jo released Burden's hands and returned her gaze to beyond the window. "Sometimes I think about ten years from now and it scares the hell out of me, because it's so easy seeing myself still here and I don't want that."

"I'm not stopping you."

Jo looked at Burden quickly with a wounded expression.

"I mean, I don't want you to go, but it's not up to me what you do."

"Change scares you, doesn't it?"

"Jo, you don't . . . you don't understand," Burden began then stopped. *Just tell her, tell her what she wants to hear and that will be that,* he thought.

Tell her to go away, cousin. We don't need her around; she's only getting in the way of things.

"It isn't that easy—"

"To hell with 'easy,' Burden." Jo threw her hands in the air in exasperation. "If this is easy I don't want it. I need a change, we both do." As she spoke her eyes fell on some object in the kitchen that caught her attention.

Burden turned and looked toward the kitchen and saw the HELP WANTED sign pressed against the glass.

"Listen, Jo, I don't know. . . ." But she was already out of the van and hurrying to the kitchen. Burden watched her as she spoke to the fatter of the two cooks. In a matter of a few minutes she was heading back to the car, beaming.

"I got it!" she exclaimed as she leaned through the passenger window, collecting her purse. "He wants me to start right away. Of course,

I won't have skates till tomorrow, but that doesn't matter. I get off at twelve, but don't worry, one of the girls can take me home." She leaned in and kissed Burden. "Love you." Her mood was buoyant and the way she said "Love you," lacking the chastising tone she had used toward him, muted Burden's misgivings.

She turned to go but then looked at him, the brightness of her eyes and smile undiminished. "See how easy that was?" she said and then walked away.

That had been just over three years ago. Getting the job at the Sonic had been the first prop Jo had used to leverage herself from him. Her weekends were from that evening taken up with her work. Those evenings that were free they spent together less frequently, with one or the other finding convenient reasons why they could not be together. A year later, when Jo told him that she'd decided to attend nursing school in Charleston after graduating, he felt he would miss her, but then realized that he had already missed her, greatly, and that the newness of that misery had dulled, until now her leaving seemed only a formal recognition of a reality long endured.

And her leaving left him no alternative than to pursue his desire without reserve.

Burden pulled into a feed store opposite the Sonic and searched for Jo among the skateresses. He was aware as he waited how increasingly agitated he felt, how increasingly distant from all points surrounding, as though he were the center of a universe that had been absolved of its obligation of existence and that he was its last remaining particle, a solitary sovereign sputtering in and out of creation.

Why should seeing Jo cause him such difficulty? Part of him *wanted* to see her again, wanted once more to feel that marvelous way he'd felt when they had met on the beach in Edisto. Her moving away to Charleston had the peculiar effect of increasing her measure in Burden's mind;

for a brief time she was more alive—more real—to him than in the years they had been together. The fragrance of her flesh was constantly in his nose, the taste of her breath on his tongue; vagrant odors, that of cooking or the scent of ripening junipers or the clean aroma of an approaching storm carried on the breeze, held unexpected potency, summoning Jo before him in vivid relief. If he kept his eyes shut at these moments, she stood before him. Opening his eyes, she would vanish. In time, even with his eyes shut tightly, she was truly gone. Such feelings, he knew, could not be resurrected; they were born of the remove of distance and withered under nearness's malignant care.

Burden's gaze skipped from one skateress to another. Leslie and Lyla, trays in their hands, glided toward separate cars. Cricket stood at the window shouting in an order. But Burden didn't see Jo. Perhaps she was in the restroom or getting supplies in the back, he thought. He would give her time. As he waited, trying to spy her from across the way, a steady procession of cars pulled up next to him. He made small talk with friends, always careful to keep an eye on the Sonic.

At eleven-fifteen he gave up on finding Jo, relieved that his watch had been unsuccessful. He started the van, then leaned back, his eyes closed. A field of stars slid quickly before his inner eye, as though sped along their million billion separate journeys by an unimaginable force; whether they were being drawn toward him or pulled away he could not determine.

EIGHT

Burden drove to Old Sheldon Church a week after losing his virginity to Maude, taking with him a spiral notebook and pencil. He and Peedie had spent their last night at the church and as he strolled through its graveyard he felt something akin to fond remembrance. The trees and stonework, the patches of grass and clay had changed not at all and each spoke to him in turn of that evening. When he reached Mary Bull's crypt he sat. The sun had severed morning's yoke and had risen above the treetops curling overhead; yet the lichen-coated stonework still held night's chill, a chill that seeped into Burden's skin as he rested against the tomb's side. Even so, sitting there beside the crypt had felt right, it had felt like the beginning of things for Burden.

A handful of visitors meandered through the grounds. They were quiet patrons mostly, content to take in the sacred breath which still was imparted by the remaining walls and altar, all that was left of this twice-pillaged church. The peace was disturbed only by the occasional click of a camera and the hushed instructions of an older woman, heavy but kind looking, who pulled behind her her young, soft-faced son as she inspected each headstone. Before each marker, if it wasn't too worn, she would kneel and make a rubbing of its face by holding newsprint paper against it and scraping a charcoal stick vigorously across the paper. The boy was content to follow behind, amused by his mother's peculiar interest.

When the mother and son approached the crypt that Burden was sitting against, she offered a polite "Excuse me," approaching the crypt in such a way as to assure Burden she didn't expect him to move. But he did move just to the corner, so that the woman would have easy access to Mary Bull's final biography. The woman tore out a sheet of newsprint and held it against the tomb's side. She carried about her the fresh scent of gardenia, and each movement of her arms blew out breaths of that sweet fragrance, subduing the fusty odor emanating from the lichen-skinned crypt. "Here, Matthew," she said, motioning her son to her side, "hold the paper still while I make the rubbing." The boy did as he was asked, clambering atop the crypt and hanging his head and arms over the side. While he waited for his mother to finish, he spied on Burden and the words he was writing in his spiral notebook. When he saw what Burden had written, the boy crinkled his nose and scratched his neck.

"Matthew!" the mother chided her son when she noticed what he was doing.

But Burden didn't mind. What sense could this young boy make of his scratch marks? None.

When the mother was finished she stood back and examined her work; something in the smear of charcoal fascinated her greatly, moved her spirit in a soundless communication she alone had divined from the stone's impassive face. "Yes," she said at length, and then to her son: "Come along."

Burden followed them with his eyes for a few moments, then attended once more to his work. He was making a list, a list of names, the names of all the married women to whom he made deliveries. The list was raw, he made no discrimination based on age or shape, all that mattered was that they be wed. The excitement of executing his plan, of planning his execution, as it were, filled him with great energy and the women's names fell from his mind helter-skelter like leaves whirling in tight circles to the ground. He was at pains to put his hand on each one in turn. Letters were scribbled messily or omitted altogether. Doubtless, fully half the names were spelled incorrectly; was it Suzane or Suzanne or Suzzanne or simply Susan Miller? It didn't matter. All that mattered was that the persons drawn in Burden's chaotic scribble be recognizable to *him*.

Having collected as many leaves as he thought necessary, Burden paused to catch his breath. Across the road, a chartered tour bus sputtered into a field opposite the church. Burden watched as double-jointed doors swung back on themselves, letting escape a well-ordered row of Japanese tourists, their uniformly black-haired heads shining like polished plums in the sunlight. They gathered in a circle, waiting for someone whom Burden supposed was their tour director. After several minutes had passed, a smallish man wearing a white shirt, thin black tie, and black dress pants descended from the bus, saw that his charges were accounted for, then ushered them across the road and onto church grounds. As they drew nearer, Burden noticed that the group carried small black books, Bibles, clasped securely to their breast bones. The tour director, whom Burden now assumed was a preacher, carried a Bible larger than the others, its leaf edges dipped in gold and gleaming in the sunlight, exploding in brilliant bursts every other second or so as it caught the sun just so. The man walked slowly, with a dignified air, his chest puffed slightly out but not at all to convey pride of place. This squat, plum-headed prophet led his flock through the burned stone edifice that had once been the church's south wall. The congregation reminded Burden of spirits as they passed one by one into the open-air sanctuary without the aid of a doorway. The worshipers stood roughly in the place where wooden pews once rested, regarded one another in a brief show of fellowship, bowed their heads toward the altar, then sat cross-legged on the grassy floor. The preacher took his place at the stone altar (Burden noticed that the woman and her son had stopped making rubbings long enough to watch this peculiar show), opened his book, hesitated as in brief meditation, then started headlong into the familiar strains of a charismatic sermon. The Japanese prophet bore all the tics of a Baptist preacher, and although they were governed by his instinctual Oriental reserve, still, they were informed by demonstrative and exaggerated contrapuntal rhythms, melodic inflections of tone, extended interludes of quiet surging in sudden volume that dissolved into contemplative silence. It was, all-in-all, a beautiful interpretation of western music voiced in the Oriental scale. Still, although he appreciated the melody, Burden could not understand a single word; he could not even pick out the names of Jesus or of God. For a while he listened intently, trying by frequency of usage to understand when Christ had been spoken of, or the Holy Spirit. These were the easy nouns, he thought, but even these were lost to his ears.

At length Burden turned from the congregation and resumed work on his own redemption. With greater discrimination he went over the names a second time, screening first for age, then for weight, then a third time for looks. He whittled away fully two-thirds of the names he'd originally committed to paper. Next he drew up a second column, which he filled in with the names of each woman's husband.

Lastly, Burden scribbled next to each name a varying number of stars, the total number representing the greater or lesser likelihood that this husband or that was up to the job. Burden set the pencil down and wiped his palms on his jeans; they had grown sweaty in his contemplation of the more violent husbands. When he had finished, he had a list of twenty women, seven of which he was certain were married to husbands capable of rising to the murderous heights he required.

He felt very good. He had accomplished much sitting here in the Old Sheldon Church grounds, among the live oak and Japanese faithful. The sound of approaching footsteps caught his attention and he turned to see who was there. It was the mother and son, passing by him on the way to their car. The boy turned to look at Burden as he passed, apparently trying to catch a final glimpse of the scribblings in his notebook. With subtle daring, Burden tilted the spiral notebook over his knees so that the young boy could see clearly what was written there. *Go ahead, have a good look*, Burden thought silently. *You're the only other person*

who'll ever see what's written in these pages, and you don't have a clue what
they mean. Go ahead, have a real good look.

The mother turned, saw the boy staring again at Burden, and tugged
his arm to hurry him along.

The Japanese congregation had by this time broken up; individually,
in pairs, in small groups they trod among the headstones, gesturing with
much animation and speaking in a tongue that, Burden thought, if he
had a thousand years to study, he'd never understand the first word of.

Not withstanding the list, and no matter his efforts, it was Burden's
misfortune that he could not fall victim to any of the wives he'd noted
at the graveyard. He had naively assumed that other seductions would
quickly and naturally follow Maude's own. Could Maude have been a
singular phenomenon? Was her passionless Hubert—a toothless, claw-
less dragon—to be the only husband with which Burden would have to
contend? Notwithstanding the faint expectation he held for finding sal-
vation at Hubert's hands, Burden continued having sex with Maude, and
on several occasions Hubert returned home either during their lovemaking or just after. At first, Burden held out the hope that by some
black magic Hubert's snuffed rage would spark anew, igniting into jealousy's fatal flame, and that he would kill Burden. But Hubert never once
ventured upstairs and hence was never in a position to discover Burden
there among his possessions, would never come upon this teenage interloper with the light frosting of Maude's sexual consummation drying
to white dust on his skin.

Once, out of desperation, while Maude was downstairs helping
Hubert find an important paper, Burden knocked a lead crystal ashtray
from the dresser to the floor. The ashtray's impact produced a satisfy-
ingly deep thud as it struck the carpeting, and Burden's heart picked up
its tempo as the reverberations of that thud sounded through a tele-
graphic trembling of the downstairs chandelier. Certainly Hubert would
be compelled to come upstairs to search out the cause of so strange a
communication. Naked and with anticipation, Burden crouched next to

the ashtray, placing a hand on it and thereby giving the appearance that
he was about to put it back in the place from which he had so clumsily
displaced it. When the doctor walked in, Burden would stand—perhaps
he would place the ashtray in front of his cock in an apparent attempt
to shield his shame, but really to magnify the offending instrument while
also magnifying Hubert's rage. Burden waited.

In short order his efforts were rewarded by the sound of footsteps
bounding up the stairway. Burden lowered his head and held his gaze
fast to the ashtray so he might look up suddenly in fading innocence
when his eyes locked with Hubert's own. He counted in his mind, mea-
suring poor Hubert's progress riser by riser, footfall by footfall. For effect, he conjured forth the image of disrobing Leslie Ward, a Sonic
skateress, to plump his ebbing erection by a quarter inch or so. At last
the person was in the doorway and surely had the offending interloper
in plain sight. Burden pulled on an expression of heightened sexual glee
and with an exaggerated motion stood, his tumefying penis showcased
magnificently behind the crystal ashtray. Maude stopped short at the
bedroom door, placed a hand to her chin, and focused her eyes on the
ashtray's contents. "Ah," she said with observed languor, "this afternoon
we dine under glass."

Although Burden was too young to understand the humor in
Maude's remark, his face burned with embarrassment. Her hunger
aroused by so delectable a morsel, Maude approached Burden with such
swift steps that Burden slid his hand over the crystal ashtray from fear
he was about to be brutally assaulted. Undeterred, Maude knelt before
Burden as in prayer and removed first the ashtray and then his hand.
Helpless, Burden leaned back against the dresser, enduring the barren
pleasure of this votary's supplications. He heard the doctor's car door
closing, heard the smooth turning over of the engine, listened to its
falling glissando as the doctor—his only hope, his sanctuary—drove
away.

———

Burden continued in his lone sexual indenture to Maude a year to the day, by which time he'd abandoned hope of his plan ever taking life from the black scribbling he'd committed to his notebook at Old Sheldon Church. During this time he pursued many tactics in an attempt to make himself seduceable in the eyes of the wives on his list: He changed the way he wore his hair, he changed the soap he washed with, he changed the brand of toothpaste he brushed his teeth with. He exercised in fits and starts and to no great gain, lacking the discipline necessary for getting into shape. He spent many hours before mirrors, his bathroom mirror, the rearview mirror in his delivery van, the windows he'd pass by on the way to the doors where the wives were waiting, trying to discover what it was about him Maude had found appealing, certain that if only he could discover what that quality was, he could magnify it and transport it into the eyes of the other women. That it was not a particular of the flesh but an intangible quality of spirit which shown through or despite his flesh—and which Maude's hyperacute emotional eye was but the first to divine—he didn't understand. In his hopeless state he attempted to maintain a sense of hopefulness with each delivery, viewing each *next* household as *the* household, holding fast to his faith that *this* time the wife would see how it was that she should seduce him. But between the handing off of the last bag and the wife handing him his tip, there was never a seduction attempted. At times, when his spirit was stricken with an acute desperation, Burden wanted to whip out the list he'd made and show the wives their names. "See here," he wanted to explain to them, "you're *supposed* to fuck me, can't you read?" Over the course of this year the lethality of each husband increased fourfold, magnified by the impotence of Burden's plan. Any one husband would have done the trick; even Toady Belcher, who was nothing more than a balding stick of a man, became in Burden's eyes a monster capable of rising to quick and violent acts of retribution.

Burden's impotence filled him with no end of shame, humiliated as he was in the eyes of his cousin, to whom he'd explained the plan in great detail and with much enthusiasm. He felt Peedie shared his enthusiasm, yet as his failure became apparent, Burden found himself in the graveyard with lessening frequency, unable to face his cousin's constant questioning of how he was progressing, of how near he was to coming to stay with him permanently. So infrequent did his visits become, that laid over the weight of guilt he felt at having delivered his cousin to his grave came the additional guilt of abandoning him to it. This twofold sense of guilt weighed heavily on Burden's mind and had the effect of pulling shades progressively lower, so that from the inside the beam of light grew increasingly narrow, till it was nothing more than a blade striking the floor, while from the outside his eyes appeared dulled and shuttered.

Sex with Maude, which at first had been stimulating, became a rote exercise as with each encounter Burden's guilt eroded a little more of his capacity to feel; how could joy or sensation be his when his cousin, by Burden's own actions, felt nothing? The result of Burden's reasoning was a scabrous growth over his emotions, sheathing them and muting any sensation that might occur either to his body or mind.

Yet it was in this state of such overwhelming and honest a presentation of lostness that Burden's fortune turned.

Maude held to her interludes with Burden with a tenacious jealousy. At the age of thirty-six, she had finally been permitted unbridled exploration of her sexuality; erotic sensations surged within her at Burden's touch, and no request she made was refused, no attempted maneuver rebuked; Burden's sexuality was as bare a tableau as hers was neglected, and with her body she could write on it anything she desired.

She regarded Burden as her student, her protégé in all matters sexual, and delighted in every lesson he learned, every exercise he accomplished no matter how well or poorly. And she thought herself a worthy teacher.

Pleased though she was with the situation in which she found herself, Maude realized, to her genuine sorrow, that her student was growing increasingly despondent, becoming at times sullen, going about his exercises with a dutifulness that expressed none of the joy she brought to the endeavor. In the months after their first encounter, she could not deny the shadow that accompanied Burden, growing in familiarity until it became at last a constant companion. She attempted many diversions to rouse her wakeful somnambulate, indulging increasingly erotic fantasies in which Burden always was the principle player—or prop—and which she was certain would bring him to his former, more cheerful self.

However, despite her best efforts, her pupil sank into an ever deeper despair, which sank her spirits also, so that she, the counselor, was herself in need of counseling. It was in this vulnerable frame of mind that Maude confided one afternoon to Laurel Pellum, her house cleaner. And it was in her attempt to verbalize her frustration that she spoke, in retrospect, too openly about her situation, thus breathing life into the dead letters in Burden's notebook.

Maude's expression, her demeanor that afternoon had taken on an appearance similar to Burden's own, the way a still lake perfectly captures its background, however bright or glum it may be. Opening the door for Laurel, she let escape a sigh that spoke perfectly of her despondent mood.

"Why, what was that for, Miss Whitman?" Laurel asked.

"It was nothing, Laurel, darling," Maude replied.

"It didn't sound like nothing—" Laurel began, but Maude was retreating like a waning spirit to a distant part of the house and so she let her words fall incomplete. At any rate, she didn't care for Maude Whitman, and so she set aside Maude's despairing sigh and went to the wash room to retrieve the polish and dust rags. She began dusting, as was her habit, in the dining room. Maude passed by the doorway and gave a second weary sigh. Laurel looked up as Maude passed from view, knitted her brow in curiosity, then returned to her task. So this routine continued, with Laurel progressing from room to room and Maude always hovering nearby, passing briefly into view to breathe a sigh like a forgetful spirit in search of its haunting spot. By the time Laurel reached the kitchen she was quite used to her mournful companion, and, being herself a nonempathetic individual, shared not at all this spirit's blue mood. Indeed, as she gazed out the kitchen window while dusting the sill above the sink she could not suppress the gaiety of her own heart. "It's a lovely day outside," she remarked loudly enough for Maude to hear, certain her employer hovered just beyond the doorway.

Laurel's cheerful tone was too much for Maude, and like a piano teacher wanting to correct her student's errant phrasing, Maude entered the room and sat heavily in a chair at the kitchen table. She regarded Laurel with an expression meant to convey how limitlessly *not* lovely the day was.

"Miss Whitman," Laurel asked, turning from the window and her dusting, "whatever's the matter?"

"Nothing."

"Well, we're women, we have our troubles, don't we?" And for a moment she and Miss Whitman were not separated by their vastly differing positions in life but instead bound close by that single word: *trouble.*

Then Maude drew in a deep breath, and as she released it, intoned the word *trouble* with such self-reflecting disgust that Laurel was seized by the delight one experiences only when witnessing the distress of those occupying a higher station. "Miss Whitman," she said soothingly, hoping to peer deeper into that distress, "if you want to unburden yourself to me, I don't mind."

At Laurel's words Maude gave a little laugh utterly bereft of humor. "Unburden myself! If only I could burden myself *more.*"

Laurel screwed up her face. "You're making no sense at all," she said, taking a seat next to Maude and setting down her dust rag. "It's obvious something has hold of you. I won't breathe a word to another soul—but what has you so . . . so *blue*?"

Before answering Maude let out another sigh. "I've been used."

Laurel sucked in her breath and secretly smiled. For Maude she presented an expression of outrage quite at odds with the delight she felt.

"No, not unpleasantly so," Maude hastened to add, pricking Laurel's faint indignation. Maude allowed herself a petite smile, prettily fashioned like those smiles women who'd had happy childhoods indulge in when remembering a moment from their happy-little-girl past. But she hadn't had a happy childhood and hadn't been a happy little girl and so that smile quickly waned, and the bright pulp of her eyes became shadowed under knitted brows. "If only I were twice more burdened, I might not be so blue."

"Does Dr. Whitman know?" Laurel asked directly, certain he had nothing to do with Maude's distress.

Maude shook her head with a communicative silence. At length she continued. "It's not according to our will but Another's as to how we should be of service to one in need."

Laurel nodded, unsure what Maude meant.

"What would you think of a woman who was asked to teach someone . . . to lead, as it were, someone to a place, a wonderful, glorious place this person had never seen; a place this person's heart had never dreamed existed, to experience emotions and sensations this person could never have imagined possible? Would you call this woman a monster?"

"Certainly not, I'd call her a saint, God's own saint."

"But what if in attempting to reveal all these things and more, to do the Lord's work, as you so rightly put it, what if in this attempt she failed, and not only failed, but failed utterly and entirely, leaving her pupil more bereft of emotion, more ignorant of this glorious place than before?"

"Poor Miss Whitman," Laurel cooed, concealing her contempt for this spoiled doctor's wife.

"He came to me. . . ."

"Who came to you?"

"Burden."

"*Burden?*" Laurel repeated, genuinely surprised. "The delivery boy?" She was well acquainted with Burden, who came to her house once a week with groceries, an extravagance her husband had arranged midway through her pregnancy, and which, a year later, conveniently continued.

"Yes, Burden, that sad child."

"You fucked Burden?"

Laurel's tactless question took Maude aback, and she blinked quickly, as a cat does when a young boy blows in its face. Hesistantly, and showing with her expression she did not appreciate Laurel's blunt phrasing, she nodded.

"When?" Laurel continued, undeterred.

Maude calculated a time span that would not reveal too plainly her failure and which would minimize the illegality of her act. "Oh, a month ago . . . yes, one month ago to the day." That was good, Maude thought, for Burden was now sixteen years old, an age infinitely more mature in people's eyes than fifteen. "He came by my house to deliver the groceries I'd ordered, just a few items that I needed. It had been raining all that morning and afternoon"—Maude scanned her memory in search of rainy days within the past month, yes, there had been two that she could recall—"and by the time Burden reached our house, why the poor child was soaked."

"What did you do?"

"What any Christian woman would do, I offered to relieve his suffering. It was nothing extravagant, you understand, I offered him only a dry towel and a warm drink. But for him it must have seemed much more and as I passed the cup to Burden, our hands touched." Maude fell silent and blushed, throwing her gaze toward the sink and remembering Burden and how delicately she had parted his robe. At length she continued. "He didn't withdraw his hand. Instead, he looked deeply into my eyes and said with naked honesty: 'Miss Whitman, I have always wanted to touch your lips.' " Maude brought her fingertips gently to her lips as Laurel brought hers also to her own lips.

"And?" As Laurel spoke her moistened hand fell to her lap; unconsciously her fingers twitched across the folds of her jeans.

"Who was I to refuse so simple a request? Burden has lived through such tragedy, after all, and I felt it was my duty to comfort him in whatever way I could. I was certain of the absolute purity—the unstained charity—of the act, and because of this I allowed Burden to do as he asked; his fingertips brushed my lips with the weight and persuasion of a child's prayer, lingering there against my skin. An absolutely

beatific smile parted his lips, breaking through the sadness in his eyes—
it was as though he had been caught up in a rapture, which I must
confess was communicated to me so completely that his rapture became
mine also. Innocently, *spiritually* he asked if he might kiss them, my
lips. . . . 'Yes,' I said. 'Yes you may.' "

"Good Lord," Laurel interjected, "you didn't." She felt herself warm-
ing under the influence of her fingers and Maude's words.

Maude nodded violently, her eyes closed. "He kissed my lips with
a trembling awkwardness that broke my heart; it opened instantly for
him, pouring out a compassion that swept us both up in the unrelenting
tide of Christian love and I knew at that moment I would yield whatever
he asked of me. . . ."

Laurel leaned forward and with the fullness of her eyes begged
Maude to continue.

For her part, Maude felt giddy, her head light and swimming under
the ether of her confession; she felt emboldened to continue, even
though a voice within warned her toward prudence. Quietly, in a tone
simultaneously refusing no pity and accepting no judgment, Maude said,
"I yielded to him."

"Was it good?" Laurel asked bluntly.

Maude shut her eyes against her shame and nodded.

There passed between the women a moment of silence. Laurel's
contempt toward Maude became for a moment displaced by a sharp
jealousy at her good fortune.

"But toward what end?" Maude wailed, roused suddenly from her
silence. "I have failed—a soul once only melancholy has sunk into a
state of despondency encouraged, nurtured, and cultivated by my own
hands." Maude lifted her hands to expose the offending instruments of
her failure. "I've put this soul to death and it refuses my every effort to
resurrect it."

Laurel clutched Maude's hands and brought them to the table. She
shifted anxiously in her seat. Her jealousy returned comfortingly to contempt for Maude's ineptitude. She was twenty-three, married four years
ago and only recently a mother. She had often complained the past

thirteen months—although certainly not to Maude—of her husband's dissipated sexual appetite, which had dried up in direct proportion to the swelling of her womb. She hadn't experienced a dick-induced orgasm for ten months. Even after she'd given birth, her husband seemed to regard her as an untouchable, though whether this was from a sense of repugnance or reverence she didn't know. Sitting there, listening to Maude's woeful tale, she experienced an elation, a welcome elevation of mood that flushed her cheeks and warmed her genitalia with a sadly uncommon sense of urgency. Silently she composed a list of groceries. She regarded Maude, poor middle-aged Maude whose hand she patted in heartfelt condolence for her failure to deliver Burden from his despondency. What, she asked herself, could a sixteen-year-old possibly learn from a thirty-six-year-old apart from the feel of skin bled of its youthful moisture and softness? She would succeed where Maude had so abjectly failed. She would resurrect Burden's soul. And she would come. She would.

Yet when it came down to it, Laurel hadn't a clue how to seduce Burden. It had seemed a natural enough act as she listened to Maude's confession, as though "Hello" naturally led to "Do you want to fuck?" But the longer she contemplated how to bring young Burden under her spell, the greater became her uncertainty. She spent several days and nights in contemplation, making mental notes and then crossing through them. By week's end her fixation had simply made her hopelessly horny, and, in urgent need of groceries and still without any good ideas, in desperation she called in an order and decided to improvise.

Yet even her improvisation caused her great stress. The day Burden was scheduled to come, she waited for her husband to leave and then hurriedly set out several dresses on the bed. But none satisfied her and so she put them away. Then the baby cried and she took him up and fed him, only he didn't nurse very long and this left her with a vaguely unpleasant feeling, almost of sexual dissatisfaction. She returned her baby carefully to the crib, then backed from the room.

She had broken her morning routine on account of Burden. Perhaps that was why—in the very act of scheming Burden's seduction—no scheme revealed itself. Deciding to make the rest of her day as normal as possible, she put on a pot of coffee. When it was ready she poured a cup and sat down. But before she took her first sip, she looked with sudden horror at the room. The house was a mess, she realized. She couldn't have Burden come over with the house looking like this. Although she had never been bothered by the uncleanliness of her own house before, she jumped up, grabbed a rag, duster, and mop, in that order, and attacked the filth ceiling to floor as though her life depended on it. She would have vacuumed also, but dared not lest she wake her baby. By mid-afternoon, she had a very clean house but was, herself, filthy with sweat and house grime. Looking at the clock she cursed: Burden would be by any moment. She ran to the bathroom, tossing off clothing with each step, and jumped under the spray of water while it was still cold.

With the soap not entirely rinsed from her hair, Laurel turned the shower off and began toweling her body dry. She trembled with anticipation of what might be, and surprised herself to learn just how much her soul hungered for the act of lovemaking. Staring into the mirror at her naked body, she examined its every detail, pleased, but apprehensive as well with what she saw. She was young, her flanks were still firm. She had lost much of the weight she'd gained during her pregnancy. Her breasts—

The doorbell rang. "*Shit!*" Throwing on her bathrobe, Laurel hurried into the bedroom to find a dress she could quickly slip into. The doorbell rang a second time. She grabbed a brightly colored summer dress and untied her robe and began to take it off when she chanced to look in the dresser mirror. With her hair wet, clinging to her face in pitch strands, with her breasts glistening under a legion of water droplets, with her robe clinging suggestively to her body here and there, she realized that by accident she had happened upon just the right look. But she had to act quickly, for her disheveled appearance had to maintain its look of spontaneity rather than of contrivance. There came another knock at the door and she smiled. Walking calmly to the bathroom, she splashed a little more water on her collarbone, spread the robe a bit more at the neck and then cinched its material under her breasts. *There.*

She met Burden at the door with a smile (slightly surprised and embarrassed and not very much contrived), her bathrobe, and her bare feet. Her feet were clean.

"Morning, Miss Pellum, ma'am," Burden said. In his haste to get out of the store that morning, he had overpacked the bags, and they weighed heavily in his arms.

"Good morning, Burden." As she stood in the doorway she tried doubly hard to think of how to proceed. Her lips moved in thought.

Burden shifted the bags in arms that were growing weary. "Miss Pellum?" he said at length.

Laurel started from her concentration. "Oh, Burden, yes. I'm so sorry, of course, come in. Here, just put those bags on the counter." But how was she to begin? She felt suddenly jealous of Maude, whom she regarded as her physical if not social inferior. Her hands fell to the belt of her robe and for an instant she considered simply flinging the robe open, like a reclusive exhibitionist, and pouncing on Burden.

But she did not do this. He must want her; that was part of the game of seduction, to make the one being seduced believe he is doing the seducing.

Burden put the bags on the counter and turned around to face Laurel. He offered her a pale smile, but his eyes remained in shadow, giving him a forlorn expression. He looked down and noticed Laurel's bare feet. They were clean, he thought, but not attractive, being too stubby and broad for his taste. But her toenails were nicely trimmed and painted, and it was clear that she doted on them a great deal. "If there's nothing else. . . ." he said.

"Wait," Laurel said quickly. But saying this she again fell silent.

"Miss Pellum?"

Oh, fuck, Laurel said to herself, her lips moving so that Burden could understand what she'd just thought. She sank into a deep despair and was about to send Burden on his way when, from the other room, her baby stirred from his nap. By the timbre of his cry she understood that he was merely hungry, and not in any discomfort. Her eyes brightened at the sound of her child's voice.

"How's little Jake?" Burden asked.

"Oh, he's a doll. I just love him to death." Laurel's eyes shone brightly as she spoke of her baby. Then her eyes narrowed. "Would you like to see him? Do you have the time? You must have to run, what with all the work you do." As she spoke, Laurel manipulated the knot on her robe. She was conscious that she was swaying, like a screw being twisted right then left, right then left. "I'm a frightful sight," she said with exasperation, and she raised her hands shyly to her face and pulled back the strands of wet hair clinging to her cheeks and secured them behind her ears.

"Not at all," Burden said. His own forlorn expression did not change. Laurel had made only his initial list, the one that was simply a regurgitation of the names of all the women to whom he delivered groceries. But he'd struck through her name on the second pass precisely because she was then newly pregnant, and this made him feel apprehensive about using her in his scheme. "I'd like very much to see him."

Laurel led Burden to the baby's room. Burden peered down into the crib and studied the peculiar, pink-skinned bundle wagging its chubby arms and legs all about. The baby cried again and Laurel scooped him up.

"Oooo, baby's hungry," she cooed. Before she had time to analyze her actions, before she had a moment to reconsider what she was about to do, Laurel pulled back the robe from one breast and brought her child's searching lips to her nipple. A thrill of illicit excitement burned her face, and she was certain she was blushing. But she steeled herself, and turning to Burden to see what his reaction had been she said calmly, "He's such a dear young thing."

"Yes," Burden said with some difficulty.

Laurel looked down to her child with eyes at once loving and rapacious. "And he's just growing so fast," she said in the distracted, third-person voice a mother falls into when directly addressing her child. "Yes, he is, and he needs his mamma's milk all day and all night to help him grow. Doesn't he?"

"Yes," Burden said, immediately realizing his error that she had not been speaking to him. He reddened intensely.

Laurel looked at Burden and smiled at his blunder. She studied his eyes, which were sad and distant. Yet she thought she saw a sparkle of interest in them as he gazed in a sideways fashion at her breast as it was being suckled by her baby. Seeing that sparkle emboldened her and calmed her. The path to his seduction was suddenly clear to her: the path was his own lust and nothing more. She could not have known then that the lust she thought she detected in her prey's sad eyes was actually the working out of a calculation. She could not have comprehended that Burden was even then recalling all he knew about her husband: Did he have the will to kill Burden for fucking his wife? Equally, she could not have anticipated that his accepting the offer she was about to tender was for him merely a first step, a setting of the scene, one might say, for the final, bitter, and blessed confrontation with his destiny. When his eyes brightened, she thought only that it was the lust in his heart for her that shone within them and not the light of sick fancy.

"Burden?"

"Yes, ma'am."

"This is a beautiful thing, newborn life. Isn't it?"

Burden nodded.

"Your heart, I can tell it feels things others can't. Your eyes, they see things others are blind to. No, look here," she said as Burden turned shyly from her. "I envy you your youth, the things you'll soon experience, the places you'll someday go. God, to be a teenager again with my whole life in front of me and no responsibility. . . . Instead, I'm married and now I have little Jake, here. Don't get me wrong, I wouldn't give him back for anything in the world. It's just that," she paused as she felt her own emotion welling up within her heart, rising above the calculated nature of her speech. "It's just that there is so much I'll never experience now that . . . now that . . . ." Quite unexpectedly, a tear fell from her eye and ran along her cheek, turning along its brief course to die on the corner of her lips.

The baby cried, as though her grief had been transmitted to him through her breast. But really he was only full and wanted to rest again.

"I should go."

"No," Laurel said as she held little Jake to her shoulder and patted his round back. "No, don't go. Not yet." When she felt the little burp, she tenderly placed the infant into his crib and worried over his blanket, that it should cover him just so. As she stood there, bent sharply over the crib railing, her robe fell open. As though the act was an unconscious one, she placed her hand on Burden's hand, which gripped the rail.

She thought it best that she not say anything more, lest she dissolve into tears and drive Burden away for good. Instead, she stood up from over the crib, and with her hand still on Burden's pulled her robe from over her other breast, so that now she stood before him in something just next to all her glory. She caressed her breast, the one the baby hadn't nursed from. "My breasts ache terribly when little Jake doesn't feed long enough. A man couldn't possibly know. I'm in such need of relief, Burden, I cannot tell you. . . ." Laurel's voice grew quiet as she brought Burden's hand to her breast. With only the provocation of her eyes, whose gaze fell silently to her breast and then back to Burden, Burden fell to his knees, and at first with tentative care and then with confidence and finally with abandon, began suckling her nipple.

A tremulous wave of sexual pleasure swept through Laurel at the sensation of Burden taking her into his mouth. She stumbled backward and collapsed back onto a trundle bed, pulling Burden on top of her. They bounced as they struck the mattress and Burden removed himself from her breast and looked into her eyes, which were rimmed with tears just as his lips were rimmed in her mother's milk. "Take me," she said.

Burden nodded. He kissed the spot between her breasts and worked his way down. He lingered at her belly button so long it seemed he might go no farther. Then, partly at the insistence of her hands, which were pressing downward on his shoulders, he descended lower. At that moment when his lips met hers big Jake came into the room and froze, his mouth agape. When Laurel saw her husband standing in the doorway she thought she might scream. But before she could, her husband collapsed to his knees and buried his face in his hands. He began sobbing uncontrollably. Moaning insensibly into his palms.

Burden spun around, alarmed, thrilled, horrified that the moment had arrived. Only, why was her husband crying into his hands like a lost child? And why hadn't he gone for his gun? At length, Jake rose to his hands and began crawling toward the two lovers. "I'm sorry," he said. "Oh, my God, I'm so sorry."

Alarmed, Laurel asked, "Sorry? Sorry for what? What are you sorry for?"

"That I've driven you to . . . to *this*." He pressed his face into the thigh of her left leg. Burden yielded him some ground, but continued to hold on to her right leg.

"What do you mean? What have you driven me to?" There was panic in Laurel's voice. From his crib, little Jake began to bawl, throwing his blanket from atop him in a fit of fury, his stubby arms and legs flailing wildly.

Between sobs, big Jake said: "To the arms of another man. To *revenge*. . . . Oh, God," he blubbered with excruciating volume, "why did I ever do it? Why? Why?"

"Revenge?" Laurel said, her face twisting sickly at the implications.

"I swear to God, she meant nothing to me. Nothing!" he moaned. "Neither of them did." Big Jake foraged along her thigh in search of solace. He wrapped his arms around her waist and Burden fell back against the wall, disgusted.

"What do you mean, 'neither of them'? You bastard," she yelled, boxing his ears, "have you been fucking around on me?"

But all big Jake could do was to sob with greater vehemence into her moistening lap.

In a grand, striking movement, Laurel rose to her feet. Her eyes glared down at her husband with an expression of righteous anger so total that Moses would have trembled upon looking at her. She raised a hand high into the air, at the ready to dispatch its terrible swift justice. "Who? Tell me, goddamn it. Who've you been fucking?"

"God, please don't ask me that—"

Whack!

"I asked who, goddamn it."

"God—"

Whack!

Burden stood and left the room. Turning at the door he cast a glance back at the sad scene, remembering the other reason he had crossed Laurel so quickly from his list: Big Jake was a pussy.

NINE

Burden read through the stack of grocery lists, shuffling each page, searching for common items as he made his way down the aisles. On the sixth list he stopped. 'Pruella Boaz' was written at the top of the paper in his sister's careful script. Below the name was Pru's address on Fishburne Street, a listing of twenty-five items, and finally the brief notation *l.d.*—last delivery. Burden separated her sheet from the others, then creased the remaining lists, tapping their folded edges against his lips; in reading through the items he saw that among the usual canned fruits and vegetables, among the starches and detergents, Pru had included a request for a box of condoms, yet neglected to list the item most important to Burden: Eugene. No doubt Eugene had left Walterboro on a long haul and wouldn't be back till late tonight or possibly even tomorrow afternoon. In Eugene's absence, she would expect Burden to come to her, to relieve her of her boredom, of her being alone.

Because he had a good feeling about Eugene, who did six months in jail when he was nineteen for beating a man unconscious, Burden had initially been content to bide his time with Pru, certain her husband would do the trick. At first he played along, engaging Pruella in her rapacious sex play without the threat of Eugene's returning home, hoping that in time he could coax her into a moment of unguarded lust, a moment when she would be mindless of the time or the nearness of Eugene's return. And in those days, which became weeks then became months, he felt nearly consumed in the complete abandon with which Pru asserted her sexuality. Insatiable in her appetite and feral in her movement, Pru stalked Burden throughout the house, a naked savage intent on making a meal of him. Cornering Burden, she would pounce, skidding sharp nails across his skin, leaving lustful imprimaturs in their wake. She demanded almost always to be on top, in this way being in control not only of her pace but of Burden's as well. At moments of particular frenzy, she would batter Burden with her body, bruising him, beating him into submission with that most supple of feminine weapons, then retreat from the field so he would not die too quickly. Quietly, she would linger in her trench, speaking to him in hushed tones from across the bed or table or carpeting or whatever else had become that moment's battlefield, trying to convince him that his situation was not so hopeless as it seemed and that peace might still be attained. But appeasement merely signaled the beginning of her final charge when, with overwhelming force, she would sweep over his body, making his copulation a capitulation to her will.

Her untiring defense of sensual satisfaction elevated fucking to a communication, albeit a simple one. In those moments when she would descend upon him, jackhammering the foundations of his body, in those moments Burden felt—even without the threat of Eugene's imminent approach—a latent anxiety, believing, *hoping,* that she might quite literally consume him, flesh and bone.

"See Jo last night?" Sue asked as she rang out the grocery items.

Burden maintained his rhythm as he bagged the groceries. "Went by, didn't see her."

"You go by the Sonic?"

"Yeah. Why?"

Sue held up a bag of apples. "Fuji or Macintosh?"

"Fuji."

Sue entered the code for Fuji apples, weighed them, and set them aside, then picked up the box of condoms. She stopped and regarded the box for a moment, shaking her head. "As many boxes of these things as Miss Pru goes through, Eugene is done going to be worn to a splinter."

Burden attended very carefully to just how he put the apples in the bag.

"Hey," Sue said, suspending the box in the air before Burden, "you don't suppose she's got herself a lover, do you?"

Burden snatched the box of condoms from his sister's hand. "You shouldn't be holding on to these things, waving them around; it's not a proper thing for a girl your age." Sue had stated her question with such joyful curiosity that Burden thought she in no way implicated *him* in Pru's sordid affair. Still, he could not be certain. "Anyway, I'm sure I wouldn't know. None of our business no how."

"Just asking." Sue scrunched her lips as though she'd eaten lemon pulp. "Girl can wonder, can't she?"

Burden thought to ignore her question but was saved from this feint by the sharp sound of breaking glass carrying from a far aisle, a despairing "oh" following in the sound's wake. Burden rolled his eyes as he shoved the final bag into the cart. "I'll get it," he said.

A squat, ancient woman hovered over a shattered jar of spaghetti sauce, immobilized by her embarrassment at having brought attention to herself. Red paste pooled around her feet and the fragments of glass, staining the jar's torn label and dotting the items near where the sauce had splattered. Wheeling a bucket and mop before him, Burden approached the woman with a smile, a trick taught him by his father. "Good morning, Miss Lucy," he said brightly. "You're out early, aren't you?"

"I'm so sorry, Burden. I'm afraid I've made quite a mess, the jar just slipped from my hand. Please, let me help." She made a motion to stoop

down, an attempt so revealing of the infirmness and physical degrada-
tion age had committed on her body that Burden's heart was tugged
simultaneously by pity and repulsion.

He cast his gaze to the floor to remove her pitiable image from his
mind. Crouching to collect the larger glass pieces, he said, "Now don't
you go worrying yourself, I'll clean it up—that's what my dad pays me
for." Drawn by an almost unclean curiosity, he looked up once more
and gazed at her gray sagging face, the phantom paleness of her skin
which looked so fearfully fragile, as though a good pinch and a tug
could easily separate it from the muscle underneath. He looked down
at the floor, saw her feet, saw her thick ankles like skewed pilings, the
geography of bone lost beneath a covering of flesh and fat run through
with threads of purple and green veining. Both the slippers she wore
and her ankles were sprayed with pinhead-sized red dots, shining under
the fluorescent lighting like red spider eyes. "Don't worry yourself at all,
Miss Lucy. You go on, you finish your shopping—oh, and here you
go"—Burden retrieved a second jar of sauce from the shelf—"don't forget this."

The woman nodded in thanks and shuffled away, the pads of her
slippers making the sound of a mother quieting her child as they
skimmed across the tiled floor. Burden followed her a moment, unable
to conceive of such an age for himself. As he contemplated the infirmities
awaiting all those with the misfortune of continuing into old age, he fell
into a shallow depression, which lifted only with the reassurance that
such an advanced age, such seemingly inescapable infirmity would not
befall *him*. Buoyed by this thought, he collected the last of the glass
pieces and tossed them into a small cup hooked onto the bucket, then
he pumped the mop a few times to get it good and soaked and drew it
through the spill.

When he was finished, he crouched a final time and checked under
the shelving for glass he might have missed. Seeing no other fragments,
he stood and rose into the restraining grasp of a calloused, thick-fingered
hand clamped heavily atop his shoulder.

"Boy," a rough voice called to him. Burden recognized the voice immediately. He dipped down from the calloused hand's grasp but it refused to yield its hold on him. "Boy," the voice called again and Burden did not want to turn around, did not want to look into the eyes that awaited him. "Boy, look here."

A visceral revulsion seized Burden, a bitter taste swelled his tongue and his heart tightened in dread; with an effort he choked back the bitter taste. The man's hand twisted over Burden's shoulder as he turned, still unwilling to relinquish its grasp. "Yes?" Burden said, making no attempt to sound polite.

Silas Stoaks, a bent, burnt trunk of a man, stood before Burden. "You've moved them again, haven't you? Haven't you? You're hiding them from me," Stoaks said accusingly. The man was as old as the devil himself; far older than Miss Lucy, who seemed by comparison to walk in the faintly cooling autumn air rather than the late winter cloak shrugged over Stoaks's shoulders. His body was a pale, palsied apparition clothed in stained flesh and faded rags; the smell of ash and decay lifted from his skin and permeated the air, and Burden breathed shallowly so as not to bring too much of the man's rancid odor into his lungs. Gray irises grew from perpetually moist, grizzle-colored sclera like lichen growing from gray stones. His face was pallid, and overall his features appeared under stress, as by some lingering infection. Liver spots encrusted his skin, sprinkled under his eyes and gathered around the bridge of his nose, while across his crinkled cheeks there flared numerous faculae, which deepened the dimness through which his grizzled eyes peered. "Where are they?"

"What are you looking for?"

"My chew," Stoaks said.

"All tobacco products are up front, behind the counter. Sue can get whatever it is you're after."

For the past thirty years, Silas Stoaks had been slipping ever deeper into dementia. He was the type of man about whom people spoke in subdued voices, in tones that connoted fear, their hearts confused as to what they should feel toward him, their minds what they should think. The charitable argued pity, while others wanted Silas off the streets before further harm came to anyone. But whether it was charity or con- finement that was argued for, universally there was an apprehension borne almost of superstition that his dementia might be communicated to any who approached him. For this reason he was left alone and untouched, observed from the safety of distance as he walked the streets, his lips sputtering wetly, muttering long stretches of nonsense directed at no one, anyone. He would be overcome by sudden and brief episodes of lucidity, but these moments, as he neared ninety-three, had grown preciously rare.

Burden glanced down at the hand on his shoulder, then looked back at Stoaks's soulless gray eyes. "You want me to fetch your tobacco for you?"

"What?" Silas demanded.

Burden saw the focus in the old man's eyes falter. For a moment he was somewhere far from this place, perhaps in another time altogether. He drew in a breath, a breath that rattled with the watery reverberations of phlegm and flesh. When Stoaks released this breath, Burden could smell the sulfuric decay bleeding from his body, could detect the handi- work of time eroding the old man's bones, eating away at his organs. "This way." Burden grasped Stoaks by the wrist and removed the old man's hand from his shoulder. He turned, not caring if Stoaks followed, hoping the murderous wretch would not follow. But the old man kept hard on his heels, his crooked shadow falling over Burden, making Bur- den feel unclean.

When Sue looked up and saw her brother and Stoaks walking to- ward her, she gave an involuntary shudder.

"Sue, Silas here needs his chewing tobacco." Burden turned to Stoaks, regarding him icily. "Red Man, right?" Stoaks absently nodded. Burden turned hastily back to his sister. "Would you get him a packet?"

"You shouldn't rearrange things where a man can't get it for hisself," Silas said.

"Can I get anything else for you?"

The old man hesitated. Burden could see the glaze of incompre- hension draw over his eyes, a fog eclipsing a shallow light. Then it was another deep breath, another burst of sulfur and ash. Stoaks took hold of Burden's hand and he recoiled at the old man's calloused touch. "I know you," Stoaks said, bringing his face close to Burden's. The man's grasp was surprisingly firm and sure and Burden was at pains to break free. "Now I remember: I seen you hanging 'round my place. Yes, at dusk, just at the edge of my field."

"I'm sure I don't know what you're talking about, old man," Burden replied in a purposefully impolite tone.

"I seen you standing there in the evening. Why do you stand there and stare at my house?"

Sue approached the grim-faced pair. "Here you go, Mr. Stoaks, sir," she said, hoping to draw his attention from Burden so her brother could escape.

But Stoaks held fast to Burden's hand, peering with an incriminating zeal into the accused's eyes. "Tell me, boy."

"I ain't never been out to your place, old man," Burden replied with icy contempt. The statement was a lie, but the sentiment could not have rung more true.

Sue drew in her breath when her brother said *old man*.

Stoaks held onto Burden a moment longer, trying to divine the truth in his eyes, then at length cast off Burden's hand. "You're lying," he stated flatly, then turned to Sue. "How much I owe you?"

Burden backed away, backing into the carts holding his deliveries, sending them across the linoleum floor. He tasted the bitterness of his tongue as it became steeped again in bile and fought a growing nausea. Turning, he grabbed hold of the carts and pushed them forcefully through the front double doors. Once outside he found a bench and collapsed onto it. He leaned forward and spat and felt the acid as it lay on his tongue. He expelled as much of the old man's foul odor as he could, blowing out his breath until his lungs burned for want of oxygen, then drew in fresh air.

In a moment, Stoaks was outside, but he turned in the opposite direction from where Burden sat and so did not see him. Burden looked after the old man, studied his gait and the way his legs never fully extended as he walked, studied the shuffle of feet too weary with age to luxuriate any longer in sweeping, gliding movement. But he did not feel pity for the old man, only hatred. And he wondered if he would dream of him again tonight.

"Burden!" Pruella exclaimed, throwing her arms around Burden's neck and nuzzling his face. He felt a wet warmth spread over his cheek and the rough hide of her tongue flicking out between her lips as though she were scenting him. "Lord, am I glad to see you," she continued. "You've come just in time to save me from this empty house. I couldn't have stood it by myself for another minute." Pru stepped back and turned her eyes up at her beau, careful to keep hold of his hands. "Look at you, don't you look like you've had a day of it already and here it is only two-thirty."

Burden's fingers twitched in Pru's closed hands. "Weren't many orders today," he said to her. He turned his head slightly, averting Pru's direct gaze.

"Well, the work day's over now, right? And here you are—*Lord,* I thought I'd never make it through the morning waiting for you to get here. Oh," she said, her voice falling into a whisper, "did you bring them?" Pruella fell to her knees and went through the two grocery bags on the floor. When she found the box of condoms she pulled them out and squealed.

With an appalling suddenness, Pru fell silent and turned up her eyes softly to Burden, her lips pulling into an inscrutable grin. "I have something special planned for us this afternoon. Can you guess what it is?"

Burden shook his head without considering her question.

"Well," Pru began, running her finger underneath the flap of Burden's zipper, tugging at it, "my sister is apartment-sitting for this bigtime lawyer or some other in Charleston. Only she has to be gone most of today and tomorrow herself, and asked whether I wouldn't mind coming over and spending the night there, just to help her out."

Earlene Lovejoy-Carter's prideful face glimmered in Burden's mind then faded, leaving a transparent stain on his eyes which he rubbed away with several vigorous blinks. He had met Earlene on two previous occasions, neither of which had gone well. Pru had evidently gone on at some length about her "new lover," recasting Burden into something much more than what he was to put herself in a better light in her sister's eyes. When the true Burden had finally been revealed to Earlene, she had looked at him askance and judged him harshly. A little sadness had shone in her eyes, a shadow of disappointment that here before her stood a lost opportunity, a boy rather than the robust young man Pru had described to her.

Pru was twenty-five, having a twenty-one-year-old lover was having a lover whose cultural reference points were similar to her own. Earlene was thirty-four years old, had married when she was twenty-eight and divorced when she was thirty-one. Since her divorce she had carried with her a mistrust, a dislike even, of all things carrying the stench of maleness. Perhaps it was because of this antagonism that her attitude, her every unconscious action, reflected a strident maleness of its own, a maleness that kept well-fed a strong self-loathing, which in turn animated a fabulous contraption built of hostility and reproach, of hatred and reproof. Earlene's image glimmered dimly once more, indistinct in itself but brought more strongly in relief like a fading, glowing wick in a lantern just extinguished. Burden blinked vigorously again: however Earlene figured into Pru's plans for the day, he was certain he wanted nothing to do with her.

"What did you have in mind?"

Pruella leaned forward and wrapped her arms around Burden's waist and kissed the slight roundness of his belly. There was that warm wet sensation again and he felt himself puff up a little at her attention. In his mind he envisioned himself secluded on a lake, the hot sun beating brutally down on him, his body literally wilting under the heat, flaccid flesh sagging underneath his shirt and jeans, rubbery feet wrapped in sweat-soaked socks. He concentrated on this image and not on the reality of Pruella on her knees kissing his belly.

At length Pru relinquished her kiss and turned her face up to Burden. "I thought you might take me prisoner and drag me against my will up to Charleston," she purred. She kissed his belly once more, quickly, keeping her eyes fast to his. "And then you could lock me up indoors in that cramped little apartment and make me do your every bidding." The devil was in her eyes. "I'd be at your mercy." She kissed the smaller pocket tucked into his right jeans' pocket and Burden thought harder on the sun and the lake. But his flesh refused to melt, mesmerized and made firm as it was by Pruella's torrid breaths.

He knew perfectly well who was being taken prisoner, he knew very well under whose beneficence mercy would be dispensed. This knowledge made him quake.

"What about Eugene?"

At the sound of her husband's name, Pru released Burden and sank to the floor, sitting on her legs and peering up at Burden like a perturbed young child. "Oh, forget Eugene for once. Eugene is gone for the day and the night, as well. He won't be back till tomorrow evening at the earliest."

"He on a haul?"

Pru puffed her cheeks and then blew out warm breath. She held her hands out to Burden, which he took, helping her to her feet. "If you really must know, he went to Kingstree, visiting some old high school buddies or something. Why're you so interested in Eugene when I'm *dying* of boredom right before your very eyes?"

"I just want to make sure he's not going to miss you."

Pru pressed her palms against his cheeks and scrunched them together, touching the tip of her nose to Burden's nose. "You worry so. He ain't going to miss me. He ain't even going to know I'm gone." She kissed him, pressing firmly, her tongue moving in warm, languorous sweeps inside his mouth. When the damage was done, she released him and took a step back. "Now, are you taking me to Charleston or aren't you?"

It occurred to Burden that until very recently Charleston had been Jo's town. He had not been to Charleston since Jo had moved up there three years ago to study nursing; he didn't think of it as his having been avoiding the city—or, more precisely, Jo—but Burden could not escape the sense of lightness, of ease of movement knowing she would not be there. It was possible that he and Pru might pass by the nursing school, and that, as they walked along the streets to the apartment, they might unknowingly pass one or more of Jo's haunts. *Haunt,* yes, that conveyed just the right notion, for Jo would not be present in flesh, only in the spirit of Burden's memory. She would be no more than a ghost and if they met she would pass effortlessly through him and he would close his eyes to her, only feeling the coolness of her spirit as it distilled through the alembic of his body. This possibility apprehended Burden with a gentle unexpectedness, and he found it pleasant to contemplate such possibilities.

But Jo is right here, a voice reminded Burden, *right here in Walterboro.* All the more reason to flee, if even for the day, to Charleston. He blushed, ashamed of his cowardice. He had tried to find her, had tried to face up to her, had made the attempt. But that reflex toward action had abandoned him, and now the mere thought of meeting Jo terrified him.

Pru wrapped her arms around Burden and pressed her body into his and Burden could feel her breasts against his ribs, could feel that she was aroused. She clasped his buttocks in her hands and drove her groin into his.

"Well?" she demanded.

Burden turned his face down to Pru, whose own face beamed upward at him, a sun-burnt, freckly oval. The shadow of Jo's features passed fleetingly over Pru's own and Burden gave a quick shudder. In a moment the vision evaporated, leaving him to wonder at its occurrence. "All right," he said at length, his mouth dry, "let's go."

The hour ride to Charleston was passing quickly, with every other moment occupied by Pru's observations on the landscape, the sky, what song was playing on the radio, inconsequential thoughts about inconsequential people, or guesses as to how nice the apartment would be. When she was not filling the air of the van with her vapid banter, she visited such distractions upon Burden as kisses, caresses, petting, all deliberately designed to provoke some response from him, the more piqued the better. Burden had driven half off the highway twice while Pru teased him with tickling fingers. He drove off a third time when she sank her tongue, soaked in its warm saliva bath, into his ear, its radiant heat lulling his mind and making his eyelids grow heavy. She was laughing around the body of her tongue as she held it in his ear, its muscle moving with the liminal movement of a python. Only when the two right tires of the van had left the asphalt and began bouncing atop the uneven berm, did Pru withdraw her tongue. Laughing harder than she had yet that afternoon, she bounced over to the passenger door all agiggle, accidentally biting into her tongue and giving a little squeal.

"Kiss it," she demanded. "It's your fault I bit it, so kiss it and make it better." She jutted her tongue from her mouth.

Burden glanced sideways at the wounded, pink prong of muscle. "Where'd you bite it?"

Pru pointed midway along the left side to a small imperfect disc of red. "Rye heya." She forced her tongue out a fraction farther and it trembled.

Burden eased off the gas and leaned over to give Pru's tongue a quick peck. But when his lips touched her tongue Pru turned to him and forced her mouth rapaciously over his. He did his best to keep his eye on the road but the angle was too severe. A car passed to their right. Burden kept his eye on the car, gauging his pitch left or right by the vehicle's nearness. Seeing that he was swerving too close to the vehicle, he overcompensated leftward toward the median, felt the slope of the road's edge, then jerked the van rightward toward the passing car. The driver looked over at Burden and Pru locked in their mortal kiss, his eyes widening in comprehension of his peril as the van swung dangerously close. In a moment he was gone, having sped to safety.

Pru released Burden and leaned back against the door, satisfied. "Hmm," she said, "that was nice."

Burden faced forward and straightened his shirt. "You're going to get us killed doing shit like that, Pru."

"But what a way to go, don't you think? Two lovers entwined, then suddenly—*crash!*—in an instant it's all over. Isn't that romantic?" she mused. "It's so romantic."

Burden gave Pru a quick, queer look. Her sentiment should have aroused a fraternal sympathy within his breast, but instead an anger flared there that felt like the anger of when a person steals a cherished idea, or perhaps more precisely like when someone forces a dare.

"But then you're not a romantic, are you, Burden?" Pru asked. "No, you're all physical and artless—not rough, mind you—just artless and to the point. Of course, I've never really been an art lover myself. You and me, we understand each other, don't we?"

"What do you mean?"

"I mean, Burden, dear, that we know what we want from each other, and we're only too happy to give what the other wants in return." Pru placed her fingers against Burden's head and began stroking the lobe of his ear with her thumb. "Now Eugene, not only is he an artless lover, he's an inconsiderate bastard, as well. No foreplay, no touching, he barely even kisses me, the prick, just sticks it in me like I'm a piece of meat and he's a fork. Afterwards—'afterwards' taking all of four minutes, mind you—if he has any energy left at all, it's barely enough to get out of bed to sit in front of the TV. Otherwise, he rolls over and grunts himself to sleep, doesn't even get up to wash himself off, just oozes onto my sheets like some common garden slug oozing its slime trail.

"Now you, Burden, may be artless, but you are a very considerate lover."

Burden shrugged off the compliment.

"I mean that. You're the most agreeable lover I've ever had. Your only sin is that you never know when to quit. The way you linger afterwards—I'm very flattered, don't get me wrong—but the way you hang around after we're through, when you know Eugene has to be coming home eventually . . ." Pru paused and sucked in a reflective breath. Breaking into a bright, broad smile she said, "But of course, I see it now—that's where you find your excitement, in the possibility of getting caught; that's when you really get off, isn't it? Isn't it? Tell me."

Burden pulled a bland expression over his face.

"That's okay, whatever floats your boat. Only don't be too surprised if Eugene ain't a tad more than upset if he ever catches you."

"And what if he did? What would you do?"

"Why Burden, I'd cover you with my body and not let him harm a hair on your precious little head."

"I wouldn't ask you to do that for me."

"I know you wouldn't, but I'd do it just the same." Pru brought her hand from his ear and faced forward. "Anyway, it won't come to that. Now please, let's not have any more talk about Eugene; I want to *enjoy* my stay in Charleston."

It was an ugly sound to Eugene's ears, the ugliest he knew of; the shrill repetition of it soured his stomach and squeezed his chest with anxiety.

"Come on, Eugene," Delbart called from the other room, "it's your shot."

Eugene waved him off and turned toward the wall phone that was speaking to him in such an ugly voice. "Goddamn it, Pru, pick up," he said.

"*Eugene*," Delbart called out again.

"Give me a fucking minute," Eugene replied testily. *Damn it, Pru, where are you? Why ain't you home?* Eugene had been counting the rings, but they had grown too high in number and so he stopped counting and hung up the phone. He walked into the pool room and retrieved his cue stick from the barstool it was propped against.

"Don't get excited, I didn't leave you anything," Delbart teased.

"What?" Eugene looked at the pool table, looked across its ball-strewn field of green felt. For several seconds the scene made no sense to him as the unceasing ringing echoed in his mind, taunting him with its shrill, ugly voice and the truth he supposed it held. "She isn't home," he said in a forlorn voice to the pool hall's smoky atmosphere.

"What?"

Eugene stared a moment more at the pool table; slowly, and beyond his will, its shapes and components returned to his understanding. In that moment he knew what he had to do. He looked at his watch, it was a quarter past four. "Let's finish up here and get some dinner. I can't stay the night, I need to get home."

"What? Why, Eugene?"

Eugene bent over the table and sighted the cue to the three ball. "Something's come up." He spoke with surprising ease, with a resigned certainty that, contrary to reason, makes a man secure even if in his own doom.

Delbart glanced down at the floor and grinned when he noticed Eugene's pant leg hitched up over his boot. A silver polished pistol grip showed between folded jean and boot rim. "When'd you start carrying a gun?"

Eugene glanced down then hastily drew the pant leg over his boot. "Mind what you see," was all he said as he scanned the hall, trying to determine if anyone else had seen the weapon.

Not one to take offense, Delbart simply grinned wisely and chuckled under his breath.

Satisfied he had not been otherwise found out, Eugene drew the cue stick back and then snapped it violently forward, terribly miss-hitting the cue ball and sending it spinning forward like a delirious dervish, smashing into the three and sending that ball forward with a sudden jolt, caroming off a rail and crashing back into the remaining balls with a sharp *crack-crack-crack* like the sound of breaking fingers.

"Jesus, Eugene, what kind of pussy shot was that?" Delbart asked, laughing gaily now, amazed at how shockingly badly Eugene had hit the cue ball.

"I'm tired of this shit," Eugene said, dropping his cue stick onto the table. "Let's eat."

———

The apartment was one section of a sprawling, three-story Victorian house that had been subdivided into three separate living quarters, one per floor. Tucked away along the mansions of Broad Street, the house, painted entirely in white, seemed like a plump white elephant nestled between the other, more garishly colorful Painted Ladies on the block. A back stairway gave entrance to the third-floor apartment. Inside, it was evident by the order and cleanliness that a person of some wealth lived here. However, just as the exterior had been transformed into a pale ghostly structure not at all Victorian in color scheme or attitude, so too had the interior been pillaged of almost every vestige of the Victorian era. Tripartite walls had been painted over in subdued hues of white and blue; druggets had been rolled up, discarded, and replaced by wall-to-wall carpeting; portieres had been shorn from doorways and lambrequin from the windows, leaving them naked and vulnerable. The only touches remaining from the Victorian era were the ceiling medallion in the parlor and three small windows inlaid with carnival glass in the master bedroom. The whole effect was of a vibrant personality shamed into reticence, of a body leeched of its life blood, almost to the point of death.

Still, the apartment spoke of wealth, eloquently so, by the orderliness, the tidiness of the furnishings; there simply was nothing out of place in the several rooms of the apartment. A bookshelf, thick with leather-bound books, stuffed to their gilded edges with legalese and case law, lined one wall of the parlor. Burden pulled one of these books down, opened it, marveled at a language he did not know, and then sheepishly replaced the book among its brethren.

"Isn't this the most?" Pru said with wonder, her voice echoing flatly as she flitted through each room.

Burden left the bookshelf and walked over to the turret built out from the northeast corner. The carpet stopped at the room's threshold, revealing an octagonal pinewood floor stained almost to the darkness of molasses. An antique globe stood at the center of this small space. Its maple pedestal grew from the wood floor and exposed three roots of equal size. The globe was tattooed with blotches of forest green, Sahara tan, and sky blue, and here and there transcribed with a faded black ink. All in all, the globe seemed out of place among the other furnishings, as it alone exuded a timeless quality equal to the era from which this house had been born.

Burden spun the globe, prematurely halting its rotation when an emerald-headed pin rose over its miniature horizon. He leaned forward to read the faded ink script and saw that the pin had pierced a nameless island among the Polynesian island chain, the green island skewered like an uncatalogued butterfly pinned to a collector's tray. Burden spun the globe again but found no other telltale pins and he wondered if the person who lived in this apartment had ever been to Polynesia, or if he were there now. Or was Polynesia only a dream, a secret promise that the man kept for himself? This second possibility unsettled Burden, bringing forth a reproach in his heart that *he* had no dream of his own that he looked forward to, at least not one that was not barren and dry like dust.

Shaking off this desolate sensation, Burden stepped to the east window. In the distance, not very far away, the white spire of St. Michael's shimmered in the late afternoon sun. The first traces of dusk burnished its white body and brought to glimmering wakefulness the brass numerals of its clock. Below, the street teemed with unwashed tourists, and even from this remove, Burden could see the casual rudenesses dispensed from one person to the next; here a refusal to give ground, there a blithe cutting off of another's progress, there a stubborn trespassing on a family's photograph. Unconsciously, Burden searched the faces spilling forth from the crowd, expecting to find likenesses of Jo among their number. There were many similarities, but only fragments, nothing he could piece together to form a satisfying whole.

"*Bur-den?*" Pru sang his name, a simple, happy two-note melody. Burden turned from the window; she was calling to him from another room and her voice echoed and sounded hollow. "Look here."

Burden never mistrusted Pru more than when there was joy in her voice. He didn't like her singing his name either, rather than simply speaking it. Jo had never sung his name; she had never twisted its vowels or exchanged its consonants or otherwise distorted, maligned, or ridiculed it. His name, when spoken by her, when carried on her breath, had always sounded reassuring and good, as though her giving it voice made his name a thing of substance. He moved forward, then hesitated on the cusp of wood and carpet.

"*Bur-den?*" Pru sang to him once more. Her voice had the quality of a second-rate Siren, attempting to entice Burden to his delight and damnation.

He continued with halting steps that skimmed across the floor, and found Pru in the dining room. She was kneeling atop the dining room table, an elegant three-leaf affair built from mahogany. Its surface was heavily lacquered and Pru's twin, somewhat dimmed, met her knee-to-knee. She held a sliver of foil, within whose folds was a condom. She waved this foil before her as though she thought it a charm to bedazzle Burden.

But Burden remained where he stood, unbedazzled. He scanned the room, which bore the same white and powder blue walls as the other rooms, the same white ceiling, the same light-colored berber, making the table a dark, beautiful blot set in the midst of the room's bland cheerlessness.

"Isn't this the most beautiful table you could imagine? It's fit for a grand feast. Why, a person could seat ten guests here and there's not one of them who would bump elbows." Pru spoke as in a type of ecstasy from her high-lacquered mount. But the joy of her discovery waned visibly and quickly, and she sat down on her legs with a heaviness of spirit that dimmed her features almost to the dimness of her twin. "This is what money buys you, Burden," she said with quiet reflection, "Happiness. I'll never have a table as fine as this one. I'll never live in an apartment so nice, so lovely as this apartment."

Pru closed her eyes and tried to hum a schoolgirl's melody from long ago, the kind of simple, sweet melody that reassures and comforts the young heart. But the tune, such as it was, was not remembered so faithfully, and the melody it rendered was unpleasant to Burden's ears.

The hum collapsed into an only slightly grating droning noise that descended to the deepest register of which she was capable. The tickling vibrations this hum produced apparently buoyed her mood, for when she reopened her eyes they once more sparkled with the dangerous joy that so often possessed her. "Come here," she said, rising once more to her knees, once more brandishing her foil charm.

Burden scratched at a sudden flaring itch at the back of his neck and mumbled an unintelligible response.

Pru untucked her blouse and unfastened the clasp on her collar. Each button she opened magnified her smile. When her blouse was entirely unbuttoned, she drew its halves of fabric to either side, revealing a satin bra, below which was framed the shadow of ribs and a tight knot of flesh captured in her belly button. Her hands swept downward to her skirt and she tugged at its material, teasing Burden, hiking it higher on her thighs. "Come here." Her voice was no longer a song and no longer melancholy, but an assured, throaty enticement.

"You want to do it on the table?" Burden asked.

"Mm-hmm." Pru pointed a finger at Burden and then curled it up, beckoning him closer.

Tables were always a good substitute for a bed in Pru's thinking, and he and Pru had struggled more than a few times on her dining room table back home. But here, fucking on this table, a place people whom he would never know dined, gave Burden pause.

Realizing her prey was reluctant to approach, Pru reached back and unclasped her bra, catching it as the cups peeled from her breasts and holding it in front of her for a moment. Then, with what she believed was a smoldering seductiveness but which was not, she slid the bra away, straightening her back so that her breasts jutted outward in a supposedly tantalizing display. Burden looked down at the table, saw the roundness of her breasts reflected in the thick lacquer coating and wondered at how different they looked; he wouldn't have thought them hers at all.

"Come on over here, little boy, come see what sweet thing Mama has for you."

It wasn't fear, not so much fear, that made him hesitate. He would never tell her this, but what he felt most was disinterest; looking at her, half-clothed, he wondered why he was not in the slightest aroused. Was it only that there was no threat of Eugene bursting inconveniently through the door to find them that stole his desire? Was it that here, in Charleston, where Jo had spent the past three years learning and growing and living, that he felt it was somehow a profane act to have sex on her territory? He lifted his eyes to Pru, taking in the features that he had come to know so well, the hair the color of rusting nails with bangs that nearly touched plush, rust-colored eye brows, the pale freckled skin of her face and shoulders where a few freckles also had settled, the half-fullness of breasts, the slender waist, the white belly that once he thought he found erotic. All these things, here, in this apartment, failed to breathe the merest breath across the unfueled flames of his sexual desire.

Pru shifted atop the table. She caressed her breasts, pushing them together and upward in a manner she supposed was sexy. "I'm so lonely," she said with a little girl pout. "This table is so big and I'm up here all by myself. Won't you come and save me from being alone?" A stray finger slipped into her mouth and she suckled it as she cut her eye at Burden.

Burden looked over at the door and closed his eyes tightly. In his mind, the door no longer let onto Charleston but instead onto Pru's backyard. And this dining room was not in Charleston anymore but in Walterboro. It was late, Eugene would be getting home soon; he'd be tired and hungry and grimy with the sweat of a day's hard efforts, he wouldn't be in any mood to come home to find another man humping his wife on his dinner table. Burden envisioned with perfect clarity the gun rack hanging in Eugene's living room, he could see the lever-action .30-.30 cradled in its lowest rack. Certainly that would be the gun Eugene would bring down. It was powerful—one well-placed shot would do the trick—and if he missed he wouldn't pepper the walls with lead shot the way he would if he missed with the .12-gauge. Burden felt the first timorous twitch in his dick. Wasn't that the sound of Eugene's truck just a few blocks away, chugging closer? His arousal strengthened. Opening his eyes he looked at Pru once again.

"What if we got caught?"

Pru laughed at such a foolish notion. "We ain't going to get caught, Burden. Who is there to catch us?"

Burden stepped forward. He felt the semihardness of his dick pressing against his pants.

"But what if we did? What if this was home?" he asked, offering Pru a different fantasy, a fantasy more to her liking. "What if this was your home and this was your table?"

Burden's supposition changed the connotation of Pru's smile, making it a feature both knowing and wise. "I see what you're doing," she answered him. She took hold of her skirt and lifted its hem to her belly, exposing her panties.

"Only it's awful, awful late in the day," she said. "Eugene could wander home any minute now to this fine, fine apartment of ours." She slipped the fingers of one hand below her panties. "Only I don't care," she moaned. "I want you now. To hell with Eugene—fuck me."

Burden unzipped his jeans, carefully navigating the steel pincers over his swollen dick, and pushed his pants down. Stepping forward, he stumbled slightly, stopped, kicked off his shoes and removed his pants from around his ankles, then continued toward the table.

Pru smiled at Burden's stumble but recovered her composure quickly. "Come to me now, Burden, while there's still time enough," she cried. She pushed her panties down to her knees. Her hands glided over her thighs, plowed the furrow of her pussy and traced upward toward her belly.

Burden shoved a chair out of his way and clambered atop the table. Pru crawled to him and met him at the table's edge. "Fuck me," she breathed hotly into his ear. "Fuck me right here on my fine, beautiful table." As she spoke, she ripped open the package and withdrew the condom from its womb of foil.

"I think I can hear Eugene's truck."

"I don't care," she said, unrolling the condom and slipping it, with able maneuvering, over Burden's dick. "Let the bastard watch us, only fuck me here, fuck me now!" Pru fell backward, pulling Burden down on top of her. She kicked off her panties, and they flew through the air, landing on the brass handle of the china cabinet. Burden's fantasy had whipped her into a frenzy; art, tenderness, even consideration were far from her mind at this moment, as far as east is from west. All she wanted was to feel Burden inside her. With artless force she grabbed his prick and pulled it into her, giving a little moan at the pressure.

Burden's lips tore at Pru's flesh. His eyes were closed and in his mind he was kissing Pru while Eugene stood beside them in a rage, pummelling Burden's back and shoulders with callused fists. Ribs splintered, muscles became bruised and torn. His spine snapped under the brutal attack. This image hardened him further, bringing a higher degree of sensation, causing him to apply himself to Pru with greater vigor.

Another moan escaped Pru's lips. Then, without warning, she leg-locked Burden and rolled him over, so that she was now on top and in control. Burden's arm and shoulder blade jutted over the table and without Pru's counterbalancing weight, he would have toppled to the floor. Reaching out, he grasped the chair nearest him and attempted to push himself to securer ground. But the chair flew backward under his weight, and wedged at an odd angle against the china cabinet's handle. Pru's pubic thrusts continued unabated, inching Burden nearer ruination and he felt more and more of his body hanging precariously in midair beyond the precipice of wood and lacquer. Pru's expression betrayed an intense inward focus, and Burden recognized that her surroundings no longer mattered, the precariousness of her situation meant nothing to her, and if in another few thrusts they should both tumble to the floor, she would continue fucking even in free fall.

With redoubled effort, Burden stretched his arm across the table, touching with his fingertips the opposing edge's smooth lacquered curl. But he could not wrap his fingers securely around to the underside. With tremendous effort he arched his back, lifting his buttocks and Pru into the air—at this Pru gave a loud whoop—then, pivoting on his one solidly grounded shoulder blade, twisted his torso a fraction closer to the table's center. At last, the edge was firmly in his grasp. Sucking in his breath, he gave one strong pull and slid over the lacquered surface. When he was out of danger, at least from the danger of falling, Burden relaxed his muscles and concentrated once more on the mortal scenario being acted out in his head. Now that Pru was on top, Eugene had abandoned his hands and had gone instead for his .30-.30 lever-action rifle, the same rifle with which he'd frightened numerous deer and killed countless trees. Storming back into the room in a fiery rage, Eugene placed the barrel's opening snugly against Burden's temple. The blue metal carried the sting of ice pressed to his skin.

"I'm going to kill you, you motherfucker!" Burden's Eugene screamed.

"Do it," Burden taunted, speaking aloud. "Just go ahead and get it over with, you goddamn prick!"

Pru planted both feet on the tabletop and arched backward. "No, not yet," she pleaded. "Not yet—just a little longer."

Eugene cocked the lever and sited Burden's temple, a needless extravagance since the barrel was, in Burden's mind, embossing a red circle in his flesh.

"Do it!" Burden insisted.

"No!" Pru cried.

Burden grabbed Pru's ass and dug his fingers into the flesh, forcing her downward with gaining ferocity. "Get it over with, you fat, shit-eating, goddamn, cowardly cocksucker!"

Burden's curses released a reservoir of sexual energy in Pru's body that had not been tapped in years. A torrent of orgasmic delight rained down through her flesh, boiling her blood and dilating her pupils and curling her toes, causing her to quicken the momentum of her pelvic thrusts to a maddening pace. A fine heat rose from their conjoined genitals, and had the light in the dining room been dimmer, a faint glow, like that of a super-heated ingot, might have been visible.

"*Yes!*" Pru cried with abandon as she came. "*Yes!*"

Eugene's trigger finger twitched spasmodically, tensing and flexing with anticipation. Under this imminent threat, Burden's penis gorged itself on a final ounce of blood soup, petrifying its flesh and sending a fatal quiver through Pru's loins.

At last Eugene pulled the trigger and the rifle's muzzle exploded in a pinkish plume of smoke. Burden arched his back in a death spasm, lifting his buttocks and Pru into the air, every muscle held still as in a momentary suspension of animation. Pru's voice dissolved into a wet, quavering moan of pleasure. For a moment her voice was all that Burden heard. All else had become quiet and he was momentarily blind with orgastic delight and trembling with exhaustion. Then, faintly at first but soon very loudly, a scream, a horrified scream, filled his ears. It was a scream that sounded so very much like the screech of brakes issuing from a train wrenching to a sudden stop, that he believed for a moment a train had somehow burst through the apartment's walls. And it lasted, Burden thought, about as long as it might take a train to stop.

The scream trailed off to silence. Burden waited, unable to breathe. Utter silence. Then a voice cried out with savage, disbelieving fury. "*Jesus Christ!* What in God's name do you two think you're doing on Mr. Remley's dining room table?"

Pru—exhausted, limp, wet, satisfied—turned to her sister and said with calculated aplomb, "Well, dear sister, we *were* fucking, but we're done now."

Earlene stood stiffly in the doorway, her body slanted forward like some faltering stone idol, quaking in anger. At Pru's words, her face reddened and plumped up the way a finger does when squeezed. "That's a goddamn Prudent Mallard, Pru, it's an antique, for Christ's sake. Do you have any idea—any idea at all—how expensive that table is? Do you? I'll tell you: It's expensive enough that you *can't fuck on it!*"

Pru's shoulders slumped downward and she looked very much like a sad mime, and Burden thought he might have to catch her, but she was not falling, only expressing her exasperation with her sister. Heavily, she climbed off of Burden and sat on the table, dangling her legs over the side and crossing them at their ankles.

Burden felt the cool evaporation of his nakedness now that Pru had dismounted him. He felt more sharply the shame of his nakedness. Drawing up his legs, he scooted backward several inches so that he half-hid behind Pru, using her body to protect himself from Earlene's judgmental gaze. Looking down, he saw the latex protuberance bouncing with waning life and pushed it down, trapping it between his legs and hoping Earlene hadn't seen him doing that.

"Earlene, what's it matter how much something costs?" Pru said with languid disregard for her sister's sensibilities.

Pru's remark provoked a deep crimson shade and increased plumpness in Earlene's face. "You disgust me. What Mama would have thought of you . . . I'm only glad she isn't here to see this . . . this sad spectacle."

So am I, Burden thought. Reaching below his legs, he tugged at the condom and it sprang off him with a loud snap that made him wince, not because it had been painful, but because Earlene had heard the snap and had stopped for one moment to glare at him. He knew his place in her world, that much was certain.

Pru turned away from her sister and studied the lovely graining that ran in swirls beneath the lacquer. A portion of her willfulness drained from her expression.

"Honestly, Pru, you're no better than one of those West Street whores."

Burden felt a reflexive twinge, a weak impulse to defend Pru from the sting of this last rebuke. But before he could organize his defense, Earlene turned her wrath on him.

"And you, you're nothing more than a lazy little boy who refuses to grow up. Running errands for your father and delivering groceries is boy's work. Just when were you planning on growing up?"

"Leave Burden out of this, Earlene. It wasn't his idea to come to Charleston. I was the one who dragged him up here."

Earlene shook her head in a show of deep disappointment. "I don't know which is worse, selling peeks at your tits for five dollars when you were in high school or screwing around behind your husband's back—

and with *him* of all people," Earlene poked her thumb at Burden for derisive emphasis. "When you were young, you were foolish; now you're older, you're supposed to know better, act better."

"I act the way I please."

"Obviously. But this isn't your house, Pru. Hell, it isn't even my house. I don't want you fucking on the dining room table; I don't want you fucking in the living room or the study; I don't even want you fucking in the bedroom. In fact, I don't want you fucking here at all. Do you understand me?"

Pru blew out a sigh as she bent over and reached down to the chair seat next to her to retrieve her blouse, which had secreted itself there at some point during their tussle. Although she attempted not to show the wounds her sister's words inflicted on her, there was a diminution of spirit in her eyes, a retrenchment against Earlene's castigation.

Pru reclasped her bra and retrieved her panties from the cabinet handle. With her panties in hand, she approached her sister. Quietly, in weak defiance, she said, "Mama was damn proud of me. Don't you forget it." Coldly, she turned from Earlene and walked toward the kitchen. "Come, Burden, let's go. We won't inconvenience Earlene any further."

Burden glanced toward Earlene, searching for any show of pity in her eyes. But the whole of her stony features remained steadfastly prideful and flushed with a righteous anger as she stood in the doorway, entrenched in her indignation. At length, he swung around the side of the table opposite Earlene, righted the chair that rested akimbo against the china cabinet, then collected his clothing, retreating finally to the kitchen.

As he entered the kitchen Burden looked back; Earlene had approached the table. With a scowl on her face she bent down in close examination of its surface.

"Sorry, Pru," Burden said as he dressed.

Pru turned to him with hardened eyes that seemed, for that moment, incapable of compassion. "What are you sorry for?"

Although he realized her anger was not directed toward him, still the shortness of Pru's tone caught Burden off guard. All he could offer in response was a shrug of his shoulders.

Pru collected her purse from the counter. "Don't, Burden."

"Don't what?"

"That look. Don't be sorry for me. I don't like it. I won't have it."

"*Jesus!*" Earlene screamed from the adjoining room.

Burden and Pru glanced toward the doorway leading to the dining room, both wondering what new horror had struck Earlene.

"Jesus," she exclaimed a second time. "There's pubic hair on the table!"

"Good day, sis," Pru called in a deliberately blithe tone. "We'll be on our way, now." She turned to Burden and a wry smile briefly brightened her expression. "Come on, let's go home."

Eugene drove wearily along Highway 52. In his rearview mirror, Kingstree was fast becoming lost in the haze of miles. Charleston lay ten minutes ahead. He thought of a tavern there, a low, squat, squalid, and dark abode that he often would visit when passing through the city on a haul. The smoke-gray air of the tavern was thick with the smell of the syrupy sweetness of whiskey and of the beer that flowed from the taps and from the patrons' pores and breaths in equal measure. Sounds that individually were garrulous and quarrelsome, fused in that sweet atmosphere to form an almost melancholy melody that never failed to move him.

But he would not stop there tonight; he would take the turn off at Highway 17 and press on toward Walterboro because he was not supposed to be in Walterboro. It scared him to think where Pru might be, it scared him to think what he might find when he got home. The fear sickened his stomach and he thought again of the tavern and that he wished he could go there and wash the sourness from his stomach. But he would not stop. He would go home.

The ride back to Walterboro was considerably more subdued than the trip into Charleston had been. Pru no longer remarked on the passing scenery or the weather, which had turned nasty ahead of them. She remained quiet, tucked against her door, smiling an almost wistful smile as she gazed at the darkening sky ahead, a smile that spoke of deep contentment or deeper detachment.

Burden thought several times to place his hand on hers where it rested on the seat between them, but each time the impulse was stifled by his recognizing how little comfort that would be for her. He remembered what she had told him earlier, that she wouldn't stand for his feeling sorry for her; that would be the only reason he would touch her hand and because of this he did not.

A bolt of lightning flashed in the distance and very soon there was the languorous roll of thunder shaking the air. As if loosed by the thunder, dark clouds poured down a rain so intense that it bled approaching images into obscure palettes of gray and lifeless blue.

"I've always loved the rain," Pru said, roused sleepily from her thoughts. "Grandmother used to hide under the bed every time a storm threatened. Me, I'd want to run outside. There's nothing more refreshing than the sudden coolness that comes right before a good rainstorm. Nothing. And then afterward, once the storm has passed, there's a sweet quality to the air that makes me feel at peace."

Burden glanced down at Pru's hand. Her fingers curled and relaxed, curled and relaxed at her side. He thought to place his hand on hers but again did not. Then, with a delicacy he did not associate with Pru, she placed her hand on his thigh. Her touch was in no way erotic, but rested there lightly, as though her hand were a sparrow that had tired and decided to rest for a short while to regather its strength.

"Grandmother would have fits," she said, a wise chuckle in her voice, "but mother always understood. She was like me, a free spirit, she couldn't be caged. . . . Where are we?"

"Just north of Jacksonboro. Why?"

"I have to pee. Would you mind stopping at the next store?"

Pru's hand fluttered on his leg and took flight. Opening her purse, she took out her lipstick and a fresh tissue.

The rain abated, falling in a drizzle that did not leave them blind.

"There," Pru said, pointing to a small grocer's store. "That'll do nicely."

Burden pulled the van into the parking lot. The store's exterior bore a dismal facade: What little paint that had not long ago peeled from its concrete sides had faded into ghostly hues, the two plate glass windows were encrusted by road grime and neglect, and proved to be poor eyes for peering either into or out from, and the store's name, which was its proprietor's name (an equally dismal person) and which had originally been pressed against the building in large wooden letters, had so many pieces missing that the name could be discerned now only by the slightly less faded design in the shingles they had once covered.

"Won't be a minute," Pru said, kissing Burden's cheek before stepping from the van.

Burden watched Pru enter the store, watched her stop to ask an unseen clerk the way to the bathroom, watched her as she turned down the aisle when all he could see of her was her head, a rust-colored balloon bobbing softly atop the bread and crackers. When she was gone he closed his eyes and leaned back into the seat. He felt exhausted, was exhausted, emotionally, mentally, physically. He wanted nothing more now than to close his eyes and sleep for a long, long time. But closing his eyes, he found he could not keep them shut, for the fatigue that overwhelmed him was of the type to keep its victim awake, and wide awake at that. A cataract of mist formed on the windows. Reaching behind the seat, Burden fished out a small towel that he used to wipe away the sweat that collected on his face during his deliveries, and rubbed it across the windshield. When he was finished, he tossed the towel on the seat next to him, partially covering Pru's purse where it lay open.

Burden settled back once more against the seat, determined to steal a moment's rest while he waited for Pru. But as he closed his eyes, a hard knock came at his window, startling him. He turned and glared out the driver's side window, angered and alarmed. Through the thin strata of fog clinging to the glass he could just make out the unpleasant and slightly swollen features of Eugene Boaz. His hands and elbows grew numb with chill.

Eugene rapped his thick knuckles a second time against the window and Burden felt constrained to yield his meager defense. With a numb hand, he cranked the window knob, sinking the window into its narrow sea of rubber, leaving him face-to-ugly-mug with Eugene.

"I thought that was you, boy," Eugene said, his breath foul with the lingering odors of garlic and beer. "I said to myself as I was driving along this road, 'Eugene, that looks an awful lot like Burden's delivery van parked in front of Henley's Market.' " Eugene burped up a coarse laugh that filled the compartment with a congealing, greasy odor. "And damn if I wasn't right."

Burden offered only a weak smile. His eyes darted toward the store front and then back to Eugene.

"So, what's going on here? You with someone? Waiting?" Eugene's smile faded and the echo of his laughter died to a malevolent silence.

"Waiting? No." Burden shook his head.

Eugene bent down and spat between his feet, and a little of the spittle flicked on the door rim and a last portion clung thickly to Eugene's lower lip like venom on a snake's scaly mouth. He made no attempt to wipe away this foamy dollop as he continued. "Really? That's funny, 'cause I've been watching you the last couple minutes and you just been sitting here."

"I don't feel well, a little light-headed is all. I pulled off to sit for a minute till the spell passed."

Eugene nodded. He looked down the length of the van then returned his gaze to Burden. For several moments his lips moved in silent speech as he engaged himself in an inner dialogue. At length he asked, "Where you going?"

Burden found it difficult to maintain Eugene's gaze, but he held bravely to it with a tenuous and trembling grip. "Not that it's any of your concern," he heard himself say with a too apparent meekness, "but I'm meeting a buddy up in Monck's Corner." Burden's hand fell from the steering wheel to the seat and he touched the cotton material of the towel and remembered Pru's purse sitting beside him. As he made this motion Eugene's eyes darted a fraction to the right, looking into the compartment then snapped back onto Burden. *Did he see the purse?* Burden wondered. How was it that every time he and Eugene met it was under half-incriminating circumstances, yet absent the sexual sedative he needed in order to fully provoke the lethal beast slumbering within Eugene's breast? He dare not move the towel, better to deny its significance; after all, Eugene may have seen nothing, and Burden didn't want to chance drawing his attention to the damning evidence. Were Eugene to discover Pru's purse and perfidy, Burden thought it likely Eugene would not kill him but only afflict him with wounds that would hurt but which would heal in time.

"I do believe you look a might pale, boy. Sure you ought to be out?"

"I'll be fine." Burden turned to look in the store windows. He saw Pru's head through the smear of grime, she was peering at him just above a row of bread loaves. "In fact," he said, turning back to Eugene, "I'm feeling better as it is." He twisted the key in the ignition and turned the engine over. "Think I'll be heading on."

Eugene did not move. He remained with his arms folded over the door, looking hard at Burden; his nostrils flared as in heavy labor, sniffing out any telltale odor. His face reddened as though under some sudden stress, and Burden could see a sheen of sweat break free on his upper lip. All in all he presented the picture of a man taken inexplicably ill himself. Then, without a word, the fever of his expression broke and he was smiling, smiling as freely as a man may smile. He stood and shoved his hands in his back pockets.

"Yeah, guess I'd best be getting on, too. Got to get home."

Burden nodded his head in mute agreement. He very nearly said, "I thought you weren't supposed to be back tonight," but had the presence of mind to hold his tongue. After a moment he said, "Evening," and pulled the van from the parking space.

He drove away slowly, using his side and rearview mirrors to keep a watchful eye on Eugene. Eugene stood in the parking lot, unmoving, alternately staring at the store and then at the ground below his feet. Taking the first road off 17, Burden turned around, stopped, and walked to the highway where he could see the store.

Eugene remained there, a lonely figure, hands planted in his pockets, eyes intent on his shoes. Then, with a furious motion, he spun round and got into his truck, the engine growling with a mechanical ferocity as he sped off toward Walterboro.

Burden hurried to the van and returned to the store. Pru came out as he pulled up, her eyes wide and white and her mouth spread in an involuntary and pained grin.

"Oh, my God," she repeated several times. "Oh, my God, that was close."

Burden stepped around the van and opened Pru's door. He took her hand, which was trembling, and helped her inside.

When he got in she asked, "You don't suppose he was following us, do you? You don't suppose he saw us?"

Burden wasn't sure what to think, but he was certain what he shouldn't say. "He didn't see anything."

"How can you be sure?"

"I'd have seen it in his eyes. Trust me, he doesn't know." But Burden was not as certain as he let on.

Pru's hand fell from her thigh to the seat and landed on the half-hidden purse. "Jesus," she said, gazing at the infernal object. "I made him buy me this purse for my birthday. He must know. What if he saw us in Charleston? What if he's been following us all afternoon? Shit, I didn't think he could be such a . . . such a *goddamn* sneaky fucker."

When they were once more on their way to Walterboro, Burden asked, "Where should we go?"

Pru turned and regarded him with a silent and sickly stare.

"Where should we go?" he repeated. "We can't very well go home, Eugene'll be waiting for you there."

The change in Pru's expression indicated she'd just apprehended a doom worse than the doom she had previously conceived. She stuck the tip of her thumb in her mouth and bit at its flesh, sucking schemes and plans and options from the sworls in the skin. Burden found himself driving ever more slowly and with increasing caution, being passed by more and more cars while he waited for Pru to divine her solution. At length she removed her thumb from her mouth and turned to Burden, her expression not so vacant of hope as moments just prior.

"Take me to Jewel's. She'll cover for me. Take me to Jewel's and I'll have her take me home."

"What about Eugene? What're you going to tell him?"

"The truth: that I've been out shopping with Jewel." Pru relaxed a little where she sat, and the set of her eyes very nearly brightened; "truth" for her was a wonderfully amorphous and pliant object, able to assume many aspects and many guises. If even the smallest kernel of truth could be roused out from a store of lies, then the sum of it all became a great and gleaming truth. "In fact, I think I will go shopping. Hell, I still have time. That'll show Eugene. We'll go shopping and I'll buy myself something fine and expensive . . . well, not too expensive, maybe something on sale. A dress. Yes, something to make me feel better because he's gone so damn much and neglects me terribly." Pru's plan aroused a jollity in her that accosted her and transformed her from a fretful adulteress to a figure triumphant: a successful adulteress who had nearly gotten caught but who had outwitted her husband and the Fates through her cunning. She began to laugh, and her shoulders convulsed with great risings and fallings that shook her small frame. Burden looked over at her as her laughter crested to a mad cackle.

"You okay?"

Pru shook, not from fear, but from the sudden release from that fear. A moment more and her mad laughter had passed, recollected by occasional fits and snorts. "I think I know now," she began as her seizures subsided, "I think I know now why it gets you off."

Burden regarded her quizzically.

"Getting caught—or should I say the *threat* of getting caught. God, I feel so giddy I can hardly stand to sit here. I want to get out and run wildly through the trees." As she spoke she wrung her hands along the length of her thighs as though she were wringing wet towels. "Stop here," she demanded when they approached a gas station. For a moment Burden feared she really intended to run amok through the woods, and he had no stomach to chase her down. But then she spoke again and allayed his fear. "I want to call Jewel to make sure she's home."

TEN

I'm going to do it, Burden thought. *Holy Jesus, I'm actually going to do it.* He glanced at Peedie. A car passed—only the second car that had passed them on this otherwise desolate road—and as its headlights momentarily caught the compartment in stark brilliance, both boys exchanged cool, aware glances of silent understanding. Peedie nudged Burden with his knee and gave him a grave nod of the head indicating his support.

Beyond Peedie, Burden saw the dozing, rubbery-faced Whalie, passed out, his lips slack and moist, his mouth open, his head pressed against the vinyl padding that was worn and ripped. Beyond Whalie, through the slim opera window, there was a blurred image suggestive of trees, their limbs burned to black by the night, their tips momentarily caught alight by the Monte Carlo's headlights. Whalie snuffled loudly, then snorted, appearing to wake as his eyes creaked open, revealing narrow slices of glistening, gray wetness. But this wakeful period was short lived, and soon Whalie was secreted once more in his private dream world.

Burden looked at his hands, at how his palms kindled like embers in the red glow of the receding taillights. He returned his cousin's nod with his own, then reached down for the Coors and drank the last of it deliberately. He felt giddy, removed from the moment. The sound of the bullet whizzing past his face echoed in his memory and the uncontainable emotions the incident had provoked in his chest stirred again. He felt his oddest desire could not be denied—that he was justified, even, in yielding to the impulse. He felt that he could commit any crime with impunity. Setting the empty beer can on the floorboard, he leaned forward and hunkered low, as though by doing so he had gained surer protection in the car's close confines.

Peedie drew in his breath. Waited.

For a few seconds it seemed as though time had stopped, that the world had become frozen, that Burden would remain hunkered down for an eternity. Then, as with the snapping of a rubber band, movement returned with swift vengeance. Burden sprang forward swiftly, his hands sliding through the air, eager to dispense their venom. Hands skimmed over the front seat, passing a hair's breadth above Sulah's pale bare shoulders. Hands fell with quickening speed toward her tube top-encased bosom, a vaporous heat lifting from the skin drawn thickly over her collar bone. Hands touched the soft material where it puckered in a thousand miniature hillocks and felt the sudden deep freeze coldness of her breasts. With a mixture of fright and purpose, Burden sank his fangs into fat, into flesh, into soft, cool tissue, releasing his venom into her, and then retreating to what he hoped was the haven of the back seat. He believed also that he drew his hands to his lap and hid them between his legs. He had planned to do as much. Why, then, why were his hands still clutching Sulah's breasts? Why were they unwilling or unable to disgorge their prey? Was it the shrill banshee wail resounding loudly in his ears that froze his hands? Was it the thought that, the sin committed, the safest refuge was continued sin? He could hear the sound of his apology—*I'm sorry*—a soft murmuring submerged below the banshee's wail. He coughed to clear his throat then said it again, but it was no use, no words could unstick his suddenly palsied hands; they were the talons of the great hunting birds that he'd seen in a museum once when he was a child, positioned immobile around struggling prey. Like those talons, his fingers had grown as rigid as stone.

Peedie stared gape-jawed. In another moment he would laugh, even now he could feel a gale bubbling in his stomach, but for the moment he was rendered silent by disbelief and joy.

The Monte Carlo shot suddenly to the right, skidding off the road and onto the shoulder. The car shuddered violently, jouncing its occupants as it rumbled over the uneven surface. Yet even this violent shaking could not loosen the death grip Burden had on Sulah's breasts. He held on tightly, feeling the cold gelatinous quivering of her fat in his palms as the car shuddered forward. Trees lunged toward the car from every angle, threatening to crash through the windshield, only to leap at the last moment to the left or right.

"Holy shit, Sulah," Ricky shouted, unaware of why she had just elbowed him in the ribs with such force or why she was screaming in his ear to so high a holy hell.

"What the fuck—?" Sutton bellowed, looking down at Sulah's hand-clad breasts.

Then Burden felt the first bite of pain. Sulah, overcoming the shock of her attack, cut her nails into Burden's fingers and ripped them from her tits. She lifted them, and as she did so she squeezed them vicelike, bending them backward and making Burden sit up from his seat and lean over her shoulder.

"Shit!" The profanity barely squeezed through his throat.

Sulah flung his hands behind her, and in the moment of relative calm that followed Burden thought, *That wasn't so bad, I could take that.* He thought this with some pride, as though he had overcome a tremendous obstacle or escaped a grave danger. Then, as from a great dark distance, a giant figure loomed above Burden, rising from its limbo, awakening with savage fury. Sutton wedged his body between the front seat and headliner and glowered down at Burden. "What the fuck—?" he repeated in his giant's bellow. And then there was a dull, meaty sound as Sutton's fist swooped down from the minimal height of the passenger compartment, landing hard against Burden's cheek. The ridge of knuckles struck and pulled the loose flesh, and Burden could feel the inside of his cheek split as it was mashed into his teeth. It felt as though a rock had been wedged between skin and bone. He raised his hands and felt a second blow strike his wrist and then a sharp pain, white and cold, shot across his palm and traveled toward his elbow.

And then it was a storm of fists as Sutton found his rhythm.

Peedie began striking the hands striking Burden.

"You little shit," Sutton spat as he backhanded Peedie across his face.

"I'll take care of *him!*" Sulah said. As she pummeled Peedie's forehead with the meat of her open palm, she leaned over the front seat, huffing and puffing, her bulbous bosom jiggling from beneath her tube top like two bloated jellyfish wrapped tight in a pink bag.

Whalie struggled from the depth of a dream and looked about him, perhaps uncertain whether the scene erupting in the car was nothing more than a continuation of his dream. "What's . . ." he began, his tongue thick with sleep and his mind steeped in alcohol. "What's going on—?" But his slow, thick words were cut short by the force of a palm to his forehead.

"That's for being his cousin," Sulah said.

Whalie stared at Sulah for a few dreamy moments, looking hurt, moved his lips around a bit, slumped against the window, and went back to sleep.

The blows continued against Burden. He felt the sting of swelling flesh around his eyes and the coppery taste of blood on his tongue. "Okay! Okay!" he pleaded.

"You think you're funny, huh, funny boy?" Sutton bellowed, discharging stale beery clouds with each word. "You think that was a funny thing to do?" Another blow pounded already wounded flesh. "Why aren't you laughing now, funny boy?"

"I'm sorry," Burden cried, his voice tremulous, on the verge of tears. "I'm sorry. Okay?"

"You're going to be sorry, all right, you little shit." Sutton turned to Ricky. "Stop the car!" he bellowed. "Stop the goddamn, fucking car!"

When they were stopped, Sutton kicked open the door and got out. He reached back in and pulled Burden through the narrow opening between the front seat and door, throwing him hard to the ground. Burden sprang to his feet to run, but Sutton snagged him with a single hand and pulled him back.

"Where you running to?" he taunted, his face pressing against Burden's.

Peedie scrambled awkwardly through the door and jumped on Sutton's back and tried to wrap his arms around his neck. Sutton, a true giant next to these two fourteen-year-olds, flung Peedie from his back with scant effort.

Sulah stepped out of the car. "Beat the ever living shit out of him, Sutton. Beat him till he cries for his mama."

Sutton looked at Sulah, his eyes narrowing for a moment. He motioned to her tube top. "Your titties is hanging out."

Sulah looked down, saw the purple-veined slabs of fat, distended and pale, hanging over the material of her tube top, which had been pushed down during the scuffle.

From the ground, Peedie pointed a finger at her and began laughing madly. Sulah pulled her top back over her breasts and then kicked Peedie in the shin. "You shut up," she ordered, kicking him a second time.

"What's going on? Why've we stopped?" Whalie asked, his head hanging over the door. He looked very much like death.

"You going to beat the shit out of him or not?" Sulah pressed Sutton.

Sutton gripped Burden's collar more tightly, twisting it in his fist so that it fairly strangled Burden. "I don't know," he said at length.

"Sutton," Ricky said from behind the wheel. "Sutton, they're just kids, you'd kill 'em."

"Goddamn right," Sulah said. "Kill the goddamn both of them."

"Sutton . . ." Ricky repeated.

Sutton turned to Ricky, whose expression was one of concern. He turned back to Burden, seemed to consider something awful in his mind, smiled, then shook his head. "Naw," he said. "Ricky's right. They're too puny to hit no more." Saying this, he tossed Burden to the ground. Burden remained there, heavy and aching.

"What's going on?" Whalie repeated. They seemed to be the only words he could recall from all the words his mother had ever taught him.

"Your cousins are both a couple of little shit freaks," Sulah told him. She turned to Sutton. "What're you going to do about it?"

Sutton stared down at Burden, who panted where he sat, crimson-cheeked and puffy lipped. "Ah . . . shit, I figure I done hit him enough for one night."

Sulah's cheeks puffed and reddened with anger. "You just going to let them get away with that?"

Burden looked up at the giant towering above him. His vision was blurred, but he thought he saw a passing light of compassion flicker in Sutton's eyes. But then the glimmer died and it seemed again just as likely that the ever living shit, as Sulah suggested and hoped, would be beat out of him. Powerless to fend off yet another attack, he set his teeth hard together and dug in as best he could.

But at the end of what seemed interminable minutes, Sutton shook his head. "I ain't going to hit them no more." His tone was almost sorrowful, like a kid who had beat his dog too hard and now couldn't bear the look of hurt in the dog's eyes.

Sulah grabbed Sutton's arm and spun him around. The freckles lining her lips began to weep. "Then what are you going to do?"

Sutton cast a doubtful gaze toward Ricky. "What do you think?"

Ricky shrugged his shoulders. "They learned their lesson. Put 'em in the back and tell 'em to keep quiet—and to keep their hands to themselves—and let's get the hell on home."

"What?" Sulah said, her delicate nerves near to breaking. "You can't just let those two peckerheads back in the car."

"Sulah," Sutton began.

"No. *No*, Sutton. I'm not riding in the same car as them two. I won't. I absolutely won't."

"Hell, put 'em in the trunk," Ricky suggested.

Sutton rubbed at his neck as a light breeze shook rain from the trees, tickling his skin. At length he said, "Where you boys say you was from?"

"They's from Walterboro," Whalie said, for a brief moment lucid. Burden looked over in time to see his cousin slump between the front seat and door jamb, his hand hanging lifeless.

Sutton rubbed again at the back of his neck. "Well," he said, without a trace of malice in his voice, "that's not so far away I guess, Walterboro. Leave them here, they can walk home."

"That's twenty miles," Ricky said.

"They're lucky it ain't twenty more," Sulah spat. "They're lucky we ain't in Bum Fucking Egypt and they have to crawl on their hands and goddamn knees through a blinding rainstorm."

"A rainstorm? In Egypt?" Ricky asked.

"Shut the fuck up."

Sutton looked down at Burden. "You okay with that?"

"What are you asking them for?" Sulah protested.

Sutton cut her a hard look, the force of which quieted her at once. He turned back to Burden. "You okay with that?"

What can I say? Burden thought. *Thanks, but couldn't you beat me up some more, instead?* He nodded his head.

Sutton turned to Peedie. "You okay with that?"

Peedie stared intently at Sutton, fire in his eyes.

"Well?" Sutton kicked Peedie's foot.

"Yeah," Peedie said finally, his voice joyless.

Sutton looked back down the road they had been traveling. "The church ain't but a mile away, go on back there. You two should stay there for the night . . . start out tomorrow for home."

"Spend the night in hell, for all I care," Sulah said under her breath.

"That's enough, Sulah. These boys've learned their lesson or soon will." Sutton looked back at Sulah. "Come on, let's get home."

"Wait!" Burden said, feeling suddenly panicked. "You just going to leave us out here with nothing to protect ourselves with? Ain't you got a flashlight, at least?"

"Shush, Burden," Peedie said, "we don't need no flashlights. I know these woods better than I know most anything else."

Sutton laughed at Peedie's bravado. "You all'll do just fine." He turned and shoved Whalie from the door jamb and into the backseat, then ordered Sulah into the car. When he settled into his seat, Ricky said, "You shouldn't leave them with nothing."

Sutton scratched his chin, considered Ricky's words. "You're right," he said. He reached into the beer cooler behind him, pulled a Corona from the ice, and popped it open. "Here you go. You earned it," he said, holding the bottle out for Burden. He dropped it and Burden caught it just before it hit the asphalt. "It's the last one, so you two'll have to share. Good night, now, and careful of them ghosts out there, hear?"

Sulah leaned forward and shouted, "Rot in hell, peckerheads," and Sutton cursed at her and pushed her roughly back against the seat. He turned again to Burden and Peedie, and as the car pulled away he gave them a reassuring smile and a thumb's up. " 'Night."

When the sound of the car was gone and there was nothing but the sound of the cicadas and bullfrogs and the soft, feathery sound of the drizzle that fell everywhere in the night, the road seemed not 20 miles but 120 miles, 220 miles from Walterboro; it seemed they were on a remote island bound by perpetual darkness. The road was a barely visible shadow underneath their feet, and the stars, what few were visible, had to struggle through the thick tufts of scudding clouds. Burden stood and shook a chill from his spine. Although it pained his lips, he drank from the bottle and asked, "What you want to do? Think we should start heading home?"

"Hell if I know." Peedie stood and took the bottle from Burden and started to drink from it but stopped himself short. Handing the beer back to his cousin, he said, "Here, take it, it'll help with the pain. And anyway, Sutton is right, you earned it." Burden took the beer and as he drank it Peedie gazed into the night sky. At length he said, "Maybe we should just go back to Old Sheldon Church. We can sleep there for the night and get up first light tomorrow morning. Then we can hitch our way back to Walterboro."

"There's bound to be a car come by soon."

"Might be," Peedie replied. "Night like this has a lot of crazies wandering round in it—not counting the three who just left us. I think we'd be safer at the church; ain't nothing can touch us in the church."

"It'll be quiet there, that's for sure."

"If we could get these goddamn crickets to shut up, it would be," Peedie said. He began laughing with a levity quite at odds with their situation.

"What?"

Peedie continued to laugh, and it was only after several minutes that he could compose himself well enough to answer. "That sound . . . that sound that Sulah made, you know, when you—" Peedie broke off and started braying in a fairly accurate imitation of Sulah's graceless note. "What," he asked after he had exhausted his lungs of brayish song, "did they feel like?"

Burden thought on this for a moment, giving his cousin's question serious consideration, wanting to be precise. After much pondering, he answered, "Squishy."

"Squishy?" Peedie repeated.

"Yeah, and cold."

It was after 2:00 A.M. when they reached the church. A chill breeze called with despair high above them, but the air around them was death-still. Their eyes were well adjusted to the darkness now, and occasionally a cloud break allowed narrow spikes of moonlight to strike the ground; then the grass and road and trees took on different hues of silver and blue. It was during one such period of relative light that the boys entered the grounds. The remains of Old Sheldon Church rose wearily above them, its walls glowing specterlike in the stray moonbeams, its punched-out windows staring down at them like blind, impassive eyes.

A tail of Spanish moss swished Peedie's face and he swiped it away. Then, stopping, he reached up and tore the moss from its limb. He continued collecting moss as they walked until he held a sizable clump loosely between his hands.

When they reached the tomb of Mary Bull, Peedie stopped. "We'll sleep here," he said, settling to the ground.

"You can sleep?"

"Sure 'nough." Peedie pressed the Spanish moss he'd stolen from the trees into a flat pillow and placed it under his head. "Shit, what I wouldn't give for a real pillow, though . . . and a real bed."

"I don't think I can sleep," Burden said. He gently prodded the swollen, split flesh above his cheek; during their walk the pain had turned to numbness, but now the pain, duller, deeper, was returning, throbbing in rhythm with his pulse. It hurt to blink his right eye. "I don't think I can sleep."

"Then don't. You can keep watch, only don't wake me unless you see a real live ghost, hear?"

"That ain't funny," Burden said, casting off a shiver. He leaned back against the tomb, wrapped his arms round his knees, and rested his chin on the poor table they made. His eyes were wide at first, alert for any movement, attentive to any spirits drifting hither or thither through the moss-strewn darkness. But soon his eyelids grew heavy. His head tee-tered. He felt for a moment as though he were falling and then wasn't aware of this sensation. Then the throbbing discomfort in his cheeks and lips ebbed. Soon after the pain left him he fell asleep.

Burden awoke with a start. For a moment he still smelled the wet spar-kling air of that night seven years earlier; for a moment Peedie was still at his side, his voice resounding in his ear and memory. But pushing himself from the sodden grass dismissed the spell, and he was once more in the present and alone. He wiped at his cheek and struck off several blades of grass clinging wetly to his skin. There was the leafy smell in the night, the clean, clear odor of air and earth freshly scrubbed. The granite of Peedie's marker shone where a coat of dew caught frag-ments of moonlight.

In the distance an owl called out to the darkness, its voice falling with the vibrato of a neighing horse. Infrequently, cars passed over the highway, their tires hissing across the wet asphalt and splashing shallow puddles. A breeze lingered in the branches of the cemetery trees. Beyond these Burden heard no other sound.

"Thought I was coming to be with you for good tonight," Burden said. He made fists of his hands and rubbed his eyes to chase away the sleep that was in them. "Almost." A point of pressure pressed into his back and it felt as though one of the departed patrons had pushed his arm through the sod and touched Burden with the death coolness of a bony finger, but it was only the remembrance of Eugene, Burden realized, and nothing else that chilled his back.

And it amazed him, that chill, because he knew it was the child of uncertainty. Uncertain he had never been before, not regarding his end. When he conceived the idea for his death he had embraced it, espousing it to his heart with the zeal of a recent convert. In the years and frustrations that followed he had never wavered in his belief that his goal was just and proper, a punishment appropriate to the crime. But in recent days, beginning with Jo's return and continuing to this evening's untimely encounter with Eugene, he felt more like a struggling apostate than an apostle. A seed of doubt had been thumbed into the soil of his heart, and as it grew it caused him to question the wisdom of his plan. *Is there still a chance of being with Peedie again?* Yes, but that time is drawing to a close, that train is soon departing, that opportunity is quickly passing and if you do not reach out and take hold of it . . .

But do I want to take hold of it?

As he had waited in the parking lot, the odor of his sin still full in his nostrils, Eugene hanging his swollen face into the van, Burden had taken a sip from the bitter cup that he himself had prepared. The taste sickened him and he was not certain if he was capable of swallowing the cup whole. This was the doubt, this was the questioning that weighed on his mind. Perhaps it was true that the journey would last only a moment, yet even if the time were half that, a troubling voice in Burden's mind said the way would be too harsh.

He gazed down at the marker, at the rectangle of sod holding Peedie close in its bosom. *Are we so far apart?* he wondered. But of this also he was uncertain. He eased again onto the wet ground and rolled onto his back. With his ear close to the ground, he thought he heard the murmur again much as he had when he was younger. The soft immutable rhythm lulled his mind and eased his worry with the gentle persuasion of a mother's voice. Soon he felt himself drifting to sleep again, and in the twilight of wakefulness believed he heard Peedie's voice barely distinct above the murmuring. "Soon," Burden said. *A promise is a promise, cousin.* "Soon." Then he thought of Jo and the image made him wince. There was no good end, he realized. "I lose everything if I go. I'm lost if I stay." This thought guided him to sleep.

ELEVEN

Jo stood in front of her bathroom sink, coaxing a stain from her uniform. A ray of late afternoon light slanting through the window caught her bra and slip alight and turned their winter white to the warmer colors of autumn. The beam crept upward, moving in counterpoint to the declining sun. The light fell also through the bedroom window, stretching along the carpeting and climbing the drawers of her dresser. Continuing its countervailing course, the beam fell upon a pair of white stockings draped over the dresser's edge.

Next to the stockings lay the book of poetry Burden had given her the day he had taken her to the old beech tree. Inside, just past the fly leaf, was a picture her mother had taken of Jo and Burden. They peered shyly into the lens, as though anticipating the judgmental eyes that someday would look back at them. Burden's hand peeked out from behind Jo's shoulder, and her hand lay across his leg, her thumb and index finger pinching the seam of his pants where it folded upward at his bent knee. A brief inscription along with the date the photograph had been taken was written on the back of the photograph in her own precise script. As she worked the stain, Jo would, from time to time, glance over at her dresser. Her eyes thus falling on the book, fragments of cantos she had visited many times would glimmer in her mind like colored stones strewn along a riverbed. However, such recollections did not bring her joy, only consternation, and she would quickly turn away and concentrate on ridding her uniform of its blot. Then, forgetful, her eyes would drift back to the dresser as silently as the sun's expiring light. She thought of the underscored passage.

Jo had purposely left the book behind when she went away to college. She had packed it in a box that was in turn consigned to a high, darkened shelf in the closet. She did not think often of the book when she went away. Eventually, with the distraction of classes and new surroundings, she did not think of it at all. Not until the first evening after she had returned home, after three years away, did she recall its lines.

Lying in bed that first night home, Jo had listened through the open window to the familiar sounds of her neighborhood; small details had changed, yet so much remained unaltered by time, escaping the pillaging years between adolescence and adulthood. There was so much more to her now than when she had left, and she had feared the town would feel cramped, confining. But three years away could not change what it was in her heart that responded to home. It was then that she thought of the book buried safely in the box hidden securely in the closet. Rising from bed, she rummaged through the closet, brought the box down, and set it to rest in a pool of moonlight so that she might see into it. With a breath she removed a patina of dust that had settled atop the box, making a star field in the light, then removed its lid. A lace sachet, its lavender ribbon frozen to blue by the beam, was the first article from her youth she retrieved. The sachet once smelled of lilac; she could almost recall the fragrance when it had been fresh and new, but pressing its cloth to her nose, she smelled only the odor of musty neglect. She put the sachet at her side and returned to the box. There, under her framed high school diploma, was the book of poetry Burden had given her. She rescued the slender volume from its limbo and thumbed through its pages until she found the photograph her mother had taken of her and Burden. The photograph marked the page containing the poem Burden had underlined. She read through its verses, her whispered words lingering among the soft shafts of moonlight, her breathing in time with the poet's rhythm. She reread the lines several times before closing the book.

In that moment Jo understood she had returned because a portion of her spirit had remained here all along. A portion of her had lingered in Walterboro so that she could, in the fullness of time, return to complete what had been left unfinished. And she realized that although the book had never intruded into her conscious thoughts, it nonetheless had animated her emotions with a subliminal power.

Jo had closed the book and put it on the dresser. As she had crawled into bed again that first night back, listening again to all that made Walterboro her home, she wondered if she would ever know how to leave finally and forever.

Jo stirred from her thoughts with the sudden awareness that she was being watched.

"Sorry," her mother said. She stood in the doorway, leaning against the jamb, her hands entwined before her waist. "I forgot how much I missed simply looking at you."

Jo offered her mother a self-deprecating smile as she wrung the water from her uniform and hung it over the shower curtain rod. Only after she had made a show of washing and drying her hands did she look at her mother, regarding her with a diffident expression. "Mother," she said simply.

Her mother walked in and took her hand. "I'm embarrassing you, I know," she said with good humor. "It's a mother's right."

"Of course." Jo gave her mother a quick kiss. Walking to the dresser, she retrieved the stockings and pulled them on, her gaze settling absently on the book.

"Have you been downtown yet?"

Jo detected a second question lingering among her mother's words. *Have you seen Burden?*

"I haven't had time, what with settling into the new job."

"I'm curious to hear from you how much the town has changed in your eyes. After all, Walterboro certainly isn't Charleston."

Jo turned and faced her mother, regarding her gently. She was struck by the uncertainty lying quietly beneath her mother's assured expression. Or perhaps it was certainty, a certainty that a life was passing inexorably from her by degrees, that caused the disquiet in her mother's eyes. She had come home, but perhaps she had come home only so she could eventually, with a greater finality than college offered, leave. "You're right, it isn't," she said at length, trying to make her voice reassuring the way her mother's had so often been for her when she was young. "It's home."

TWELVE

"Burden, dear, do come in," Maude said, swinging the mud room's screen door open. She lingered in the doorway so that he could not help but brush against her as he passed. "You can set the bags on the kitchen counter."

Burden walked to the kitchen, feeling Maude close behind. After he set the bags down he turned, giving Maude her first good look at him.

Maude leaned against the counter, her back bending in a sensuous curve that had the intended effect of pronouncing her pelvic bone, which was merely a subtle suggestion, hidden demurely underneath loose folds of raw silk the color of winter wheat. She sipped delicately from a glass of iced tea, then closed her eyes and drew its side across her forehead, dispelling a tremendous heat. She brought the glass down. "May I fix you a glass?"

Burden nodded. "If it's not too much trouble."

"Not at all." Maude retrieved a glass from the cupboard and ice from the freezer. The ice protested as the tea flowed over it, creaking and cracking as it settled into a loose pack. She approached Burden with catlike smoothness and when she offered Burden the glass she made a point of keeping her arm close in front of her, so that to take the glass Burden's hand would have to graze her breast.

Then, as though suddenly accosted by a vagrant thought, Maude spun around and paced to the far counter in the kitchen. She turned, faced Burden, took another sip of tea and said, "You've been ignoring me." Her brow was knitted sternly, but her lips bore a puckish grin.

Burden sipped from his glass.

"See?" Maude continued. "I tell you you've been ignoring me and you simply go on drinking your tea."

"What do you want me to do?"

Maude set her glass on the counter. "I want you to come here, to me, I want you to stop ignoring me and instead make me feel as though I'm somebody special. Come. Come." Maude held out her hands.

Burden pointedly took a slow drink of tea, then set the glass on the counter and wiped his mouth.

"Come." Maude flicked her hands, beckoning Burden to her. When he approached, she wrapped her arms around Burden and held tightly to him. "I've got you," she said, kissing him deeply. At length she yielded her kiss and said to him, "I have a surprise."

"A surprise? What surprise?"

Maude held a finger to her lips. "Shhh," she whispered, taking Burden by his hand and tugging him from the kitchen. They made the trek through the front parlor and foyer and ascended the staircase to the master bedroom.

Burden made a quick search of the room for anything out of the ordinary. On the end table next to the bed a small towel was drawn over several objects, one of which stood some six inches high, making the towel a type of circus tent in miniature.

"What's under the towel?" Burden asked.

"Never you mind about *that*," Maude said, unbuttoning Burden's shirt. She eased him to a sitting position on the bed and kissed his forehead. "Just be patient. I have something special planned." Maude pulled his shirt off and ran her hands across his shoulders and down his back, bringing her breasts close to Burden's face; he smelled something akin to a poached magnolia blossom rising from her bosom. "You're tense; I can feel it in your muscles."

"I'm just wondering what's under that towel."

Maude gave a delicate laugh. "It's nothing to be frightened of, Burden. Would I do anything to harm you?" She leaned back and took his face in her hands. "Don't you trust me?"

Burden smiled but his lips faltered.

"Let's just say that I've been doing a little research."

Burden screwed up his expression.

Maude stood and stepped back from Burden. Reaching under her skirt, she pulled down her panties, then returned to Burden and pushed him onto the bed and straddled him. "It's been *so long*," Maude complained softly in his ear. "And I know how hard it is for you when we haven't been together for a while."

Burden frowned in understanding, for while he had proven himself adept at tricks of the tongue, there was often a too quick consummation of their lovemaking that left Maude wanting (once, he caught her looking at the bed clock, surreptitiously timing his endurance).

Burden studied the towel-covered instruments on the table as he drew his tongue along her neck. He wasn't worried, but he was concerned about what it might be hiding.

Maude drew her hand over Burden's groin and then tickled his belly with the tips of her fingernails. When he shrank from her touch she quickly rubbed the tickle away. "I have something that I thought might help you"—here she paused with some awkwardness, and with his expression, Burden prodded her to continue—"last longer." Maude buried her face in his neck as she said this, as though to soften an unavoidable insult.

"What is it?" Burden asked.

Maude hesitated. Then said: "Have you ever been to a store that sells massage oils and body lotions?"

Burden shrugged his shoulders. "I've seen them."

"You know how they can heighten the sensation of touch . . . of pleasure?"

"Like when you had me rub baby oil on your breasts and then we slid against each other?" Burden remembered how long it had taken in the shower to wash the slippery feel from his skin and how he had smelled like a baby's ass for two days afterward and he hoped she hadn't bought more baby oil.

Maude smiled shyly, "That was a crude version, yes. But I have something more medicinal, something you might say a certain doctor we both know unwittingly recommended to me."

Burden took Maude's face in his hands and studied her features, trying to divine what devilment played in her mind.

Maude removed his hands, kissing each palm lightly, then pulled them over his head. "Close your eyes," she whispered.

Against his better judgment Burden did as instructed. Blind, he felt Maude's weight shift over him, sensed that she was reaching above him, perhaps for the instrument under the towel. An object of moderate weight was placed beside him.

"No peeking," Maude warned. With care, she undid Burden's pants and slid them from his legs. "I got to thinking that everything in this world has its opposite. Black has white, joy has sorrow . . . Burden has Hubert. And," she concluded with unerring logic, "brief has long." She slipped her fingers below his underwear and tugged them to his knees. There was the sound of a cap being unscrewed and then she said, "If there are things that sharpen a man's sensation, why, there must be things that do the exact opposite."

Burden smelled an odor that he could not place, but to which he had an immediate and negative reaction, and which brought an unpleasant taste to his mouth, as though triggering an unpleasant memory. Ignoring Maude's warning, he opened his eyes. She was tipping a small plastic tube into a large cotton ball. "What is that?" Burden asked, alarmed.

"Shhh," Maude said. "It's nothing that's going to hurt."

"What is it? I want to know what it is." Burden raised himself on his elbows. "What are you going to do with it?"

Maude righted the bottle and snapped its lid shut.

Burden tried to scoot from under Maude, but she lay heavily on his legs. "What is it?"

"It's Emla. There, you've gone and spoiled the surprise. Satisfied?" Maude said with pouty indignation. But spoiling the surprise didn't keep her from pressing the cotton ball against his prick just as vigorously as if he had requested it.

The cream was cold to the touch, and in an act of penile preservation, Burden scrambled back across the bed, dragging Maude with him. "Stop that," he demanded.

"Really, Burden," Maude said testily as she struggled to apply the cotton ball a second time, "there's no need to be a baby about this. Hubert uses it all the time on his patients when he has to give a painful shot."

Burden swatted Maude's hand away. "I don't care," he said hotly. "I don't give a shit if he uses it on every goddamn grandmother's ass in Walterboro, I don't want you rubbing it on my dick." Burden grabbed Maude's knees and pushed her backward and then kicked up his feet. Maude fell backward, tumbling over the bed. Burden heard a dull thud and the quick escape of breath. "Holy Jesus," he cried, his hand around his penis, "I can't feel it, it's like half of it's fucking missing." He slapped it then shook his head. "This had better wear off, and soon. I swear to God, you've done some crazy shit, Maude, but this is the goddamn dumbest thing you've ever done." Burden looked up, didn't see her. "Maude?"

There came a sob and then quickly another. Burden sighed and shook his head, feeling sick at having been so ugly toward her. "Maude," he began, subduing his voice, "Maude, it's okay, I'm not angry." He walked around the bed. Maude lay on the carpeting, her legs drawn to her body and her arms curled into her chest, the fluff of cotton poking between clenched fingers. Her eyes shone wetly. "Maude," Burden said softly. "I'm not angry, I'm not. I was just scared is all."

"I was just trying to help you, I was just trying to make it better, so that we could . . . we could both . . ." Her voice, small and childlike, faltered.

Burden sat next to her. "I know that," he said, stroking her hair. "I know you wouldn't do a thing to hurt me."

"I wouldn't," Maude said, nodding her head, her voice pleading. "I only wanted to make you happy. Don't you want to be happy?" A second sobbing fit seized her. She tried to still herself as Burden held her tightly.

She'd intended no insight, yet Maude's question cut Burden deeply; it was clear to him that the last thing he thought he could ever be was happy. He brushed her cheek with the backs of his fingers. "Maude," he said in a whisper, "there're not many women who'd treat me better than you." Maude had composed herself and she looked up at him, sniffled, smiled. "God's truth," Burden continued, "in all the years I've known you, you've been nothing but a saint to me. I owe you more than I'll ever have time to repay."

Maude snuggled into Burden's lap. "Yes, I have, haven't I?"

Burden drew in a breath and held it, as though deciding suddenly not to release it as a word. At length he said, "I've been thinking." He hadn't intended to say today what he was going to say; he'd intended to come to Maude for, what, comfort? solace? Yet the alleyways of his mind conducted him to this sad, neglected square of conversation that, as Maude must have realized by the way she squeezed her fingers into his waist, admitted no joy. "I've been thinking . . . about us."

Again Maude flexed her fingers and Burden felt the shudder of hard breath. What he had to say would cause her pain and the emotional distress she transmitted through her fingertips gave him pause. For several moments he withheld his words as in a suspension of time.

But that miniature infinity ebbed and at length he could do nothing other than continue forward. "What we're doing . . ." Burden paused in thought and then added for Maude's benefit, "although every moment has meant something to me . . ." He hesitated again, the flatness of his sentiment making him wince as surely as Maude had, if for different reasons. "But it's weighing too heavy on me. It's wrong—"

"It *isn't* wrong," Maude interjected, tightening her grasp around his waist.

"It is," Burden insisted gently. "It is and I can't continue. It's not fair to Hubert, and it's not fair to you." Burden was amazed at how clumsy, how sublimely foolish the words he spoke sounded even to him; he felt as though he were in high school and that Maude was not a mature woman but some lovestruck freshman.

"Oh, to hell with Hubert. He's a man with a corpse's heart."

"That may be, but he's still your husband." Burden guided his fingers through her hair, drawing out tangles. "Listen, Maude." What Burden was about to say made him smirk, and it confused him how the truth could sound so empty and utterly untrue. "I have great affection for you. You know I do. But what we've been doing these past few years . . . it has to end."

Now it was Maude who grinned with ironic appreciation. "When I was younger," she said in a hushed, unhurried tone, "not much younger than you are now, I would have given anything to hear a boy saying those words to me, because if he *were* saying those things, then it would mean there had once *been* something special between us. I never had that—something special—with anyone." Maude ran a finger lightly over Burden's belly, stroking the soft patch of blonde hair that sprouted there. "I would have given anything to have had those sad words fill the emptiness in my heart. But I had no idea, no idea at all just how painful they would have been for me to hear." Maude paused, and Burden felt her breath tremble. "Now I know." Her words were gently accusatory.

"Maude, I'm sorry," Burden said quietly, touching her cheek with his fingertips.

"Now I know how deeply they wound, but I can't regret hearing them, even this late in my life."

Maude turned her face up to Burden's and he was struck by how pretty, simply pretty, she looked, even with, or perhaps because of, her sad, tear-stained eyes. Their years together had meant nothing to him, but he would not let her see this as he regarded her.

"I married Hubert," she continued, "but I never fell in love until I met you."

For several minutes they were silent and Maude's self-judgment remained a pungent presence between them. Then Maude shifted and the silence was dispersed as easily as dust is unsettled by a footstep. "Love is a fool's game, but you did love me also, if only for a moment or two?"

Burden nodded. How easily one lie followed another.

"Then that is all I need." Maude's hand descended from his belly to his groin, her fingers timidly playful. "But there is one thing, one last thing."

"What?"

"I want us to make love a final time, so that we can look back and remember that we parted as lovers."

Burden wanted no such thing and his initial impulse was to decline her request. But then he recalled that he had *never* been emotionally engaged in their lovemaking, and passion's absence this time would not be felt to any greater degree. His hand moved to her breast in acquiescence.

Maude wrapped her fingers round his penis and gazed at it. "You really can't feel anything . . . here?" she asked, prodding the top of its shaft.

"Not a thing."

"But, dear Burden, I notice that this lack of sensation isn't lessening its ripeness." Maude abandoned her sadness and allowed herself a smile. "And that means Maude is a very smart woman, after all."

They made love, Maude with an apparent sorrow that made her motions frantic, Burden with a more detached emotion, but with a sadness also because he could feel in Maude's touch and her checked breath the anticipatory pain she felt in this last afternoon with him. Afterward she did not rise to prepare a warm towel for him but rested against him, her hands a bouquet at her chest. They did not speak, and when finally Burden could wait no longer, he rose and she rose also, cleaning themselves and dressing.

After dressing they descended to the first floor, still silent. Burden thought what last words there might be and found he hadn't any that would not be wounding in their commonness. They reached the foyer, and Maude slipped her hand into Burden's and together they continued to the kitchen. Pulled down by the gravity of self-reproach, Burden's eyes skimmed along the area rugs and planking passing beneath his feet, hearing nothing but an inward echo of "good-bye" sounding in his mind, in his own voice. Maude squeezed his hand and sniffled. Why did these small actions make him feel so guilty? Why should he feel anything for her? But then he found he could not feel callous toward her, and the guilt he felt was the transformation of sadness for her, a sadness he thought himself incapable of.

Soundless and sightless they continued toward the kitchen. Because they walked thus they did not hear the sharp clinking sound of a spoon knocking with a desultory rhythm against the sides of a ceramic cup. And it was not until they had committed themselves to the kitchen that they registered the dark burnt odor of coffee in the air. Maude looked up, her eyes no longer blind. Her hand flexed strongly in Burden's hand and so Burden lifted his eyes from the floor and looked before him.

Dr. Whitman sat at the kitchen table, looking lost, the coffee cup grasped by one hand as the other weaved a spoon absently through its contents. As he gazed downcast at the table, it seemed possible he might have been sitting there for an eternity, simply stirring. When Maude and Burden entered, he heard them and looked up; the spoon, belatedly, was relieved of its chore. The doctor took a sip and set the cup down, regarding Maude and Burden with a distant, distracted appraisal.

For his part, Burden felt he'd been apprehended by an impotent potentate, one so powerless and so not to be feared that all he could do, upon discovering their perfidy, was to deny the evidence before his eyes. Still, powerless or not, Burden felt a depthless desire not to be standing here before Dr. Whitman when inferences of transgression could be so easily drawn; it seemed an affront to a decent man. Burden felt something, something physical, and looked down to see his hand still in Maude's.

"Hubert," Maude said, her hand unwrapping itself from around

Burden's and rising to her chin, as though the maneuver were meant to dispel any illusion of sin. "I didn't expect . . . aren't you scheduled . . . ?"

For all the cool repose Maude had demonstrated on previous occasions, with some pride and vanity on her part, her words now faltered. Burden looked at the doctor, looking fatigued and insubstantial behind his cup of coffee, the skin below his eyes adorned by sunless quarter moons and every crease running through his aging face seemed like erosions of some softer material, permanently marking every storm he had weathered.

"Hubert?"

"Stuart's gone. I lost him," Hubert declared softly, in a detached manner that slipped from his tongue with deceptive ease.

Although he gathered the gravity of the situation, the name meant nothing to Burden. However, the name instantly transformed Maude's expression from one of guilt and surprise (and not a little anxiety) to sympathy.

"Hubert," she repeated, the word tempered by intonation. "Oh, Hubert." Maude walked to her husband and from behind leaned down and wrapped her arms round his neck, burying her face in his fine gray hair and kissing him lightly on his pinkish crown.

Burden stood, somewhat awkwardly, observing the scene of Maude and Hubert entwined. The emotions appeared genuine, with the doctor in obvious emotional discomfort (though muted by a professional and male remove), while Maude exuded empathy and caring as she protected her husband with her arms. But where was the anger? Burden thought. Did the sorrow of remorse trump the rage of betrayal? Perhaps. But standing here, looking now with fearless eyes at old Hubert Whitman, Burden thought it possible, likely even, that had the doctor merely come home for an unexpected late supper and caught him and Maude walking hand in hand, that the expression, the emotive force of his eyes would be no different. *Here sits a pathetic man,* Burden concluded. *Here is a man who has sold or abandoned or willfully renounced his passion.* He was sorry for the doctor that Stuart, whoever Stuart was, had died. Still, what cold and obscenely composed heart must animate him, that he could discover Burden and his wife together and yet regard him with such supreme self-possession?

Maude turned her eyes up to Burden and motioned toward the door. How opportune this Stuart's death was for her, how timely that she could subsume the hurt in her heart with another's deeper despair.

Burden walked to the door and stopped at the threshold. He turned to look back at the doctor and Maude. She had sat down next to Hubert, was urging the coffee cup toward him with one lovely and sympathetic hand while the other stroked the back of his neck.

Dr. Whitman looked at Burden and his expression registered not the slightest difference as he said, "Good afternoon, Burden."

Burden returned to the store, helped with odd chores, left again and drove through town looking for Johnnie White. He turned down the roads Johnnie most frequented when hawking his boiled peanuts. But he didn't find Johnnie and so drove home. He stayed long enough to eat half his dinner, then jumped up, with a mounting agitation, and drove back to town. The sun had set and only fragments of colored light remained. Along the streets, lamplight shone brighter and the storefronts came to quickening life. Burden lost himself down by-roads and pock-marked streets that curled around like rutting snakes; he traversed the city and felt with an ever increasing awareness that he was not where he was supposed to be and wondered if he ever would feel otherwise. He pressed forward or slantwise, whichever way the roads led, and when he sensed the van needed to rest he brought it to a stop, with prophetic alacrity, across from the Sonic. For there, under the fluorescent lighting (which transformed her normally pale complexion into an ethereal gloss), stood Jo, looking crisp and clean in khakis, an ivory blouse tucked loosely into the waist.

For a moment, Burden heard nothing, felt nothing, as though suddenly imprisoned within a bell jar. Then Jo, who stood with several of the skateresses, talking, laughing, and touching each other on their arms as they laughed, turned and saw Burden. Her laughter fell silent and her mouth melted into a tentative smile. Then she cast a broader smile and waved to him. *Come here,* she seemed to say.

Burden remained still. Hearing eluded him, but he felt, with timorous touches, the beat of his heart, felt it in his chest, felt it transmitted through his throat and temples, felt the tips of his fingers quiver as by some internal rhythm. The sound returned. *Come here.* A distant echo.

"Burden," Jo called. His reticence appeared to embolden her, for she took several steps toward the road, making sure he saw her.

Unconscious of the act, Burden started the engine, and in a convulsion of terror and ecstasy, crossed the highway.

THIRTEEN

As Burden made his way across the highway, on the other side of town Eugene, bloodied and fatigued, lurked in the heavy night in an empty lot just down from his own house. Short of breath and sweating profusely in the humid summer air, he was bleeding from the knuckles of the index and middle fingers of one hand and from both palms. Blood trickled also from a swollen gash running vertically along his lower lip, which made his mouth taste bright and coppery in contrast to the shadows he hid in. He had received these injuries while stealing his way clumsily through the woods bordering his subdivision. The woods were relatively young, and the spindly limbed trees engaged their intruder with adolescent mirth, tweaking his face and neck and twice tripping him. The first spill had produced the split lip, with Eugene whooping in fright as he fell through the dark abyss into whose arms he knew not. (The arms turned out to be those of the binoculars slung around his neck, whose right lens cover was now christened with a few drops of his blood.) He lay on the ground, nettles pricking at his cheeks, fearing he'd been heard. Frozen in this awkward position for several minutes, he waited and listened to the bay of a distant dog, its lonesome-sounding voice echoing among the night and trees. When he was satisfied no other creature more intelligent than himself or the dog had heard his whoop, Eugene stood and continued, took two steps through the fog of night, and stumbled again. This second fall produced the wounded knuckles, which left their skin on the bark of a pignut hickory. A tight curse choked in his throat but otherwise he made no sound other than that produced by hitting the ground. Thinking better of walking through the course of blind obstacles, he covered the final fifteen yards on his knees, enduring the occasional patch of nettles that punctured the skin on his palms.

He stopped two lots down from his house and dabbed sweat from his eyes with the bloodied cuff of his shirt sleeve. When he could see well enough again, he peered through the foliage toward his house and counted the lighted windows—one, two, three, four—then staked out each window in turn, training his binoculars on them and waiting for telltale Siamese shadows where only one should be. His stomach burned with a sour heat that left him famished yet without appetite; each minute that passed without revealing the shadows he feared, far from easing the pain in his stomach, served only to increase the dyspepsia tormenting him. He felt a sting at the back of his neck, slapped it, then inspected his hand; more blood, this time from the burst body of a dead mosquito.

Eugene had devised his plan to catch Burden and Pru together as he stood in the parking lot, after speaking with Burden. His plan had seemed simple enough: He would pretend to leave on an overnight run but would return, lying in wait for the young lovers to commit their crime. There had seemed little opportunity for mishap, and because of this he had not anticipated the hurt his body would endure, with his legs tugged at by brambles and his neck and face assaulted by dried twigs that scraped across his skin like needles, or the smell of dog shit stuck to his boots and pressed under his fingernails, or the goddamn mosquitos swarming round his head. Was it not hurt enough that his soul ached in his chest like a burst and bleeding heart? Was it too little agony that his mind, with maddening detail, taunted him with visions of his wife and Burden in bed together, laughing at dumb Eugene who could never quite figure out what was going on while he was away? Tonight his agony was complete—body, mind, soul. He slapped at and missed a second mosquito.

Eugene didn't expect Burden to drive up in his delivery van this late at night; that would be too obvious (indeed, a similar incident had nearly gotten Eugene caught when he was screwing a fair, petite married woman in Summerville). He figured Burden would steal up to the house on foot, perhaps sneak round through the side yard and enter through the back, and so Eugene remained vigilant for the quick faint flash of white sneakers in the lamplight scudding along the sidewalk and around to the side. But it was approaching midnight and he had seen no such faint flash. And because he believed it possible Burden had somehow eluded detection, he spied on each lighted window with mounting anxiety.

A shadow passed briefly over the curtains of the living room window then disappeared. Eugene pricked up his ears and tensed his muscles at this movement, holding a point with his binoculars as steadily as a bird dog scenting quail. But the shadow did not return and, what was more, the window fell dark.

Eugene slapped his ear to chase away another mosquito and then worriedly scanned the three remaining lighted windows, which were bundled upstairs. But like the ten little Indians whose numbers dwindled one by one, the eastern-most second-story window went dark also, this time without the foretelling shadow. The only illuminated windows remaining were those looking into the master bedroom. With the curtains and sheers drawn and with his binoculars pressed to his eyes, Eugene had an excellent view into this room. Pru walked to the bed (which, from this angle, Eugene could see only with his mind's eye) and pulled off her shirt. She walked to the window, wearing only her bra and shorts, and hesitated, as though hearing or seeing something outside.

"Christ, Pru," Eugene muttered, "have some goddamn modesty."

As though hearing Eugene's remonstration, Pru withdrew from the window and went into the bathroom. After a few moments she dashed back into the bedroom. Her sudden movement alarmed Eugene, who for a moment forgot his purpose and suspicions, fearing she was being chased. When he was satisfied there was no intruder, he breathed more easily. But this easiness was short-lived, for Pru had only hurried to retrieve the phone. Eugene studied her face as she spoke, thinking she wore an expression of pleasure. Who was she talking to? he wondered. Burden? Were they engaging in some sort of sick phone sex? Or were they laughing at Eugene and planning their next rendezvous? Pru approached the window again, the phone pressed to her ear. She was dressed in a sheer nightie which Eugene, with his aided vision, could easily see through.

"Christ Almighty," he muttered. He slapped at his right ear and felt the warmth of blood signaling a dead mosquito. "Got you, you motherfucker."

A breeze blew through the open window, catching up Pru's nightie and revealing her even more plainly. She closed her eyes and seemed enraptured by the breeze's embrace. Or, Eugene thought, his stomach foaming sourly, could it be Burden's words giving her such pleasure. "Goddamn son of a *bitch*."

Pru stepped from the window and set the phone down. She returned a last time to look out on the night-shrouded street, fastening her nightie with delinquent modesty. At length she turned and vanished atop the hidden bed. The last Eugene saw of his wife was her arm reaching up for the lamp switch. Then darkness.

Eugene remained crouched on his own dark throne for several long minutes after Pru had gone to bed. Each breath brought the foul stench of dog shit deeper into his nostrils, but he did not perceive the odor any longer, and as he smacked mechanically at the mosquitos teasing his ears, he could think only of what a dumb fuck he must really be—certainly as dumb as Pru and Burden took him for. He felt betrayed and this made him feel sorry for himself, which in turn made him feel angry. Above all he felt powerless, powerless that he could not support any of these miserable emotions with the consolation of hard proof, having to satisfy himself with only circumstantial evidence and grave suspicions.

But he would be patient. He felt in his bones that the day was not far off when he would spring upon the two lovers unaware. On that day he would have his revenge. On that day he would restore a measure of his wounded pride. On that day Pru and Burden—especially Burden, the miserable prick—would find out just how smart Eugene really was.

He studied his bloodstained hands, their red charred black by the night, then spat a bloodied glob between his knees. *Damn you, Pru,* he thought in misery, *damn you for putting me in this position.*

Eugene stood and wiped his hands against his pants. As he made his way through the thicket and brush and wove through the pignut and pine, he knew he must do Pruella great harm, not physically, but in a no less permanent way. It was not until he had happened upon Burden and Pru as they were driving back to Walterboro that he had seen how he would do this. He suspected Pru was being unfaithful to him. But what he had been too weak to acknowledge for the truth revealed itself plainly as he watched Pru step from the van and go into the store. His idea had manifested itself while he stood talking with Burden. And after Burden had driven away, leaving Pru behind in a craven act of cowardice, he knew there could be no other course but to kill him. Reflecting on his decision brought peace to Eugene's mind. Killing Burden would accomplish three things: First, it would remove Burden from their lives; second, he would have his revenge; third, Burden's death would fill Pru with such depthless remorse, that it would leave her no choice but to repent of her sinful ways. And because Eugene would make certain to catch the two in the act and only then shoot Burden, he felt certain no jury would convict him of murder. Surely they would see that he had every reason, a God-given right—a duty even—to kill Burden.

Eugene felt an abiding calmness possess him. His mind grew composed, his thoughts serene, his heart felt very nearly without weight or substance as he contemplated Burden's death.

FOURTEEN

When Burden reached the Sonic he cut the engine and hurriedly stepped from the van. Finding an empty picnic bench, he sat down, and when Jo approached he motioned to the seat across from him.

"Please," he said, the timbre of his voice casual but its power faint.

For all the time that had passed since they had last sat and spoken to each other, Jo placed her hand on Burden's own with such lightness and ease that it seemed as though not a single hour had been lost. That ease, that lightness of touch and presence, had been hers on the beach the afternoon they had met; it had been hers after Peedie's death when she sat silently with Burden, coaxing him through the hours; and it had been hers the evening she told him she was leaving for Charleston to attend nursing school and that she thought it better if they didn't see each other anymore.

But you wouldn't feel so free, you wouldn't feel life was so easy if you carried in your head the images I carry, Burden thought. *I know you would be different.* Why couldn't he have made her understand that there was no changing destiny, not his? He'd caused too much pain for others, and had peered too deeply into a world he had no right seeing into and from which he could not turn away. It was these things that sealed his fate, he reasoned; it was these things, the inescapable images that had been woven into his mind from which he could not turn away, that justified all his pursuits since Peedie's death.

"It's good to see you again." Jo's voice was pleasant, but Burden was relieved to detect the faintest quiver; knowing she was not entirely at ease made him feel on more equal ground.

Bending forward, Jo tried to kiss Burden's cheek but he shied away. "Sue told me you were back in town."

Jo settled onto the bench. "How is Sue? I've been meaning to come by the store to see her."

"Sue's Sue," Burden said, shrugging. His nervous state would not allow him the luxury of a lingering gaze, still, he took quick note of how the intervening years had changed Jo; only traces of the young girl he'd known remained in her face, and he felt regret at that other person's passing. Yet many promises of early youth had matured, gathering the remnants of girlhood and recasting them, so that a face that was once pretty had grown lovely. Her eyes, he noticed, reflected a more melancholy aspect, gazing at him with such intelligence and clarity that he could not escape the feeling his thoughts had somehow been laid naked before her.

To protect himself, he cast his gaze down to the tabletop and it fell on his hands wrapped in hers. He recalled the many times he'd kissed her hands, studying them silently when she was resting with her head against his chest and her fingers laced across her belly. He recalled how he would hold her hand as they raced through the woods, and how it had been the touch of her fingers to his that seemed the only real thing to him as they fell forward through the mote-speckled rays of sunlight and blue shadows. He recalled her hands on his arm and how perfectly they rested there. And he recalled how they had touched his face and how he would flush with heat and that they would be points of comfort. These things and more he recalled as he withdrew his hand from hers.

Ignoring the slight, Jo brought her hands together and rested them on her lap.

There followed several moments of awkward silence between them, with Burden feeling a sharp discomfort in an environment that had once been a second home to him. He understood from Jo's posture that although she was outwardly composed, she felt no less out of place than he, even if only because he was here.

"Evening, stranger," a voice called out from behind Burden. He turned to see Leslie gliding toward him.

"Haven't seen you in a mess of years," she said. "Where you been hiding?"

Burden turned to Leslie and opened his arms as though to indicate, somewhat sheepishly, that he had been powerless to make it otherwise. "I'm very busy."

"So I hear—a real man about town." Leslie gave him an enigmatic smile and a wink that indicated neither awareness nor ignorance of his many affairs. "Well, I'm glad to see we finally put something on the menu to make you come back," she said, tugging on Jo's blouse sleeve.

Jo's composed expression faltered at Leslie's remark and her pale complexion pinkened in a blush.

Burden also was caught off-guard by the remark. He turned to Jo and shook his head. He meant this as a gesture of reassurance—although how it could be construed as such he did not know. He saw at once from the tensing of her brows and the slight upward tilt of her head that Jo felt she had been insulted.

"Order up, Leslie!" barked the cook from behind his glass cage.

Leslie turned and wagged her hand at the cook. "I hear you!" She turned back to Burden. "It's good to see you again . . . both of you." She tousled Burden's hair and bent to give Jo a kiss on her cheek then glided off to retrieve her order.

While the silence had been awkward prior to Leslie's speaking with them, now Burden additionally sensed Jo's wounded feelings, a wounding demonstrated by the tightening of her lips and the way her posture had grown more correct. He hadn't intended to insult her, but the words of an apology—or at the least of explanation—escaped him.

What he wanted to say was that he was overjoyed seeing her again, that he adored her as dearly this night as he had when he had first seen her on the beach so many years before. But such adoration frightened him, and he was uneasy with the emotion's power. He wanted to tell her this also, to confess his sins and weaknesses, all of them. Sitting with Jo, it felt as though all the emotions he thought dead had merely been compressed and shunted aside to a remote area of his heart, and that seeing Jo, merely sitting with her, had released these emotions from the restraints of absence and willful neglect. He wanted to fall to his knees, to hide his face in her lap, to close his eyes against everything that had transpired the past six years and the emptiness that lay inside him, to reclaim the joy that his sick desire had stolen from them both. Even now, gazing upon her face, he felt a tremor faintly reverberate within him as he comprehended the enormity of his loss. But the emotion was of such great force that he feared releasing it, feared its consuming him with its ungoverned vitality, and so he struggled to rebind the restraints, to subdue his feelings with greater determination. This yielding to fear sowed shame in his heart, and this shame blossomed into anger. To mask the terror and anger he felt, Burden tightened his expression, allowing no reflex to betray either thought or emotion.

Such efforts reshaped Burden's features in an ugly fashion, till he fairly grimaced with displeasure. Unwittingly, his expression infected Jo also, who responded to Burden's apparent displeasure with a noticeable infolding of her own body. In this mood, neither was able to offer the other the expected civility of normal conversation, and with a child's irrational sullenness, Burden wondered why he had ever had it in his mind that he cared to see Jo again. This thought, though discomforting, did not frighten him as much as his adoration of Jo did.

Turning away, he sought a spot on the ground upon which to concentrate and collect his thoughts. At length he subdued the confusion in his mind and spoke again, affecting a more placid tone, which sounded uncaring. "How's school going?"

When she had spotted Burden across the road, Jo had been seized by a desire to tell him all she'd experienced during her years at school, to revel in the pride of her efforts. Perhaps by doing so they might begin to reestablish the bond that had once been so strong between them, the absence of which she realized left her incomplete. She thought of the book Burden had given her, how she had hidden it, had tried to forget its existence, as though by putting it aside she could also put aside her feelings for him and get on with her life, unencumbered by another's tragic past. But these efforts were of no use, for she knew there remained between them a cord she could not cut. Yet now, with Burden scowling at her, a prideful anger flared within her and she attempted to persuade herself that it was untrue a long-dormant part of her had reawakened the moment she had seen him again. This humble-jumble of emotions, this willful pride and rekindled affection for Burden, left her confused and uncertain as to how she truly felt.

As before, the awkwardness of the moment was temporarily relieved by Leslie, who set between the apostate lovers a single root beer float run through with two straws. Giving them a smile and a wink, she skated away wordlessly. And again, as before, her intervention only deepened the dark mood that had captured and bound their hearts.

Jo looked at the float and gave a slight ironical smile. She had a great weakness for root beer and ice cream and in an almost automatic response she reached for the glass.

"I don't care for any," Burden said.

Jo touched the glass and tapped her fingertips against its perspiring side, then pushed it away, her smile gone. She drew in a breath. "School was difficult," she said, as though only just now comprehending his earlier question. "But I won't be going back."

Burden looked at her, misunderstanding her, and in his ignorance was caught by genuine surprise at her words. His surprise momentarily softened his expression. "You won't?"

"Of course not," Jo said, her tone chiding. After three years of study and hard effort, how could they not now be over?

Burden's features hardened again. "I didn't realize . . ." he began then stopped. The puzzled expression overcame him a second time and admitted a brief warm ray. "And now you're back here." He said this with some incredulity, meaning the Sonic.

Jo compounded Burden's error with her own, thinking he was referring to Walterboro and her returning indicated failure after her time
away at college. In a chilly tone she responded, "Why not here? This is
where I grew up, this is home." Her tone was made all the harsher
because in truth she did feel shame at having come back after what she
believed had been a permanent break. What she mistook as Burden's
mocking attitude made her feel that shame more acutely.

Burden shook his head and laughed, not out of malice but a sense
of deepening befuddlement.

Jo reached for the root beer float just so she could push it farther
away, tightly squeezing her fingers around its glass fluting. "What's so
funny?"

Burden truly felt no malice toward Jo. In fact, he felt himself beginning to warm once more to her. "It's just that . . . you were the one so
anxious to make something of yourself, to move out of here . . . to get
away. I would have thought—"

"What?" Jo interrupted hotly.

"Well, it wouldn't have taken me three wasted years and God
knows how much of my daddy's money just to realize I needed to stay
right . . . *here*." Burden opened his arms to indicate the Sonic, shrugging
his shoulders in a show of incomprehension.

Jo stood, her face crimson. "What do you mean 'wasted years'? I've
worked hard—damn hard—to get where I am now."

Burden blanched and looked around at the diners in their parked
cars, whose faces he could just make out through the glare of fluorescent
lighting reflecting against windshields. He could feel their numerous and
inquisitive gazes and this made him uncomfortable. "Do you want to sit
down?"

"No, I don't. Why would I want to sit with you when all you've
done tonight is insult me?"

"Insult you?" The timbre of Burden's voice rose as he tried to
demonstrate, without increasing his volume as Jo had done, that he
could remain reasonable while standing his ground. But why did he
have to stand his ground? The adoration he had felt minutes earlier,

and which he struggled against so mightily, evaporated, making it no longer difficult to hide this now obviously erroneous emotion. "How have I insulted you?"

"How?" Jo responded, her voice growing louder. "First, you assure me that I could *never* be the reason you would come back to the Sonic, for which I thank you for letting me know my place. Then you ridicule my career choice and tell me all my education has been nothing but a waste of time and money."

Burden's eyes skipped across the parked cars and he drew into his shoulders in increasing discomfort. "I—"

"No, you be quiet—you be quiet and listen to me, Burden. I'm going to tell you something I should have told you a long time ago."

A young woman in one of the cars yelled out, "Go, girl!" which made Burden flinch as visibly as if she had boxed his ears.

"You may think you have your life—such as it is—figured out. Well, I don't. Okay? For me, almost every day of these last three years has been a struggle to make myself better, to believe that I could make that happen. But I wanted to be someone so I accepted that challenge. I want to make a difference in other people's lives. You . . . all you care about is . . . honestly, I don't know what you care about, but it isn't us. I don't think it ever was."

A car engine started up and immediately died and Burden heard a girl's voice arguing with her boyfriend. "Wait, not yet," the girl said.

Burden stared helplessly at Jo, uncertain how to recover his balance.

"I can never know what it was like to have been there at Peedie's side when he was killed, but somewhere along the way you forgot that he was the only one who died that evening. He didn't have a choice, you did; you had a choice to live and God knows how often I tried to convince you to take it, but you wouldn't. One day I came to see that two young boys instead of one *had* been left dead in that field after all."

The nascent light mood gathering among the patrons in the Sonic parking lot darkened with these words, and the curious, smiling faces became merely curious.

"I didn't ask to fall in love with you . . . not the first time," Jo said, catching herself short. When she continued, her voice was quiet and the anger bled from her eyes as they glistened in the fluorescent lighting. Remaining silent a moment longer, she gazed down at Burden with unexpected melancholy. "But I swear to God I won't let it happen again. I can't love a ghost, Burden, and a ghost is what you are."

Burden felt a kick in his gut that had the curious effect of straightening his back.

Tears rimmed Jo's lower lids and coursed along the round fullness of her cheeks. When she spoke her voice faltered and she had to screw up her resolve to finish her thought. "And I know now I can't make a difference in your life—I thought I could once, with enough time, with enough patience, but I see now that helping you is beyond me." Incongruent with her words, Jo took Burden's face in her palms and kissed him with a desperate passion. Then, standing, she wiped her eyes harshly. Her voice choking, she said, "Good luck with your life, Burden, whatever you eventually decide to make of it . . . but please, let this be the last time we see each other." There was so much else that needed to be said, so much she needed to relieve herself of, years of loneliness she wanted desperately to confess to him. Yet every thought came out jumbled, and the emotion she held in her heart manifested itself in an opposite manner. At length unable to say anything more, she turned and hurried to her car, in tears and brushing off the outstretched, consoling hands of her girlfriends.

Burden remained in his seat. For several moments he could not move, could not feel, could not breathe, not deeply. Reaching up he touched his cheek, drawing back a finger wet with Jo's tears. His hand trembled, just as Jo's hands had trembled as she held his face close to hers. He brought his finger within an inch of his eyes and studied the image trapped in the tear. As his eyes focused, he discerned his own face in the stark lighting; his face was ashen while his eyes, with the glassed-over regard of the dead, gazed back at him without resolution, reflecting perfectly the overwhelming sensation of being adrift that had seized his soul. That all eyes had focused on him meant nothing now; he could no longer feel the stares or hear the whispers. There was a far greater weight on him than the few onlookers at the Sonic could exact; he felt keenly the presence of an entire lifetime pressing down on him, its innumerable years compressed to a single point in space and time and laid upon his chest. He still could not breathe deeply and began to feel light-headed. Images slid barely within perception, giving him the sensation of vertigo.

She is gone, he thought. Or had he spoken this out loud?

A car in front of him started up and as the sound of the revving engine stung his chest, he started breathing deeply again. He looked up, took in every detail, yet registered none of it, stood, looked around for his van, and stumbled toward it. Leslie approached, holding out a hand, but stopped herself short when she saw the utter anguish that blotted out Burden's eyes.

The weight moved with Burden step for step, and even as he drove off, no destination in mind, he could not escape the suffocating presence of its mass pressed against his chest. Images slipped by, moonlight spilled around him and then dried to shadow, voices and the sounds of the night accosted his ears, yet none of these particulars penetrated his senses.

She is gone, that was the single thought sounding in his mind. It was the sum total of all the years he'd spent pursuing his dream of escape from the guilt of having killed his cousin. He pressed harder on the pedal, taking corners at reckless speeds. *It can end tonight,* he thought. *Everything can end tonight.*

Burden drove through the darkness. With no destination in mind, and attempting to blind himself to the truth unfolding in his heart, he slipped into a state of semiconsciousness, continuing forward by instinct. After more than an hour of randomly chosen turns leading anywhere but to a destination, Burden stopped at Buck's Tavern. He stood from the van, steadied himself on weak legs, then entered the bar.

Hesitating at the door, Burden glanced at the counter; there he saw Blind Willie, Bobby, and Cat huddled protectively at the extreme end of the bar just under the television. Bobby stared into the TV's mutable face, lost in a reverie of color and motion. Cat was talking to Frankie, who was leaning over the counter to better hear him. As he listened, his head nodding and his lips screwing up, he absently drew a dish rag across the counter, making small circles. A shimmering trail of moisture chased after the rag, its light fading as the trail evaporated.

Blind Willie turned and saluted Burden with his beer hand.

Burden nodded. Feeling more at ease, he continued toward the bar. Still he felt the weight pressing against him, making breathing difficult. A faint sense of vertigo lingered, and he didn't trust that the ground below him was as solid as it seemed. When he reached the bar, he gripped its edge and carefully sat down on the stool.

Blind Willie apprised Burden's movements with a sideways glance. He sipped his beer and then said, "Looks like somebody's seen a ghost . . . or Eugene."

Burden motioned for Frankie, and the barkeep turned to him, his eyes bright with anticipation.

"What'll it be, Burden?"

Burden started to respond but stopped short. Tonight beer wouldn't do. He looked down the bar. "What's Cat drinking?"

Frankie gave him a queer look. "Bourbon."

"That's what I'll have."

Frankie paused, and Cat and Blind Willie gave Burden long, questioning looks. Even Bobby tore himself away from the game on the television long enough to find out what was going on.

"Burden's just ordered a bourbon," Cat said, edging close to Bobby.

"No shit?" Bobby said, curious.

In the year that Burden had legally been coming into Buck's, and the years before that when he simply came in, the law be damned, he had never ordered anything other than Corona or Coors, depending on whether or not he'd had sex before coming to Buck's. Because of this, although they did not understand its meaning, they grasped the significance of his request.

Frankie asked Burden if he was certain a bourbon was what he wanted and Burden nodded gravely.

When Frankie placed an ice-filled tumbler in front of him, Burden insisted, "No ice."

Frankie gave Willie a questioning look to which Willie nodded his silent approval. Frankie dumped the ice and set the empty tumbler in front of Burden. His hand had grown tense and it was with great care that he poured the shot.

Without hesitating, Burden upended the glass and drank the bourbon whole. He slammed the glass on the bar top, wheezed mightily, then motioned for another shot.

"Must have been a ghost," Blind Willie observed wryly.

"Take this one a little slower, son," Frankie advised. "I'll be back in a while to fill you up again soon as I take care of my other customers. Just take it slow."

Burden acquiesced to Frankie's wish and sipped the next glass, but as soon as Frankie turned his back he downed the remainder of the bourbon in a single gulp just as he had the first. He wiped his hand roughly against his wet lips, which already felt peculiar, then turned to Willie and nodded. "A ghost? Yeah, you could say that. But not like any ghost I ever dreamed of or read stories about. Jesus." A shudder ran through his body. He felt the bourbon working, but its effects were masked below his agitation. He had to slough off the weight on his chest soon or he would collapse sure as dead where he sat. "This isn't fast enough," he complained. Standing on the rung of the bar stool and craning over the counter, he retrieved a bottle of beer from the ice trough running the length of the bar. Absent an opener, he set the bottle against the rim of the counter and smashed down on its cap twice with the ball of his hand.

"You sure you know what you're doing?" Willie asked.

Bobby leaned into Cat and said, "What's Burden saying, anything yet?"

Cat waved Bobby away.

Burden got down a third of the bottle and then he began coughing foam. He wiped his mouth again and set the bottle on the counter; he felt better, the vertigo was less severe and the weight was easing and now his breathing came more easily. Closing his eyes for a moment, he relaxed onto the seat and blew out sweetened breath. He began to speak, stopped, smiled, shook his head, drank more beer. At length he said, "Ghosts? Old man, I got more ghosts dogging me than one soul can bear."

Here Burden thought of the ghost of Peedie, who was a continual shadow in his dreams and who—he believed unintentionally—ruined whatever peace sleep might have offered. He thought also of the ghost of Jo, coming back after three years away and resurrecting a past he thought he'd lost for good. Seeing her again, he understood she had never really departed from his heart, and he realized how inhumanely he had compressed her memory, squeezing and compacting it till it was safely hidden under less provocative memories. He felt humiliation at this shunting aside of his feelings for Jo, humiliation and a sharp awareness of having betrayed her. Then there was the greasy, hulking specter of Eugene lurching ever closer. From his first sexual encounter with Pru, Burden could detect Eugene's malevolence in the house, thick and suffocating like the putrescent odor of decay fouling the air. His heart had thrilled at the menace Eugene promised, and each coupling with Pru was an anticipation of deliverance that at one time had seemed unattainable but now seemed at hand.

Burden upended the bottle and consumed the remainder of the beer.

"You planning a late night or an early morning?"

Burden turned to Willie. "What?" he replied, wiping his mouth with the back of his wrist. Foam spotted his chin.

"From the looks of it, I'd say you've got something special planned for the evening."

"Maybe I do," Burden responded slyly. The twin influences of bourbon and beer had begun the numbing work he sought, and he felt that first remarkable sensation of being himself but also of being removed from himself, sucking back inside to observe his speech and movements, to critique and belittle his notions.

Bobby leaned again close to Cat's ear. "What'd he say?"

"Said he's got big plans for tonight," Cat whispered.

Without revealing his gesture to Burden, Blind Willie placed a restraining hand lightly on Cat's wrist and then released it. "So," he said to Burden with disinterest, "you telling what they are, these plans of yours . . . or are they a secret?"

"Secret? No," Burden insisted as he surveyed the counter, searching for hard liquor but finding none. He turned and called for Frankie, but as soon as he got the name out he felt a tapping on his shoulder.

"I'm right here, kid," Frankie said. "What do you need?"

"Oh," Burden said, turning back around. He smiled at his friend's magical appearance. *Yes, that's it, everything is magic, all of it,* Burden thought. Nothing was real, nothing at all; for a blessed moment in time, the ghosts haunting him were only figments of his imagination. Eugene? Nothing more than the remnants of a foul odor, utterly harmless. Pru? Nothing but an unpleasant, conniving bitch of no importance to him. Maude? A pitiable phantom conjured by his own desire to help the less fortunate. Peedie? A horrible, horrible accident that probably never really happened. What proof was there beyond his constant nightmares? *And Jo?* Burden's thoughts faltered; he could not dismiss Jo so easily, who, even above Peedie, haunted his soul. He could not conceive of her as anything more substantial than flesh and bone, and as a result was incapable of disbelieving Jo from his life. Burden found he could not disbelieve in anything that haunted him, and he believed with a renewed fervor that his ghosts were entirely real. He raised his tumbler. "Another bourbon."

"Look, you sure you wouldn't prefer another beer instead?"

Burden looked at the bar counter and saw the empty bottle he'd discarded. "Ah, yes, I was going to pay you for that—"

Frankie shook his head. "That ain't what I'm worried about."

"Okay, Frankie, but while I figure out what it is that you *are* worrying over, how about another shot?" Burden shook his glass.

Exasperated, Frankie huffed and shook his head, muttering to himself as he poured Burden's glass.

Burden thanked him and dispatched the liquor with the swiftness of the executioner's blade falling on its victim. "Sorry, Frankie," he said, his eyes imploring the bartender's understanding.

Willie said to Frankie, "How about serving me up a bourbon, too. No sense our boy walking the road to oblivion all by his lonesome."

"Sure thing, Willie," Frankie said, setting the old man up with a glass. He asked if Willie wanted any ice and Willie shook his head.

Burden did not feel well. The emotional vertigo that had accosted him earlier had been momentarily tamed by the bourbon, but now the liquor itself was beginning to play spatial tricks of its own on his eyes and inner ears; that part of him that was removed registered the lurching of his stomach as the room began a languid, clockwise movement. He grasped Willie's forearm to steady himself.

"Two of these and you see God," Willie said as he raised his glass in a toast. "To your dreams, Burden."

Burden's eyes widened in horror and excitement at Blind Willie's words, as though focusing on an object so overwhelmingly hideous and frightful that it possessed an undeniable beauty; he clutched the old man's shoulders tightly, bunching up Willie's shirt sleeves in his fists. "You remember that story you told me long time ago?"

Willie laughed kindly. "I've told you lots of stories, son, which one you talking about? The one about the one-legged whore up in—?"

"No. No, the one about that old car of yours . . . you know, and . . . and the bridge," Burden sputtered excitedly, clutching more tightly to Willie's sleeves.

Willie thought for a moment and then his eyes brightened in recollection. "You mean the trestle? Ah, yes. You're talking about when me and Deacon Wells took my father's Ford and drove it onto the tracks."

"Yes!" Burden said wetly. "That's the one. Tell it to me again."

Willie chuckled softly, in wonder at his former recklessness and the young boy he hadn't thought of for many years. "Well now, let's see, there isn't much to tell. We went off with my daddy's car late one Saturday night. We weren't going anywhere. Hell, I guess we were just out to be seen by the girls and the other fellows."

Bobby tapped Cat's shoulder. "What's going on now?" he whispered lightly enough that Willie wouldn't hear him.

"He's telling Burden about that time when he and Deacon Wells rode his daddy's car up onto the tracks."

"Oh, Jesus," Bobby snorted, rolling his eyes in mockery. "I thought he'd put that old story out of its misery a long time ago."

Cat shushed him. "Kid asked to hear it again."

Bobby rolled his eyes and turned back to the television. "Jesus."

"That's right," Burden said to Blind Willie, his words spilling over themselves with excitement. "You took your daddy's car up on the tracks."

"Down at Green Pond—we were heading for Jacksonboro and thought it'd be a hoot to see how far we could get."

"It was nighttime, right? Full moon. You could see a mile down the track easy—"

"Easy enough."

"You'd have seen any train coming toward you long before it come up to you."

Blind Willie nodded. "Pretty much straight track all the way to Jacksonboro, just a couple of shallow curves."

"Only when you did finally see it—the light—you figured it couldn't be real."

"I suppose Deacon and myself, we were too scared to believe the light was real. We were about a hundred yards west of the Ashepoo," Willie said, meaning the Ashepoo River. "Beyond the trestle was a curve off to the north. We could see a faint glow shining on the trees, that's all we could see. Deacon—"

"Wanted to turn off right then, but you wouldn't do it."

"*Couldn't* do it," Blind Willie said, correcting Burden. "Deacon wanted to pull off right then and there, but we were going too fast. You see, when you're riding the rails, you can go as fast as you dare, the devil of it is to keep your hands off the goddamn steering wheel, that's what kills you; just let the car ride along those rails." Willie saw by the narrowing of Burden's eyes that he had dissembled too much. He coughed into his hand and continued. "Well, if we'd've tried to turn off then, our speed would have flipped us into the woods like a silver dollar."

Bobby touched Cat's shoulder with his own. "He done yet?"

"Just reaching the trestle," Cat replied.

"The trestle," Bobby repeated solemnly as he turned back to the television.

"We had to slow down, and fast, before I dared to turn her off the tracks."

Burden drank from Willie's glass and set it loudly down on the counter. "But there was a bridge between you and the light, and you couldn't just slow down—" Burden stopped as his inner self observed the slow, carousel turning of the bar and its patrons. Even Willie appeared to undulate on his barstool.

"Slow down? Goddamn it if we didn't have to *speed up*, right toward that goddamn locomotive heading right goddamn for us." Willie laughed heartily as he remembered the two young boys in his daddy's car, their faces alight by the locomotive's blazing lamp.

Burden renewed his clutch on Willie. His eyes widened in the terror of realization. He brought his face into the shadow of the old man's and spoke to him in a voice mimicking the terror in his eyes. "I'm in that car, Willie, I'm in that car right now. Goddamn if I don't have something terrible coming for me, and there ain't a goddamn thing I can do but go faster."

"Burden, what've you got coming for you?"

Not hearing Blind Willie's question, Burden sprang up violently and ran to the door. Stopping at the entrance, he turned, his eyes ablaze in private torment. "It's too late," he stammered and several of the patrons turned to see what wild man stood at the door. "Jesus, it's too late."

Blind Willie stood but Burden was already gone. He walked outside to see if the kid was still in the parking lot, but heard only the sound of the van's engine fading into the night, then silence.

When Blind Willie returned inside and sat on his barstool, Cat and Bobby gave him questioning looks.

"Think we ought to call the sheriff?" Frankie asked.

Blind Willie shook his head. He remained silent for a moment; he could remember the flame of passion that burned him in his youth, and he understood such passion was as much torment as ecstasy. At length he said, "No, Burden'll be all right." But he wasn't at all certain of his prediction, and he turned to the others as though for confirmation. Not seeing any in their expressions, he repeated to himself, "The kid'll be all right."

FIFTEEN

Burden sped along the wet Walterboro streets, but whereas before he'd had no destination, this time he knew perfectly well where he had to be. He'd had a revelation sitting at the bar speaking with Blind Willie, experiencing a sudden shifting of vantage point that placed him behind the wheel of Willie's old Ford. He could smell that night's damp air, feel it sweeping across his skin, could smell the sweet fragrance of jasmine and juniper in the surrounding woods and the clean, cold odor of the steel tracks passing swiftly underneath him; he could hear the crushing of the stone bed and the rhythm of the ties as the tires clattered over them. And he could see the glare of the train's lamp, a mournful eye all ablaze, gyrating sickly in its iron socket. He had felt the terror in that instant, the terror of approaching death. Peedie sat next to him in the passenger seat, and he could see the ugly, grim joy in his cousin's eyes and the mirthful twist of his lips set before a desecrated face whose flesh had been shot through with lead; the ice-chill touch of Peedie's hand on Burden's ran him through with terror as together they rushed headlong toward their doom and reconciliation.

As he approached the cemetery, its stone walls and iron fencing gleaming in the van's headlights, Burden maintained his speed, deter-mined to continue down the road. He braked only at the last moment and by the same damnable grace that had protected him his entire life-time, the van stopped before it could crash through the locked gates; he hadn't even nudged them, although a passerby would have been hard pressed to explain how the van had stopped in so short a distance. Yet this demonstration of dark grace did not register in Burden's mind, so inured to its oppressive presence had he grown. He stepped from the van and walked in halting, lurching steps to the wall, falling against its iron fencing and grasping its bars tightly. His eyes burned and, asham-edly, he felt on the verge of tears, but he fought against this weakness, biting hard on his lips and cursing obscenely into the still night.

When he was sufficiently composed, Burden mounted the fence and hoisted himself to the top. This he did with great difficulty in his drunken condition, for the bars seemed to twist about in his palms, bending and flexing and otherwise offering such passive resistance that he could not hoist himself up except with the greatest exertion. Then, hanging precariously astride the iron crosspiece, a row of daggerlike posts to the front and rear, he found he'd caught his pants leg in a section of iron scrollwork. He yanked at the material but it would not come free; indeed, trying to free it only wedged his jeans in more tightly. He remained captured in this position for several minutes, raging against the work of angels and devils alike, uncertain from whose cold heart the ironwork had been spun. It was only when he drowsed for a moment and teetered from the fence in a dead fall that the hem of his jeans tore away, freeing him. He tried to right himself but couldn't, and fell to the soft peat—again without injury—picked himself up, and surveyed the grounds.

A full moon hung high above, its light intermittently blocked by lumbering clouds. Just now the moon's light was unobstructed, and its rays filtered down through oak limbs and lit pale patches of Spanish moss, which hung in the trees and lay strewn in lifeless clumps on the ground. Here and there the brass of grave markers glimmered like night eyes, and granite tombs shone dully with a faint spectral glow. During these periods of relative brightness, the clay road was clearly defined, and formed a line of pale yellow cut between squares of blue sod. At other times, when the moon was hidden by a cloud, the roads and tombs and grave markers would dim to the barest glow, as though they were, each in their turn, winking from existence.

Light or no, Burden stumbled forward. He gave no mind to his steps, and didn't care if he walked on the road or trod over grave sites; in this senseless state he tripped many times, and on several occasions fell blindly to the ground. Each time he picked himself up from the damp grass or clay, hovered unsteadily for a moment, then pressed forward. His mind was in a frantic state, and even had he been sober it was unlikely his thinking would have been any more coherent. Stopping to rest, he leaned against an old oak that rose with an arthritic malformation into the night sky. The grounds fell into a dreary darkness; an owl called out from its gloomy perch as an image, unrelated and unremarkable, flashed in Burden's mind and suddenly the tears that he had held back with such effort came flowing out unhindered. Covering his face with both hands he sobbed, his body bent over with as much disfigurement as the tree possessed. His shoulders shook, his chest heaved and burned with fiery breaths, and his throat caught in knots of unvoiced words. This fit endured several minutes at which time the sobs subsided, and his tears, while they continued to course along his cheeks, fell without the shameful, wretched sound of crying. He twisted his fists into his eyes, then stepped from the trunk of the tree, teetered, and fell back against the oak. He pressed a hand against the trunk and pushed himself away a second time, and looking up through the tree's limbs saw a pale disc of moonlight brightening behind a thinning cloud like a candle drawn near to parchment.

Burden stumbled forward again. The weight that had pressed so heavily, so suffocatingly on his chest, had vanished with the first sobs. Now, in that weight's absence, Burden felt a void opening within him, as though he were expanding inwardly to an immeasurable distance, and that each vital part of him—his soul, his mind, his heart—grew impossibly remote from the other. In this mood, his reasoning became insensate, his emotions illogical, his sense of existence impenetrable. He was everything and nothing at once, he felt an exquisite torment yet also a simultaneous detachment that was as exhilarating as any pleasure he'd ever known, as though it were some other unfortunate creature and not himself suffering so terribly. But this sense of exhilaration quickly died, and once more he stumbled forward through the gloom of night and the deeper gloom of his soul. When he reached Peedie's grave he collapsed to the ground.

"I'm sorry," he sobbed into the earth, repeating these words to each face that glimmered like the grave markers in the darkness before him: He offered these words for Peedie, for Jo, for Maude, for Eugene even, whose thick-fleshed features scowled at him with particular scorn. Envisioning Eugene filled Burden with a resurgence of self-loathing and fear. How many times had he promised his cousin he would someday come be with him? How satisfied had he been in the certainty of his guilt and the rightness of that judgment of death? Yet here was delivered to him the executor of that self-will, and now Burden wanted nothing more dearly than to tear apart any agreement he'd ever made, be it with the devil or God. *Coward!* a voice said, accosting Burden with a physical force that made him flinch. *Coward and a son of a bitch! Don't run from me—come here, boy!* But whose voice was that? Burden thought. In his delirium the voice seemed twinned, like lengths of chilled and burning cords woven into a single rope, as though Peedie and Eugene spoke with a single voice. *Come here!*

Burden covered his head with his hands and pressed his face to the sod covering Peedie's grave. The damp odor of dirt and grass filled his nostrils. "Go away," he insisted, "go away. I can't come with you, I can't do it . . . it's too much. It's too much for me." Again his voice broke and became choked with sobs. Mucus rattled deep within his chest with each hard breath shaking loose from his body. Anxiety seized him, halting his thoughts. In his delirium, a veil drew over his eyes, blotting out the waxing moonlight brightening the brass of Peedie's grave marker, absorbing into its folds the grounds' whispered noises and shielding Burden from the desultory wind that loitered among the trees and granite tombs and that stirred the spirits to restless impatience. No longer afflicted by these normal sensations and undisturbed by his sobs, which had quieted to a pitiable crying, he relaxed into the sod with the weariness of a penitent, and fell into a troubled sleep.

Burden stirred drowsily. He dully sensed a chill passing over him, waking him enough to make him want to turn over. A strand of moss adhered to his cheek as he rolled over, tickling his lips and causing them to pucker in a kiss. Drawing an arm over his eyes, he settled peaceably back to his thoughts. He'd been half-dreaming, half-thinking of Jo, this wonderful new creature who had so recently come into his life. She had come over Wednesday—their second date, if he dared call it that. She had eaten dinner with his family, and thinking back on it now he could feel again the eagerness and uneasiness he felt eating with her in front of his father and mother and his sister. Sue in particular vexed him, cutting her eyes at him throughout the meal, scrunching her lips together and blowing kisses through the air. He kicked her under the table with increasing force until at last she whimpered and his dad had asked what was going on. Both looked sheepishly into their dishes and that was the end of the kissy lips.

Beyond these taunting kisses, Burden also had to endure the discomfort of his parents' questions, especially those of his mother, as they drew details from Jo about her family and other matters.

When at last the meal was over the two escaped outside. Burden meandered through the yard, unsure where they should go, perhaps afraid to reach any destination in particular. He had too much nervous energy to sit any longer, and preferred instead to walk the evening away. But when Jo discovered the bench swing hanging from an old oak in the side yard, she insisted they sit and it seemed to Burden like the best of ideas. They sat, neither talking as the cool evening breeze sifted through the limbs and the sound of the easy, steady rhythm of the chains creaked softly above them. Then the breeze curled around Burden and it brought to him the freshness of Jo sitting so near to him. In that moment he smiled for the evening sky, which had muted to a bruised, shimmering light; he smiled for the northern breeze that swept through the air, cooling his skin; and he smiled for the knowledge of this girl, pale as moonlight and who smelled as fresh as the breeze.

At length their silence ended, and when they spoke their conversation was unhurried, flowing from one topic to another the way conversations will when two strangers try to divine each other's thoughts and likes. At some point their arms drew close and touched, and Burden liked the sensation this produced and hoped she wouldn't pull away. Jo didn't pull away, and through his skin Burden drank in the soft feel of her arm pressing against his. He wondered crazily whether they might forever touch this way; he would gladly spend his time on the bench sitting next to Jo, feeling the softness of her arm and breathing in her freshness.

"The fire dies so quickly."

"What?" Burden asked, embarrassed he hadn't heard her. He had been thinking what it would be like to kiss her, wondering if her lips were as soft as her arm.

"The fire, the sunlight. Evening comes and brightens the sky with all its colors, and gazing into it you think it will last forever. But then you look away for a second and when you look back it's all changed, all gone.

"I wonder," she said, craning her neck as she looked at the sky through the limbs above her, "do you think sunsets look the same all over the world?"

Burden shrugged his shoulders. "I don't know, I figure they do."

"I hope they don't. I hope that a person could run away and find a different sunset waiting for her wherever she went. Wouldn't it be boring otherwise, if all the sunsets looked the same no matter where you were? And the stars, too. Why go anywhere if nothing ever changes from how it is right here?"

Silly, Burden thought, then, *Kiss me.* But he didn't give voice to his desire, only turned and studied her profile as she in turn studied the last flame of twilight, her mouth set in a delicate smile, her lips barely parted. *Kiss me.* But it was no use, she refused to hear his thoughts.

Then, suddenly, Jo turned and caught him studying her. He looked quickly away, horrified; he heard her laugh and his face grew hot in a blush, then he felt her hand on his. Turning slowly back, he saw her smiling, her teeth bright against her lips. He wanted to confess his thoughts to her at once; what use was it to deny his guilt? Indeed, it seemed a greater penalty to say nothing and to receive nothing. *Tell her, tell her,* a voice demanded. *Tell her—*

"Burden," his mother called out. "Burden, where are you?"

With the greatest reluctance, Burden turned from Jo and called back to his mother. "Over here."

"Time to take Jo home, your father's bringing 'round the car."

"Okay," Burden said, his voice sounding pitiful, deflated. Indeed, he thought ruefully, nothing *can* last forever. Then, turning to tell Jo they had better get going, his half-parted lips met Jo's. Her breath warmed him, and the sensation warmed him throughout his body, steeping his flesh in a sensuous heat, the likes of which he had never experienced. As quickly as she kissed him, her lips were withdrawn and Jo was standing over him, holding out her hand for him to take.

They did not speak in his father's presence on the way to Jo's house, but as they sat in the backseat their hands entwined, secure that the veil of darkness drawn over them would protect their secret intimacy. When they arrived at her house and they were standing on the porch, he said, "Would you like to do something this weekend, a movie maybe?"

Jo nodded.

"How about Friday?"

"No," Jo replied. "I can't Friday night. Saturday?"

Burden shook his head, feeling an anguish (it was the first time he had felt anguish). "I can't. I'm going with Peedie to our cousin Whalie's in Beaufort. We promised a ways back we'd come over and help with some yard work."

"If you'd like, Burden," Jo began, and the anguish Burden felt vanished at the sound of his name falling from her lips, "you could come over Sunday for supper."

Burden nodded. "I'd like that."

Jo looked at the front door with some anxiety. "I'd better go in."

It was more than he could hope for to receive a second kiss from her, but when she touched his fingers with her own and then quickly disappeared inside her house, he experienced something similar to disappointment, or was it more akin to being discontent? Whichever it was, as he walked back to his father's car, Burden began scheming how to get Jo back on that swing where it seemed all her kisses might be dispensed.

These were Burden's thoughts as he lay at Mary Bull's tomb next to his cousin; the remembrance of Jo's kiss warmed him. But then a murky chill passed over him, dispelling the comfort of his memory, and it was at this point that he stirred in his half-sleep, rolled over, and swiped at his tickle, kissing it as though stealing a second kiss from Jo.

He wished nothing more than to revisit the events of that recent night again but felt his body being rudely shaken. Irritated, he opened his eyes, and wiping the mist from their corners, saw that Peedie had him by his arm and was shaking him as he peered into the distance.

"What is it?" Burden asked, hiding none of his irritation at having been awakened from his dream of Jo.

Peedie held up a finger to silence Burden, then motioned to the far end of the cemetery. Burden had to raise himself to his knees to see where his cousin was pointing. Again he wiped his eyes. "What is it?"

"Over there," Peedie said in a whisper, pointing at the cemetery's northern boundary. "There's two of them. See them?"

The moon's light had pooled behind a cloud bank, casting the whole of the grounds in darkness. It was all Burden could do to delineate the brick of the church, with its tall, open arches, from the cemetery's gloom. Other than the church itself and two prominent tombs—which were but suggestions of form in the darkness—he saw nothing. Then, as though he had been looking directly at them the entire time and had only just now realized he could see them, two dim figures appeared, their bodies glimmering in the backdrop of night. They walked closely next to each other, peering down at the ground and seeming at once comfortable in the darkness and at the same time wholly unaware of that darkness.

"I was sound asleep," Peedie said, still in a hushed whisper, "I was sound asleep and then I felt this deep cold pass through me. I woke up at once and when I opened my eyes, there they were, walking right past us. I think maybe that they walked right through us. . . ." While he might have been expected to be in a fit of uncontrollable fear, or at the least in a state of uncontainable excitement, Peedie spoke in measured tones. There was evident tension in his voice, but all in all he took the appearance of this spectral couple with a remarkable calm.

"I didn't feel anything," Burden said, and as he spoke he remembered the chill of his half-dream and gooseflesh rose on his arms.

"I should be pissing my pants, but I don't feel at all afraid of them. Do you?"

Although Burden had seen something—or *imagined* he had seen something—whatever had been there was no longer visible, for the moonlight that had been held in abeyance by the clouds now rained unimpeded to the ground. Now he was no longer certain he'd seen *anything*. But turning to his cousin, he saw that Peedie was following an object with rapt attention. Burden turned back to the church and searched again for the two figures, if that had been what they were. "I don't see anything," he insisted, a yawn overtaking him.

"Sure you do . . . or you did, I can see it in your eyes. You saw them—a man and woman, walking hand-in-hand."

Burden sank back to the dirt and rested against Mary Bull's tomb. "Okay," he began sleepily, "suppose I did see them. Who do you suppose they are?"

Peedie shrugged his shoulders. "I don't know, a man and wife? Lovers? Maybe they died somewhere around here, somewhere near the church. Maybe they're buried here." Peedie paused in thought. "Maybe they were *murdered* here."

Even though Burden was confident he hadn't seen anything, his cousin's words squeezed a shudder from his body. But as the shudder subsided, he felt his eyes growing heavy with sleep once again. Peedie said something to him, but he didn't understand him.

"I said I wonder if this is some sort of sign," Peedie said again.

"I don't care if they're a sign. All I want is my own bed to sleep in." *And to see Jo again,* he added silently.

Peedie looked down at Burden and frowned. After a moment he said, "Don't worry about that, cousin, tomorrow night you'll be safe at home and all this will be over. Still, aren't you curious who they are?"

Burden was too tired, too sore for curiosity, and welcomed the pleasing, light-headed, free fall sensation of approaching sleep, which he didn't care to resist. He burrowed deeper into the indigo folds of slumber and Peedie's words became intertwined with the chirping of the crickets and of the breeze that blew down drops of cold rain clinging to the trees, and then Burden confused the true details of the night with the false details one conceives while nodding off. For this reason he could not be certain, when he awoke the next morning, whether Peedie had actually roused him from his dream of Jo, or whether Peedie and the two specters had been merely a dream within a dream. To compound his uncertainty, Peedie said nothing of the incident the next morning, and Burden was not inclined to ask him anything about what had very likely never happened.

The morning was cool and humid, unable to shrug off the previous day's wet weather. The grounds were choked with fog, and Peedie, who was already awake when Burden stirred to life, stood beside a tree, pissing on its roots. In the mist he looked as much the specter as the two figures of last night, except Burden knew Peedie was real and not a ghost or dream.

"What are you doing?" Burden teased sleepily as he pulled himself up to a sitting position.

"Making holy water."

As Burden grew more awake he felt more intensely the conse-
quences of last night's beating. His cheeks felt puffy and gave off a heat
even in the morning cool, and having spent a night in the damp outdoors only increased his discomfort.

When Peedie walked back to Burden, he shook his head, as though
rendering judgment at the sad sight. Furrowing his brow, he appeared
disgusted with something or someone. But his expression quickly
changed, assuming a forced calm. He offered his cousin his hand. "We'd
better get going if we want to make it home before supper."

"You wanting to walk?" Burden complained, massaging his jaw with
light strokes. "Shouldn't we wait for Whalie?"

"Whalie? I don't figure we should count on Whalie picking us up.
Hell, I don't figure we should count on him waking up before noon.
Nah," Peedie said firmly, "we should head out now. It's not but about
twenty miles home."

Burden told Peedie that he knew how far from home they were and
that he could make it, but he grumbled about it all the same. He suggested that they might wait for the church visitors to start arriving and
maybe hitch a ride with one of them. Peedie considered Burden's suggestion but then tossed it aside; he'd much rather walk, he said, ex-
plaining that there would be more adventure in walking than hitching
a ride.

"We're not supposed to be home till four anyhow, so this is free
time for us. Now come on," Peedie said, "let's get some distance between
us and all these dead people."

The two boys walked several miles along the narrow country road,
whacking at tree trunks and tall grass with slender, dried limbs they'd
collected at the church. Neither wore a watch, but Peedie estimated that
they had started out around seven, and that if they hurried they might
get home just after three; however, Peedie was in no mood to rush and
Burden wasn't inclined to hurry him along by telling him about his date

with Jo. As the occasional car passed, Burden furtively glanced at each one, hoping that by some luck the driver would stop and offer them an easy ride home. None did.

Morning's cool was giving way to the warmth of afternoon, and shadowy puddles were drying into the trunks of trees and fence posts, sopping into Peedie's and Burden's sneakers as they walked alongside the road. When noon arrived they were only slightly better than a third of the way to Walterboro. At that rate, they wouldn't get home until early evening. This knowledge gnawed at Burden's mind and itched his heels to move faster. Yet again he silently demurred to his cousin. When a break in the woods opened up, revealing a dark, winding path, Peedie looked at Burden and suggested they take it to see where it led.

"Will it get us home quicker?" was as near to what Burden wanted to say as he could get.

"Maybe, maybe not," Peedie replied. "You aren't in any hurry are you?"

Burden tossed the limb he'd been swinging down the path. "No," he managed after a bit and in seconds they were down the berm and tramping onto the path's damp soil.

The path wove upward promisingly for several hundred yards, meandering in a northeasterly direction, then hastened downward, threatening to become a bog. But although the earth grew moister and the smell of sulfur and loam filled their nostrils, the ground beneath their feet held them up; not wishing to turn back, the boys pressed forward. As though rewarding their faith, the path began a second incline. This incline was of greater distance, and set them on firm ground once again. Their luck held for more than a mile before the path swooped violently upward in a curl of earth crested by small trees and ferns. The path appeared to die at the curl, and for a moment both Peedie and Burden felt with greater acuity the heaviness in their feet, thinking how many steps had been wasted. Now it was likely they would have to turn around.

"Here," Peedie said at length, "boost me up." He grabbed the gnarled

finger of a root jutting from the ground, and with Burden's help scam-
pered up the steep rise.

"What do you see?"

"Give me a minute," Peedie said, disappearing into the limbs of the
trees, and the only thing Burden could hear then was the fading sound
of snapping twigs. Without Peedie's distraction Burden became aware
of a heaviness in his heart greater than that in his legs, a feeling of
isolation that had begun at the church the previous night. He thought
of Jo and of their date this evening, and wondered if he'd make it home
in time. But that concern became muted in Peedie's absence for he felt
alone, as though he were in so remote a spot that home and Jo might
never be reached. That he was the cause of his condition only compounded his dread. Had he not acted so foolishly by grabbing Sulah's
tits, he and Peedie would be home and not lost. He would be anticipating his date, and he would know nothing of this dread feeling. Several
minutes passed in this manner, with Burden's self-recrimination spiral-
ing him into an increasingly darker mood. Only as he was about to slip
into a mild depression did Peedie reappear above him, his face beaming
as he poked out from the green foliage curtain.

"Well?" Burden asked, brightening with relief.

"You're not going to believe this," Peedie replied excitedly. He
bent down and offered Burden his hand. "Hurry—you don't want to
miss it."

"What?" Burden asked, catching the excitement that bubbled forth
from his cousin, grateful his despair had lifted. "Miss what?"

"Just wait. You'll see."

When Burden had mounted the ridge, he again asked Peedie what
it was he might miss. But his cousin gleefully ignored his entreaties and
continued through the trees. "It's pretty thick for maybe a hundred
yards, after that there's a clearing. I figure we must be somewhere near
Yemassee, that's still a long ways from home." Peedie spoke with a con-
trolled deliberateness, but underneath that reserve were the brighter
tones of devilment known fully only to young boys.

The trees pressed thickly together just as Peedie had described, seeming to want to stand in the boys' way, but eventually the pale brilliance of open land appeared between the most distant trees, forming thin lines of whitewashed golds and greens spreading wider as they neared the woods' edge. When they were very near the break, Peedie stopped. Turning to his cousin, he took him by the shoulders and said with great solemnity, "What I'm about to show you squares you and me concerning Pruella."

"What—" Burden began to say, but Peedie put a hand to his lips to quiet him, leaving him to imagine what was out there in the clearing.

Peedie compounded Burden's anxiety by warning him to stay quiet, and, turning, he proceeded along his former course, stepping gingerly and crouching low as though stalking a deer.

A glade opened beyond the tree line, a short rise of clear land covered by lush field grass swirling under the influence of a light breeze. So accustomed to the shadows of the path had Burden's eyes grown that he had to make slits of his eyelids at first and bring his hands to his forehead in order to see. But the breeze felt sensuous against his face, and carried with it the gaining warmth of the afternoon sun and fragrance of the open space of the field. He looked around. "I don't see anything," he said, disappointed.

"Wait." Peedie fingered Burden's belt loop and pulled him forward toward the crest of the hill. Two-thirds of the way up Peedie fell to his knees, pulling Burden down with him, and they continued toward the crest on their hands and knees. The field grass tickled Burden's nose and lips and he had to constantly scratch at his nose to relieve a dozen itches that sprang up spontaneously, for he understood a sneeze meant disaster. "Wait here," Peedie said and he scooted through the grass alone. But this time he was never out of Burden's sight, and so Burden did not feel remote or abandoned. Indeed, he felt the tense excitement one experiences when colluding in a crime, only he wished he had some idea of the crime he was committing.

Peedie returned and whispered to Burden to follow him. Burden crawled after his cousin quietly. Only after his vision cleared the tall grass did he appreciate his cousin's excitement.

While their approach to the crest had followed along a leisurely incline, the far side of the crest fell away precipitously, looking as though its earth had been scooped out with a giant's broad spade. Where the incline ended, the field became level and stretched another thirty feet, beyond which lay a dirt road bordered by more woods. The road snaked out from between two large oaks on the edge of the far woods, followed a shallow curve as it edged along the field, then slithered back into the woods several hundred yards to the east. Splotches of damp soil were visible here and there where the road had not yet fully dried from the previous day's rain. A truck sat to the side of the road, its fenders and doors frosted with mud dried to an ashen gray; its windshield likewise had a light frosting on it, formed around two scallops of clean glass. The truck was parked on the far side, under the shade of trees. On the opposite side of the road a young man and woman lay on a faded, red-checkered blanket. The two were lying side by side, and the man, whom Burden guessed to be in his late twenties, had his hand on the woman's arm. With his thumb he was pulling the material of her blouse from her shoulder and kissing her skin there. Burden could see the white of her bra strap, exposed for all the world and him and his cousin to see.

Peedie looked at Burden, smiled, and whispered, "Well, are we square?"

Burden did not speak, or rather could not. Before Jo, he'd kissed only one other girl—and that had been only a single kiss. He'd tried kissing her a second time but she had backed away, yet with that single kiss he thought he had captured the essence of what a female was: her odor, the feel of her body against him as they stood close to kiss, the sound of her breathing suspended for a moment of time, the taste of her tongue, which held a day's worth of flavors. However, this blessed awareness had lasted only through that night and half of the next day, and in the end he was left no less frustrated and puzzled by girls than before the kiss. Now, as he looked at the young man and girl, the young man seemed poised on the brink of some tremendous discovery that Burden could never hope to undertake.

The girl sat up, and with her lover's assistance shimmied from her blouse. They kissed and she laughed nervously as she fell back onto the blanket. Now the young man began kissing her neck and the girl bent her head back in pleasure and laughed again, covering a fine mouth with her hand; the echo of her laugh carried softly across the field grass, bending their slender staves as though they had been touched by a breeze. The man slipped her bra strap from her shoulder and the girl struggled playfully for a moment and then a moment more, then settled back and became very quiet, very still, very intent. Burden looked on, enraptured by the scene; he felt his own body tremble and ache in response to what was happening; he felt great fear, and greater wonder. He thought of Jo and how it would be to kiss her the way this man was kissing the girl, to touch her the way this man touched the girl.

Afterward, after the young man and girl had dressed and gotten in the truck and disappeared into the woods, Burden remained silent, staring at the spot where the two had made love. Peedie observed his younger cousin with the air of the sophisticate, as though what he had seen was nothing extraordinary. He seemed to gain the greatest satisfaction from this attitude, that of exposing his cousin to some new experience to which he had long ago grown accustomed. At length he shook Burden by his shoulder. "What did you think?"

Burden could not look away from the spot on the field where they had lain in the grass. He had no words, no emotion for what he had seen; he had imagined such scenes many times, with himself playing the lover and any number of girls he knew playing the girl's role, but he realized now that he'd had no idea *what* to imagine, that his fantasies had all been formless and inaccurate, and that he'd fumbled along in his daydreaming as certainly as he had fumbled after that second kiss.

"Well," Peedie said after a short while, "we can follow that road, it should take us in the direction we want to go." He stood and shook dirt and chaff from his knees. "You ready?" he asked, offering Burden a hand to help him up.

Burden looked up at Peedie, his eyes holding the soft focus of some very distant and wonderful object. After several moments, he took Peedie's hand.

The two boys made better progress following the dirt road. Still, Peedie's estimation of when they would reach home had been woefully under-calculated. It was evident they would reach home no sooner than early evening, and realizing this, even with Peedie at his side, Burden grew despondent. His heart held the impatience of youth, with everything that was not at that moment feeling as though it would never be.

Apart from the still very present pain in his cheeks and lips, he sensed a gnawing within him he could not place; it was a vague aware-ness of some part of his nonphysical self being out of joint. This sen-sation, indefinite though it was, cast all he looked at, all he thought on in the blue filter of melancholy. It did not help that he'd awoke hungry, and as the morning gave way to noontime, his hunger pains came to him in increasingly powerful twists in the stomach; for minutes at a time he would feel nothing and almost forget he was hungry, then with an errant step or thought an acute pain would take hold of him. At these moments, which were growing more frequent, he would rub his stom-ach and gnash on his tongue so that his mouth would salivate. After a short time the pang would subside and he would be fine until the next episode.

When the pang of hunger was not distracting his thoughts, Burden played and replayed the scene of the young man and girl making love in the field. Each time a different detail would manifest itself; the pale relief of flesh beyond the young man's tawny cheek as he kissed the girl's breast, the swale of her torso between rib and belly, which swelled magnificently into a compact mound, the strong sunlight that struck her shoulders and which looked like shimmering patches had been sewn onto her skin. Considering these things, Burden was conscious of his having passed into a new chapter in his life and of something old passing away; it was too much to say that he felt born again, but only barely.

"Want to rest?" Peedie asked, his voice coming to Burden as from a great distance.

Burden nodded.

They sat on a recently felled tree that was still struggling to live, with half its roots jutting into the air in a tangled, petrified web clogged with the prey of soil and dead leaves.

Peedie looked up through the limbs of the overhanging trees and wiped his brow. "Sure could go for a soda right about now," he said. "Or ice cream. How about you?"

Burden shrugged his shoulders. He was in between hunger pangs at the moment and was concentrating on the girl, remembering the funny perspective of her upside-down face. It had formed a soft triangle, the angles of which haunted his memory.

Peedie poked Burden in the side to rouse him from his reverie. Burden turned and was about to say something but stopped. He blushed.

"What?" Peedie asked.

Burden blushed more deeply as he considered his question.

"Come on, Burden, what are you thinking? Wait a minute. I know, you're still back there, aren't you?" Peedie pointed down the road they had traveled, back to where the man and girl had been. "You ain't said two words since we saw them," Peedie chided Burden. "You might as well tell me what you're thinking, 'cause you're probably getting it all wrong up there." Peedie poked Burden's temple as he said "up there."

Burden flinched but he smiled also. At length he decided that the shame in asking his question, which would show his cousin how meager his education was concerning such matters, was outweighed by the satisfaction of a good answer. Gathering his will, he glanced at Peedie but turned away at once. Blushing, he closed his eyes and said in a rush: "What does it feel like? What does it feel like to be with a girl?"

The awkward, naïve quality of his cousin's question took Peedie aback. His impulse was to laugh at what he felt was a ridiculous question, but the earnestness with which Burden had asked it quieted his mirth. Unable to lightly dismiss the question then, Peedie gave it serious thought, which made him uncomfortable because he hadn't a good answer. "I don't know," he said finally, the tone of his voice making his answer sound like a shameful confession.

Burden turned to Peedie, surprised. "But I thought . . . I thought you and Pru—"

Peedie threw up his hands and shook his head; a feeble grin bent his lips. "Just 'cause a girl'll sell you a peek at her titties doesn't mean you get to touch them."

Burden turned away, crestfallen. After a moment he recovered a little and said, "You mean . . . you never . . . ?"

"Guess I should have done more chores; maybe if I'd had more money on me at the time I'd have a better answer for you."

The absurdity of Peedie's suggestion made Burden laugh, lifting him from his blue mood. He would have liked it better had his cousin had an answer for him, but a part of him realized that had the mystery been revealed in this secondhand manner, he would have felt the pangs of jealousy as strongly as he now felt the shame of ignorance.

"Still," Peedie said, looking out into the depth of trees, "still, it's got to be some kind of wonderful, don't you think?"

Burden nodded. Yes, he thought, it had been some kind of wonderful, the most wonderful thing.

Peedie placed a hand on Burden's shoulder. "Don't know about you, but I'm starving. The sooner we get home, the sooner we eat. Ready?"

Burden nodded and stood.

The boys continued along the road for several more miles, but when it made an abrupt southern jog that appeared permanent, they took once more to the woods. The day wore doggedly on as they walked. The trees, which in the afternoon light had come alive in sudden brilliant bursts of green and yellow, lost their vibrancy as the sun began its downward glide. Verdant colors once bright deepened and took on hues of gold and amber at their fringes. As the leaves began to shed their covers of sunlight, shadows of indigo welled up from the ground and gathered below the limbs of trees and clung to the underside of the countless leaves. Fiery specks of red and orange glinted from between distant trees, and directly overhead the sky's blue began to fade as a gloom descended with twilight. Under other circumstances, Burden might have found a certain peace at this quiet hour, but he was tired and hungry, his legs were pained with fatigue, and he could not shake off the melancholia that had overtaken him. Jo must have given up on him by now, thought he'd blown her off, and the thought of this pained him.

"Do you hear that?"

Burden turned to Peedie, his eyes questioning and still thinking of Jo.

"Do you hear those cars? That's seventeen, it has to be," he said, meaning the highway running in front of their parents' houses. "We reach that and we're almost home for sure."

Burden's expression brightened. *Almost home?* he thought, amazed at how good those words sounded. *Maybe it's not too late.*

Peedie took hold of Burden's shoulder. "Come on, cousin, let's hurry."

The boys broke into a spirited trot, laughing now as limbs scratched their arms and cheeks. *Laughing, yes, that feels good,* Burden thought, and his lungs began to sting pleasantly from the rush of oxygen his laughter produced, and his thoughts felt lighter. *Soon I'll be home,* he continued, *and I'll call Jo and . . .* Along this line did his thoughts flow and he experienced a surge of joy as he raced forward, overtaking Peedie and punching his shoulder as he passed.

"Beat you to the road," he yelled in a jolly voice.

Peedie reached out to grab him but missed. Grimacing, he sped up. "No you won't," he said, calling after Burden.

As they neared the break in the woods, the glittering shafts of late afternoon sunlight slanting between the trees became glaucous panes of color, shimmering beyond the present blue gloom. Both boys focused on these luminous displays, and they whooped and hollered with joy, for they understood how close to home they might be. In truth, neither had anything but a rough estimate, or more likely an earnest hope, of where they were. It was possible that they were still miles from home, or perhaps only a few houses; they wouldn't know for certain until they escaped the woods. What they knew surely was that the road beyond the trees did in fact lead home.

But when they broke from the woods they stopped short and their laughter died and their expressions fell in sick recognition. The gloom, which they thought they'd shaken off and left behind them in the woods, settled on them once again and with greater weight. This bleak emotion overtook them not because they were still far from home—indeed, they were only three miles from home—but because they had come out on a parcel of land so dismal, so laden with dark stories, that the sight of it shook the joy from their hearts: They had come out on Silas Stoaks's property.

Stoaks had a reputation in Walterboro for being difficult and peculiar. For most of his life he'd farmed corn. Now that field, sixty acres deep and ten long where it ran beside the highway, lay not fallow, but bloated by the crop of two seasons ago. Desiccated ears of corn, their stalks brittle and brown with age, stretched in front of the boys and hid the highway and home. Stoaks offered no reason why he would not harvest the corn, simply shut himself up in his house and let the whole of his property go to rot and ruin.

For the boys in town it became a game to sneak up late at night and spy in Stoaks's windows. These boys told stories to their younger brothers about how Stoaks sat in his chair, listening to an old console radio whose face glowed eerily in the dim parlor light, how his lips never stopped moving, as though communicating some silent litany. His eyes, they said, had attained the fiery gaze of the devil's own. Indeed, many a young boy speculated that Silas had seen the Old Man himself, and that it was this meeting that had beguiled him toward madness.

Some nights he could be seen with a shotgun cradled under his arm, keeping sentinel, wandering the rows of dead stalks, arguing with himself in speech that boomed with thunder and pitched to silence, carried by a cadence natural only to the most eloquent or most divinely insane speakers. Burden knew of Silas only what he'd seen of him when the old man came to the store for food. Peedie knew him only slightly better, having worked as a field hand the season Silas departed the rational. Peedie had helped with the seed bags, and had fetched here and there for tools and such. Where others despised Silas out of fear of him, Peedie only thought that he was an odd old man, nothing more. Still, he respected the shotgun in Silas's arms.

"What should we do?" Burden asked, breathless from their run. "Go around or cut through?"

Peedie approached the corn stalks. He took a dried leaf in his hand, tore it from the stalk, and crushed it to dust. At his feet lay strewn the remains of ears of corn, their kernels gnawed clean by deer and 'coon and mummified by two summers' sun.

"It's faster cutting through," Burden continued.

Peedie peered into the lavender bruise of twilight. "Yeah, but that old devil's out there somewhere."

Burden shook his head; he felt fully the day's weight, felt the impatience itching his heels again and the weight of his legs. "We can't be sure about that. Anyway, going 'round means another half hour. I think we ought to get home—I'm hungry and I'm tired." He did not speak the reason most important to him.

"Well, all the same. . . ." Peedie's voice trailed off as he contemplated the twilight sky. There was still light, but it was fading fast. Turning, he studied Burden's expression, which betrayed exhaustion. "You really want to cut through?"

"I want to get home, Peedie. I want to get home now."

Still indecisive, Peedie kicked at an ear of corn.

The muscles in Burden's jaw flexed. The promise of home was too strong a temptation. Even if going around Silas's property added only thirty minutes time to their journey, still, the night and day they'd endured made those minutes too dear a price to pay for caution's sake. It was true that had he not grabbed Sulah's tits they wouldn't be here now contemplating cutting through Silas's field. Still, it was Peedie's suggestion in the first place that had put the foolish idea in his head. This reasoning made his desire to cut through, the desire to get home as quickly as possible to see Jo, seem not so selfish to him. "I don't want to wait. I want to get home now," he repeated. "There isn't any harm in cutting through, not if we stay well clear of the house."

Peedie smiled weakly. "You don't have to worry about that, cousin," he said, "we won't go anywhere near Stoaks's place."

But they both knew that was a lie, they would have to walk by Stoaks's house eventually, for its disheveled hulk sat on the northwest corner of the field just off the highway, standing between them and home. "We'll cut through at a diagonal," Peedie said. "That'll dump us onto seventeen far enough from Stoaks's place that we won't have to concern ourselves with the old goat.

"Stay close behind me," he continued, taking Burden's shoulder for a moment. His hand was damp and cool. "And don't go slow—I don't want to spend a minute longer in this field than I have to." This said, he dove through the dried stalks, splitting them and felling several as he brushed past them. Burden hung back in sudden fear, hesitating even against his strong desire to get home and to see Jo, feeling his heart beating powerfully in his chest. Only when he was about to lose sight of his cousin did he leap into the field.

They could not have picked a worse location for skulking stealthily, for every step brought the snap of dried husks and stalks. Burden looked back at the swath they were cutting and the fine ashen cloud their steps produced. If old man Stoaks was deaf, Burden thought, he surely wasn't blind as well. Above the crest of stalks he glimpsed the gabled peak of Silas's two-story house. His heart beat soundly in his chest upon this sight, and he felt his mouth drying not with thirst but apprehension. Stalks seemed to tower over him, pressing from the front and both sides, and this made him experience a certain suffocation. Yet looking back at the gash they were leaving behind, he felt utterly exposed; every few steps he glanced back, certain he would see Stoaks, shotgun in hand, bearing down on him and Peedie. The consequence of his impatience became clear to him and he wanted out and away from this horrid place. He hastened his footsteps and crashed into the back of his cousin, who had stopped.

"What are you doing?"

"Shhh," Peedie whispered sharply, cupping his hand over Burden's mouth. He stood silent, intent on some distant noise, his eyes searching.

Burden waited, silent also. Whether the noise his cousin thought he heard was real or imaginary, Burden could not guess, for he heard only his heart beat as it sounded loudly in his ears and thumped solidly against the back of his head.

Peedie held up a finger. "Hear that?"

Burden listened: He heard nothing beyond the dull echo of his pulse. At once, Peedie seized him by his shirt front and hollered, "*Run!*" Without a moment's hesitation, Burden burst into a run. Why he did so he did not know, for beyond Peedie's sudden shift in demeanor, no particular had changed in the field. He twisted back, looking behind him, and saw no one. He turned forward and lost his cousin for a moment when Peedie cut to the left. "Peedie! Peedie, wait for me!" he called out, no longer mindful of being quiet. A hand reached from between stalks and grabbed his shoulder. "This way," Peedie said.

Stalks fell to either side in the boys' headlong rush. Several times Burden lost his footing scrambling across the chewed out corn cobs. Peedie cut suddenly right. Burden stopped, dug a toe into the ground for traction, and started to the right also. But his foot landed on a cob instead of solid ground and slipped from underneath him. He fell into the stalks like a clumsy giant crushing a forest, landing hard on his hand and knocking the wind from his chest. For several seconds he lay among the splintered corn stalks, trying to suck air back into his lungs. Breathless and terrified, he listened for telltale sounds. He easily picked out the fading sound of Peedie's retreating footsteps; he tried to call out after his cousin but his emptied lungs allowed him no voice. Then he heard a second sound, a second set of footsteps, approaching, not retreating. In another moment Burden heard a voice, incoherent and bound up in depthless fury. There were no words, only the guttural sounds of an insane mind.

Burden forced himself to his feet, tottered weakly, then hurried into the wake of felled corn stalks, despairing of ever catching up with Peedie.

But as he rounded a sharp corner where his cousin had taken a sharp turn, he saw Peedie coming back toward him, his face lit up with equal measures of excitement and fear. A smile was on his lips but his eyes were white all around.

"This way," Peedie shouted. Burden hurried after him.

A shotgun blast thundered close by and Peedie and Burden fell to the ground. There was the bright sound of pellets punching through the stalks above them. Burden looked back; a small cloud of bluish-hued smoke rose above the stalks. As the sun's rays lit upon this tiny cloud it gave off an iridescent shimmering of lavender and orange, floating higher, higher. The shotgun blast was followed by a burst of cursing that swept through the stalks. It was Silas, marching through his sacred field, gun at the ready. Peedie looked back at Burden, the excitement having bled from his expression, leaving his face a pallorous white. "Come on."

They leapt to their feet, their legs carrying them with the swiftness of prey. A car horn blared then faded in the near distance, telling them that the highway was very near. Rather than head directly for the road, Peedie cut hither and thither through the stalks, hoping to deny Stoaks the easy shot.

Burden looked to his left and saw a flash of color through the ashen stalks as a car passed along the highway. Turning back, he saw Peedie was still running parallel to the road, apparently unaware they were so close to the field's edge. He stopped and shouted, "Over here!" and before Peedie turned to face him, Burden rushed through the final rows of corn. When he burst from the stalks he fell to the ground, partially from relief, but also because his legs refused to carry him any farther. Silas's house loomed ruinlike above him to the right, and beyond the house lay the road, no farther than a hundred and fifty feet. He pressed his forehead to the dirt and sucked in as much oxygen as he could; his chest burned hotly, his eyes stung, and his legs felt thick as pilings and as cumbersome, too.

Someone burst through the stalks several feet ahead. Burden tensed as he looked up, then relaxed when he saw Peedie shaking free of the field. He stopped and leaned forward, putting his palms on his thighs as he caught his breath. He looked up at Burden and smiled darkly, shaking his head.

Burden sat back on his haunches. He looked again at the road, at freedom.

"You all right?" Peedie asked from the distance, out of breath.

Burden nodded.

"That was a hell of a shortcut you picked, cousin," Peedie said, teasing now that they were free of the field. With his eyes he motioned toward the field. "Think you can make it just a little ways more?"

Again Burden nodded.

"Good," Peedie said, peering at the cornfield with a wary eye. Assuring himself they were safe, he started toward his cousin, but froze at once. Silas, stepping with the lightness of a ghost, padded out from the corn stalks, a .12-gauge cradled in his arms. From the first he had the boys in sight and when he trained the weapon on Peedie, Burden heard his cousin suck in his breath.

"Don't move, damn you," Silas said, his voice harsh, sounding as dry as the leaf Peedie had crushed. "Don't the neither of you move a goddamn muscle." Silas looked all the world like a worn-out machine, rusted and broken in a hundred different places, kept going only by infernal will. But he had run hard through his field, and the aged machinery of his body showed its every weakness in tremors that shook his limbs and bowed his back. He trudged toward Burden, stopping when he was within ten feet. As though buffeted by an unfelt wind, he tottered side to side where he stood, cursing as he summoned strength to his legs. His arms trembled with a visible infirmity under the shotgun's weight, and his forefinger likewise trembled, tapping against the trigger with epileptic insistence.

With Silas standing so near, shotgun in hand, it seemed a folly to Burden that he should have been so eager to see Jo. Every action he'd taken over the last two days, he thought bitterly, had spiralled him further downward and he did not think it was possible to make things right. He turned and looked up at Peedie, and saw that contrary to Silas's command, he was moving forward, crouched low with his arms held up in front of him in a show of submission.

"Evening, Mr. Silas, sir," Peedie said. His shoes scraped through the dirt as he spoke, edging closer to Burden.

"I said don't move," Silas barked.

Peedie stopped.

"What're you boys doing on my property? The truth, damn you, or I'll shoot you sure as dead."

Burden wanted to vomit; the dull burn of acid was in his throat and on his tongue. Why had he touched Sulah? He wanted to take it back, to wind back the clock to that fateful moment and keep his hands in his lap. If only such a thing were possible.

Peedie looked down at his cousin, showing him an expression of reassurance, then fixed his gaze once more on Silas. "We were lost, Mr. Silas. We were walking through the woods and ended up at your field by accident. We didn't know where we were, not till we saw your corn, then we said: 'We're at Silas Stoaks's place.' "

Burden listened to his cousin's voice, its tone aggressively concili-atory and nonthreatening; in his despair, he did not think Stoaks would comprehend Peedie's words. What good was there in talking sense to a madman? Turning toward Peedie, he saw only a young boy dressed in dusty shoes and filthy pants, his face flushed and sweating from the chase, his fair hair matted darkly to his forehead. But what demon Silas Stoaks divined through the prism of his insanity, Burden could not fathom.

When Stoaks did not respond, Peedie straightened in gaining con-fidence. "Yes, sir, we were lost," he repeated. "But we know where we are now, and we'll be going."

Stoaks moved toward the boys, faltering like a man stepping through darkness, the shotgun slipping in his hands. Gathering himself, he snapped straight and took another few steps toward the boys until he was now only four feet from them. His lips jabbered in rubbery fashion, sputtering a dozen invocable thoughts. Then, with a sudden vicious snarl, he said, "Bullshit, bullshit you was lost—you was stealing from me. You was stealing my corn."

"No, sir, Mr. Silas. We surely weren't stealing your corn. No, sir." Burden heard the dying confidence in Peedie's voice. "But we do apologize for troubling you, and we'll leave you be if—"

"I said not to goddamn move, boy, now stay where you are!"

A tremble disturbed Burden's flesh, bringing with it a numb, freezing sensation. His muscles ached from the awkwardness of his position, half-raised on his arms as though in a perpetual moment of rising. Yet he feared that collapsing to the ground would provoke Silas to murder, so he remained determinedly immobile.

"All right," Peedie said with soothing grace, "all right, sir, if you think we were stealing from you, then you ought to call the police, have them take us away."

"Police, bah!" Silas spat. "*I* know how to take care of thieves." He pointed the shotgun at Burden and sighted him. "You there, you on the ground, stop whimpering like a whipped dog. Stand up so I can get a good look at who's stealing my corn."

Burden peered up at Peedie. What escape could they possibly have from this madness? he wondered.

Peedie nodded and motioned with a slight movement of his hand for Burden to stand. "It's okay, Burden," he said at length. "Mr. Silas here is going to call the police. I'm afraid we'll have to spend some time in jail." As he spoke, his eyes held fast to Silas as though willing him not to shoot. He edged closer to Burden, and when he was within a foot of his cousin, the old man cocked the hammer back and trained his shotgun on Peedie and told him that that was close enough.

As he stood before the boys a shadow passed over the old man's face, and he faltered. Then, as though suddenly overwhelmed by an unbearable weight, he stumbled forward and the shotgun slipped once more in his hands. As he tried to right his twisted frame, the shotgun swung toward Burden like a reeling canon on a floundering vessel. Burden felt his cousin's hand grasp his shoulder, felt his fingers cinching the material of his shirt in an effort to pull Burden away from the shotgun. But Burden could not take his gaze off the old man; the gun's barrel pointed dead on at his face, and he could see the bore hole's utter blackness. In that moment he felt an infinite fear and blindly swept his arm in front of him, brushing the shotgun to the right. The force of Burden's swipe toppled Stoaks from his precarious balance, and the old man tightened as he stumbled forward, using the gun as a counter balance. There then slipped past Burden a moment which he could not, for its enormity, perceive, as though he had winked out from existence for a split second only to rematerialize to find everything he'd known changed. Peedie's fingers bit into his skin, only for an instant, then released him. Though he had not perceived the cause, he now saw the lingering blue smoke of gunfire suffused with a fine pink mist wafting above him, felt the warm wetness clinging to his face, smelled the discharge of burnt powder, heard the ringing sound of a blast mingled darkly with his cousin's voice, forced suddenly silent. He could not turn around, he dared not. For in the mirror of Silas Stoaks's twisted-up face he perceived perfectly the reflection of his cousin's dead body. The old man collapsed within himself as the meaning of this most horrendous act became clear to his ravaged mind. His lips began jabbering again, spitting out nonsense. He stumbled backward, the spent shotgun hanging limp at his side. He dropped the weapon to the ground and turned away, wandering toward his cornfield and the gaining night.

Burden fell to his knees and vomited. He collapsed and curled onto the ground, his eyes blind with tears. Like the old man before him, his lips trembled, and between choked sobs incoherent sounds gurgled from his mouth. Unable to stand, his body convulsing in spasms of horror, he gathered what power he could and swiveled slowly around on his arms, dragging his face across the ground as in penance and tasting dirt on his lips and in his throat. Bits of flesh and blood lay splattered on the soil before him, like fallen rain commanded by a lunatic god. He reached a hand out and grasped his cousin's shoe, feeling the unresponsive foot caught within it. His eyes stinging with tears, he drew himself up to his cousin's legs and pressed them to his face.

But he could not bear to look any more closely at his cousin, could not bring himself to gaze at the fatal wound.

A new voice called out from the distance. It was a man's voice, deep, commanding. By his tone, Burden understood the man had asked a question of him but hadn't the presence of mind to comprehend its meaning. The man approached, asking again his indecipherable question, but this time the man's voice wavered and he fell silent. "Oh, Jesus," Burden heard the man mutter, his voice wrecked.

Burden learned in the days following Peedie's death that the man had seen the flash and heard the report of the shotgun from his car as he was driving by. The man had stopped and approached Burden and Peedie, and when he saw the young boy lying on the ground, the flesh of his face and chest shredded by the shotgun's blast, the man had hurried back to his car and summoned help. It was only after the paramedics had arrived and tried to separate Burden from his cousin's body that Burden found the courage to look at Peedie in full. Overcome by a paroxysm of grief, he tore himself from the arms of the paramedics and heaped himself once more onto his cousin, clinging to him and screaming with the abandon of one for whom sense of pride and self are utterly departed, thinking madly that he might with his tears resurrect Peedie's lifeless body.

Somebody help him. These words echoed as memory in Burden's mind for weeks afterward, as sharp to his ears as though he were still speaking them. *Somebody please help him.* These words were with him still.

Burden felt a poking at his side. He heard words, indistinct but directed toward him. He opened his eyes. It was morning, an aged black man stood above him, and behind the man a white boy, a teen, stood. The boy held a rake in his hands, its worn gray handle pressed under his chin as he studied Burden with an expression of apprehensive curiosity.

"What you doing on this grave, son?" the black man asked.

Burden lifted himself on one arm and looked around. His clothes were damp and clammy against his skin.

"Grave's only meant for one person at a time, son," the black man continued. "Didn't your papa ever teach you that?" The young boy smirked at the man's remark. He removed the rake handle from under his chin and tapped it against his cheek.

Burden fell to the grass and rolled onto his back, shielding his eyes from the morning sun. His head throbbed with pain, and his joints burned as he flexed them, feeling on his skin the grime of a night spent outdoors.

"That your van out front? Outside the gates?" the man asked.

Burden said nothing. With an effort, he rose from Peedie's grave and stood on unsteady legs. In a moment he had found his balance and started toward the front gate.

"I was about to call the police . . . have them take it away, yes sir," the man called after Burden. "Lucky for you I didn't call the police."

Burden stumbled to the front of the cemetery. The gates had been swung open and his van parked just inside the grounds. He got in, looked for the keys, which he discovered still in the ignition, and started the van. He sat there for several long minutes, letting the engine idle. He could just make out through his clouded vision the black man and his young assistant; they pretended to rake the plots, but really were looking at him. After a time his vision cleared, and giving the two groundskeepers a parting look, he drove away.

SIXTEEN

Eugene rose only after the morning sun had shed its vibrant color, its light falling in a pale slant through the motel window. He had been awake for several hours, immobile, his eyes barely blinking as they soaked up the ceiling's angular pattern. Yet though gazing heavenward, his mind perceived only a hellish anguish. *Have I been wrong?* he asked himself. *Have I been wrong all this time about Pru and Burden?* That he might have falsely accused his wife of sleeping around on him caused Eugene much distress. How could he have been so callow? How could he have grown so insecure in his relationship with his lovely Pru, his darling wife?

At other moments, like the broad sweep of a lighthouse beam across his darker thoughts, Eugene was convinced he had not been wrong but stupid, and he clearly saw Pru's and Burden's perfidy; they were fucking each other, only they were too smart for him, anticipating his every effort to catch them in their devil's game. At these moments, his thoughts illumined by jealousy's brilliant beam, he grew enraged. His hands knotted into fists and twisted the sweat-dampened bed sheets under his body, his flesh trembled in fury, and his teeth clenched as in a death grimace. Relief found him only as his mind focused on Burden's bloodied body lying lifeless at the foot of his bed.

It was this confluence of emotion, this alternating feeling of depthless guilt and vengeance, that caused Eugene to lie immobile but hopelessly awake, his pistol unholstered and near his side. He touched the gun every few minutes as though it were a charm or ticket that he dare not lose. As the hours slipped by, taunting him with the languor of their movement, he remained prone like a lame man or a man very nearly a corpse. Then the first colors of morning showed through the narrow gap in the curtains that he had failed to draw completely closed. A world awoke beyond the motel window while inside his room Eugene felt his tormented mind pulling his body to oblivion. Then, as the scarflike colors faded to lifeless yellow, a single blade of light, thin as a razor blade, cut across the ceiling of his room and slid silently downward onto his bed. The passing minutes piled atop the pale blade, and it fell as on an ebbing tide of time until it settled across the length of his body, from his forehead to his steel-tipped boots. As though roused from another dimension, he forced his aching head up and peered at his boots' metal tips, which blazed with the fire of brilliant distant stars. The light suffused him with a weary energy of sorts, enough so that he stirred from his immobility and rose from the bed.

Stumbling to the bathroom, he studied the haggard, harried face staring so listlessly back at him. His eyes had grown dusty and seemed mired; fleshy jowls likewise were cast in darkness under a two-day growth of stubble. His lips were puffy and he looked as though he'd been in a fight and had lost. All in all, he felt a sharp revulsion looking at the pathetic piece of shit trapped in the mirror. Peering into his own expressionless eyes, Eugene teetered forward until his nose touched the mirror's glass; he searched those dusty globes for some answer, any answer that might at last relieve his torment. Not knowing one way or the other was the greatest torment of all. He could live with Pru's infidelity, and he could live with her innocence. What he could not handle much longer was his own uncertainty over which was the truth. *Inno-*

cence or guilt? he thought. *Reconciliation or retribution? Which was it?* He knew he would break—and soon. He knew that soon his mind would shatter from the ambiguity of his predicament, and the destruction of his body would quickly follow. If only he could be certain at last what his position was and what his choices were. He gazed with disgust at the fool in the mirror. Behind him the blade of light fell upon the pistol, and a bright flare glinted off its silver body. As he smiled grimly at this image, a voice spoke to him. It told him that soon everything would be revealed.

Eugene's eyes brightened at this dark prophecy. He walked heavily but with force from the bathroom and picked up the gun, and in touching it a fleeting image appeared in his mind, the image of a bloodied corpse. He stood in the numinous light and felt its heat warm his greasy, sweating face. The image produced an elation in his spirit much as had overcome him the night before, when he'd settled on killing Burden. Spreading his arms into the air, he leaned back and braced his body against the light, then, rather awkwardly, he fell to his knees. "Thank you, Lord," he stammered in his delirium. "Thank you for revealing to me Your divine will." Here the dark image bled once more into his eyes, causing him at once to shudder and smile. "Yes, O Lord. Yes. Thy will be done."

But as he prayed his prayer of thanksgiving, the light withered and then expired and he was forced to conclude his supplication in an atmosphere of gloom. He stood and swung the motel room door open. Above him a storm front was unfurling its gray canvas across the sky. A cold gust of wind burned his tired, dusty eyes, and he felt an infinite remove from his spiritual warmth of a moment ago. Still, he felt he'd been delivered of a revelation, he had been shown the path that led to the end of his torment and despair. He had understood the image, unmistakable in its portent of death. Only whose death? Here he paused. For while the condition of the body he had seen lay clearly in a deathly repose, its face had been turned from him, so that its identity remained a mystery. Was it Burden or—and at this thought the muscles in his gut convulsed tightly—had it been himself?

Burden drove into the dull gloom of the gathering storm. The air cooled precipitously and before he reached home a wall of chill wind pulled down a heavy rain. Reaching his house, he raced inside, not out of fear of being soaked, but because he believed that his end must be near and he dare not lose even a single moment to sloth. No one was home—his father and sister were at the store and his mother was at church. He hurried upstairs to his room. When he got there, he fell on his knees and dragged a box from under his bed. The box lid was thick with dust, and where his wet fingers touched it, the dust pooled in dirty miniature mud puddles. Opening the box, he rummaged through its contents without a care for ever putting the things in it right again. At length, unable to find what he was looking for, he upended the box, spilling its load onto the floor. Pushing through the various objects, his eyes finally found and his fingers finally seized upon that one thing he desired: the notebook in which he kept the list of the women he'd slept with and those others he hoped still to sleep with. He flipped randomly through its pages, smearing the ink entries with his moistened fingers. He scanned the first of three columns, the names of the women, then scanned the middle column listing their husbands. A final column contained notes on his prospects: Some entries read simply "no," while others spoke of future possibilities with multiple tiny question marks scribbled in an excited hand. There was Pru's name, at the end of the list, for he had been delivering to her house for only a year. He scanned the other names—there was Laurel, there was Nathella and Jacine, there was Lurline. Failures all, glorious failures.

A sound came from downstairs, that of the kitchen door opening and closing.

"Burden?" his mother called up to him. "Burden, are you home? Where have you—"

Burden leapt to his feet and rushed downstairs. His mother waited for him at the landing, standing there in her fine church dress, a Bible in her hand and a small purse cradled in the crook of her elbow. Giving no mind to his filthy state, Burden embraced her, clinging tightly to her as though he were being led to his execution and this would be his last opportunity to feel her against him. But when he let her go and stood back from her, his eyes gleamed widely in a type of ecstacy and he smiled so that his teeth showed.

"Why, Burden, what's—"

"I love you, Mamma" he said, and embraced her again. He gave her no chance to reply as he let go of her and dashed out of the house.

The rain was falling with greater insistence, and as Burden crossed the lawn, helpless against the storm's onslaught, he stopped. He looked up as in surrender and spread his arms wide to either side; he even spun once, laughing gaily and collecting the cold water in his mouth. The rain felt bracing against his face, and for a moment he hadn't any care, no care at all.

"Burden?" his mother called from the porch, confounded.

Burden spun around and looked at her. He grinned and called out over the din of the storm. "Gotta go, Mom. I love you!" And then he headed for the van.

Jo sat in the employee lounge. Three large windows stretched from floor to ceiling before her. Since starting here, she often would look out of these windows and see the moon or the bright lights in the parking lot that made the cars underneath them shine like pieces of colored slag. But now it was morning, her shift nearly over. It was a dismal, gray morning, already wearied by a rain that had lasted through the night. With the aid of this dark daybreak she saw a reflection of herself in the glass, her image translucent and absorbing something of the outside gray. She stood up, feeling peculiar, as though something was fluttering inside her body, tickling her in a pleasing manner, but also making her feel anxious. Her hand reached into the pocket of her smock as she walked to the window, and her fingers brushed against the edge of the poetry book. "Why did I bring this with me?" she asked herself. *And why can't I let it go?* She did not want the book, did not want the memory it represented, did not want to recall how she had felt the afternoon Burden had given it to her. Yet she realized she could not throw the book away, or even hide it again in its box in the closet. For it spoke to her, spoke to her more clearly than her own thoughts. Involuntarily, she brought the book out and opened it. The spine had been broken long ago, but now there were numerous tiny fissures paralleling the largest crease that marked the place where the book naturally fell open. She scanned the lines and ran her fingers along the faded pencil underscoring. "I don't need this," she said aloud. "I don't want this." But even as she spoke she knew her words were untrue. Knowing this frightened her, made her feel faint by its implications. There was still a need in her heart for Burden, and more than that, a desire.

"This can't be," she said. "I'm different now, I don't want Burden anymore." Only it wasn't want but need that she fought against, and a desire that she had not consciously summoned and therefore could not extinguish.

I'm leaving tomorrow, first thing, she remembered telling Burden.

But I thought you weren't leaving for another two weeks.

And she could see it in his eyes, still, after three years, the odd mixture of relief and hurt, of confusion and determination. And it tore at her with no less misery than it had that night.

"The dorm room I'll be staying in has become available ahead of schedule, so I thought I'd go in early and get settled. It'll make it easier for me once classes begin."

"Of course."

Jo looked at Burden, his expression had clouded over, obscured by powerfully conflicting emotions, making it difficult to read him. His thoughts, his feelings, had grown increasingly concealed, which they had never been at first. She remembered him as wonderfully open to her, and this above all other things had drawn her to him. Even after Peedie's death, Burden, while often silent, had never withheld through his expression how he felt at any moment. But over the past two years it was as though a veil had been pulled over his features, as if he were purposefully withholding his emotions. His eyes were often dark, but if she asked what was bothering him he would deny that anything was wrong. He would grow short with her questions and so she learned to keep her thoughts of concern to herself.

But she could not live with him this way, not knowing. At first she believed he had grown disenchanted with her, and this made her feel sick inside. But she came to understand that it was not her but something greater with which he'd become disenchanted; it was as though life itself had become an encumbrance to be thrown from his shoulders. He never spoke about the future. When she brought the subject up, when she spoke about her desire to leave town and go away to college and wasn't there something that he too wanted to do, he would become distant. He would seem angry with her for asking such difficult questions and she again learned not to speak of such things with him.

"Part of me didn't really think you'd leave."

Jo drew in her breath and held it. Above the trees the stars shone with a wavering light. There was a new moon and so the sky was dark save for the stars and she studied them as they lay scattered like dust across the night sky. *Will the stars look the same in Charleston?* she wondered, hoping this would not be so. *Will I come back some day and find these same stars unchanged?* "I used to think that I couldn't be any happier than if you and I settled together here in Walterboro," she said.

Although she didn't take her eyes from the stars she might never see again, she sensed that Burden had turned and was looking at her.

"After a while I began to think, wouldn't it be wonderful if Burden and I went away, left Walterboro behind us and found a place that was new and only for us?" *And at night we'd look up and there above us would be stars we had never imagined before, new stars that would tell us we were home. But it isn't the stars that change; they'll be with us wherever we go, looking down at us from a place we can never reach.* "And now it's come down to this—that I'm leaving and you're staying. I can't pretend it's what I wanted, but I know it has to be this way."

With a word Burden could have kept her home, could have prevented her from leaving for Charleston. She would have given up her desire for a fresh start in a new town and instead would commute to

Charleston if only she knew she had a hope for a future with Burden. But Burden had no words to offer her because it seemed he'd stopped believing in a future for himself. As it stood now, his continued silence had driven her to the sanctuary of Charleston early. There was no dorm room waiting for her to settle into. For the next two weeks she would stay with a fellow nursing student with whom she had become friends, then move into the dorm when it opened. But she could no longer afford to give Burden the opportunity to speak. She no longer wanted him to speak, to keep her here.

"I'll come back," she said, assuaging the guilt she felt for leaving. But she wasn't at all certain she would return. As she gazed at the stars, she waited for Burden to respond. He might have said, *There's always something to bring you back,* but he remained silent. At last she quit the stars and looked at Burden. He stared forward, his expression inviting no interpretation. She grew furious with his silence and determined anew to leave without regret, finding a life as far from Walterboro, as removed from Burden, as possible. Why then, with such surety of intent, did she feel such depthless remorse?

"Jo?" a voice called softly to her.

Jo turned, saw her supervisor standing a few paces from her.

"You're needed in 207."

"Yes, ma'am." Jo closed the volume and slipped it into her pocket. She lingered by the window a few moments longer remembering that night, looking at the rain but really studying the reflection of her face, peering into eyes that appeared frightened only because at last they comprehended her future.

Burden had a plan of action sketched out in his mind, although the details were hazy. His only sure thought was to reach the Sonic and find Jo. She had to be there, had to be. He approached a traffic light and stopped, taking the opportunity to close his eyes, for he was weary nearly beyond his ability to continue; his mind hummed and his feet felt the chill of exhaustion. How could he have lost so much? he wondered. At what point could he have made things different? He felt a hot torment as a hundred different pasts rolled into impossible futures in his mind, futures he could never hope to enjoy now. But was it too late to wrench his present off the tracks? He had seen the light coming around the bend easily enough, he felt the train coming down hard on him, heard the thunder of its body passing through time and space to crush him. But was it really too late? Couldn't he simply stop now and get out of the way of the train? Or would escape come only if he sped ever faster toward its steel death?

"Cousin?"

Burden's eyes opened wide. He turned toward the passenger seat.

"Where're we going, cousin?" Peedie asked.

"We're—*I'm,*" Burden corrected himself, "going to the Sonic. *I'm* going to find Jo."

"Hadn't you better get home? I've been waiting for you it seems like forever. When you coming home?"

"I am home, Peedie. This is my home." The light turned green and after the driver in the car behind him blew his horn, Burden drove on.

Peedie shook his head.

"It is, too, Peedie. I can't go with you, I can't. I've got to make things right." This was the first time that thought had consciously occurred to Burden. *Make things right.*

"But you promised. We had it all planned out." Peedie paused. Studying Burden, looking him up and down, he smiled as though he was the sole possessor of a fantastic secret. "He's waiting for you, you know. You don't have to screw things up this time."

"Who's waiting for me?" Burden replied, alarmed.

But Peedie only turned away and remained silent. After a few moments he said, "You promised you'd come be with me. . . . I don't know, I never see you anymore. You never come to visit even for a short while. I think maybe you've forgotten about your cousin and would just as soon not be bothered by me."

What could Burden say? What defense did he have against the truth? "I can't do it," he said.

"Can't or won't? It's you who has a choice. It's you who's made a promise. If you don't want to keep your word—"

"I would have, Peedie, believe me, I would have earlier . . . but—"

"It's that girl, isn't it? She's come between us again, just like the last time. I thought she was gone for good. Guess I was wrong. She's got you thinking all strange and everything. She's making you forget where you belong . . . where you belong by right."

"It wasn't my fault—"

"Whose decision was it to go into that cornfield, cousin?"

"Listen to me, you want to know why I chose to cut through Silas's cornfield?" Burden asked hotly. "It was because I couldn't wait to see Jo. I couldn't wait even a few minutes longer than I had to to see her again. I chose her over you that evening and I've been trying to make it up to you ever since. If I'd have known what was going to happen, don't you think I'd have chosen differently? I'm sorry as hell and God for what happened but I can't come home with you, Peedie. I've got to make things right."

Peedie gazed impassively at Burden. There was a chill about him greater than the chill of the storm. "You can't make it right, cousin. It's too late. He's coming for you, he's coming for you even as we speak. In a little while you'll be with me and then we can be together forever."

Burden slammed on the brakes. The van skidded across the wet road, fishtailing and threatening to cross into the oncoming lane of traffic. Burden subdued the van and pulled into an empty parking lot. "*God*damn it, Peedie, listen to me—I didn't die that evening. God knows I haven't been living these last few years, but those days are over. Over, do you understand? Damn it, I love you . . . but I can't take this talk of coming home anymore." As he said this, he felt a bracing self-contempt and freedom simultaneously. How could he speak these things? Yet equally, how could he not? "I don't want you in my head. I don't want you to come by at night and stand outside my window. Jesus, Peedie, I miss you something terrible. I'd move heaven and earth to bring you back if that was what it took. But it won't and I can't.

All I can do is be here. *Here!* That's what I want, it's what I need. I haven't been anywhere for so long now, and I'm dying inside." Burden pressed his palm against his chest. "There's almost nothing left and it's almost too late. I've got to—"

"Make things right," Peedie said in a mocking tone. "But you never made it right with me." Without opening the door, Peedie began to move from the van. "Can't change your destiny, cousin," he said levelly. He started off for the trees at the far end of the parking lot.

Burden jumped from the van and ran toward Peedie, stopping short when Peedie turned on him. In the rain he screamed, "Damn it, I love you, Peedie. I love you but you've got to let me go."

Peedie held his gaze silently for several moments. At length he said, "He's coming for you, cousin. Nothing I can do about that now. Nothing either of us can do." Saying this, he turned and started once more for the woods. In the rain and distance his body faded till when he reached the woodline he was not there at all.

Burden walked back to the van, his head hung low. When he got in, he buried his face in his hands and wept. "And I've got to let you go, cousin." Saying this, he willed himself under control and the crying stopped. He thought of Jo, concentrated hard on her face, only in his mind he couldn't make her smile or remove the shadows from her eyes.

The storm's fierce edge had begun to abate when Burden pulled into the Sonic. He parked crookedly, jumped out, and ran under a narrow central canopy. There were no other cars and no walk-up customers. Leslie stood by the galley, leaning against the large glass wall and smoking a cigarette. Val stood next to her and was talking to the cook through the glass partition.

Leslie waved at Burden and offered him a smile as he approached.

When he reached her, Burden took her by the shoulders and looked searchingly into her eyes. "Where's Jo?"

Leslie did not lose her smile, but her eyes narrowed in puzzlement. "Now, why would I know that, Burden?"

"When's she on? What time does her shift start?" Burden realized he sounded frantic, but also that he didn't care. "Tell me!"

Leslie's smile broke. "She doesn't work here, Burden."

"But she was here the other night, Sue said she was getting her job back."

"Why would she want that? Jo went to school to become a nurse. That's what she is now, Burden—a nurse. She just stopped in the other night to chat. That's all." Leslie laughed gently then stroked Burden's cheek with her thumb. "Poor Burden."

The strength in Burden's fingers waned and he released Leslie's shoulders. He turned away, lost.

"Go down to the hospital, that's where she works. They can tell you when her shift is."

But Burden was not listening. He understood now why Jo had become so angry with him, and he felt the fool for having not seen how far she'd come. *She's different now,* he thought. *She's become something more than what she was before, and I am still just me.* He could not see her now, dared not. His shame was too great. "*I didn't ask to fall in love with you,*" he heard Jo say and his heart felt dead within his chest. "*I won't let it happen again. I can't.*"

He could not have her love anymore. Of this he had no doubt. He wondered now if he could at least gain her forgiveness. But he had done her so much wrong, he had taken away so much in his errant quest for redemption. Of necessity she had turned her back on him and severed their relationship with a finality he could not resist. Better not to see her, then. Better to let her go, better not to fuck up her life anymore.

Eugene finished his fourth cup of coffee. He felt better, fresher, clearer-headed than he had in months. He felt light. He felt renewed. He felt born again. He felt an understanding of the world, as though he had been given an intimate glimpse at the mechanisms whirling clockwise and counterclockwise deep within the universe's core. His eyes alone had perceived such wonders, and they showed him also what he must do. It was easy now, thinking of the task ahead. The knowledge had set him free; he no longer fretted over Pru's possible infidelity or Burden's duplicity. In a little while all his problems would be set right and the debits of hurt and humiliation he had suffered at Burden's hands would be paid.

He stood, threw a few dollars on the counter beside his cup and saucer. He winked at the waitress and grinned a coffee-stained grin.

"You leaving so soon?" the waitress asked.

Eugene nodded. "Some things I got to take care of back home."

The waitress looked at the crumpled dollars on the counter; she quickly counted twice the amount of his bill. "Well, you come back soon, mister, you hear?"

Eugene nodded a second time and left.

The storm's fury could endure for only so long. By early afternoon gray clouds still billowed thickly, and the sky was dark in a false night, but the rain came down with an almost remorseful dreariness rather than with rage. Burden sat in his van, listening to the rain. Through a continual falling sheet of water, he gazed up at the hospital; the thin cascade of rain softened the building's perfect and harsh lines, yet there was nothing soft in Burden's heart. Like the rain, his heart poured forth a remorse that could not satisfy the aching guilt and the overwhelming sense of loss he felt.

Make things right. Indeed! Burden saw now how monumental a task that would be, and he doubted he was up to it. He picked up the notebook and flipped through its pages. There were so many women, so many husbands, so many failures. In a fit of rage, he started ripping the pages out of the notebook, crumpling the pages into tiny balls and throwing them to the floor. He did this with each one until he came to the last, where he read Pru's name. *He's coming for you, cousin.* Yes, but here was a first chance to make things right. If nothing else, by going to Pru's and ending their relationship, Burden would have one less worry. He held no hope for bringing Jo back into his life, but he understood that if there was to be any chance at all, it would come only after he had severed his ties with his recent past. And the most recent was Pru.

When Pru opened the door and saw Burden standing on her stoop, a soggy, sad mutt, her face brightened; in spite of his condition, she wrapped herself around him tightly. "Burden!" she cooed. Then sense returned to her thinking, and she looked anxiously at the surrounding homes and then yanked Burden indoors. Once inside, Pru spun Burden around—he had yet to utter a word and she had yet to notice—and sprang upon him, wrapping her legs around his waist and her arms around his neck. The force of her body against his carried him backward and together they tumbled to the floor. Pru kissed Burden deeply, she kissed him with a rapacious hunger, but Burden could feel the tremors of laughter shaking her ribs and belly as they lay on the floor. At length she gave up her kiss and, sitting up on him, began laughing with aban- · don. Then, with a violent suddenness, she became quiet, regarding him with a look nearing reproach. "I was afraid you weren't going to come. I was afraid I'd missed you, and with this being Sunday and what with the storm—oh, but you're here now and that's all that matters." And again she dove down and attacked Burden with her tongue.

From her words, Burden gathered that Pru had called in an order. This meant that Eugene would be gone for some time, which was good, although Burden didn't think he'd need very long to finish what he'd come to say. If Maude had taken their breakup with a melancholy grace, Pru, he realized—*feared*—would be a torrent of emotion, of many emotions, and all springing forth here and there like spikes being run through paper. It would be a tumultuous but brief ride, but all he had to do was hang on and walk away clean when it was over.

"But look at what a mess you are, you're soaked to the bone, Burden." Pru ran her hands along his belly and down to his crotch, which she grasped playfully. "Every last bone." She bent down over him, breathed hotly into his ear, and whispered, "Guess who *won't* be home for dinner?"

Instead of answering, Burden made a motion to rise, trying to free himself from underneath her.

"Hold on. Where do you think you're going? I called in an order, and damn it, I expect to get it." As she spoke, she seized Burden's hand and ran it under her shirt, clasping it to a breast.

But Burden pulled his hand out and tried again to free himself. "Look, Pru," he said as he strained underneath her, "look, we've got to talk—I'm serious, Pru, let me up."

"No," Pru said, taking Burden's wrists in her hands and pinning them to the floor. "Not until you kiss me back."

"Pru. . . ."

Pru tightened her grip and frowned gravely at Burden.

"*Kiss me.*"

Exasperated, Burden closed his eyes and sighed. He felt her lips brushing his; he opened his mouth and let her explore him with her tongue as he explored her mouth with his. The juices of her mouth were hot and tasted sweet, almost of strawberry jam. He was chilled from the rain, and the warmth of her kisses, once he yielded to them, chased a little of the chill away. Then there was the heat of her body on top of his, it was as though she had only a moment ago been lying under the August sun. She felt good, but only to his body, for his mind was in as much torment as before, and she hadn't a cure for that.

After they had kissed for a short time, Pru raised up and looked dreamily at him. "That's better, Burden, I liked that." She began kissing his neck. "I wanted to call you yesterday but some friends came over unexpectedly. Eugene was going to be home this morning—no, don't worry, he called last night to say he'd be home later than he thought, couldn't get home before six tonight." Pru chuckled lightly. "If I didn't know better, I'd swear *he* had a honey on the side somewhere. Fuck if I care, though—*I* have you, my delicious, considerate Burden."

This was not going well, Burden thought. He should have told her they were through the moment he'd come in. He shouldn't have kissed her. He shouldn't be underneath her. This was not going well at all. "Listen, Pru," he began.

Pru stopped kissing his neck and looked at him. "What is it?" Her smile was gone.

Burden looked away. *Make it right,* he thought, and was surprised when Pru asked, "Make what right?" for he hadn't realized he'd said it aloud.

"Burden, you're losing me. Look in my eyes—make what right?"

But Burden closed his eyes, searching for how to begin, just the first word or gesture, that was all he needed and then everything would properly follow. His eyes were closed for several moments as he thought, several long moments during which he felt Pru's intent gaze boring into him. At length he said again, "Listen, Pru—" but Pru placed her hand firmly over his mouth.

"Shhhh," she said, her smile returning. "Don't say another word, not here." She stood and gave Burden her hand and pulled him from the floor. "Follow me," she said, holding jealously onto his hand and leading him upstairs.

"Pru," Burden protested. Pru turned on him and, with a stern expression, bid him to remain quiet.

As was inevitable, she led Burden to the bedroom. They stopped at the foot of the bed and then Pru let go of Burden's hand and opened the window. Because the wind had died down and the rain had slackened to a dreary cadence, very little rain fell on the sill. She pulled back the curtains and curled them around the tiebacks to keep them from becoming damp, then breathed deeply. Burden could see her frame rise with her breath and fall with that breath's exhalation. "It's the most marvelous fragrance in the world." Burden shrugged his shoulders even though Pru's back was still turned to him. When she turned around her face glowed with a devilish fire. She approached him, put her hands on him, and where she touched him he felt the warmth of sexual desire warm his skin.

"But you're trembling, Burden," Pru said. She untucked his shirt and began unbuttoning it. She did this with the confidence of an older man undressing a beguiled younger girl.

"Pru, I need to tell you something about you and me," Burden said, but Pru kissed him to quiet him. He could push her away, have his say and leave. But he felt constrained, feeling almost as though this was a moment preordained and that he could not alter its course, that he simply had to follow where events dictated.

Pru pulled open Burden's zipper. She parted the jeans slightly and kissed his belly. "Remember what you called me in Charleston?" she asked coyly. "What was it? Oh yes, you called me a 'goddamned cowardly cocksucker.' " Pru laughed. She pulled Burden's pants and underwear to his ankles and then playfully kissed his belly a second time.

Burden felt his penis swelling against Pru's neck. "This isn't making things right," he said quietly. His voice sounded forlorn, as though he were a young child lost and had said, "This isn't the way home."

"I'll make it right for my Burden," Pru said. She took him in her hand and began stroking him.

"I shouldn't be here. I should go." The same young lost child.

Pru wrapped her other hand around his ass. "Not so fast, Burden. What's your hurry?" And saying this, she pressed him tightly to her. Her face was in his hair and Burden could hear the rough breaths and feel their warm discharge on his prick. A moment more and he was inside her mouth. He tilted his head back, felt his body sway. *Jesus, this is so far from making it right,* he thought. *I'm insane and this is an insane thing I'm doing.* He felt as remote as he had felt the afternoon in the woods when Peedie had left to scout the terrain ahead; then he seemed a single object in the universe, unknown and unknowable by anyone else. This was how he felt at this moment as Pru worked on him with her mouth. But toward what end? *Where am I going?*

These thoughts weighed heavily on his mind, becoming so oppressive that he grew insensate to his surroundings, even to the hot, moist cradle of Pru's mouth in which he was rocking. In this removed state he was not aware precisely when the rocking had stopped and she had given a halting breath, removing his prick from her mouth. After a few seconds he opened his eyes, saw the open window and the waning drizzle that fell outside. He saw this, but he sensed, too late, that he and Pru were no longer alone.

Eugene stood just inside the doorway, a pistol in his hand. Burden turned to him. *How long has he been standing there?* Burden wondered. But then he realized this one detail more than any other didn't matter. Eugene did not appear angry. He did not, to Burden's eyes, even appear disturbed by what he was witnessing. In fact he was smiling. True, it was a sickly, pale smile, but it was a smile nonetheless.

After what seemed an interminable period of time, during which he simply stood in the doorway, Eugene shifted on his feet and took a step closer. His expression transformed to one of supreme benignity as he brought the gun up and pointed it squarely at Burden. "At last," he said, his voice tinged with mirth bubbling from deep within his body, threatening to boil over into the room. "At last I know for sure. My God, you can't imagine what a relief it is . . . just knowing."

Pru wiped her lips and shifted uneasily on her knees. When she made a motion to stand Eugene turned the gun on her. "*No.*" Then, calmly, "Stay right there." Still smiling, but eyes cold and hard. "Excuse me if I want to enjoy the moment."

Pru threw her hands in front of her face and let out a little cry. "Christ, Eugene—" she said, her voice trembling. Burden winced at the terror it so clearly evidenced.

"It's me that you want, Eugene. Not Pru, me."

"I'll get to you soon enough, boy," Eugene said. As he regarded the two, his expression began changing between that of rage and humor, like a coin slowly spinning on its edge and revealing both faces alternately. His tone likewise was at moments malevolent in its intent and then unaccountably gay. Overall he gave the appearance of a man consumed by the joy of some horrible knowledge.

"All I wanted was your love, Pru. Your fidelity."

"Eugene . . ." Pru whimpered. Her eyes were red with tears and her body shook in tiny tremors. She could not look at her husband, but instead gazed intently at her palms, which she held close to her face. "Sweet Jesus, Eugene, don't kill me."

Pru's words wounded Eugene, and he straightened a little where he stood. "I would never hurt you, Pru," he replied in a reproachful tone. "How could you say such a thing? I love you more than the world, I love you with all my heart. You're my wife, you're my greatest possession, I'd never harm you."

Burden felt little relief at Eugene's words. He studied the open window and then looked down at his ankles, which were bound in his pants. All he needed was a couple of steps and he could hurtle himself through the window and take his chances with the fall. A broken bone or two, at any rate, would be better than a bullet between the eyes. But could his feet, constrained, give him those two steps?

"I would never harm you," Eugene repeated. "I just needed to show you how far down you've driven me. My mind is a world of worry, and my heart, it's full of hurt and sick over your unfaithfulness to me."

Pru collapsed slightly as her husband spoke, making by degrees a ball of her body there on the floor.

Eugene stepped forward and trained the gun again at Burden. His hand shook in rage and fear and he was, at that moment, in a fit of high anger, not at all gay. When he spoke his voice broke, and he sounded pitiful. "I just wanted you to witness what you've brought me to. I'm doing this for you, Pru. I'm doing this to save our marriage." When he said "save our marriage," tears brimmed in his eyes and he sniffed loudly. Then he fired. The bullet whizzed past Burden's ear and shattered the glass of a wedding photograph mounted on the wall. "Shit!" Eugene said. The sound of the shot instantly changed the dynamic of each person's perception in the room. Eugene seemed startled by the sound the gun had made, or perhaps that he had missed Burden from such close range. Hysterical, Pru pressed herself to the floor and covered her head with her hands and began wailing. Burden made an attempt for the window, but with his ankles bound together he could not step over Pru.

Eugene fired again and shattered a vase in the corner of the room. "Goddamn it," he spat in frustration.

Burden tripped over Pru and fell to the floor like a loosely tied bundle. He kicked his feet furiously, trying to free them from his pants. But he could not get them over his shoes and all he managed to do was to turn them inside out, so that they dragged behind him like a paralyzed tail. There was the report of another shot and the carpeting in front of Burden's face exploded in a plume of fluff and wood splinters.

"Goddamn fucking shit!" Eugene bellowed.

Pru crawled toward her husband. "Jesus, Eugene," she said in tears, her voice wrecked with panic, "that's enough! Don't shoot no more. I'm begging you, for the love of God!"

Burden's eyes teared and he wiped at them to remove the bits of carpet fibers plastered to them. Then, gripping the sill, he pulled himself up. He looked back at Eugene. Pru had reached her husband and had her arms wrapped around his knees. He aimed again at Burden and just as he fired, Pru reached blindly upward, sweeping her hand in the air and knocking his aim off, which corrected it. The bullet chewed into the meat of Burden's calf. At first Burden didn't realize he'd been hit, not until he saw the broad smile, almost of astonishment, on Eugene's face. Pru looked back and screamed in horror.

"I've got you now, you goddamn cocksucker," Eugene said as he took a fresh bead on Burden.

In a final furious burst of strength, Burden hoisted himself up to the window and dove through it. There was another shot and the window shattered, raining down tiny shards of glass onto his body.

"Damn it! Damn it! Damn it!" came Eugene's voice from inside.

The damning grace dogging Burden for so long was exorcised the moment the bullet struck his calf, and as he spilled over the sill and onto the roof he felt for the first time in years the liberating uncertainty of how this night might end. So slick had the rain made the shingles that he couldn't gain any traction, and his momentum sent him skidding headlong over the edge as easily as if the roof had been a slide, tumbling through the air like some wildly inept acrobat, his pants fluttering behind him. He hit the rain-soaked ground hard, landing on the point of his right shoulder. A sharp pain shot through his shoulder blade and clavicle as they broke. Mud became impacted in his eyes and as he peered up at the open window all he saw were dim images, a foreshortened square of amber light shining against a background of storm clouds. He expected at any moment for Eugene to poke his head through the window and take dead aim at him where he lay on the ground. Of course, he hadn't so much a worry of Eugene's taking dead aim at him as of Pru's possible attempt to block his shot, thereby assuring that the bullet would find its mark. But only a stream of cursing—both male and female—issued from the window, as the sounds of intense verbal sparring suffused with the subtext of reconciliation. "Give me the gun!" was heard repeatedly, along with "No!" Then a shot rang out and Burden flinched, even though it was not possible that he could be struck by the bullet.

Rain shook through the trees, cooling a heat gathering under Burden's skin. As he lay in the mud, dimly perceiving the conversation carrying out above him, a fit of laughter seized him. This fit was followed quickly by a fleeting awareness of overwhelming grief, an emotion that shook tears from his eyes as easily as the wind shook rain from the overhead limbs. In the ensuing moments by turns he laughed uproariously and cried with selfless abandon.

"It's yours," Burden spoke to a point somewhere beyond the lighted window, somewhere above even the rain. "All of it. Take it, I can't bear it any longer. . . . It isn't mine anyway, not anymore." His voice choked in his throat and the words stopped, but there flowed from his heart the polluted waters of six years' emotional upheaval and turmoil. Images, names, odors, sounds, sensations, faces all passing before him and from him on laughter and tears, as though in that moment he was witness to all that had occurred since Peedie's death. As these sensations of memory passed from him they became impotent recollections—possibly not even his own. How long this process took he was not certain; perhaps had he counted the drops of rain striking his face he might have an accurate idea of the passing time. The outpouring could have lasted several minutes or been accomplished in a mere moment. In the end, a vagrant peace settled over Burden as he willed his guilt to the rain and night. He thought of Peedie, how now he was leaving his cousin behind, if not for good, then for at least a lifetime. He saw perfectly the gallows life he had erected over the past six years and understood that it was not so easily torn down. But here was the first positive act of its dismantling.

A heavy object splashed near Burden's ear. He craned his head as best he could and saw Eugene's pistol half-submerged in a mud puddle. When he saw the gun, he breathed a sigh of relief.

He turned and gazed up through the tree limbs and into the storm-blackened sky. A gust of chill, wet wind seized the tree limbs and shook a final clot of rain from their leaves. Hearing the wind, Burden thought, *It's only the wind and nothing more.*

Pru thrust her head out the window and looked down at Burden. When she saw him move, she said, "Oh, thank God, he's not dead." She turned and looked back into the room and said, "Call an ambulance." Then she disappeared inside and after a moment Burden heard her yell, *"Goddamn it, Eugene, just how long do you want to go to jail for? Now call the fucking ambulance!"*

Burden settled once more onto his back. His vision, already cloudy with flecks of mud, began to grow fuzzy, and the intensity of the pain racking his body lessened until he felt almost high. A soft, out-of-focus, wind-borne rain anointed his face, and it was a marvelous sensation. It felt to him as though countless cold, moist fingertips were pressing gently into inflamed cheeks and chest, his belly, his genitals, his thighs and ankles. It was all very wonderful, and he felt a light-headed bliss overtake his thoughts.

A siren sounded in the distance, seeming to come nearer yet at the same time fading. And the more the siren's sound grew louder and yet faded, and the more out of focus the raindrops became as they fell toward Burden, the greater bliss he experienced. He smiled as he thought of Peedie, his sight growing dim. And then all was darkness and silence. All was peace.

SEVENTEEN

The hours following Burden's tumble from Pru's window were marked by a worrisome oblivion studded with brief episodes of hallucinatory wakefulness. Undiscernible faces hovered above him like earthbound balloons; disembodied voices asked questions composed of an English overgrown with the sounds of a hopelessly foreign tongue. Of the few faces appearing above him he thought he recalled Dr. Whitman's glum, owlish features. But he could not be sure. The doctor—if indeed that was who it had been—peered at him through a pleasing darkness from which Burden was rudely wrested, his mind invaded by a brilliant, inescapable light, absolutely without tint or heat. Then there was a second face and more questions and his feeble attempts at answers; then a coolness swept up through his arm, spreading across the plain of his body. But he wasn't afraid, for the coolness sopped up the unwanted light and lowered him on backward steps to a quiet, dark place.

When he awoke, Burden's first conscious thought, freighted by the lingering effects of the anesthesia, was that he had died anyway despite his late embracing of a desire to live. But if he was dead, where had he wound up? If this was hell, then hell was not so unpleasant as he'd been led to believe; in fact, it had something of a chill to it, and seemed banal rather than tormenting. If this was heaven, then likewise heaven was not so acceptable as he'd hoped. He thought for a moment that he was in purgatory, then remembered that he did not believe in purgatory. He hoped he hadn't been wrong about *that*.

While he was working out his cosmic locus, a face of indeterminate gender and beauty hovered above him. "You're awake," the doubtful face said. The room—be it heaven, hell, or wherever—was brightened by a milky luminance, and the face floating in the air above him shone starkly as though struck by the beam of an artificial moon.

Burden tried to move—a hand, leg, foot, anything to test the bounds of his reality. To his dismay he discovered he was nearly immobile. Craning his neck (an excruciating exercise in itself), he surveyed his body and found fully the right half of it either imprisoned within plaster (his shoulder and arm) or shrouded underneath gauze and white tape (his calf). In addition, his right leg had been slipped into a sling and hoisted above the bed. Of his left side, he could manage only the most sluggish of movements. It was as though he'd forgotten *how* to make himself move.

His vision gradually improved while he lay there, which in turn quickened his memory. He understood now that he was indeed in a type of purgatory: a hospital. Slowly and with care his mind reconstructed the events that had led him to this bed. He recalled the pelting rain, his mother at the foot of the stairs, Peedie, the Jo-less Sonic, Pru's bedroom, Eugene's cheery countenance as he shot at Burden, his own fall from the window (which produced a sympathetic and dully painful spasm from his body, like the involuntary jump prior to sleep).

The face returned and hovered over Burden again. He could make it out more clearly now and saw that it was a she. The woman was full-jowled and graying, with pressed-in lines radiating from the corners of every particular of her face. She smiled without warmth and produced a thermometer magicianlike. Its body glinted in the false moonlight with as great a chill as her smile. "Let's just get your temperature, shall we?"

Before Burden could open his mouth, which he could not have done quickly in this present circumstance, the nurse drove the thermometer down, piercing his closed lips with a studied adroitness.

"Where am I?" Burden managed after the nurse had removed and read the thermometer.

"Recovery." The nurse seemed pleased to impart this information, and her smile increased till it was as warm as the winter sun.

Recovery. Of course, Burden thought sluggishly through his mental torpor.

The nurse began asking him questions and taking additional vital signs. After a few minutes of this mental and physical prodding and poking, she departed, saying with a chirpy foreboding that she was going for "the doctor." As much as he could, Burden eased back into the bed and closed his eyes. His will and the lingering effects of the anesthesia made him want to slip back into that pleasant oblivion from which he had so recently woken. But the pain, while not acute, throbbed dully at a sufficient number of fleshy intersections to keep him from doing so. Soon he heard the sound of approaching footsteps, and the vague remembrance of a face that earlier "could have been" Dr. Whitman's became not a possibility but a fact. It had been *his* aged and expressionless face hovering above Burden; it had been the doctor's faint and passionless eyes that had summoned that fine oblivion. And now they were his footsteps circumventing that oblivion's return.

"How's our young patient feeling?" Dr. Whitman asked upon reaching Burden's bedside.

Burden wasn't sure if he was supposed to answer this question or whether it was merely a pro forma ritual—a verbal uncluttering of the mind, no more meaningful than clearing one's throat. Thinking it best (and because he could not help but feel awkward in Dr. Whitman's presence), Burden kept silent.

"I would hazard a guess that you're in some bit of pain, certainly groggy," Dr. Whitman said as he scanned Burden's chart. By his expression, which at no time deviated from what it had been the moment previous, he might not have spoken at all; Burden might simply have imagined his words. Setting down the chart, Dr. Whitman took Burden's face in his aged, soft fingers, turning Burden's head a fraction to the left and then a fraction to the right to examine his color. This motion produced sharp pains in Burden's neck, chest, and jaw. "Very good. Well, we should have you out of this bazaar and in your own room shortly. How would you like that?"

Another rhetorical question, Burden guessed, finding it incredible that Dr. Whitman could address him in tones so civil, so devoid of historic insight, as though Burden were just one more patient, vaguely known by the doctor and not the person who had been so flagrantly cuckolding him these past six years. That this willful ignorance and forced civility might have been the doctor's only means of protecting his true feelings, which may well have been wretched, did not occur to Burden.

"Nurse," Dr. Whitman called, "have a room prepared for our patient." Then, to Burden, "That was a nasty spill you took." He stroked the cast and then tapped it gently. "Cassidy's work. He's good. We'll keep our hopes up about your recovering full extension of your shoulder. Had a patient once, a truck driver. Involved in a head-on collision. Broke both his arms. When they took the casts off, he couldn't extend his arms any farther than this." Dr. Whitman held both arms aloft, their elbows bent at 100-degree angles. "Poor fellow. Still drove, though." As he related his story, the doctor's eyes possessed a half-wistful expression, while his mouth admitted no mirth in its lines. "He didn't have Cassidy. You did. You'll be fine."

The doctor fell silent, having exhausted his banter, and stood by Burden's bed awkwardly. Fishing his fingers in his coat pockets, he withdrew from one a piece of paper on which was scribbled a short note. He gazed at the paper in some surprise, as though he'd forgotten the note entirely, then plunged it back into the depths of his pocket. "Your family is waiting down the hall. I'll send them in," he said, turning to leave. He stopped short and turned back to Burden. "Oh, and I know one young woman who'll be glad to know you're making fast progress." Dr. Whitman imparted this bit of information with the same curious mixture of wistfulness and professional decorum that made his emotions inscrutable. "I'll let her know you're doing well."

From Recovery, Burden was taken to a room on the second floor. Burden's parents came into the room briefly. They had spent much time with him in Recovery and wanted only to make sure he was comfortably settled before leaving for the night. They assured him that Sue would be by first thing in the morning. "And I'll be by in the afternoon," his mother added. When they were gone, Burden lay alone in the room's transparent darkness, against which a dim night-light above his bed struggled. The hallway's antiseptic light slipped through the partially open doorway, and the objects in the room glimmered much as though struck by the rays of a quarter moon slipping through a crack in the clouds.

Burden had slept too much since his surgery to sleep well now. He felt a frequent returning to a light slumber, like repeatedly wading ankle-deep into a lake, but he was never long immersed in sleep's depthless waters. Once, sometime after midnight, he stirred from a light sleep, prodded to partial consciousness by the uncomfortable sensation of a full bladder. He imagined he saw a figure standing just inside his room, obscured within the confluence of light and shadow. He did not move, but remained intent on the person veiled in shadow. At certain moments he would concentrate so singularly on the figure that it would disappear altogether, and he would have to look away briefly to see it again. Finally, after one such moment, when he looked back, the figure had vanished.

"I can think of better things to do with a Sunday afternoon than getting shot and falling out a window," Cat said after the nurse had left the room. "Lots better." He had been eyeing the nurse, his lips set in a lascivious grin, for while she was not abundantly attractive, her relative youth still held great charm for an older man such as himself. He had kept a close watch on the nurse as she tended Burden, touching him here and there and speaking so kindly to him. When she left, Cat smacked his lips and said, "Still, almost makes it worth it, huh?"

Blind Willie, who was gazing out the window, had ignored Cat. Now that the nurse was gone, he moved to Burden's side and nudged him knowingly on his good shoulder. "How about it, kid, thirsty?" he asked. Without waiting for a response, he reached into an inside pocket of his coat and produced a half-Thermos, like one that goes in a child's lunchbox, which is just what it was. "Corona," he announced. "Frankie sent this along, figured you might could use one 'bout now." Willie unscrewed the Thermos, poured a little of the beer in the cap, and handed it to Burden. "Still cold, too."

Burden took the cap awkwardly and studied it.

"Go ahead, son, drink up," Willie said. "You earned it. More than ever before, I'd say."

But Burden kept studying the cap. His initial impulse had been to drink the beer, but he found that beyond the impulse there was no desire. In fact, he felt indifferent to having a drink. At length, with a shy look of thanks, he returned the cap to Willie. "Tell Frankie I appreciate the gesture, but all the same, my stomach's a bit messed up. Maybe later."

"Sure thing, kid."

Cat intercepted the cap and raised it to Burden. "To Burden's speedy recovery," he said, drinking it whole. When he was finished, he wiped his lips and said, "So how is it, the leg? How's it feel?"

Burden screwed up his lips in a show of indifference. "Hurts a little, I guess. The bullet nicked the bone. That's why they had to operate; otherwise they'd have just fished the slug out. Pretty much I don't feel anything with the pills they're giving me."

Cat took the Thermos from Blind Willie and poured a second capful as Bobby said, "You're lucky he didn't shoot your pecker off." To which Cat raised the cap in a second toast and said, "To Burden's pecker; may it ever stand proud."

"They treating you nice?" Bobby asked.

"Like being in a five-star hotel. Waiting on me hand and foot." Burden held up the call button. "All I've got to do is press this button and they come running. 'Nurse, I'm thirsty; nurse, my leg itches; nurse, I can't reach the bedpan—' "

" 'Nurse, it's time for my bath,' " Bobby interjected wryly.

Cat eyed Bobby with uncertainty. "What're you talking about?"

"Well, our boy can't very well wash hisself, can he?"

Cat turned to Burden with an expression comprised of equal measures of disbelief and hopefulness. "No shit, kid, that woman's been washing you up?"

" 'Course she has, Cat," Blind Willie answered, "that's her job. From his head to his toes and all stations in between."

"Holy sweet Jesus," Cat said, incredulous.

"Yep," Willie continued, "just a nurse, a bucket of water . . . and a bar of soap. God's gotta love that."

Cat turned and looked out the door to see if he could spy the nurse. "Lord, ain't that something—from your head to your feet and your dickie in between."

Bobby clasped Cat's shoulder. "That's worth a bullet in the leg any day. Huh, Cat?"

Burden looked at Willie and smiled; it was the first time he'd truly smiled since waking from surgery. "Well, Cat, I'm sorry I can't say for certain if she's washed me up yet or not. If she has, I've been too out of it to recall. But come back tomorrow and I'll tell you for sure all about it."

Cat turned from the door and gave Burden an imploring look.

"Don't look so all pitiful eager, Cat," Bobby said, chuckling. "Ain't no nurse in her right mind'd get close to you. If that was you lying there in bed rather than Burden, the nurse'd just as soon toss that bucket of water on you as to bathe a sorry dog like you."

"Screw you, Bobby," Cat said, turning for the door.

"Ah, now, where you going, Cat?" Bobby called after him.

"I'm hungry. They got any goddamn snack machines 'round here?"

Bobby touched his stomach tenderly, as though Cat's admission had stirred a sympathetic hunger in his own belly. "Hold on, I'll come with you."

When they were gone and it was only Burden and Blind Willie, both felt a sudden awkwardness, with Burden looking like some sorry spectacle people would pay a quarter to get a look at. Without making a show of it, Willie took the chair from against the wall and slid it to the bedside. Sitting now and not lumbering over Burden, there was a greater equality of position and ease between the two friends.

"Guess I really fucked up this time, huh?"

Rather than answer, and having either to admit what he thought or lie, Willie gazed down at his shoes and blew out a breath, the sound indicating only that life rambles where it will, which was the sum of his philosophy. "You survived," he said at length. "In the end, that's what's important." He gave a derisive laugh. "Shit, I always knew Eugene was a coward and a fool; I suppose it was only a matter of time before he did something like this. Still, always comes as a shock whenever a fool *acts* like a fool."

"*I'm* the fool," Burden said quietly. "Eugene was only protecting what was his."

"Well, all the same, I hope whatever wild hair you've had up your ass has been plucked out of there. Or do you like being shot at?"

"Has its advantages," Burden said, teasing, then he fell silent. His eyes studied the middle distance between his chest and feet, as though something had sprung up there that only he could see. "Willie . . . " he said after a short time. "Willie, I want to thank you." Burden's voice was subdued as his eyes beheld the object they alone perceived. "I want to thank you for the help you've been."

"Help? Shit, son, if I'd have been any real help, I would've locked you up in the stockroom at Buck's and kept you there till I forced some sense through that skull of yours."

The object levitating above Burden's torso evaporated and he blinked away its remnants. He turned to Willie and took his hand. Without shame, he held his gaze to Willie's. "But you *did* that . . . you made me open my eyes to what I'd blinded myself to for six years. You saved my life."

Although Blind Willie did not withdraw his hand, he did turn away, with an uneasy expression at the depth with which Burden's eyes regarded him. He said, "Well, leastways now I figure you know enough to keep your pants on." He was about to say something more when there came a sound at the door. Maude had been standing at the doorway, listening, and was trying to back out. She blushed deeply at having been discovered. She walked haltingly into the room, her expression apologetic.

"Maude," Burden said, surprised to find he was glad to see her.

The tone of Burden's voice evidently reassured Maude, for she strode to his bed with a confident air.

Willie stood. Although he had never met Maude, he knew much about her as related by Burden. This knowledge—wonderfully anatomic in its detail—he tried to suppress as he regarded her, dipping his head in greeting.

Burden introduced the two, and Maude offered Willie her hand with accustomed grace. But Blind Willie only fumbled his hands along the buttons of his jacket, managing a second dipping of his head and a poorly voiced "Hello," to which Maude tactfully lowered her hand.

"Suppose I ought to be going," Willie said. "We'll come back tomorrow to check on you. I'll bring along another present from Frankie, see if you're not in more of a mood for it then." He turned to Maude and dipped his head a third time. "Miss Whitman," he said, fumbling with his buttons again, "was a pleasure meeting you."

When Willie was gone, Maude sat down in the chair he had placed at Burden's bedside. Then, possessed by an impulse, she stood and leaned over Burden and kissed his forehead tenderly. As she bent over him, a lock of her hair brushed his lips softly, and he caught the fragrance of a well-tended garden rising from her breasts. For a moment he felt fifteen again, an innocent young boy who hadn't any sickness in him. But only for a moment.

"You look well," Maude said, settling down once more in the chair. "I was expecting worse from what Hubert told me."

"Guess I didn't look half so well yesterday," Burden replied in a self-deprecating tone.

Maude grasped the bed rail, her slender fingers pale against the chrome bar.

"Why don't you lower that? I won't fall out. I'm pretty certain I've got all my falling behind me."

They shared a smile and after a moment of fumbling, Maude lowered the rail. She scooted the chair closer and rested a hand on Burden's hip. "Yes, that's much better. My," she said, her manner more relaxed now that the bed rail had been lowered. "I can't tell you the horror that seized my heart when I'd heard you'd been shot. Of course, I imagined the worst; it's the safest thing to do. Until I learned that you would be all right it was as though my whole world had died; my heart shrivelled inside me and I felt disconnected from everything, especially with not being able to come down here to see you right away—people talk enough as it is. I had to content myself with whatever drabs of information I could get out of Hubert last night. . . . This morning when I woke up I said to myself, 'Hubert and Walterboro be damned, I'm going to see my Burden, I'm going to look into his large, wonderful eyes and reassure myself that he's still here with me . . . with us.' And well, here you are, just as bright and beautiful as a woman could hope for."

Burden blushed and waved her compliment away. "It'll take more than Eugene and a gun to kill me, I suppose."

"That beast," Maude said, shivering. "I don't know how a woman could stay with a man like that. It can't be love. . . ."

Burden withheld a wry smile, wondering if Maude heard her own words.

Without warning, tears welled up in Maude's eyes and she was crying softly as she flung her arms around Burden's neck. Her words were warm and wet as she pressed them against his skin. "Oh, I know we're through, you and I, but God, I couldn't have stood it if you'd have been taken completely from me, if I couldn't see you again, if you were nothing more than a memory. You can't know the despair I felt thinking you were gone."

Because she was draped over his good arm, Burden could do nothing to console her, and the fingers of his injured arm fluttered in the air, caressing nothing. After a minute or so, as gingerly as he might, he retrieved his good arm from under Maude's heaving bosom and, as her sobs subsided, patted her curled locks. "Don't cry, not over me, Maude. And anyway, I'm right here, I'm not leaving or gone. I'll still be around. I'll still deliver your groceries to you just like I always have."

"But it won't be the same," Maude moaned quietly, and Burden felt her words again, humid and warm against his neck.

"There isn't anything that can be the same forever," Burden replied. Maude shook her head in agreement and Burden felt a belated tear moisten his bed gown. "But I'll be your friend, Maude, for as long as you'll have me."

Maude stood and wiped her nose with a tissue that blossomed spontaneously in her palm. She smiled wanly, in a placating manner, in the way people agree to appear cheerful in the face of disquieting news. "Yes, well, we'll see how long it is before I grow tired of you."

Burden ran his fingers along the lapel of her blouse. "Not too soon, I hope." Now that he was rid of her, he felt no irritation with Maude, and was pleased with the reservoir of good will he held for her.

Maude clasped Burden's hand to her breast in an intimate rather than sexual manner. "Not soon at all," she said, her voice still unsteady as she gazed at her lost lover with a longing that, in its very tenuousness, surrendered the satisfaction of that longing.

There was a knock at the door. "Excuse me," said the nurse who had been tending to Burden. "The doctor's making his rounds. He'll be by shortly." Her voice was level, avoiding any untoward implication.

Maude turned and nodded, dismissing the nurse. She turned

back to Burden and her heart seemed to break again as she studied him. At length she fell on him a last time, although without tears as before, and kissed him deeply. When she rose her face was composed; all that was needed was a dab or two of her tissue. "I shouldn't come by anymore, you need your rest. But I'll call to check on you. To cheer you up."

"I'd like that."

Maude lingered a moment longer and then, composing herself, departed.

The parade of souls marching through Burden's room ended shortly after lunchtime. Johnnie White had come while the doctor was examining Burden, bringing with him a walking stick made of birch that had once been his grandfather's. "I figured you could use this," he had said, "for a while at least, once you get on your feet." The stick's head had been worn smooth as polished marble from all the years the elder Mr. White had braced his palm against it, imbuing it with the fragrance of all those lost years. Burden's mother sent word through Sue that she had been delayed but would be by in the evening. Sue had arrived at the same time as his lunch, and she delighted in picking at the food, comparing the mashed potatoes, chicken, and cherry cobbler to old kitchen sponges and floor mats. She insisted on feeding Burden, which she did with an increasing zeal until Burden believed his sister was trying to pierce his tongue. To protect himself, he shut tight his mouth. After much pleading to let her continue feeding him, Sue relented and put the fork down.

"You're no fun," she groused. "I'd hoped falling out a window would at least've made you funner." Unable to make further sport of Burden's tongue, Sue grew bored; making certain he didn't need anything else, she complained that she had twice the work to do with him gone and that she figured she ought to go.

After lunch, the nurse administered two pain killers, and in the absence of additional visitors Burden spent the next three hours in a cycle of light naps and pleasant semiwakeful periods that never broke to the sunlight of full lucidity. He could have struggled to a clear-headed state had it been necessary, but preferred to remain for a time in a condition that demanded so little.

Toward late afternoon a nurse and an orderly entered the room. The orderly was wheeling a patient on a gurney. The nurse made a cursory inspection of Burden, who was at that moment vaguely awake, then pulled the privacy curtain around his bed. Not feeling in the least slighted, Burden turned lazily and peered out the window. Outside, the sky seemed fatigued, as though its colors ran through veining perilously bled. In the distance he could make out the tops of clouds that soon would burst into roseate flame with the approach of evening.

"How is that?" Burden overheard the nurse ask the patient after he had been transferred to the bed. The only response she received was a disgruntled grumble holding the vague form of an obscenity. But although ill-formed and indistinct, something of the word's tenor made Burden start from his indolence. "We'll come and check on you again soon," the nurse answered, ignoring the patient's surly tone.

In an act that seemed a communication of emotion she dared not direct toward the patient, the nurse snatched hold of the curtain and forcefully pushed it three quarters back, revealing for Burden the patient as far up along his body as his shoulders. The man's arm, pale and vitiated, with sagging skin that adumbrated bone rather than muscle, fluttered heavily in the air. "What in damn hell'm I in here for?" the man demanded, his words slurred as they struggled up through the wreckage of carnal decay. "I've no need to be in here, goddamn it—ain't nothing wrong with me." His voice held the quality of death as it rattled hollowly out of a body withering around a chilling soul. Despite his declaration, the man's words so exhausted him that his arm plummeted to his side as though it had been a buzzard shot from the sky.

Still, the man's voice had a bracing effect on Burden's mind, wrenching him back to lucidity. He was seized by an inconsolable need to rise from his bed, to rise and flee, flee to home, flee to anywhere that would be an escape from that most unholy voice.

The nurse looked at Burden and silently apologized, arching her eyebrows as though to suggest she'd just as soon turn the patient onto the street. Out of reflex, she fluffed Burden's pillow and then placed her wrist against his forehead. Her brow knitted as she withdrew her wrist. "You feel a little cold. Would you like another blanket? Some hot tea to warm you?"

Burden shook his head gravely.

The nurse glanced back at the old man with an expression nearly of contempt, then bent closer to Burden and in a quiet tone said, "Sorry about your new roommate. He gives you any trouble, just buzz me and I'll be right over to settle him down."

Burden nodded.

Before leaving, the nurse pushed the curtain open the rest of the way, but Burden would not look at the man. For an hour he stared at the ceiling, barely blinking. Occasionally the man would grumble, and Burden could discern now and again a curse, a disconnected rant, gibberish. Beyond the window the clouds flamed briefly as the sky's pale blue skin darkened with early evening. The moon's ashen face materialized in the ebbing daylight and became brighter by imperceptible degrees till it peered through the window with a disapproving scowl. Still, Burden would not look at the man.

Then, as though it were a breathless sound loosed from an opened tomb, the man spoke. "Boy."

Burden's fingers fidgeted with the call button, his thumb at the ready. He thought of Johnnie's walking stick, thought to take it in hand. *But why?* he thought, feeling foolish. What could the old man—the *dying* man, for that was surely the case—do to him from his bed?

"Boy," the man intoned again, like the sonorous hymn of an iron bell.

The man fell quiet, Burden relaxed his grip on the call button. Then the patient's voice exploded sharp and loud. "Boy!" The word was violent, clipped, vanishing rather than fading.

Burden started in his bed. He turned, bathed in deep chill, and looked at the old man. "Mr. Silas?" he said, his voice faltering in fear and dread.

Old Silas lay immobile under the sheets. It appeared that his body had already passed away, lying there with an effortless rigidity and expiring a thick, sickly sweet odor as though his flesh had been bathed in rancid perfume. Only his face betrayed signs of life, and those so slight that Burden felt, as he stared into Silas's soulless eyes, he was witnessing a second passing. Yet, like a machine locked in perpetual motion, the mechanisms of Silas's face never surrendered the final tick; his lips trembled as they mumbled silent words, his eyes glistened as they took in something more than the room. And his face, as pale as the moon's, hanging ghostlike beyond the window, quivered ceaselessly. "Boy," he said again. But Silas was not looking at Burden, and Burden supposed he was not addressing him either. Rather, the old man was holding a dialogue with a person only he and the angels perceived.

Still, having gathered the courage to look at the old murderer, Burden found himself unable to turn away. He held his eyes fast to Silas, and as he quelled his fear, tried to see beyond the mask of death threaded loosely to his face, to peer into the man, and not his conception of the man. Try as he might, however, Burden could not divine a soul, and barely even a person underneath the features he had come to loathe. And he realized that of the three of them, it could be said none had survived the events of that tragic evening, that all three occupied a lesser land than this earth. Peedie had been entirely freed of these bonds, while Silas and he were mired in the onerous path of the condemned, Silas by his nature, Burden by desire. How difficult it was now for Burden to wrest his legs from the muck of self-loathing and a desire for death.

But remove them he must. And holding his gaze on Silas, Burden sensed a growing pity for the old man, perceiving a little of his torment, whether self-induced or ordained by fate, that fueled his hours. And in his pity, Burden felt a fleeting brush with the divine, felt for a moment that he was on the border of spiritual revelation. Then he retreated, seeking again the old revulsion, so comfortable and well-worn. He turned from the old man, who had grown silent while his lips still quivered, spilling forth soundless words. Burden sensed Silas keeping an eye vaguely on him. But he understood also that Stokes had descended to a point where his eyes apprehended less his physical surroundings than those things awaiting only his final breath.

"Jo," Burden said, waking with a start. He had been dreaming of her. They were walking, she several paces ahead, he trying to catch up but unable to. He had called to her repeatedly but she refused to turn around. The path threaded through a dense wood, running on at great length, with its end, if it had one, obscured by countless bends and innumerable limbs. They seemed to walk thusly for an hour, with Jo never slowing or turning, and Burden calling for her to look at him. Then he awoke, feeling for a moment that she was standing near him.

Silas murmured in the darkness. Burden gazed at the old man; he had scarcely changed position from hours earlier. It was night now and the room lit only by a dim night-light hung over each bed. In this light, Silas's features became a degree paler, and the liver spots that peppered his face grew more pronounced, making his flesh appear diseased. His eyes were open, and he stared with deathlike dispassion toward the ceiling. Burden could see them glistening dully, their cheerless gray refracting a demi-beam of light like a moon ray passing through soot-clothed glass. Age and infirmity had let him escape justice after having killed Peedie. Now that same age, that same infirmity was bringing down on him a sentence no soul could escape.

Silas's voice continued in a monotonous drone, and Burden felt a deepening despair; there was the dull ache of his past, but what accosted him more painfully was the fact that Jo had not come to see him, where she had every opportunity as well as every reason to see him. Had he so completely sundered their relationship that she would not come even for a few minutes to wish him well? Beyond the window the moon had moved on, leaving only the dark of night and a few faint, scattered stars. He closed his eyes to this night, and wished for sleep that he might dream again of Jo. It did not matter that she would not turn to look at him; it was enough that he should see her, and that he should know he was not alone.

EIGHTEEN

Burden dreamed again, but not of Jo. He was locked in a fierce struggle with an adversary he could not see. An object of great weight pressed down on him, stealing his breath, and in a detail mocking his present condition, he could not lift his arms to fend off the attack. Calling out, he woke himself from this somnolent struggle. But upon waking, Burden wondered if he hadn't simply risen to another dream, a dream more vivid in detail, with the addition of weight, shading, and odor enfolded into the already peculiar alchemy of dream images.

Silas had climbed atop Burden and taken him by the throat. The old man glowered down, his goitrous eyes wide in rage. "Away! Away with you!" he screamed petulantly, spittle spraying Burden's face. "I know who you are," he continued, his voice piteous for all its rage. "I know why you've come, I know but I won't go. I won't."

Silas's full weight bore down on Burden's suspended leg, causing it to burn hotly with renewed pain. Of itself, Stoaks's attack was not over-powering, but because Burden was handicapped by the use of only one arm—the strength of which was dulled by medication—the best he could force was a stalemate. Managing barely to loosen Silas's grip from around his throat, he yelled out for the nurse. His first sounds were feeble and quiet, but when he found his full voice he didn't care that he sounded frantic; he wanted only to survive this attack, to get this wretched corpse off him.

"God*damn* you," Burden spat between clenched teeth as Silas discovered an ounce more strength and reclasped his fingers around Burden's neck. The old man's fingers were dry and rough as parchment, the brittle shafts of bone running through them poorly dressed underneath a paucity of flesh.

"You're not taking me," Silas hissed, pressing his goatish face against Burden's own. "I'm not going." Rearing up, Stoaks regarded his prey, his eyes afire with a mad illumination. In that moment, Burden saw clearly the utter conviction they held, a conviction bordering on a religious certainty that demanded Burden's death. Clearer still, he understood the reasoning buttressing that conviction. Oddly, this understanding calmed him, and while he did not cease his struggle, the panic that had so recently seized him vanished.

"You recognize me," Burden whispered hoarsely as a rolling wave of heat swept across his face, chased away at once by a waxen chill. "You know who I am. . . . You remember." Burden's words expired on the most ethereal of breaths. But his thoughts continued, and where they led amazed him, for he realized the old man had only the same goal in mind as he himself had these past six years: to destroy the one object capable of recalling that fateful evening and thus of haunting his every hour. For Silas, killing Burden would kill his past.

The surety of this revelation collapsed any immediate outrage he might feel toward Stoaks. Had he any air left in his lungs, Burden would have regaled his attacker with robust laughter fed on the knowledge that his quest for redemption was finally drawing to a close at the hands of the very murderer who had set him on his dark course. But it was a course he no longer cared to follow, an end he no longer desired, and so, lacking the weapons of his hands or even at this point his voice, Burden fought back with the only weapon left to him: his will. *I won't die.* The force of this single thought shook Burden's flesh, and he felt his body tremble within Silas's grasp. *I will not let you win.* The thought flashed through the breadth of his mind like a torch alight, sparking and then igniting his long-dormant will to survive. Yet it was perhaps a battle too late joined, for to Burden's eyes, Stoaks's features descended into shadow. This darkness was as a pale light against a deeper, more abiding blackness sweeping across Burden's vision, bringing a lightness of being as though he had somehow shrugged off a heavy coat or troublesome thought. A peace was contained within this darkness, but it was, as never before, a peace to which he had no desire to surrender. Then, without warning this blackness was for a moment vanquished by a flash of brilliant light as, like a winged creature, Silas took flight into the room's far reaches.

"*Mr. Stoaks!*" a voice spoke hotly. Then a second voice said: "What're you doing, you crazy fool?"

Spangles of multicolored light burst through the blackness of Burden's vision, their discs resolving into the room's common forms. Two nurses and an orderly wrestled with Stoaks, struggling to settle him into bed. The old man flailed his arms and legs, spitting venomous curses at his helpers.

"Get the restraints," the first nurse instructed heatedly. "Got 'em," the orderly answered. The trio subdued Stoaks in short order, but although his limbs were restrained, Silas continued, with increased fervor, to spew invective into the room. When the doctor on duty came to examine Silas, Burden struggled to watch the spectacle, curious to learn the resolution of the old man's attack. For the doctor's part, after satisfying himself that the patient had done himself no grave harm, he ordered Silas sedated.

Noticing Burden's interest, the orderly closed the curtain as the nurse prepared an injection. The doctor stepped around the curtain and checked Burden for injuries. At length he too was declared unharmed, and rather than a sedative being ordered, was asked if he wouldn't prefer one.

"No," Burden said. While he curiously bore Silas no ill will for his assault, still he did not trust the restraints tying Silas to his bed and therefore did not care to sleep, especially to sleep soundly.

"Very well," the doctor responded. As he was leaving, the doctor paused and took the nurse aside, instructing her to look in every half hour to make sure Silas remained quiet.

Returning to Burden's bedside, the nurse and he shared a wary glance toward the curtained patient. Silas's voice rose from behind his veil, caught in a maniacal dialogue only one side of which they were privy to. But his words were grinding slower and it was evident that they would soon cease.

"Are you sure you're okay?" the nurse asked as she straightened his gown.

Burden nodded.

Reaching across the bed, she retrieved the call button and rewrapped it around the railing, setting it near Burden's hand. "He so much as makes a sound, you press this button and I'll be here quick as a whip," she said. Grateful for the concern in her voice, Burden nevertheless felt a grudging sorrow. How much better would it have been to hear such concern coming from Jo, whom he pictured walking the hospital halls on her rounds, purposefully avoiding *this* room. "Don't hesitate," she continued. "You hear?"

Burden nodded.

The nurse gave a final glance toward the curtain and then at Burden. "I know it's difficult, but try to get some sleep. I'll be back soon to check on things."

When the nurse was gone and the only other person in the room was Silas, Burden felt an immeasurable loneliness. The old man had grown quiet, yet his inchoate words still disturbed the silence with a random rhythm that allowed no lasting peace. For several minutes Burden lay barely blinking. Toward Silas Stoaks he felt nothing more than waning apprehension. Far stronger and more disturbing was the sense of abandonment that settled over him, a condition he accepted as having brought upon himself. Recalling their conversation at the Sonic, if Jo chose to sever their relationship, then he could do nothing other than accept that also as the consequence for having behaved as he had.

Silas fell silent, then, like the final ounce of water released from a drying pump, he spoke quite clearly, almost with humility: "Forgive me, I didn't mean to shoot the boy."

Burden's ears pricked up at these words. In the ensuing silence they echoed sharply in his mind. Exhaling, he realized he'd been holding his breath for some several moments. "What was that," he said at length, his voice tentative. "What did you say?"

Stoaks offered several minutes of silence, disturbed only by his measured breaths. But just when Burden believed the old man had slipped into sleep, Silas said: "I didn't mean to shoot the boy. Forgive me."

Burden's blood ran cold. "Forgive?" he repeated in a quiet, mocking tone. "How can I forgive you what you did?" The revelation he'd experienced peering into Stoaks's eyes had broken the abhorrence he felt toward the murderer, but he hadn't contemplated the question of forgiveness . . . he did not believe he could.

Again Stoaks fell silent, as though waiting patiently for a dispensation of grace. After several minutes he repeated: "Do forgive me, Lord. Forgive me and I'll not tarry here any longer." His voice had grown contrite, convincingly so, as though conceding defeat after an interminable struggle.

The sea change in Silas's voice, with its piteous tone, pierced Burden. He stumbled over the unfamiliar emotional terrain, uncertain of his true attitude toward the man who had killed Peedie. Was it conceivable that within his heart he harbored compassion for this monster? Was grace a possibility? He had put aside his hatred, but forgiveness would put the lie to his struggle. It was one thing to reach the conclusion that, for all his trying, he no longer wanted to die. It was another thing entirely to admit that the impetus for those years was in error. Yet another, quieter part wanted this to be so, as if by embracing this newfound grace he could release finally and entirely all that tethered him to an errant and tragic past.

Silas lapsed into a deep slumber, his breathing growing grave and regular, his breaths finding voice as they wound through the decaying hollow of his throat. Burden still did not wish to sleep, believing such respite impossible. Yet he was overcome by an exhaustion equal parts physical, mental, and spiritual. If his recent years had been a journey to find escape from the guilt of a single act, the events of the past few days, and especially those of the last few hours, showed how futile, how empty that journey was. He wanted nothing more now than to reach an accord with his past, and if he could not erase the lethal act of his youth, then at least to reassure himself that he still had a future in which to struggle through his redemption. Now he was tired, so tired, and if he did not wish to sleep, still his body craved it in remembrance of the rest it once held. There was a moment, as he was drifting away, when he stirred slightly at the sound of the nurse coming to check on her patients. She was at pains not to disturb them, Burden thought, for she remained at the threshold, content to study her charges from the shadows.

"Jo . . . ," Burden whispered, wishing her to be his final thought as the gaining weight of slumber pressed down upon him. At this word the nurse seemed to hesitate, then stepped from the shadows, but when she reached Burden, he was fast asleep.

Burden's sleep was anything but restful, for it was wrecked by disquieting images which invariably woke him. But on waking he felt an abiding despair, his mind clinging to dream images as though they were fact. At these moments he would lie in the darkness and concentrate on Silas's breathing. How labored the breaths sounded, bearing the weight of nine decades and countless privations. They were a pitiful sound, and in an attempt to absolve his mind of its despair, Burden found he could not hate the man so much as a moment before. Then, fatigued by this slight dispensation of grace, he would sleep again and dream again disquieting images, only to wake and repeat the cycle.

In the lost hours, where the division of night and morning becomes for a moment obscured, Burden woke fully. He listened to the strained rhythm of Silas's breathing, which had grown shallow, separated by a more generous interval. Burden understood the significance of this rhythmic change, and he felt sorrow for Stoaks. Before, he would not have thought himself capable of feeling such an emotion for the old man; yet now, listening to Stoaks's slackening breaths, he could not conceive of feeling any other way. In breaking off his relationship with Maude, and especially with Pruella, he had taken outward steps toward a new beginning. Now, he realized with much more fear than attended those first steps, he had to perform an act that was wholly internal. No one ever need know of it other than himself and Silas, and it was only this assurance of privacy that gave him the strength to speak.

"Mr. Silas," he began haltingly, pausing, as though waiting for a response he knew would never come. Silas's breaths grew more labored and so Burden continued, sensing an urgency. "I need to confess something to you. I need to make something right." Again Burden stopped, listening to the timbre of the next breath to see if perhaps Silas hadn't woken. At length he said, "I figure you know how I feel about you; all the same I need to tell you directly—I hate you, sir. I hate you with all my heart for what you did to Peedie . . . for what you did to me." The confession was instantly liberating. His heart raced, sped by the whip of truth. "With a single act you destroyed two lives . . . three," he added, thinking of the old man himself, for now Burden could admit that the events of that evening had ruined Silas's days as well. This sharing of grief diminished Burden's own, like a tributary breaking from the main stream and diminishing that water's destructive force. "Peedie's gone, there's no changing that. Me? I've been dying ever since that evening, fading a little more every day just like my memories of Peedie's voice. Seems to me I've done my best to destroy everything you left standing that day. No more. I can't bring Peedie back, I understand that. Hell, I don't even know if I can ever bring myself back to what I should have been, if I can find what it was I would've been if Peedie and I hadn't wandered onto your property, if I hadn't insisted on cutting through." Stoaks's breathing faltered and Burden caught up his own breath in his throat. After a moment he continued, uncertain of Silas's condition, certain only that his time was short. "But I can do one thing—I can do what you asked of me. Truth is, I don't want to hate you anymore . . . I don't think I even can. I feel like it's all wrung out of me, everything, good and bad alike. So, if it makes your passing any easier . . ." Here Burden's voice stumbled over what he knew he must say. Before he continued, he offered a silent prayer to Peedie, begging his understanding, for Burden understood he was betraying his cousin in the final way it was possible to betray him. Then, at first with his eyes closed but then with them open and staring at the veil hanging between himself and Silas Stoaks, he said the last words he had for the dying man. "If it's what you want . . . I forgive you. I forgive you everything."

Stoaks's breath creaked from his body at these words. Drawing in a final shallow draught of air, the old man held preciously to it, then expelled it with a sound as quietly horrifying as any Burden had ever heard.

"Mr. Stoaks?" Burden said, his voice a whisper. He took the walking stick Johnnie had given him and stretched as far as he could toward the curtain and drew it back, revealing Silas Stoaks bit by bit. When at last he had drawn the curtain back completely, Burden gazed at the dead man without bitterness. Silas's body lay still underneath bindings incapable of restraining what at last had passed from his flesh, and he seemed to stare back in repose, his eyes fixed precisely on Burden's own. But this illusion lasted only a moment, and afterward it was as though a mannequin had been secreted in Silas's bed. For the face that Burden apprehended bore no resemblance to the man he once feared. It was as though all that had been Silas had been contained in his eyes, and that the light, the awareness (however meager that awareness had been in life) had utterly vanished. This sudden darkness left his eyes destitute, and there was no longer any feature the old man could claim as his own.

Burden pressed the call button, and as he waited for the nurse to arrive, he held his eyes intently on what remained of his past. For a moment he was unencumbered by thoughts of an uncertain future. But later, as the sheet was pulled over the old man's face, Burden was struck by a quiet panic, and as Silas's body was borne away, he felt the severing of the final physical bond between himself and his cousin. "Goodbye," he said at length, as the old man's body passed from the room. "Goodbye."

Alone, Burden lost himself in the morning's gathering light, which collected in the square of his room's window and spilled across both his own and Silas's now empty bed. While he concentrated on the brightening sky, memories arose unbidden, only to evaporate in the gaining light. He felt empty, at peace, but a peace borne from losing everything and reconciling those losses. One thought vexed him, however, disturbing this doubtful peace: When he finally was reunited with Peedie, whenever and wherever that might be, would his cousin understand that he had had to let Peedie go entirely to regain himself? Would Peedie forgive him that final weakness?

He was delivered from these troublesome thoughts by the entrance of a young nurse's aide, come to bathe him. Wordlessly she went to the closet and brought out a small wash basin, which she filled with warm water from the bathroom tap. Setting the basin and a container of liquid soap on the cart next to Burden's bed, she said, "Time for your bath," as though pressed to explain the presence of the soap and water. As she began unfastening Burden's gown a voice called from the doorway.

"I'll take care of this patient."

Burden looked toward the door: Jo stood within the threshold. At the sound of her voice, he experienced simultaneously a fear and yet a relief so overwhelming that his fear was at once vanquished.

The young girl looked questioningly at Jo.

"It's all right," Jo said, taking up position beside the aide. "I'll tend to this patient. You go on to the next room."

The girl appeared uncertain how to proceed but did as Jo instructed.

When they were alone, Burden gazed up at Jo with a mixture of hope and questioning. His face brightened with a smile. But Jo rebuffed his expression by maintaining a professional demeanor, and, more pointedly, by not looking into his eyes. She leaned over him, reaching behind his shoulders. "You *could* help me," she said, "by leaning forward, just a bit."

"You smell fresh, like a flower," Burden said, propping himself up slightly with his good arm. Jo ignored his observation and undid the straps holding his gown together. When they were untied, she pulled the gown from his left shoulder and folded it across the right side of his chest.

Burden breathed deeply. "I remember that smell." But then he also remembered many other things as well, some causing him great shame, others regret. What he recalled most clearly was the recent evening at the Sonic. If he could do anything it would be to put himself and Jo back on that bench at the Sonic. There he would tell her every good thing in his heart he felt toward her. That night's potential fortune had escaped them, just as their future had escaped them years ago through his foolish actions. It might never be put right, but for the moment Burden luxuriated in the prospect of a possibly brighter future. "Whenever I'd pass by a garden at a house I was delivering to, I'd think for a moment that you were behind me. Sometimes I'd close my eyes and pretend that if I reached out my hand I could touch you."

He spoke rapidly, unheedfully, the way the arrested speak quickly of their crime in an attempt to absolve themselves of their guilt. For Burden, his guilt reached back to the Sonic, to his inability to understand what Jo had been struggling through, and for his further inability to speak honestly to her rather than filtering his words through his pride and hurt.

Jo wet the sponge and pressed a dab of soap onto it. Squeezing the water from it, she drew the sponge across Burden's forehead. "You always did say the most foolish things," she told him, her eyes still averted from his gaze. "I see that hasn't changed any."

"I always said what I thought . . . even when that wasn't such a smart thing to do."

A trickle of water pooled in the corner of Burden's eye and Jo deftly removed it with the tip of her pinky.

"Jo," Burden said, but she turned deliberately away as she rewet the sponge. "Jo," he repeated, placing his hand on her wrist.

Jo hesitated, her gaze lingering on the basin. After a moment she relented and turned toward Burden, trying to preserve the refuge of her professional remove.

"I've been thinking . . . thinking about how we were before . . . about what I've done"—he gave a bitter laugh—"*especially* about what I've done."

Jo turned away and tried to remove her wrist from Burden's grip, but he wouldn't release her. Her expression faltering, she turned back to him.

"No, listen to me. Have you ever felt a desire so deeply," he began, "that it seems nothing can keep you from making it come true? Have you ever felt a need so strong inside that it becomes more a part of your life than the people around you? You'll lose everything for it if that's what it takes. Everything you do, every thought you have, every waking moment is consumed by this one desire. Then one day it's within your reach, everything you ever thought you wanted, everything you ever worked for, all you have to do is close your hand around it and it's yours." Burden fell silent for a moment and turned away. *This is a beginning,* he thought, *this is what I have to explain.* "The thing is," he said, continuing more slowly, looking again at Jo, "you discover you don't *want* to close your hand. You realize someone else has been inside your head all this time. It wasn't you but you have to live with it just the same." Burden released Jo's wrist and, with an automatic movement, she continued washing him.

Burden's gaze stole into Jo's eyes. "I drove you away. Deliberately."

Jo stilled her hand and cast her own gaze at the bed, averting her eyes from Burden. "You did no such thing. I chose to leave."

Burden's features softened in understanding, but he would not yield the point. "I couldn't have you near me, you weren't what I needed, you weren't what I wanted."

Jo looked questioningly at Burden, her eyes shadowed by feelings of hurt.

"At least, that was what I thought. How can I explain?" Burden's eyes searched desperately for some inward resource he might call upon. After a moment his eyes fixed once more on Jo's. "When Peedie died," he said, struggling to give "died" the precise intonation it deserved, being neither too dramatic nor too casual, "I felt I didn't deserve anything good. It was my fault for what happened to him, what right did I have to go on with him gone?"

The expression in Jo's eyes softened with Burden's words, their aspect opening to Burden the way a friend might look at another whom she has not seen for some time. With this simple gesture, she encouraged him to continue.

"I thought that following after Peedie was the only thing I could do." As Burden spoke, Jo drew the sponge along his shoulder, the act becoming with each pass less a dutiful touch and more a caress. "But to do that, to follow after Peedie, I had to drive away the only thing keeping me here, the only good thing I had left in my life—" He peered up at Jo as his voice failed him, his eyes imploring her to understand what it was he could not speak.

"Burden. . . ."

He turned away and his voice was small as he continued. "I thought I had everything figured out. Everything. Finally, after years of failure, I had what I'd wanted in my hands, all I had to do was take hold of it. Only, when you came back it was as though I saw for the first time what a godawful, miserable thing it was I was chasing after. Jo," Burden said, grasping her arm, "all this time I thought I was afraid I couldn't go on without Peedie, but I see now I was afraid because I knew I *could*. I didn't want that guilt. That was what I was running from. I can go on, but"—Burden paused, the focus of his eyes dissolving into despair—"but just when I've discovered I can go on, there's no reason *to* go on. Not without—" He fell silent, releasing Jo's arm and turning away. "Jo, what happened at Stoaks's place that night I can't undo anymore than I can undo the things I did that brought me and Peedie to that cornfield. I can't talk to Peedie for real and tell him how sorry I am for what happened. And I can't tell him how much I miss him or what he meant to me and have him hear me. But you're here; I can talk to you, Jo."

Jo remained still, her slender frame trembling. She submerged the sponge and wrung it out once more, then traced its damp edge along Burden's brow. "I heard you speaking to Mr. Stoaks this morning," she said simply.

Burden closed his eyes and his skin flushed hotly with embarrassment.

"I was standing just by the door, watching you. I'd been by several times at night to do that, to watch you. After we spoke the other evening at the Sonic I wanted to hate you all the more, I wanted to hate what it was you did to us, for bringing me back here only to show me again how hopeless it all was. I wanted to gain some satisfaction seeing you lying there in the hospital bed, helpless. But I couldn't hate you."

Burden's eyes opened, yet he hid his gaze from Jo's.

"And I couldn't feel indifferent toward you either, and it angered me that I couldn't simply let you go. It was what you deserved. It was what I thought you wanted. But watching you breathe, watching the way you struggled in your sleep—with what, I couldn't imagine—my heart broke for you. And when I listened this morning as you spoke to Silas, I realized I could never feel any differently about you than I felt that first afternoon on the beach."

They were silent for several moments and then Burden asked, almost of the far chair, "What happens now? What happens to us?"

Jo said nothing. Burden looked at her and saw she was crying quietly. The hope that had risen in his heart on seeing her at his bedside, the hope of righting his future's course, died when he took in her expression. She appeared to be in some faint torment, as though struggling with a vexing and grave decision. Abruptly she turned her back to Burden, abandoning the wash basin and her patient. With each step she took toward the door, Burden felt his own presence a little less.

Jo stopped just inside the doorway. Not turning, she reached a hand into her pocket. Drawing in a labored breath, she asked, "Do you remember that you once gave me a book?"

Burden thought for a moment, his expression darkening then brightening in recollection. "Under the beech tree? Is that the one you mean?" By the barest possible movement of her shoulders Jo answered him affirmatively. "I remember."

Still facing away from Burden, Jo asked quickly, with perhaps too great a concern, "It was a book of poetry. Do you remember that you underlined a particular passage for me?"

"Perfectly," Burden said without hesitation, for at her words he could see the page again and the pale pencil line he'd scratched underneath the poem's lines.

"Did you mean it then? Did you really think I was that girl?"

"Yes."

"And now? Am I still that girl?"

Burden began to speak but fell silent. He could not divine the correct answer, thought there might be no correct answer.

"I'm not. I realize that, but that's okay because I wasn't then either."

"Jo."

"Tell me, what would it have been like if it had only ever been just you and me?" Burden gave no reply. "Do you want to hear something awful?" Jo asked, giving a nervous laugh. "After he died I used to try to imagine your cousin never existed. I used to try to imagine what it would have been like for us then. There would be nothing haunting you, nothing for you to hold on to, and nothing to come between us. But the evening Peedie was killed has always been between you and me, and until I heard you speaking with Mr. Stoaks last night, I thought it always would be."

"For the last six years I've pretended Peedie was still here, encouraging me in my—" Burden paused, realizing he was about to speak too frankly. "I loved Peedie, he was closer to me than anybody ever was. But I'm through pretending, I'm through being haunted by ghosts that won't die. Peedie is gone, I'm not. But now. . . ."

Jo remained with her back to Burden a few moments longer. Then, as though commanded by a will superior to her own, she turned, her gaze falling without inhibition on Burden. "But now?" she asked, her voice tentative yet defiant, her posture braced to withstand any word Burden might offer.

Burden held Jo with his eyes, communicating silently what words, by their inadequate nature, would fail to impart. At length, when he saw by the change in her expression—no longer tentative, no longer defiant, but with a weary awareness, wholly accepting of the peace he offered her—he said, "I've lost years from my life, maybe I've lost my future as well. But if you would forgive me the harm I've done to you . . . if you would forgive me then I think I could live with what's left."

Jo hurried toward Burden and wrapped her arms across him, pressing her cheek to his chest. "I forgive you, Burden, everything." She was crying, the sound not of sorrow but relief.

"Do you?" Burden asked, his own voice breaking, his eyes stinging with tears. "I need that, I need that more than anything, I need you to forgive me."

Jo raised up and looked into his eyes. In them Burden saw possibilities of joy he dared not admit.

"What happens now?" he asked again.

Jo stood, placing her hand on his. Nothing in her eyes had changed from a moment ago, they were still wonderfully open to him, yet he could see a shadow darkening their light. She struggled against this present darkness. At length she shook her head. "I can't say, Burden. I'm not sure what happens now."

For all her uncertainty, Burden's furtive hope of retrieving something of his future did not falter with her words. Indeed, he thought that had she said anything more encouraging it would have spelled their end, as though a false hope had been temporarily offered to make the ultimate unpleasant truth easier to accept. "Will you walk with me?"

"What?" Jo asked, her face brightening at Burden's odd request.

"I know this spot over at Edisto, just where the river meets the shore, where a person can catch more blue claws than he can eat. Would you walk with me there? Would you keep me company on the beach while I hunt blue claws?"

Jo smiled, her posture easing in remembrance of that warm afternoon. Worrying over stray locks of hair falling wetly across Burden's forehead, she leaned down and kissed him. Then she nuzzled his ear, and with the barest breath, whispered, "I will walk with you."

NINETEEN

Burden crouched in the shallow and clear water near where the Edisto River flowered into the ocean, tempting a blue claw close enough to catch it up in his net. His bait was a catfish head, filament run through its eyes, and Burden waited minutes at a time before tugging the head closer. He felt fine and lazy, his thoughts lulled by the warm touch of an August afternoon. The urge to sit in the cool water was strong, but he dared not move while the crab was still free. Another moment, perhaps two.

A body glided through the surf several yards off shore and Burden looked up from the blue claw and out toward the person. It was a young girl, perhaps in her early teens. Willow-limbed, she swam with little effort, her long arms lifting and stretching above her in graceful arcs as fluid as the sea itself. At times she would stand, the water coming to her belly, and walk, her chin touching her chest and her eyes peering intently into the water as though searching for something she had lost there. Her lithe frame and nimble movements reminded Burden very much of Jo when she had been that age and he thought of the first time he had seen her here on the beach. The girl must have felt Burden's absent gaze for she turned and looked at him, showing him an impish smile.

"What are you doing?" the girl asked, turning and wading toward Burden.

The girl's question reminded him what it was he had been doing, and Burden looked back down to check the crab. "Catching blue claws," he replied. The girl continued toward him and Burden was afraid her movements, although smooth, still would scare off the crab. Reaching as far forward as possible, he brought the net behind the crab and then splashed his free hand in the water, sending the blue claw scurrying backward. As he lifted the net from the water he winced at the slight pain the movement produced in his shoulder.

"Can I see?" the girl asked. Now that she was standing beside him Burden could see how pretty she was; he could also smell that she held the fragrance of the sea and sun on her dark skin.

"Ever eaten one of these?"

The girl nodded, her eyes intent on the crab as it tested the surety of its prison. "Daddy catches these sometimes." She looked over at the bucket set in the water. "How many you catch so far?"

"This one makes seven. I figure that's enough for one afternoon."

The girl peered inquisitively into the bucket, surveying the crabs. "You going to eat those all by yourself?"

"I could, I guess."

"Could you spare one?"

Burden laughed gently. "What are you going to do, eat it raw?"

"My parents have a place up a ways on the beach. Mamma'll boil it for me."

Burden studied the girl. She smiled for him helpfully, a pretty smile that pushed tawny-colored cheeks softly against her eyes. After a moment he said, "Why not? If you can carry him all the way home he's yours."

Burden untangled the crab from the net and turned its body upside down and to the girl's advantage, so she could safely take hold of it from the back, clear of the claws. "Careful you don't drop him, I don't want the time it took me catching him to have been for nothing."

"I won't, I promise. Thanks, mister." The girl's beaming smile brightened and seemed to hold a hint of many other things; Burden thought in that moment that he would have gladly given her the entire bucket had she but asked. When she was gone Burden rolled up his net, set it atop the bucket, and sat down. The water was cool against his skin, rising and falling gently in the slack tide. He wound the filament around his fingers and when he reached its end he removed the fish head and tossed it far out into the surf.

Leaning back, he rested on his elbows, letting the surf wash over his chest. The sun was warm where it touched him but the water was constantly erasing this warmth with cool touches of its own. With his eyes closed he thought briefly of the young girl and this made him think again of Jo as she had been at that age. He thought maybe this was a memory that would never abandon him, would never become altered or made false by passing time; this picture of a young Jo, dressed in the fine garments of a summer's day.

There was a momentary flurry of activity in the bucket as two of the blue claws attacked each other. But the fight was short-lived and served only to rouse Burden from his thoughts. Standing, he took the net and bucket in hand and walked north along the surf, liking the feel of the water kicking at his ankles and calves.

Burden set the bucket next to a beach umbrella planted in the sand. Jo lay under the umbrella; a book held loosely in her hands rested open but face down on her chest, rising and falling on shallow waves of breath. He sat, careful not to awaken her.

Jo stirred anyway, embarrassed she had fallen asleep. Then, recovering, she stretched lazily and gazed up at Burden, offering him a smile every bit the equal of the young girl's.

"Didn't mean to startle you."

"You didn't. I was reading."

"I saw you were reading."

"Well, I *was*."

Burden brushed his fingers along her knee, drawing them up along her thigh. She had tried to remain under the umbrella's shade, but falling asleep had allowed that shade to slink away, leaving the skin on her legs pink and hot.

"Anyway, let's not talk about what *I* was or wasn't doing. What I want to know is whether you found us supper."

Burden nodded.

"Oh, good. How many did you catch?"

"Six."

"Only six?" Jo teased.

"Was seven, but a sea nymph came and stole one away."

"Right."

"Honest," Burden insisted as he pressed a finger into Jo's skin and withdrew it, watching the white circle his touch produced slowly fade back to pink. "That's going to sting in a couple of hours. Maybe you should stick to reading indoors."

"I think someone's been spending too much time around doctors."

"Not for much longer." Burden slowly swung his right arm in a circle. He winced only slightly and then smiled for Jo.

Jo touched Burden's hand where it rested on her thigh. "Of course, I suppose a little cold cream wouldn't hurt. Care to lend a hand?"

It was night now and the sea was thirty miles and several hours behind them, yet Burden still could hear it in his ears and smell it on his arms, which smelled of brine that rose from his skin upon a fine heat in the cool night. A new moon stood aside, letting the stars shine clearly above the pine and making easy work of following the Milky Way's faint, twisting tail. Nights felt good to him now; he had faith they would feel even better. All the old ghosts had slipped away, either to shadow or memory, or to a place perhaps they had for a time forgotten was their true home.

There was the sound of a screen door opening and closing, and then that of footsteps approaching over dampened grass. Jo walked up behind Burden and handed him a beer.

"I need to leave soon."

Burden set his beer at his side and held up a hand to her. "Just a little while longer."

Jo took his hand and sat next to him, easing against his shoulder, closing her eyes and letting herself become seduced by the sounds of the night and the warmth of his body.

They did not speak, which was fine with Burden as he held his gaze fixed to the stars. He wondered how it was he had paid them so little mind before, wondered how it was he had missed their quiet beauty. In the weeks following his release from the hospital and during his recovery, he'd grown fairly enamored of the night sky, contemplating its wonder work of constellations as he rested long into the evening on his parents' back porch. Now that he was well, he'd taken to lying in the backyard, where he would gaze heavenward for long stretches of time, his thoughts tangled somewhere among the stars' limitless number. They were the true fields of the Lord, he thought, where souls ran till they found their second breaths; where the departed, be they mothers or grandparents, sisters or lovers, peeked down from time to time, not to judge or pity or scold, maybe not even to anticipate or mourn, but simply to see and remember what had been theirs and perhaps glimpse what was yet to be. One night Burden would fall asleep and wake to play in those fields. He would search till he found Peedie, or perhaps Peedie would be there waiting for him and together they would run. Some night this would happen. Only not this night.